THOU SHALT NOT...

Copyright Information

Contents

4. Thou Shalt Not... Violate the Day of Rest

5. Thou Shalt Not... Dishonor Your Parents

6. Thou Shalt Not... Murder

The Ten Commandments

And God spoke all these words:

"I am the LORD your God, who brought you out of Egypt, out of the land of slavery."

1. "You shall have no other gods before me.

2. "You shall not make for yourself an idol in the form of anything in heaven above or on the earth beneath or in the waters below. You shall not bow down to them or worship them; for I, the LORD your God, am a jealous God, punishing the children for the sin of the fathers to the third and fourth generation of those who hate me, but showing love to a thousand generations of those who love me and keep my commandments.

3. "You shall not misuse the name of the LORD your God, for the LORD will not hold anyone guiltless who misuses his name.

4. "Remember the Sabbath day by keeping it holy. Six days you shall labor and do all your work, but the seventh day is a Sabbath to the LORD your God. On it you shall not do any work, neither you, nor your son or daughter, nor your manservant or maidservant, nor your animals, nor the alien within your gates. For in six days the LORD made the heavens and the earth, the sea, and all that is in them, but he rested on the seventh day. Therefore the LORD blessed the Sabbath day and made it holy.

5. "Honor your father and your mother, so that you may live long in the land the LORD your God is giving you.

6. "You shall not murder.

7. "You shall not commit adultery.

8. "You shall not steal.

9. "You shall not give false testimony against your neighbor.

10. "You shall not covet your neighbor's house. You shall not covet your neighbor's wife, or his manservant or maidservant, his ox or donkey, or anything that belongs to your neighbor."

When the people saw the thunder and lightning and heard the trumpet and saw the mountain in smoke, they trembled with fear. They stayed at a distance and said to Moses, "Speak to us yourself and we will listen. But do not have God speak to us or we will die."

Moses said to the people, "Do not be afraid. God has come to test you, so that the fear of God will be with you to keep you from sinning."

The people remained at a distance, while Moses approached the thick darkness where God was.

–EXODUS 20:1–21 New International Version

THOU SHALT NOT...

Worship False Gods

Timenfaya

Lee Forsythe

Dean waited in the middle of the dusty road for the tour bus, the early morning island sun already warm on his face. He mentally kicked himself again for forgetting that nothing opened in Timenfaya until ten at the earliest. But he'd made arrangements with the strange old man to be picked up at eight o'clock.

Hungry and thirsty, he faced a bus ride of unknown length to god knew where. He hoped they'd be stopping at the cantina or roadside stand of an in-law or business partner somewhere along the way.

Of course he could bag the whole thing and return to the hotel. Running away had become his specialty lately. First his job, then Karen. How inadequate was the note he'd left her. There was no good way to sum up a relationship gone sour. Better to end it than continue on the bitter downward spiral they were on. She'd have to sort things out for herself for once. Judging from the unqualified disaster this trip had become, she might even be doing a better job than he was.

He'd wanted to escape to a remote, inexpensive place with sun and sand. After trying to push something pricier on him, the travel agent, sighing heavily, had pulled out a faded brochure for Timenfaya, one of a string of islands off Africa's west coast.

The beaches had turned out to be beautiful, but the smiling young beauties frolicking in the brochure's pictures must have been flown in for a one-day-only photo session. The average age of the current clientele was nearly deceased, and their health appalling. Enormously fat men and women with dark tans lounged side by side the length of the beach. They ate, drank, and smoked with gusto, and seemed to be enjoying themselves immensely, irritating him even more. He felt like he was stranded in the middle of walrus mating season.

With the end of his stay approaching, his boredom had given way to anxiety about finding another job. He also remembered now, despite all their problems, how empty his life had been before he'd met Karen.

Then he'd run into the old man, his bronze complexion and high cheek bones identifying him as a member of the island's indigenous population—the only one Dean had seen, except in a tiny photo in the brochure.

Deep-set eyes met Dean's gaze from under a thick mantle of black hair streaked with gray, the same color combination as his neatly-trimmed beard. The man wore a standard vacation-land costume: shorts, sandals, and a batik shirt.

"Good morning, sir," he said, smiling gently. "Enjoying your stay?"

"Not particularly," Dean answered, thinking he might be one of the time-share touts patrolling the island sidewalks, hawking condo deals.

The old man gave him a sympathetic look. "The beach does get tedious. But many visitors miss an interesting feature of our island. In 1934 volcanoes changed life here forever. Many perished. Our crops were ruined. The cattle that survived the first eruptions died within a week from breathing the ash that fell. Dead fish, from the ocean's depths and never before seen here, washed up on our shores. Few realize that several of these volcanoes remain active a short distance inland."

"And how are you supposed to get there?" Dean asked. Away from the beachfront, the island's road system was quite primitive.

"We're offering a specially priced, limited time bus tour of the volcano lands. If you are interested in something different—"

"How specially priced?"

"Oh...," the old man acted as if he were coming up with a figure off the top of his head, "for a nice young man like you, only seven dollars, payable tomorrow morning when the bus picks you up right here at eight."

Forty-five minutes after the appointed pick-up time, Dean tired of mentally cataloguing Karen's annoying habits and started back to his hotel. It was then the battered gray bus slid around the corner and rumbled toward him. It screeched to a halt with metal scraping metal, the sound of long-gone brake linings. He noticed the bald tires and the rusty, dented body.

The door slammed open and he stepped up, handing his seven dollars to the driver, a long, lean native with wild eyes, greasy hair, and a smirk. Without looking at the money, the man tossed it on the floor to the left of his seat then grabbed Dean's right hand and imprinted the back of it with a stamp from a pad on the dashboard.

"How soon can we get something to eat?" Dean carefully enunciated. The driver shrugged, slowly shook his head, and smiled vacuously. Before Dean could think of a follow-up question, the man threw the bus into gear and accelerated down the street as rapidly as the straining engine permitted.

Dean grabbed the seat backs to keep from falling and made his way down the aisle. The only other passengers, a middle-aged couple in matching jogging suits of chartreuse, red, and green, conversed in sing-song Finnish. He nodded as he passed, plunking down near the back.

He studied the red image on his hand, admiring the sharply detailed lines of a horned demon against a backdrop of flames.

The next passenger, a Japanese man, snapped a picture of the bus with one of three cameras slung around his neck. Once seated, he continued to take photographs out the window of nothing in particular as the bus wound through the narrow streets. *Click-whir, click-whir, click-whir.*

At the next stop, an empty lot on a dead-end street, a group of prepubescent girls in white blouses, kneesocks, gray pleated skirts, and Mary Janes got on with their stern-faced female chaperone. The woman complained in thick German to the driver during the stamping process, shepherding her giggling charges to their seats once the tattooing was completed.

Ten minutes later they picked up the final passengers—a fat, sunburned American and his small, pleasant looking wife, both in their retirement years. He wore a pastel-colored baseball cap inscribed Cabanas del Sol and handed a bill to the driver who threw it onto the floor with the previous fares before stamping their hands and abruptly starting the bus in motion again, sending them lurching backward.

They collapsed into seats near Dean. The man's face flushed crimson. "You stupid, third world pissant," he growled at the driver.

Less than half full, the bus moved by the last string of beachside hotels and turned toward the center of the island, the town falling behind them and the mountains looming in the distance.

Dean wondered what Karen was doing. He imagined her sitting by the window, crying softly, her brown eyes alternately sad and flashing with anger. She'd be lost without him, of course.

The moderate morning temperature gave way to the oppressive heat of the day, spurring the passengers to open the windows as the ancient vehicle labored up a rutted one-lane road. Kicked up by the tires, dust floated back inside onto the sweating travelers.

The mountains now appeared in sharp focus, some covered with black ash, others with yellow or dark red sand. Patches of bright sunshine pierced the clouds, highlighting the barren splendor of the peaks and rolling hills.

The Finns peered out, talking excitedly in what sounded like strange yodeling. The schoolgirls pointed and chattered away in German. The Japanese man, who'd temporarily lapsed into inactivity, resumed picture-taking.

They passed sloping fields of black slag dotted with white rock cairns in long parallel rows. In other places the tips of green tendrils poked out of huge craters in the rocky terrain.

Dean turned to the old man and his wife. "Really different isn't it?"

The woman turned and smiled warmly, perhaps at the sound of another English speaker. The man muttered, "Looks like the damned surface of the moon."

"Can anything be growing in that?" Dean asked.

"They say volcanic soil is the richest in the world," the woman said.

"Well *they* must be out of their minds," the man snapped. "That's just a bunch of rocks."

His wife's smile evaporated; she looked back out the window. Dean had to agree with her husband, though. The landscape was the most sterile and otherworldly he'd ever seen.

As they climbed higher into the mountains proper, the road rose, dipped, and snaked at incredible angles past towering peaks and plunging crevasses. The bus slid around a particularly sharp corner and rode up on the edge of a precipice, throwing dirt and stones into the deep gully below. Two of the girls squealed as they looked down into the dropoff.

The driver didn't slow, however; he muscled the wheel and alternately stood on the accelerator and brakes.

The topography continued to change as they approached more recent volcanic activity. Fantastic rivers of black lava had been frozen in mid-flow, their rippling currents perfectly preserved. Higher up, tiny white and yellow lichens grew on a few rocks, the only relief from the blackness.

Karen would have enjoyed the scenery with her childlike fascination for the new or unusual. He suddenly realized how much he missed her.

The bus had stopped and the tour group was filing off. They moved up a steep grade in the direction indicated by a red arrow on a weather-beaten sign. He hoped they'd arrived at the long awaited rest stop; he was feeling a little lightheaded.

A short distance up the hill the group came to a flat area where two boys waited by three holes in the earth vented by thin metal tubes extending a foot above ground level. One boy produced a brown earthenware jug and held it up at arm's length until he had everyone's attention. He bent down and poured water into one of the tubes and stepped back.

For a moment nothing happened, then, just as the crowd relaxed their attention slightly, an explosion of steam jetted up out of the pipe ten feet into the air. The tourists oohed and aahed.

The boy repeated the feat with the second tube then poured the rest of the water down all the tubes to create three simultaneous geysers, a grand finale captured on film by the Asian gentleman.

The second boy guided the group to a small opening in the side of the mountain. Enough sunlight hit the opening to illuminate some unremarkable looking rocks and the volcanic ash surrounding them. With a long metal pole tipped with a small trident, the boy speared a clump of vegetation wound together like a tumbleweed. He extended it into the opening, held it still, and it burst into a ball of flame. The group gasped in amazement and applauded.

At first Dean suspected a trick, but changed his mind when he held his hand to the opening and felt the blazing heat.

Their performance over, the boys silently escorted them back to the bus. Standing with their backs against the vehicle, three men and an old woman sized up the group as they approached.

Everyone slowed, anticipating food or souvenirs for sale. But when they saw the locals' hardened demeanor and their dark, unsettling eyes, they hurried by them to get on the bus. The natives were not selling anything—that much was clear. Dean noticed their coarse clothing, weathered skin, and the men's sinewy forearms.

The Japanese man paused long enough to snap their picture and do a quick bow, neither eliciting even a blink from the natives.

Before the driver could start the bus, Dean leaned over and grabbed the steering wheel with one hand. He pantomimed eating and asked, "When?"

The driver held up a hand. "Soon," he said.

As Dean stepped to the back, he wondered if the man had understood all along or merely remembered a convenient word to terminate unwanted questions. Whatever the case, Dean felt he had finally made an effort to take charge of this Tower of Babel bus tour.

Maybe it wasn't too late to do the same with Karen. She'd take him back, he was certain, but there'd be hell to pay for a while. He'd just have to weather it.

The bus took a turn and weaved its way through a tumble-down village. Crumbling walls of white rock from long ago were buttressed by more recently formed black volcanic stones. Corrugated tin roofs, many a patchwork of repairs, slanted at crazy angles along the main street.

On the outskirts of town they passed some citizens by the side of the road. The assemblage stopped whatever they were doing to study the faces framed in the bus windows. Some even stepped into the road to stare after them.

The bus doubled back, and soon they were ascending again. Three-quarters of the way to the top of the peak, the driver stopped, put on the parking brake, and opened the door. Everyone filed off and headed farther up the grade in the direction indicated by an arrow on another makeshift sign.

Dean trudged up the incline behind them. Another arrow, this one on a long board blocking the road that continued to wind upward, pointed to a narrow ledge flush against the mountainside.

The tourists had assembled there and were staring down in amazement into the fiery bowl of an active volcano. A sulfurous stench rose from the bubbling soup of glowing, molten rock.

Dean had speculated earlier about what kind of liability insurance the tour operator held. He could see now the answer was none. They stood above the boiling inferno without even the benefit of a guardrail. The chaperone warned the girls to stay back from the edge. Everyone else stood close to the rim, captivated by the spectacle.

Dean heard a mechanical rumble and wondered for an instant why the driver was starting up the bus already. At the sound of splintering wood he slowly turned around.

The bus driver, at the controls of a huge bulldozer, roared down upon them with a look of grim determination on his face. Additional movement above caught Dean's eye and he glanced upward.

The old man who'd lured them there stood on the mountain peak, his palms out in offering before him, his tourist clothes replaced by a snow-white robe. The boys from the demonstration knelt on either side with their heads bowed. Next to them the four peasants from alongside the bus leaned forward for a better look.

The driver lowered the dozer's blade and its gritty scraping alerted the others. Everyone was temporarily compacted by the rectangular steel slab. Dean heard a girl's high-pitched scream, a Finnish expletive, and a camera's *click-whir, click-whir* as they began to tumble through the air.

Set In Stone

Stephen D. Rogers

Blinking away beads of sweat, I watched a tiny red ant climb my thumb. Without even pausing, the ant crossed from skin to nail, apparently unfazed by the transition.

I was impressed despite myself, jealous of the ant's resilience, since I knew I would have lost my footing on the slippery slope. Even lying here prone on the rough ground I could feel the world tipping beneath me.

I closed my eyes until the movement ceased.

My legs had gone to sleep so long ago I didn't think I could ever walk from this place, but my obedience was proof of my devotion.

The red ant climbed over the edge of my thumb, onto the rifle, and continued down the barrel.

Perhaps the ant meant to march all the way to the end of the rifle, flip over the muzzle, and then crawl deep inside the dark tunnel to await sweet oblivion. Perhaps I was projecting more intelligence than the insect merited. Perhaps I was crazy.

I laughed and shifted my focus to the gravestone in the distance, a sight which cut my laughter short.

Although I couldn't read the letters from this angle, I knew the words engraved there by heart. I had filled out the form. I had selected the font. Today my daughter would have been seven, and instead of her laughter I was stuck with silent granite.

My daughter would still be alive if it weren't for the negligence of my ex-wife, who refused to believe she was to blame for what happened. Once a year, she spent an hour at the cemetery to atone for her sins, an uneven trade if there ever was one.

Not a day went by that I didn't visit the stone, the embodiment of all my hopes and dreams. The stone was my lover, my muse, and my confidant.

I'd been lying at the edge of the woods since three this morning. I'd sobered since I arrived, but my head hadn't cleared at all. If anything, my thoughts had become fuzzier. I was no longer a man with a rifle in his arms, no longer a high priest preparing a sacrifice for his god.

I could still blink my eyes, focus on the end of the rifle, see the empty space before the stone. I could twitch my index finger but didn't, now worried that I would be unable to pull the trigger when the time came.

An itch forced me to shift, and I felt the ground resist the movement, could almost hear the earth sucking at me, pulling me back to my original position.

Had I put down roots since I'd been lying here?

Did the stone wish me to emulate its inability to move? I would be the earth and the earth would be me.

A muscle in my leg tried to jump, but the ground held it firm.

I blinked away another drop of sweat, my eyelid slow to reopen, the effort almost beyond me.

Had the red ant reached the darkness inside the barrel? Should I have squashed him beneath my thumb when I had the chance? Had I ever the chance?

I sent a message down my trigger finger, saw it respond. That was good.

I should probably keep the finger moving, perhaps trace out those graven words in the dirt. I could not afford to have the digit fail me.

There was a crunch, and I tasted grit between my teeth.

I hadn't lost a daughter, I'd gained a new manner of being, an existence closer to nature, part of nature itself.

There was a buzz in my ear. Had the red ant worked his way back to stand on my shoulder, whisper the sermon of the stone to the faithful? No, there he was, walking toward me along the side of the barrel.

The buzzing became a hum and grew louder.

An engine was added to the din. As my ears tracked the approach of the vehicle, my eyelids became heavier, and I could barely blink away the sweat that continued to hamper my vision.

A blurry figure climbed from a car, bent on her sacrilegious act.

Ants didn't erect monuments to their dead, didn't understand the need for a deity.

The stone was the only thing that kept me from dissolving into nothingness, the task that still lay ahead.

A gray glob of motion approached the stone.

I could feel myself slipping away.

Now was the time.

The gun kicked back against my shoulder, and I saw the haze shift, my last sight the stone reaching out to me.

Someone crawled up inside my nose.

My friend the ant, praying to the stone, with me and for me.

Amen.

Old Ways

Barbara Malenky

Mary Grace bent low to the radio. Jesse could see the tops of her hose and the pink garters holding them up. She listened to Wally Bodine, the Friday night preacher on KW103 out of Austin.

"I can't understand a word that fella is yollering," Jesse said, but Mary Grace ignored him.

After a while, he went to sit on the porch. "He ain't preaching to me anyhow," he mumbled. A trio of crows were perched on the fence across the road, and he addressed them. "Used to be I could take down her hose when I took a notion. Now there ain't time, what with the chores and the preaching." He remembered the years before Wally Bodine and longed for the old ways. "Ain't no man got to tell me how to live," he whispered, and the crows spread their wings to rise high. Jesse watched them until they resembled ashes against the blue sky.

He gazed across the fields, bare now after the last hay cutting. They lay flat and deep green with nothing to mar their perfection, until they ran into a line of trees thirty acres off.

Mary Grace stepped out on the porch. She perched on the railing.

"He's coming here," she said.

Jesse moved his eyes on her. Her face glowed, and her hazel eyes danced brightly. She smiled big enough that her crooked front teeth showed.

"Who's coming here?" he asked, still thinking of pulling her hose down.

"Reverend Bodine," she said. Her voice filled with reverence. "In two weeks time. That's what the radio says."

"Coming here, right here, up these old steps right here?" he teased, and his gaze dropped to her hose-covered legs.

"In Siler. At the Freedom Center, 7:30. I want you to promise you'll drive me there."

"Take down your hose, Mary Grace," he whispered, not daring a look at her face.

"Promise me first," she said, and then he did look at her face. Her eyes held the same passion he heard in her voice. There was a moment when he wondered whether the passion was for him, or for the invisible entity called Wally Bodine. Then her hand smoothed over one leg and stopped above the knee. She carefully rolled the stocking down to her ankle.

"Promise me this one thing, Jesse," she said. Her eyes became heavy-lidded. Her full lips slackened with need.

"All right, I promise," Jesse whispered. He slid one hand above the stocking roll, and tenderly touched her flesh.

It wasn't until Jesse pulled his truck through the gates of Freedom Center that he realized how many people like Mary Grace there were. The crowd surged across the asphalt like a rope of slow-moving tar pitch. There was something eerie about them. They were silent. Mary Grace herself hadn't said a word from the time they crossed the Siler town limits.

Jesse followed the line of cars, searching for a parking space, then saw one near the end of the last row and quickly claimed it. Mary Grace was out of the car before he could throw it into park.

Irritated, he took his time joining her. He watched her waiting figure through the rear-view mirror. Watched the crawling line of people pass her. Not one looked her way nor spoke to her. They were all ages and shapes and colors. They reminded him of a scene in some horror movie where people are called to their deaths. He got out of the truck.

They joined the line, slipping like water into water, and were carried along the parking lot and up a tall flight of steps, then across another driveway with a row of limousines and police cars in attendance. They passed through glass doors into the lobby where Jesse filed into one line to secure tickets and Mary Grace stood in another to wait for him.

He took in everything as he waited. Slack faces and shining eyes. Some dressed nice, others in the best they owned, which was nothing to brag about. There was a solemn air in Freedom Center. There was no joy in these faces. Jesse turned to find Mary Grace. She looked pretty in her best black print dress. He stared at her legs and remembered the day on the porch. Today she wore high-heel pumps.

Jesse took her arm, and they followed the usher to their seats. Mary Grace was upset at how far they were from the stage. She twisted her hands and played with her purse. She would not look at Jesse for a few minutes, probably upset with him for not allowing her to pre-order tickets through the mail.

"You'll be able to hear him fine," he whispered. He took her hand. "I'll buy you a program when the boy comes around, okay?"

Mary Grace nodded, but pulled her hand from his.

Inside the auditorium the atmosphere was charged with silent excitement like power through a wire. The lighting was subdued and elegant. The air perfumed, cool. The faces surrounding them were softer in the light, worshipful.

A dozen young men in black suits and white shirts passed offering buckets. They stood at one aisle then moved to the next and waited for the buckets to come back. When a bucket reached him, Jesse did not contribute, and tried to pass it to the couple on the other side of Mary Grace. She intercepted it and placed a folded bill inside.

"What are we paying for?" he whispered. "He hasn't even started his sermon yet."

He didn't expect an answer and didn't get one.

Organ music filled the air, and Mary Grace gave a little gasp. They were playing "Rock of Ages," her favorite hymn.

Jesse looked at her. Since finding Wally Bodine and his gospel hour, she had changed. Following Bodine's belief that long hair and makeup tempted other men besides her husband, her hair was short and permed now. Jesse had loved her long red hair, loved to wrap his hands in it when they made love. He wished she would let it grow back, at least to her shoulders. She no longer applied makeup, opting instead to be natural like "all God's children." But the biggest change was in her expression. Mary Grace had gone serious on him. When was the last time she laughed? Really laughed? He couldn't remember. It was some time before losing the baby, and finding Wally Bodine.

And then Bodine was there, standing like Jesus on the stage with his arms outstretched and his eyes scanning the crowd. The applause was deafening. People rushed the stage, their arms jerking and stretching toward him. Some people fell to their knees, overpowered with adoration. Guards moved in to push them back and maintain order. Somewhere a choir began to sing. There was nothing to see, though, except the white-robed Wally Bodine.

He was a small man. A tortured maze of wiry hair framed his pale face. Although they were near the back of the big auditorium, too far to see his expressions or features, Mary Grace whispered that his eyes were so green. Jesse didn't see his eyes or the color. What he did see were the rays of light around his head, splaying out and upward. Jesse's gaze tried to follow one of them. It disappeared above the curtain line. He wondered what Wally Bodine took them for. Was he trying to make them think he was touched by angels instead of an off-stage spotlight?

Jesse turned to tell Mary Grace about the light rays. She was gone. He craned his neck to stare down the aisle and saw the top of her head bob along with the crowd that was moving to get down front close enough to worship at the anointed one's feet.

At the edge of the stage the light rays caught her scarlet hair and illuminated her as though she, too, was anointed. It was easy to keep an eye on her, and Jesse relaxed. He didn't begrudge her anything if it would make her feel better. He missed the baby, too. He wanted to try again for a family. Hadn't he told her that over and over in the dark of their bedroom late at night, only to have her turn her back to him, pretending to sleep, blaming him somehow?

The sermon went on and on until Jesse could hardly keep his eyes open. Wally Bodine called for patience, perfect faith, love for one another, and donations. It was the same sermon he shouted over the radio into Jesse's living room. The preacher danced like a frenzied insect. His voice was loud, soft, angry and persuasive. Finally Jesse dozed off, only to be awakened by a sudden surge of sound. The crowd burst into voice, and a hymn throbbed from a big organ at one side of the auditorium.

Wally Bodine moved to the end of the stage and stared into the crowd. He held his hand down to someone. Mary

Grace soon stood on the stage next to him, and Jesse gave a start and sat straight in his chair, boredom flown away like his religious beliefs years before. Wally Bodine leaned toward her and whispered. He wrapped his arms around her shoulders and pressed his mouth to her ear. His eyes stared into hers. He walked Mary Grace with him across the stage to the microphone. When he opened his mouth to speak, it was an unspoken command for the music to stop. The crowd grew quiet. His words were clear.

"This woman is sick. I don't know her name. I ain't never seen her before. She didn't tell me she's sick. Don't nobody have to tell me she's sick. The spirit in me knows it. This woman has come here today to seek that which she has lost. To find some relief. Well, brethren, she's come to the right place. I'm going to take her to the Lord's room, now, and he's going to fix up what's sick in this pretty little woman. The one who came with her must not despair at her absence, for she will come home and be renewed and filled with God's splendor."

He gestured to a band hidden in the wings. Music soon filled the air. "Join in this final hymn of praise to God." He disappeared with Mary Grace still wrapped in his arms.

Jesse felt the heat of shame in his cheeks. He wasn't sure what to do, so he did nothing. What could it all mean, the words Wally Bodine delivered, a message to him alone? Maybe Mary Grace would get what she needed backstage, maybe a few words of comfort or advice on how to make her husband happy; then she would return to where he waited.

The auditorium emptied. Jesse sat in his seat and watched the people leave. They would have a head start out of the parking lot. Finally, he stood and moved with the crowd, breaking off when he drew close to the stage where workers removed the band instruments and lighting equipment. Jesse asked one of them about his wife. He was referred to someone else, then to another person backstage. There was no one to help him. Nobody had seen Mary Grace. No one remembered a flame-haired woman in a black print dress and pumps. No one could tell him where the "Lord's room" was located.

Jesse shuffled down the narrow backstage hallway and stopped at each door to ask his question. He stumbled outside, and took three turns around the building, but she wasn't there. He tried to re-enter the building and found the doors locked. Soon he stood alone in the darkness. If he climbed to the top of the steps, he could see his car in the parking lot. Maybe she would be waiting for him, afraid and not knowing where he had gone. He hurried to find out. No one waited, but he circled the car several times anyway.

When the parking lot fluorescent lights flickered off, leaving him in darkness and despair, Jesse climbed into his truck and drove home.

At dawn, Mary Grace mounted the porch and knocked on the door. Jesse opened it and stared at her. She was different. Her eyes shone with love. Her skin glowed. Her hair hung loose and soft, and framed her face.

"Did you get what you need?" he asked.

She nodded, walked past him, and went into the bedroom. She quietly disrobed, taking down her hose, and stood naked in front of her husband. He saw the invitation in her eyes. He forgot his fear and anger. No words needed to be spoken. He took what was his.

Summer moved into fall. Jesse attended to harvesting his crops. He didn't sleep well at night. He had always been a restless sleeper, and since Mary Grace's delicate condition had shown itself, he was afraid that if he slept too deeply, he might somehow harm the unborn child.

A new peace filled the house. Mary Grace spent her time on the porch swing. Her hair grew long, and a tube of lipstick and a new bottle of perfume sat on her dressing table.

She didn't listen to Wally Bodine anymore, and Jesse didn't ask questions. All she needed was something to fill the empty spaces, and the unborn baby sufficed. That's what he believed, and it was enough.

When it arrived, it came unexpectedly early and in a rush that left no time to summon a doctor. Jesse helped as much as he could, but Mary Grace did all the work. The child entered the world with powerful screams to challenge the greatest orator. It was a boy and red as a lobster. A wild frizz of light hair sprouted from his scalp like tiny snakes. Its malehood was long. The legs were tiny, but already muscled, as though the kicking in its mother's belly had been more for exercise than to prove his existence. The small fists beat the air with fury, and two large bright eyes fixed on Jesse's.

"Damn," Jesse muttered. He held the baby and marveled. Mary Grace opened her arms, and he lay the infant in them with tenderness. His son, his boy.

"Let me get the Polaroid," he said. "I want something to show him when he gets big."

He aimed and shot the photo, while Mary Grace cuddled the baby and held him in a photogenic position. Then Jesse left them to fetch the country doctor.

The doctor's waiting room was full of patients. After checking at the desk, Jesse was told it would be two hours before the physician could make a home visit. Jesse settled in to wait. A woman near him flipped through a magazine. Jesse stared at it, filled with emotion that he could not identify. Wally Bodine looked out from the front cover. The night at the auditorium was far past. In his own happiness of the last months and the absence of the preacher's thundering voice from the radio, Jesse had allowed himself to forget.

Now the hateful face stared at him, and all the resentment flooded back.

When the woman laid the magazine down, Jesse couldn't help himself. He grabbed it and located the article. What he read filled him with a certain ghoulish happiness. He noted the specifics to tell Mary Grace later.

The doctor was full of praise for the success of the delivery. He checked both patients and gave a good prognosis. The little boy was a fine specimen of humanity. He wrote out his orders and left with a promise to drop by the next afternoon. Jesse couldn't wait to tell Mary Grace what he'd learned about the great Wally Bodine.

"He's dead," Jesse said. He watched for some sign of remorse, hoped for it, to appease the humiliation he'd felt at the auditorium. "He's dead by his own hand. A scandal of sexual misconduct. He persuaded dozens of his followers to commit suicide with him. What do you think about him now?"

Mary Grace remained silent, enthralled with the new being in her arms.

"I'd like some broth," she said. "I need to keep strong."

Jesse nodded, disappointed at her lack of response, then went to the kitchen to prepare the meal. He set a fire in the stove.

"I say it's good riddance to him," he whispered to himself. "The world has enough phony-baloneys."

When the soup was on to heat, Jesse picked up the Polaroid from the kitchen table. He cried out in disbelief before slinging the picture into the fire.

He watched as it dissipated into ashes. First the body went, then the face was licked away. The beams of light that splayed from around his son's head, visible only on the Polaroid, were the last to disappear.

Blood Sacrifice

Jennifer D. Munro

Fritz veered across two freeway lanes to make a sudden exit and tossed the dregs of his Bloody Mary out the driver's window.

Red droplets flew in the backseat window, splotching Genevieve's dress—her preservative-treated wedding gown, yanked after all these years from its sealed box. She had ignored the label's instruction to dryclean before wearing. She itched, envisioning the chemicals preserving her, mummy-like. Without the train and veil, the simple dress now hung plain and dowdy on her. She looked like a skeleton draped in a sheet, perfect for an All Hallows Day voodoo ritual. Yet she felt full. So stuffed that she couldn't eat, even in this city of decadent food. Maybe tonight they'd mistake her for the returning dead. Sacrifice to her. Bury her.

Wearing white had been Fritz's only instruction for the ceremony, other than bringing a sacrifice for the dead and a dinner contribution. She sat crammed into the shrunken hatchback with the cooler and drums. Fritz had tucked booze and noisemakers around her into every available crevice of the back seat.

Conversation was impossible in the mufflerless car Fritz had scavenged from a friend's yard, all four windows open to relieve the humidity. The wind pulled wisps from her ponytail. She worried the colorful bead necklaces Fritz had draped her with like a rosary.

The front passenger seat yawned with emptiness. Clara's seat, tainted, as if Fritz's wife had hacked off her long hair there and not in the white bathroom. She had gouged her scalp with the ferocity of her self-destruction, crimson blotches at her feet, drying to puce on the sterile tiles.

Genevieve stared out her car window. Faded and broken strands of Mardi Gras beads hung from electric wires, tree branches, wrought iron fences, and gallery railings. Plywood was hammered over windows of once grand mansions. Galleries warped and sagged. Magnificent, battered columns tilted. Paint faded and peeled. Litter claimed its ground between the swaybacked houses and the sucking swamp.

Above-ground tombs rose on either side of them as they drove past the many Cities of the Dead. Long ago, before New Orleans had adopted the custom of cementing corpses into small houses, buried coffins surfaced and floated down the streets during floods. The wooden coffins rose in the water-logged soil and *knock, knock, knocked* to be let out. Tonight, the ritual participants would knock on the doors of the dead, asking Les Morts to answer.

Fritz shouted at the rearview. "Don't worry, Gin, darlin'. We'll make it." He punched the cigarette lighter, although the Virginia Slim menthol dangling from his lips had not yet burned down to the filter. "This is the real stuff, not some tourist jive. Not some cockamamie vampire bunk. Priestess won't let nobody in once it starts. Interferes with the vibes. Window to the dead's most open at midnight. Ceremony's gotta finish by then so we can make it to the cemetery with the offerings. Cuttin' it close here." Fritz himself had made them late, waiting in vain for Clara to join them until well past their scheduled time to leave. As if Clara could exorcise her dark demons at the voodoo ceremony—in spite of the blood that would leach through the white Marie Antoinette wig she'd planned to wear, like brackish swamp water oozing through the sculpted lawns of Garden District manors.

The car limped into the Ninth Ward. "Worst district in N'awlins. Outside of our neighborhood." When Genevieve had called long distance to rent his downstairs rooms a month ago, Fritz hadn't mentioned the nightly gunfire and sirens. But he'd also asked no questions.

Genevieve had chosen to move to New Orleans for the Gothic houses, famous ghosts, decadent costumes, and fantastic cemeteries. The spirit that followed her was not tied to a grave, but to her body, her womb a tomb. The haunted atmosphere of this city would give him voice. The bayou phantoms would teach Gin the child's language. Decipher the tapping code. If a spirit would talk to her anywhere, it would be here in the Hoodoo swamp—a letdown so far, with kitschy French Quarter tourist shops hawking mass-produced fertility candles and pin-cushion hex dolls made in China.

Despite their tardiness, the ritual had not yet started. The open door of the priestess's house spilled light and noise onto the dark street. "N'awlins time." Fritz laughed like a car engine refusing to start.

He parallel parked in a too small space and left the car snout nosing into the street. "Made it." He stepped barefoot from the car and perched a white top-hat, festooned with a gold Christmas garland, over his thinning, static-charged hair. He wore white ringmaster's coattails unbuttoned over his bare chest and massaged his breastbone with the cigarette hand, a constant movement, as if he were rubbing a crystal ball to divine his own heart. Clara's sleek cigarette hung slender and incongruous from his cragged features.

White clothing unified the otherwise diverse crowd packed into the bungalow. Gin elbowed her way through a mash of men and women—white, black, young, old, tidy, grungy, drunk, sober, gay, straight—dressed in everything from ordinary streetwear to fanciful costumes, nurses' uniforms to marching band outfits, sheets and togas, all white. This swarm of bizarre angels engulfed Genevieve, separating her from Fritz. Her hand protected the delicate burden in her side pocket. She would sacrifice this keepsake. Beg the stone baby to talk. Translate the signal. *Knock knock.*

Dense and dark oil paintings covered every wall of the shotgun house, enormous artworks that rose from floor to ceiling. Genevieve made out flames, snakes, half-naked African figures. Fiery orbs, maniacal grins, breasts. Skeletons, cigars, mermaids, sunglasses. Fetuses, severed heads, women fornicating with reptiles, men rubbing their crotches. Riotous swirls of deep color. Sensual, disturbing images. Smaller works filled every strip of leftover wall space.

Genevieve caught a glimpse of one small work behind the heads of partygoers. She pushed toward the image of a kneeling, pregnant woman, naked. The Mississippi River flowed from her womb.

"*Yemaya,*" someone whispered in her ear. Genevieve turned to the tiny woman. Caucasian, with mousy hair brushing her shoulders, dressed in a simple, loose shift. She wore no makeup to brighten her plain face. Yet Genevieve stared, compelled. The woman smiled and turned away.

Genevieve felt out of place, an impostor, like the pregnancy mask that falsely declared her a future mother. Melasma, the doctor called it. Pregnancy hormones splotched her face like faint birthmarks. A cruel mask fixed on her in this city of masks. Genevieve's hand moved from her pocket to her belly. Beneath the caress of her fingers, a hard shape protruded under the satin of her skirt, reminiscent of the face of a child at play behind a blowsy curtain.

Like a car tailing an ambulance, Genevieve followed the mouse woman's path through the celebrants into the back courtyard. Lush foliage stirred in the evening breeze. Colored lights strung in the leaves danced on and off. The nearby French Quarter wattage drowned out struggling stars.

Genevieve was surprised that Fritz had invited her at the last minute. At first she'd been unable to decide what dish to bring to an All Saints Day Voodoo Ceremony potluck. She had pictured a spread of rooster heads, bull testicles and raw eggs, eels and locusts. At the least, local fare such as crawfish, jambalaya, and gumbo. Instead, tuna casserole, bean dip, macaroni salad, hot dogs, and Doritos loaded the table. The food was left untouched. Everyone drank instead. Fritz had suggested they split the cost of vast Bloody Mary quantities as their contribution, and many of the white-garbed strangers now sucked at the drinks, licking pulp and salt from their lips.

A tall man heaped bay leaves on a rusted barbecue grill. Pungent smoke wafted over the devotees, who trickled out the back door, following an invisible current. The fountain water's chlorine, disinfecting the toxic Mississippi, overpowered the scent of the smoldering laurel.

The tall man smiled at Genevieve. "I'm Rhett," he said, his voice quiet and warm. He shrugged at an unasked question. "Mom liked Clark Gable." Like the mouse woman, this man seemed anchored. As if he knew something Genevieve didn't.

"Gin," she said, the abbreviated name Fritz had given her when they met.

"The ceremony's starting soon. Did you bring a sacrifice?"

Genevieve stared at the flames. Tucked in her pocket, the crystal egg lay warm against her hip, as if fire were inside it.

Like the solid presence in her belly. Like the glowing, swollen abdomen in the painting.

Rhett gave her a bay leaf. "Sacrifice doesn't mean giving up. It means to make sacred. The sacrifices tonight are *mange sec*, dry meal. Without blood."

"I've never been to a ceremony like this before."

"Go with the flow. Don't fight the Loa." He pointed her toward a gate leading out of the courtyard, and she followed the stream of partygoers passing through it.

An altar of candles throned the dirt alley behind the house. An ark of white wood straddled two long poles, handles for two men to carry the offering-laden barge on their shoulders during the procession to the graveyard. The mouse woman crouched in front of the empty barge, chalking a human figure with cornmeal into the uneven dirt before it—like a victim's outline at a crime scene. Becky, the priestess and artist.

The woman's normalcy surprised Genevieve. She had expected a large-breasted, coal-skinned woman with serpentine hair and enormous hoop earrings. Like wearing white for ritual purity when she expected Gothic, black garb. Like learning the day *after* Halloween was the hallowed day. Day of the Dead.

The people gathered, silent, illuminated only by candles. Fritz danced through the crowd, a snare drum balanced on his hip. He used the palm of his hand as an ashtray. He moved close behind Genevieve. "The Vévé." He motioned to the chalked figure. "A path for the Loa, from Guinée to us."

Becky stood, wiping her hands. The devotees left a wide, empty circle around her. Becky set a painting on the altar, the colors garish against so much white, a naked man and woman, entwined.

"Marassa. The First Twins." Becky's low whisper carried like distant thunder. She told the myth of the farmer's wife who continually gave birth to stillborn twins. *Abukus*, she called the dead babies, actually monkeys who had entered the woman's womb for revenge. Only when the farmer ceased killing monkeys who ate his crop would the next set of infant twins survive.

Becky addressed the crowd. "There are no opposite forces. What is different is really the same. Death and sex are intertwined under one god. Don't be ashamed if the Loa, the spirits, seize you tonight and cause you to do the unexpected." She glanced at Genevieve.

Becky tied a white scarf over her hair and spoke in Haitian Creole, her words flowing in harmonious cadence. Fritz hummed translations in Genevieve's ear.

"To the east, to the north, to the west." Becky slugged bourbon. She crouched, spat over the chalked figure in each direction, and scattered cornmeal. "We call upon Legba to open the door to the World of the Invisibles."

Rhett sang, leading a call and response. A half dozen drummers beat an intricate rhythm. The devotees repeated Rhett's foreign song. Fritz hummed and swayed behind Gin, her skirt *swish-swishing*.

Rhett chugged bourbon. He passed the bottle to the massed celebrants. Someone's hand reached forward. A moment later, the hand returned the bottle. Rhett took another swallow and again passed the bourbon into the crowd. Someone else reached, took a slug, and returned the bottle. Soon Rhett had taken a dozen shots in rapid succession. Hands patiently reached, no one anxious or greedy. The singing and drumming continued. The neighboring houses remained dark and quiet. Fritz took a long swig.

Rhett weaved, blinked, and fell to his knees.

Becky danced around Rhett and pulled him to his feet. Coiled, rhythmic, restrained, intimate. Bodies around their perimeter moved in place, blood beating to the rhythm, still outside the invisible circle.

The music ceased.

Mysteriously choreographed like everything else, the offerings to the dead began. As Fritz had explained, the devotees sacrificed gifts to the deceased, offering something the dead had cherished in their lifetime. Having crossed into the beyond, the Loa could reach out and receive, hear the devotees, feel their heartbeat through the drums. The offerings would be carried to the cemetery at midnight. The Loa, the spirit gods, would consume the energy from the sacrifices, leaving the material remains for the poor to scavenge.

A woman stepped forward with a loaf of bread. She knelt before the altar, murmuring, set it down, and retreated into the crowd. One by one, devotees stepped forward with their offerings: cigarettes, a vial of white powder, Mardi Gras beads, money, alcohol, cigars, cola, fruit. Fritz sprinkled a Bloody Mary on the ground and set a full cup on the altar. He then set a small blank canvas, about six inches square, in front of the Marassa painting. The devotees continued their quiet, rhythmic humming. No two people stepped forward at the same time; each understood when to take a turn.

An attractive businesswoman, blonde hair coiffed, knelt in her stockings and murmured. The drumbeats and singing drowned out her words. No one filled her space when she stepped back. An expectation hung in the air, like an audience hesitating to clap, not sure if the symphony is over. Genevieve caught herself, as if drawing up short on the edge of a precipice. Only the weight of the glass egg in her pocket kept her from stepping over. Tiny fingers scratched inside her. She leaned back against Fritz.

Becky led a young man into the circle. He wore black jeans, black coattails, his chest smooth and hairless between the lapels, black top-hat, cane, and sunglasses. He strutted and posed with the swagger of a rock star. Genevieve recognized his image from a wall painting.

"A Guedeh baron, spirit of death itself," Fritz whispered. She would have guessed the devil.

The young god turned his back to Becky. His feet remained planted, but his knees absorbed the rhythm of the drums. Becky passed a small gourd filled with dried seeds across his body, shaking, shaking, shaking. She inched her way along his back, arms, and legs. He turned to her, and she repeated the process down his face, chest, and groin. He moved to the circle's center and began to dance. As the rhythm took hold of his body, his movements became exaggerated, bubbling from his pelvis and emanating to his extremities. As if he were not dancing at all, but some force danced him.

A brown-skinned, sinewy youth, clothed in flowing white, stepped into the circle. He was barely past boyhood, though he had reached a man's height. He could have passed for any of the androgynous stone angels that stared down at Gin from the city tombs she spent her days wandering through. She had ventured alone into the crumbling St. Louis I, the city's oldest, a cemetery the guidebooks cautioned against entering—not for fear of the dead, but of the living dead. Genevieve had been unafraid. Crack addicts seeking tourists to mug would look at her and see only a stone monument. All she had to fear was lodged inside her, the graven image that would not leave her.

The brown-skinned angel turned his back to Becky, and she passed the shaker along his body. The angel joined the god, whose grinding dance escalated to pelvic thrusts. The angel danced close beside him, perfect beauty shimmering in his delicate, flowing movements, his diaphanous raiment floating over muscle and sinew. Black and white cupped together, the pair remained the center while Becky worked her shaker one by one over the crowd as they each stepped into the circle. Packed into its invisible circumference, now almost no one stood outside of it.

Rhythmic, pulsating bodies filled the alley. The dancers helped themselves from the altar, the dead and the living sharing food, drink, and cigars.

Becky passed the shaker over Fritz. He gyrated and spasmed.

When Gin had asked him if the dead would reveal themselves at the voodoo ceremony, Fritz had told her, "Ain't no afterlife. The living dead are all around us." He didn't believe in any of it. Not voodoo. Not ghosts. Not God.

"Why go to the ritual, then?"

"Because it's real. 'Cause it's a helluva party, man." A phlegmy cough had caught his car engine laugh.

How many were here to feel alive by celebrating the dead? Genevieve didn't know what she believed in, except the stone baby, heavy inside her, as real as a pagan idol carved by ancients.

Fritz stepped into the circle and turned to face Genevieve, still outside of it. "Never too young to drink around here. Not even the baby." He motioned to his alcoholic offering on the altar. "Clara asked me to give an offering to the kid—smaller than my damn thumb," he snorted. "Tell her I did. She won't believe me."

"You know?" Gin rubbed the distension in her belly, like a veil draped over a dead bride.

"Clara said she wanted the abortion, but now she says I forced her. Again. Wasn't meant to be no mother. Meant to be an artist. More damn DNA not what she's here to create.

Meant to paint. Doc fixed it so she can't get pregnant again."

"But, Fritz, I thought she couldn't paint anymore. It's been years since she created anything. She's..." Paralyzed. Sterilized. Turned to stone.

Fritz leaned in to kiss her, but Gin turned away. Tomato juice and pepper on his breath mixed with his typical sweat and tobacco smell, and something else, like mulch, a compost beneath the surface. He pressed against her bony arm. He radiated fever.

Fritz frequently stepped out on his wife. Clara, suspicious and jealous, paced whenever Fritz was gone. The century-old floorboards creaked above Gin's bed with the woman's ceaseless footsteps. Gin trailed Clara through the downstairs rooms, rubbing the tumescence beside her hipbone like a worry stone. When Fritz came home, screamed arguments erupted upstairs, followed by shattering glass.

But despite Fritz's wandering ways, he had never put the moves on Gin. She understood his lack of attraction—to lie with her would be to lie in a grave.

Genevieve backed away from him. Loneliness and desperation drove Fritz toward her tonight, not desire. Gin now knew why Clara had taken the scissors to her head yesterday and torn out chunks of the long hair that Fritz adored. The jagged and bloody spikes would remind him of what he'd ripped from her, punishment for what she'd lost while he filled his own emptiness with the bodies of other women.

Gin reached out. The bay leaf crushed in her fist fluttered over Fritz's head. Fritz touched Gin's cheek as he danced back into the circle's center.

Becky approached Genevieve and pried open her locked knees and crossed arms. Becky passed the shaker over her front, back, and down each limb. Genevieve remained still, did not step into the invisible circle. She expected to be pressured, but nobody stripped her naked and wrapped a snake around her, flames licking at her feet as they howled at the hallowed moon. The tame and joyous gathering disappointed her. She craved fire and brimstone, an end to the sentence she labored under. How much easier to be the maiden sacrificed to the inferno rather than to make a choice.

Becky shook the gourd over the hard obtrusion in Gin's belly. "Yemaya cannot contain the Mississippi. Let go. It is a force that must flow. Must return to earth, blood to feed the next creation. Sex and death are the same river." Becky stepped into the circle, beckoning, but Genevieve would not follow.

Rhett moved among the tiring dancers, dousing outstretched hands from a bottle. He pulled Genevieve's hands out and sloshed rose water over them. Like everyone else, Genevieve patted the flower-water on her face, arms, throat. She patted her belly. The perfumed liquid burned like acid.

Exhausted, Becky called a halt to the music. Everyone clapped softly. "Okay." Becky smiled. "Time for potluck."

The dancers filed back into the courtyard, mud streaking their white clothing. The chalked Vévé figure had been ground into the dirt. Gin had lost the elastic band for her ponytail. Alone with her in the alley, Fritz beat the drum at his side, loud in her ears, moving behind her. *Knock, knock, knock.* The Marassa painting fell forward onto its face, engulfing the small white canvas.

"Genevieve. Please. Please, Gin."

His desire against her back was insistent and pulsing. Genevieve no longer felt such desires. She was dead inside. Turned to stone. Like the baby inside her.

Genevieve had never known sex like the lovemaking that created the child. Her husband, Vincent, ceremoniously cut a smiley into her diaphragm, but the warped rubber face looked sinister rather than happy, with a malicious jack-o'-lantern grin. With the union of their bodies calculated to create a third being, Genevieve felt ecstatic, holy, wholly connected to another human. Her sacred passion with Vincent continued into the pregnancy. She had not experienced morning sickness, only a rapturous sense of fullness.

Then the heartbeat monitor suddenly displayed no sound or motion in her womb. Doctors said her body would probably reject the foreign object and miscarry. She was instructed to save all of the tissue she expelled, so that microscopic analysis could determine whether fetal scraps remained inside her. Before modern medical procedures, embryonic corpses not naturally expelled by the body would calcify in the womb—nature's vengeful IUD. The stone baby would prevent implantation of the next embryo. Sterility caused by conception.

"How can they expect you to walk around with that *thing* inside you," Vincent said while doctors waited to see if they needed to scrape her uterus clean. "If you don't want to wait, you just tell me, and I'll make them take it out now."

Not "it." *Him.* An earlier ultrasound proved that it was a boy, showing his penis sticking out for all the world to see. They had laughed and laughed. With Vincent's words, she knew she could not trust her husband. She turned the same glass eyes on him that she turned on everyone else.

The fetus remained lodged in her belly, a hard, misshapen rock dimpling her skin. Let someone try to rip her child from her and she would turn on them with Medea's ferocity. Her talisman, her child. They would go to the grave together.

She agreed to the D&C, and Vincent dropped her off at the hospital. But she walked straight out the back doors and returned home to pack while Vince eradicated viruses from campus computers. When he returned to pick her up after the procedure, she was gone.

She had taken odd things from the house along with the suitcases: her wedding dress, the glass orb from the mantle, and the antique cradle. Things that made no sense to her at the time, but now did. The baby knew what would be needed.

She pictured Vincent now, lining up his Cheez-its like a checkerboard on the table before he ate them, working his way one by one up the rows. As if life could be so ordered. Surely he was relieved that his wife had abandoned him, taking the coffin with her.

Now in this muddy back alley, she would step forward and speak to her child. Offer the crystal egg Vincent had purchased for her after she woke from a magic dream, which told her she had conceived.

She had described to Vince the dream egg, full of exploding color and light. The glass egg became a shrine to the hope that conceived the child, to the memory of one who had never been born. *But he exists. Solid as stone. Can't you hear him knocking?* The knocking and gnawing woke her whenever she tried to sleep. *He's still feeding on my sorrow, and he remains.*

"A blighted ovum," doctors called him, stating that miscarriage would be a blessing in disguise. "The body knows what's best." They tried to comfort her.

Yes. The body knows what's best. To hang on. Not let go. Yet they would have taken him from her.

She had misinterpreted the dream as a good sign, not a bad omen. The glass egg cursed her and the baby. Vincent's gift had looked nothing like the egg in her dream: this one was a crimson flower locked in glass, scarlet tentacles licking the surface. A burden, heavy as the stone baby, but separate. She would reach across the void with this, his evil twin.

Speak to him. Ask him what he wanted. It would be sacrilege to shatter the egg, as she had been tempted to do. But she could give it to the dead, to the unborn frozen inside her.

Genevieve stood still, detached and isolated as Fritz ground against her, his drumbeat loud and insistent.

Knock knock.

I'm here.

Gin crossed into the circle and stepped onto the smudged Vévé figure. She righted the two paintings and set the glass egg next to the small white canvas for Clara's baby, twins perched in front of the Marassa. She picked up the Bloody Mary, tipped her head back, and drank.

Knock knock.

Tell me what you want.

As if she had no body, the drink flowed straight through her, pouring out between her legs and soaking the white dress.

And then she heard it. Not *knock knock.* But *abuku abuku.*

Like an inmate rattling cage bars, fists seized her ribcage and shook her. She fell to her knees, the beads tangling themselves around her neck. She clawed at them.

Abuku abuku. Let me out.

A deformed fossil tumbled out of her onto the blood-soaked earth. She knocked her fist against her smooth belly.

Don't go. Don't leave me.

Abuku abuku!

Fritz threw off the drum and staggered to her side. "Christ, Gin." He tried to lift her from behind, but could not budge her dead weight. Fritz collapsed on top of her.

Light stabbed the alley as a car swerved into the narrow dirt lane. The vehicle slowed as its headlights engulfed them, a pair of rutting monkeys. The silhouette of Clara's spiked and scabbed head loomed behind the wheel.

A shriek like a jungle macaque's pierced the air. The car backfired, then picked up speed.

Gin threw Fritz off of her, and he lurched toward the altar. She searched in the dirt for the stone child, the only thing she had ever worshipped. Her hand closed on something hard and slippery. Gin clutched the warm rock to her breast as the car struck her, vaulting her over the hood and roof. The car hurtled onward and crashed over Fritz and the altar. Metal and bone crunched. The car flattened the fence, plowed through the party, and sideswiped Becky's backyard fountain. The glass egg shattered into a glittering shower of slivered red. A spume of water sprayed over the wounded and moaning celebrants.

Gin landed face up on the altar wreckage amidst the litter of sacrilege and torn flesh. The blank canvas landed on top of her. Something crept across her smashed torso.

The car ground to a halt with its snout over the toppled grill. Flames licked at the bumper. The car groaned and shuddered into stillness, metal popping in the flickering heat.

Clara flopped from the open car door, her neck gashed. Dressed in a filmy white slip, she crawled toward Gin, trampling Fritz's legs that beetled from beneath the front tire. "Whore," she rasped. She plucked the white canvas from Gin's breast. The fountain of blood at her throat gurgled. "Had to offer this myself." A protrusion now warped the blank canvas, as if a child's face were pressed against it. She caressed the mask-like shape, smearing it with her bloody fingers.

Gin tried to reach for the baby crawling across her dress, but she was paralyzed, her spine crushed to pulp. Clara saw what Gin wanted, and lifted a strange talisman from Gin's skirt. A small penis thrust between half-formed legs. The malformed infant grinned lecherously like a baboon.

Clara pressed the stone fetus and the white canvas to her breasts, and it seemed that they tipped their mouths up to the cascade of blood washing her bodice. "Twins," she wheezed, with a victorious look down at Gin. "They run in my family."

Gin tried to scream her protest, but she lay fixed and silent, as if she were made of stone.

THOU SHALT NOT...

Engage in Idolatry

Frozen

Megan Crewe

The rite always begins in warmth. We gather around the fireplace and its wafting heat, every one of us with Grafton blood. Sparks spit through the iron grill and snap at our hair. The glow floats over the painting of Great-Great-Grandpa: stiff and young in brilliant oils, gazing across the room with lips slightly parted, as if He's about to grin or sing or breathe us in.

This evening, it was my turn on the stool. The stool wobbled because one leg was too short. I could still taste the icing of my thirteenth birthday cake on my lips. The hall wavered with the sole dim light of the fire, because Grandma Grafton didn't want us to remember the water stains on the wallpaper or the spider cracks in the ceiling plaster. I looked for Billy's face, for his eyes to hold me steady, but I couldn't find him. Then we all—aunts, uncles, nieces, nephews, Grandma, Great-Aunt Doreen, and Dad of course—went still, because Grandpa Grafton had cleared his throat. He stood behind my stool, beneath the painting of Him.

"A long time ago..." Grandpa said. His voice was rough in my ears. "...three score and seven years, there lived a man."

"A great man," said Grandma, rising beside me.

"The greatest man," said Great-Aunt Doreen, on the other side.

"Do you know his name?"

"We know it," said the aunts and uncles and cousins and Dad.

"We know it," I said.

"Do you know it?"

"We do," we cried.

"Tell me."

"Richard Grafton!"

The name rose and fell against the muted hiss of the fire. A little one twittered, and an aunt pinched him quiet so the name was not disturbed. It had to settle over us like a drift of gauze. No other time may we say it. Every other time, it's Great-Great-Grandpa. Great-Great-Grandpa watches and listens. If you push or steal, we may forget, but Great-Great-Grandpa will remember. Keep all the secrets you like; Great-Great-Grandpa will find you out. And it is He who will decide.

He stared down from the portrait, the wood smoke rose, and I remembered how Lenore had looked through the mist of evaporating schoolyard snow the day she'd smashed the disc of my science project under her glossy shoe. How afterwards she'd pursed her lipsticked mouth as I picked the icy shards out of the gravel, and her clot of friends had called me a geek-baby.

Maybe they were right. Maybe I am a baby. Now I can't remember anything. The cold is squeezing into my eyes like two twisting thumbs, suckering my skin raw like a giant leech. My nerves prickle, my bones ache. I think there's a sob stuck in my throat. I can't suck it in. I can't let it out. He will hear.

I won't cry in front of Dad, even though he thought I did, coming up on the train to Grafton Manor. The passengers were strolling the aisles and debating who was most overwhelmed by the experience of riding a train. They were all grins and toothy excitement, but I must have looked sad, staring out the window. Dad asked if I missed Mom. I didn't answer.

He ruffled my hair and said, "It's just for the weekend. This time is special."

"Mom never comes when it's special," I said.

"It's not your fault," he said. "She wouldn't understand about it."

"About Great-Great-Grandpa?"

Dad's voice went all stiff, the way it does whenever Mom mentions Him.

"Yes," he said. "And other things, too."

"She thinks they should bring Him back," I said. "Couldn't they? We learned about those new microbot medics in school last week. Mrs. Carson said they can fix all sorts of things that doctors couldn't before."

Dad frowned. "The procedure should work," he said. "But it's not perfected, especially the cryo part. Sometimes there's damage to the organs when they do the warming. Sometimes people come out wrong. We don't want to take that chance. Until there's no risk..."

"We'll leave Him be?"

"Yes," he said. "He went through so much. He deserves his rest."

Dad looked at me then in a way that seemed so far away it made my skin itch. His eyes wavered between laughter and tears. "My Fanny," he said. "Almost grown up. We'll have to wait for you and see."

He must be waiting now, somewhere outside the cold dark world and the tingling in my nose and teeth. He and Grandma Grafton and Grandpa Grafton and Great-Aunt Doreen, all half-cousins and second cousins, aunts and uncles, Billy, and Rachel, too.

When Aunt Millie picked us up in the train arrivals lot, with her stretched toffee grin and Grandpa's ancient blue minivan, Rachel was already waiting. She watched me through the windshield, from where they'd folded her wheelchair into the passenger seat. Her head leaned to the side and her bangs tipped across her eye, the one that never opens all the way now. I wasn't sure she was looking at me. Her look went far off.

I smiled at her and her lips twitched, and I felt a lump in my stomach like I'd swallowed a rock. Then Dad said, "Let's go," and I clambered into the back of the van. Matt and Tobey in the middle seat stared at me as if I was covered with polka-dots.

In the back was Grandma. She tapped the seat beside her and I sat down. In the shadow of the window shade, her face looked small and wizened as a dehydrated peach. Her gaze darted over me.

"You'll do fine," she said. "I can see the strength in you." She patted my knee with her cool hand. I couldn't speak.

She was wrong. I'm not strong, and He will see. He'll see how I fell when the boy shoved me, as I skidded over the iced cement of the schoolyard. I couldn't even hold onto the disc shards. Lenora had gone, all of the girls, the teachers, too. It was just me, and I couldn't stop it, couldn't stop the pieces from scattering, couldn't stop him from grabbing my skirt, couldn't stop my feet from slipping. The ground tasted the way my mouth tastes now, like cold.

My teeth are numb; no matter how I try to shut my mouth, it's yawning open with an icicle jabbed in my jaw. I can't open my eyes. I can't feel if they're closed. The dark is still black, either way.

It's darker, darker even than the sky after the sunlight died on the way to Grafton Manor, the Manor that is not really a manor but just a big house, with ivy crawling across the curling shingles, and windows that arc into little crumbling peaks like perpetually raised eyebrows. But even on the porch you can hear it, rustling through the rotting floorboards: the hum of His machines. Like one long exhale vibrating through the walls.

Our last visit, Mom called the house a health hazard, and Dad kept his voice calm and said his parents couldn't afford to fix it up, what with the medical bills—they were nearly as poor as Great-Great-Grandpa had been once. They were talking so quiet that I had to pretend I was asleep. Dad said they didn't want to make a mistake, like His children before. Like His son. The son, Dad said, had been greedy for money. Great-Great-Grandpa said he needed to stand on his own feet, earn for himself the way He had with His new jet engines and motor designs, and the son thought he'd earn by inheriting. Which had something to do with the thing that made Great-Great-Grandpa so sick he had to be put in the cryo-chamber, except I couldn't hear everything Dad said. And I thought, I've made so many mistakes already.

Does He know? I'm only thirteen with frost cramping my lungs, and He is going to decide. Does He see the great big mess in my head that I try and try and can never get untangled? Does He see how my hands shake when they're not numb, when I get the wrong answer, and the teacher's face goes all flat and disappointed? Does He see that I only stared when Lenora flirted with the cute guy from the high school, and I wished I was her? All I feel is the sliding and the sharp bits on the inside, and my pulse as it scatters. I'm scared.

Did He see the same in Rachel? Is that why He took from her?

No one really knows what's left in Rachel. All you can see is what's on the outside: her legs floppy like a doll's and her lazy eye. I can remember when she joked and argued and pinched me so she could take my spot at the kiddie table. Now her sentences come out scrambled. At dinner, she goes in her wheelchair to sit with the grown-ups. He judged her, and she came back, even if not so well as the others. So still she gets to eat with all the grown-ups, which means Frank and Alice and Billy, too, even though they're not much older than me. Billy always notices when Rachel needs help cutting her meat or pouring the gravy. Even before he went into the basement four years ago, his eyes were cloudy and the pupils drifted like bottle caps in the canal, but he sees.

He came over when the grown-ups were clearing their table and gave me his smile, a little ragged around the edges. "You ready?" he said.

"I think so," I said.

"Nobody is."

I thought of how he'd come up the stairs between Grandma and Grandpa, his face beaming like a new May morning, so it made me glow on the inside. "You were, weren't you?" I said.

He shook his head. "They thought my eyes were weak and I'd fall asleep. But I didn't. I stayed awake, and you know what? It was like I'd woken up, without even knowing I'd been asleep."

When we got to the hall, he stopped in the doorway and kissed my forehead.

Maybe that was all the boy wanted, three months ago, when I'd run to the wrought iron tree and he'd run after me. My palms froze to the metal as I climbed. The skin tore and bled. He tugged my ankle and leered, and my grip started sliding. Three months ago or three minutes ago, I don't remember. It seems like hours, and I can't feel the tick of my watch against my wrist. I can't tell if I'm breathing, even. There's nothing. Nothing but me and Him.

We all know His story by heart, the tale Grandpa tells as the humming swells, the tale of His sacred life.

Grandpa said, "And in His youth He learned from great scientists, and machines leapt to life beneath His fingers..."

Grandma said, "And then He heard of the distant struggle in the city of His birth, and He returned, though His parents begged Him to stay away..."

Great-Aunt Doreen said, "And through the jungle He fought to reach the tyrant's throne, and the devices of His invention led the way..."

All three: "And though He was a hero to the people, and they rejoiced for the freedom, yet He was betrayed, infected..."

We all joined in. "And He said through the swirling mist, 'Let those of my blood follow me in my path, and learn what it is to live.'

"Those will follow Him in His path, and learn what He wills that they know."

It's my turn to follow.

"May He judge her worth returning."

I should have run, vanished behind the scuffed velvet curtains that line the basement walls. But Dad was standing proud at the top step, and I kept stepping, down, down, into air that smelled of mildew. The cryo-chamber looked like a giant chrome bathtub, the dials and plugs and blinking lights. Dimpled pipes snaked into the floor. Grandpa yanked a lever, and the lid whined back with a gasp of icy vapor.

"No," I said. "I can't." Grandpa took me by the hand. "No," I said, but still I walked, up the tin stepladder. I saw Him, His stone-blue face, in the glimpse before my eyes squeezed shut and they rolled me in, and the lid snapped shut on the last sliver of light. Leaving me with Him.

His chin is touching the bridge of my nose. His ribs arch against my chest. I could sink into Him, sink in and seek out the warmth He must be hiding, somewhere, inside. Pretend the cold is just a frost duvet and His lips a frozen pillow. Let the darkness steal over.

Wake up, says Billy. That's what he did. But I'm not sleeping. Not yet. It's He who's asleep. Maybe I could make Him let me go. He wouldn't know.

The trick is, don't fall asleep. Don't fall...

Those are his arms, clamped around me. They clench so tight. Ice-hard, they crack my lungs, and the air just gushes out. The cold floods in. I'm falling into the solid wall of His chest. He's judged, He's judged, He will take my eye and my legs and my tongue, He's dragging me down, I should have run. Now I can only grab. It feels like clutching steel, like the wrought iron tree, where I thought I knew the boy would never stop tugging, but still I held.

So I hold on. I hold and I remember how I ran, how my legs skittered but held me up, how Rachel's legs dangle limp over the front of her wheelchair. How her hands flutter like mindless birds. She was the one who let go. She let go in the cold dark crushing and fell down into the black, and He decided. But my legs are mine. I need to stand on them, the way I stood when the boy swore and wandered off, and I dropped from the tree simply because I wanted down. Lenora was skulking by the fence. Her fingers, that once tied knots in my hair, trembled around the yellowed cigarette. I saw that she would rather have fallen than held on until her palms bled. I looked at her, and I was glad I was different.

I must keep seeing.

Great-Great-Grandpa tugs, and I hold on. I push Him away, His ribs, His lips, His arms. I hold onto His name.

Richard Grafton. I say it in my head. It's mine, too. Fanny, Fanny Grafton.

The grip loosens. I push, and I feel it's not so crushing. It's like when Mom squashed me against her before I left this morning with Dad. Except He has no warmth, not for me. I push, and I feel the pulse flicker in my temple.

He lets go.

I curl up on his frozen skin and hold strong to my heartbeat and the gasp of my lungs. He will lie beneath me until I scramble out into the light.

He's judged. I've decided.

I will not be frozen.

into a frigid pool of water. "The victim was found yesterday afternoon by an officer on rounds." The detective moved to the center of the empty room. Only the wan light from a narrow window provided illumination. It spilled across the filthy floor like a stagnant pool of water. "His body was found here." Matthew gestured toward a black stain near his feet. "He was mutilated...."

As I listened, my attention drifted toward the wall, pulled there like iron to a lodestone. Upon seeing the words, an icy hand seized me. The room now felt as cold as a crypt.

"Is it the same?" Matthew asked.

"*He gearwian þæt fyllo man hwa forlætan se leoht,*" I read aloud. "He serves the feast for those who have abandoned the light." The corrupted Old English script had been scrawled on the wall with human blood. It was the same as it had been nearly a decade ago.

"Are you sure, Rudolph?" Matthew asked bleakly. "Could it be someone else?"

I struggled to breathe. The chill air and its cloying odor of death and sweat and sickness stifled me. Gasping, I reflexively withdrew a handkerchief, clasping it over my mouth and nose.

Matthew waited, but he didn't need my confirmation.

"I am certain," I managed after a moment, turning about. "It is the same."

"*Damn,*" Matthew said. "There's no escapin' it this time."

The weary floor creaked beneath his pacing bulk. I willed myself to face him. "What do you mean?"

"The first time the victim was a petty thief, and an immigrant. Few in city government want money spent on investigating that sort of murder. But this, this"—he shook a fist—"this time a man of *substance* was murdered."

That seemed impossible. We were standing in a ramshackle tenement in Hell's Kitchen, not a mansion on Millionaire's Row. "Who was it?"

"Harold Van Alstyne," he said.

"While I don't take my evening stroll along the gold-paved lane of Park Avenue," I said, "I still know that a man like Van Alstyne would not be prowling around Hell's Kitchen. Even if we were to assume he had some unsavory appetite, some vile attraction to this district, men are at his beckon to manage such details. I can't imagine him even setting foot in any part of New York City below 42nd Street, except to depart to another region of the world."

"Detective," came a voice from the doorway. Startled, I spun to find a uniformed officer. "I've been called to Union Square. Some of the rabble are gathering."

I'd heard the word used often, as of late. It seemed that cold, hunger and poverty had transformed the people of the city into "rabble."

"Be gone, then. You're not needed here."

I felt the officer's stare settle upon me. There was what I took to be a glimmer of amusement at the pale cast of my countenance.

"*Move!*" Matthew roared, and like a mouse to his lion, the officer scurried away.

"It *was* Van Alstyne," Matthew said, his voice hoarse but softer. "And this city is so bloated with corruption that a murderer *must* be found. While the rabble gathers at one end of Manhattan, the wealth gathers in midtown, pulling strings to protect their own. And our politicians dance and jump like the puppets they are. All the while gangsters set up gambling houses—even in the mansions on Park Avenue. No, this one won't be forgotten. This death was one of theirs."

While I didn't share my friend's instincts in many areas, I could read into this. The dark secret we'd uncovered a decade ago, one that we'd let rest in fear of what might be uncovered, was now in danger of returning. He was correct. The city couldn't withstand this. We were facing something beyond humanity's ken. And disturbing it would result in something far worse than a riot.

...the mighty beast was slain by my blow in the storm of battle. In this manner, and many times, loathsome monsters harassed me fiercely; with my fine sword I served them fittingly. I did not allow those evil destroyers to enjoy a feast, to eat me limb by limb, seated at a banquet—

A gentle tapping interrupted me. I gingerly placed *Beowulf* on a stack of books tottering on my end table—a skyscraper of writings.

When I opened the door, I received a cheerful, "Hello!"

Jordan Gabriel stood before me, a canvas bag slung over her shoulder, and a bright expression on her soft face. "Detective Leahy suggested I pay a visit," she said.

My gloomy disposition unexpectedly lightened. "The detective is a perceptive fellow. And I suspect in league with you. Please, come in."

She possessed a jaunty step and an assurance in her demeanor. She nearly reached my height, and while she appeared slight, almost to the point of being as fragile as china, it was not so. Her fiery hair, cropped close, matched the resilient façade New York City had given her. Being a female anthropologist with little chance of acquiring tenure from a university required determination and eternal hope. Rather than professing, she catalogued at the Museum of American Indian Studies.

With a thump she planted the canvas bag on my dining room table.

I cringed at the sound, although my concern went unheeded.

"Books," she pronounced. "The type you dread so very much."

"No more," I said, closing the door. "Unless you brought them for the fire, you've wasted your time."

During my years in the city, I'd encountered the ubiquitous pulps. A low quality, formulated class of something that only approximated writing. At every opportunity I denounced them and condemned them. I lectured about them, and fed them to my fireplace. Or at least, that is what I claimed. By some inexplicable means unfathomable to me, I'd come to enjoy them. It was a foul habit, one of which I was quite ashamed. And Jordan kept me plied with volumes of the sinful treasures. But now her motives had become suspect. I couldn't help but wonder if she had surmised my horrid addiction.

"I won't read them, you know," I offered as firmly as possible.

"They are for the fire. Cheaper than coal or wood." She glanced at my end table. "Chrysler or Empire?" she asked.

I thought for a moment. "The last one was *Beowulf*. Malory would topple the lot. Therefore, it has reached its apex. It must be the Chrysler Building."

"I should have known. Chaucer or Malory always forms the foundation of the Empire State Building." She marched into the kitchen. "I'm having tea. Care to join me?"

"Indeed," I answered, while quickly stealing a glance at the contents of the bag. Books and magazines! Enough to carry me for several days, if I paced myself.

When she returned, I had the fireplace blazing, and was settled on one side of the table.

"Lucky I brought plenty of books," she said, placing cups and saucers before us.

For a long moment we said nothing. The fire hissed and popped, and the cups clanked. Finally, Jordan broached the subject. "Detective Leahy says that they've returned."

Even in the company of a roaring fire and within the walls of my apartment, a bitter cold still slipped beneath my skin, seeping into my bones. "I suspect they've always been here. Only now we can no longer ignore them."

She nodded. "Is it time to leave the city?"

"I can't. That would be too easy. I've carried this secret too long to run from it now."

"What's different this time?" she asked.

"Harold Van Alstyne."

She arched an eyebrow. A motion I found charming. "How on earth is he involved?"

"It seems that he owns a number of tenements in Hell's Kitchen, and probably every other district in the city. I've read in the papers that many people in that neighborhood have been turned out, living in the streets as they are unable to pay rent. I believe that's why he was... consumed."

"It *was* those creatures, then. The sin-eaters?"

Although I avoided using that label, it had been given to them in countless texts I had scoured in search of their history.

"I fear so. The medical examiner believes that Van Alstyne was eaten alive. Originally he stated it was an animal attack. But when pressed for the sort of beast, he recanted and proclaimed it a *human* animal.

"It seems now the guilt is being placed on the doorstep of the ejected tenants—if they had a doorstep, that is. The argument is that they found Van Alstyne and murdered him."

Softly, Jordan said, "Some men worship rank, some worship heroes, some worship power, some worship God, and over these ideals they dispute—but they all worship money."

This sudden pronouncement startled me. My surprise clearly amused her; the hint of a smile danced upon her lips.

"Mark Twain," she said.

"I've never read that."

"It was just published in his notebooks."

"Oh... right. Well, either way, it appears that Twain has seized upon the root of the problem. One of the wealthiest men in the city is turning out people, leaving them homeless, and his brethren want satisfaction. Justice be damned."

"Do you think Detective Leahy is going to arrest—capture—one of these degenerated humans you and he suspect?"

"You've examined the original bones I brought from the sewer. They are not human. Maybe they once were. Since I first encountered them, I've combed through volumes of folklore and history, hoping to make sense of them. Originally, I had traced them to a monastic order, one that believed eating the flesh of sinners would save humanity. They were persecuted by the Church, and it was said they confessed their sins and were executed."

"Instead, they hid," Jordan said.

"Yes. But I've found other writings describing such cults as far back as ancient Sumer. I don't know how long they've been lurking in the dark folds of the world. But I do know that New York has plenty of hiding places, and I've feared for many years that there may be scores of them here."

Jordan's visage darkened, concern creasing her smooth skin. "How many, Rudolph?"

"I can't be certain. But if they arrived in the 1600s when New Amsterdam was settled, then they've had plenty of time to propagate. For them, New York is a veritable paradise. Think of it. Creatures who consume those guilty of sin?" My spine felt as though Death were tugging at it from the grave. "This *is* the Big Apple."

My words had no effect. Matthew continued to load the shotgun. One shell following another.

"You are only endangering yourself," I pleaded. "This isn't a Lower East Side gang, or a few hoodlums hiding in the subways."

He fixed me with a withering gaze. "You didn't see fit to tell me this before? You've let me believe that only a few of these *things* lurk beneath the city. Now you tell me there's an army of them."

"I've refused to believe it. I've been lying to myself. I dreaded the truth. The possibility seemed too terrifying to accept."

Clad in our overcoats, we stood inside a subway maintenance house, near the tenement where Van Alstyne's body had been discovered. Our heated words formed clouds in the air. Outside traffic sputtered past.

He worked the shotgun, loading a shell into the breech. "The folks Van Alstyne tossed out have been arrested," he said bitterly, his lips white with anger.

"What evidence stands against them?"

"Ha! Evidence, you want. Then you'd be the first man in the city that required evidence to rid our grand metropolis of a few rats."

"You only risk your life," I said.

"I'm doing what's right. Maybe the cannibals won't see it that way. But I do."

Effortlessly he pulled open one of the two steel doors covering the opening to the tunnels below.

"These are more than cannibals, Matthew. They are monsters. The only reason they hide is because they still fear us—*those who live in the light.* Memories of the Church persecuting them keep them at bay. Entering their world might provoke them."

"So we just let the innocents be punished, and that keeps us all safe? Is that it, Rudolph? Wouldn't that put us on the plate next? 'Cause if that ain't a sin, then it should be. An' I'll not stand for it."

I started to reply, but my words caught in my throat, contemptible words that I could not force myself to speak. Instead, I watched as he descended, vanishing into the blackness.

Terror held me fast. I had encountered one of these creatures before, face to face. They were indeed more than cannibals. Not only did they eat the flesh of their victims, they also consumed their memories. These ghoulish monstrosities had somehow become a form of living purgatory. The humans they devoured lived on inside them. Memories persisted. Thoughts continued in new brains. They were repositories of humanity's wretchedness. Foul, loathsome vessels of evil. I knew this, but no others did. Another secret I had never uttered.

Try as I might, I couldn't force myself to follow Matthew.

Time ran on as I stood on the precipice, urging myself forward, all the while cowering inside. I had reached my wit's end. I quaked and shivered from head to toe. I locked my eyes tight and thought of my friend, and what awaited him. Unfalteringly, he'd entered the fray, with the intention of protecting those who were innocent, people he did not know. This propelled me forward, though I knew no good would come of it.

With the fury of a storm, Jordan stomped into the maintenance room, cloaked in a heavy woolen coat with her usual canvas bag hoisted on her shoulder. The door slammed behind her.

"No note? No word? You just intended to vanish into the sewers?" Blazing anger heated each word, giving them form in the cold air.

"Yes," I said flatly.

"I know!" she said. "You just don't understand, do you?" I pondered her questions, hoping to discern some hidden meaning. But I hadn't the time to give the matter proper consideration. With each second, Matthew gained a further lead.

"No," I confessed. "I'm sorry, but I must stop Matthew."

"Without a lamp, I suppose?" She commenced searching the canvas bag. Her rage had transformed into determination.

"Do you have one?"

"I do. And it is staying with me." She waved the lamp with its bulky battery, urging me down the ladder.

"You cannot follow me," I said, appalled. "It is too dangerous."

She brushed past me, and with the agility and grace of an acrobat, worked her way down the ladder. "I have the light. You'll be following me."

We plodded through the darkened subway tunnel, my ears alert for the growl of a bulleting train. But above the crunch and snap of the gravel strewn around the rails, hearing anything except the pounding of my heart and the huffing of my breath was difficult.

A pace or two ahead of me trotted Jordan. Beyond my pleadings, she refused to relent, pressing onward.

It did not seem possible that Matthew had gained so much ground. How long he had been gone, though, I was no longer certain. What seemed to be seconds might have been minutes.

The circle of light from Jordan's lamp danced and bobbed in the gloom. My eyes remained fixed upon it, while my mind replayed the same words: ...*dread of something after death, the undiscovered country from whose boundary no traveler returns....*

"Look at this." Jordan halted several paces ahead. "This is an old service duct." She aimed the lamp at a round shaft that burrowed downward, into the subway tunnel's wall. Partially buried in gravel was a rusted grate. Clearly, it had once covered the shaft, but had been ripped from its hinges.

"Matthew certainly didn't wrestle that grate open," I said, sending puffs of air before me. "I doubt he could squeeze through the opening. It would be like trying to thread a rope through the eye of a needle."

"It leads to old electrical tunnels, or the pneumatic tubes the city uses for mail delivery," she said. In the lamp's reflection, I glimpsed her face. Intent and resolute, she examined the passage.

"How on earth do you know that?" I asked.

She settled on her knees, planting the lamp on the useless grate. Then she started down the rungs anchored in the wall. "I'm an anthropologist, Rudolph. I know the strata of this city, above and below."

"Good heavens," I exclaimed as she reached out and snatched the lamp. "Matthew couldn't fit down there."

"Perhaps," she answered, her voice tinny and faint. "But his footprints stop here."

I gave a heavy sigh. I very much longed to be in a classroom on the Columbia campus, in warmth and safety. Unbidden, hostile gawking of the officers returned to me. I had only been fooling myself. A mollycoddle I was. Absolute horror gripped me every time I considered what waited beyond the veil of life. *For in that sleep of death what dreams may come?*

I hunkered down and finagled my way into the entrance.

"Is he alive?" I asked.

When I reached Jordan, she'd already located Matthew. He lay prostrate on the hard floor of the narrow passage. "He's breathing," she said, kneeling at his side. "It appears that he's taken a nasty fall." Her hand slipped from underneath his head, damp and red in the lamplight.

I dropped to his side. "Matthew? Can you—"

A slobbery growl interrupted me.

Immediately I fumbled for Matthew's electric torch. Before I could snap it on, Jordan had turned the lamp on them. Four of the gangly, gray-skinned creatures huddled down the length of the passage. They slouched forward, clawed hands swiping at the light.

"Turn the lamp away," I said. "It angers them."

Slowly, the beam glided to a spot before us.

I climbed to my feet, holding Matthew's light. I didn't understand why he was alive. He'd come upon them, and maybe even grappled. Maybe our approach had frightened them off, or some other unfathomable reason. But I was resolved to let no harm come to Jordan or Matthew. In hope of achieving this, I started to formulate a plan.

They crept forward in small, jumpy movements. With them came a fetid stench. My stomach churned and my gorge rose.

I stepped forward, planting my feet in the light. "Is Van Alstyne among you?"

"Rudolph..." Jordan's soft voice quivered. I felt her hand grab my ankle.

A chorus of hissing reverberated in the passage. Smacking sounds and more growls followed.

"I must speak to Harold Van Alstyne," I said.

"Good God, what are you thinking, Rudolph?" The words sounded close to my ear. Jordan was now at my side, the light shifting about at our feet.

"No liiight," came the answer. "Nooo. We bring to him." The guttural sound was part hiss and part slavering.

"Find Matthew's weapon," I whispered to Jordan. Turning to face her, I only caught sight of her delicate visage, swathed in the shadows. "Wake him and leave. Do not follow me."

"What? You don't intend to go with *them*? You can't."

I placed my hands on her shoulders. Even beneath the heavy coat I felt her trembling. Gently I kissed her forehead. "Don't linger," I said, and stepped from the light.

The passage seemed an endless series of twists and turns. My escorts did little to make the journey pleasant. With every step, one hissed or whimpered or released a watery hack. And the rank odor worsened as I neared what I believed to be only one of many colonies hidden beneath the city.

Nonetheless, I stumbled along in the darkness until I knew I was there. No doubts worried my mind about the final location. The overwhelming rot that permeated the air brought me to the point of retching. I struggled against the foulness, using my handkerchief in hope of filtering the stench.

The air pressure had changed as well. I sensed a large room or chamber. From every direction came an inhuman murmuring, as though hundreds or thousands were chanting in some alien tongue. Unable to tolerate it any longer, I called out: "Harold Van Alstyne!"

The chanting continued, unabated. I knew these creatures could see—or sense—me in the turgid blackness. I had expected to silence them for a moment, at the least. When no response came, I raised the narrow electric torch.

"Nooo liiight!" A force, anger or fright, I knew not, propagated the words.

"I must speak with Harold Van Alstyne," I said.

"I... am many. Alssstyne is with me."

Hoping to purchase more time, I pressed onward. "You killed Alstyne?"

A sharp hiss shot back. Snarling and slavering followed like a reproach. "Not killll. Con... sssume. He is now ussss."

My readings, be they legend or fact, told of these creatures being able to "smell" sin upon a person. Now I wondered if it was that unique sense provoking the salivating I heard around me.

"He sinned," I said, using all of my resolve not to let my voice waver. "His flesh served as the feast for those who have left the light."

Another refrain of whimpering and growling came in response. I took the noise to be an affirmation.

"Alstyne, why did you evict those people? There is no one to rent the rooms. Why let them stand empty?" I hoped a direct approach might awaken the memories or whatever part of Van Alstyne that was trapped inside the creature. If anyone, Harold Van Alstyne knew that with the countless empty places in New York City, and the thousands living in ramshackle structures in Central and Riverside Park, evicting the people achieved nothing. Almost one third of the city was on the dole, unable to do more than wait in lines for jobs and food. But if my hypothesis was correct, he would have a reason.

Something part howl and part wail echoed through the vast room. "Greeeed! Greeeed!" It was a tortured sound.

With each moment I felt my determination dissolve. The compulsion to flee flowed through me like the blood pulsing through my veins. But like the Dane who ventured into Grendel's lair, I came to seek out evil. Unable to see, I imagined myself in my classroom, about to present a theory. "You evicted the people to set up a gambling house, is that it?"

Something slammed into me. I stumbled, colliding with another wretch. The slick touch of its skin and putrid breath again set my stomach roiling. Impossibly, I remained on my feet.

"Yesss..." the thing that was Alstyne cried.

Then I knew he'd been in league with racketeers. Like many businessmen in the city, Alstyne saw more profit by tossing the destitute renters on the street, and creating a crooked gambling den to earn revenue. Contemptible as I found him, I so feared his fate that I felt only pity.

One by one the creatures started jostling, dancing about with agitation, snarling and slavering. Without the light, it seemed that I was shifting in an endless mass of the hideous creatures. Any moment, I expected them to pounce upon me. I had leaped and grabbed at virtue throughout my life, but like Alstyne, I had fallen short many times. Righteousness, like Grendel's slayer, did not attend me. I had only hoped my life might purchase mere minutes for Jordan and Matthew.

Like a man caught in a strong river current, a slimy mass of flesh pushed and pressed against me, forcing me in an unknown direction. Tempted as I was, I did not use the light, knowing it would only hasten the ending. I wanted every last moment.

Then above the repulsive sounds, I heard Matthew's voice.

"Rudolph..."

The call was repeated, but this time it came from Jordan.

No. If they entered this place, all hope would be lost.

Although I didn't know what number of people it took—two, ten, twenty? to break the dam, releasing the colonies beneath the city—I was certain at some point they would flood from the sewers and subways, pouring into the streets, frenzied by the seemingly endless feast on the surface.

I slipped through the throng, and with each step, Matthew's call grew clearer. I dared not reply for fear I would be located. The touch of the greasy skin made my insides stir until I thought I would burst. Eventually, I felt a clammy wall, and followed it with the repetition of my name as a guide. The horde that had enveloped me now seemed to recess. The disturbing chanting continued, and far off, I thought I heard a mournful cry—one like Alstyne's.

The fire crackled as Matthew read to Jordan and me from the newspaper. He reclined on the couch while enlightening us.

"*Rusty McCarron, one of the city's most notorious gangsters, was arrested for racketeering yesterday evening. Sources in the Detective Bureau believe that he was also involved in the murder of Harold Van Alstyne.*" Matthew lowered the *Post*, allowing his green eyes to peer over the paper's edge. "I'm not that source. Probably someone on a mobster's payroll who sees this as an opportunity to eliminate the competition."

"I'm sure he's murdered someone," Jordan said. She was sitting opposite me. "But he'll probably get off scot-free."

"Of that you can be certain," said Matthew, returning to the paper. "So many judges in the city are on the take that they're driving the price of bribery down. It's a gangster's market, it is."

The fire popped.

"Those pulps make a nice blaze," Matthew said from behind the paper.

I fixed my gaze on the yellow flames, trying to avoid Jordan's stare. Nonetheless, I felt it upon me.

Moments passed as Matthew read various articles to us. Eventually he fell silent, lost in the comics.

Jordan touched my hand. The warmth pushed away a portion of my chill.

Through the window I watched snow fall from the heavens, gently filling the gaps and folds of the city, silently covering it like a sheet draped over a corpse. It had been said many times that we lived in the greatest city in the world. I wondered what would be said on the day the rabble streamed from the shadowy recesses to overwhelm this great metropolis.

The Wood and the Brass

Marguerite Croft

Had I really wanted to be there, I probably wouldn't have noticed him in the first place, a strange man—pale-skinned, dark-haired, scruffy-jawed. A beautiful man.

It was week two of the fall semester, my first term in college, and the professor was lecturing on Beethoven or Chopin or Bach, some dead, decomposing composer. I smiled at my pun, knowing it wasn't the first time it had been made, especially in the Introduction to Music Appreciation class that was supposed to be part of my gateway to success in the world. And I couldn't care less. I'd get a degree in nursing or business, or become a dental hygienist, like my mother suggested, nothing more, and that would be my life.

I glanced back at the beautiful strange man. He seemed to care about the professor's lecture. His pencil scribbled heatedly across the page, and I imagined smoke coming from the lead. The strange man looked up at me and smiled. I returned my attention to the teacher, and then wished I hadn't. That's what men want, isn't it? A woman who's not afraid and will hold their gaze.

But that wasn't me. There was no man for me, no friends, only college, so I could get a job that would feed me and my mother, who really needed a live-in nurse.

When the fifty minutes were up, I gathered my notebook and pen and headed out the door. Behind me I heard a voice call, "Hey, you. Hey." I almost ignored it, didn't think anyone would be calling me, and I continued past the class-room doors and other students who seemed very old to me, though they couldn't have been more than a few years older than I. A hand touched my shoulder, and then I was looking at my beautiful man, his gray eyes gazing at me, and he was saying, "Hey. Sorry, I don't know your name."

"Amalie," I told him.

"I'm Jeanun." It was a name I'd never heard before, but I said nothing because he'd probably been told, "Oh what an unusual name," a thousand times before, and I didn't want him to think me odd. "You were looking at me in class." He smiled.

"Sorry," I said.

"Why?"

I shrugged and looked at the floor, embarrassed.

"You like music?" he asked.

"Yeah," I said. "Who doesn't?"

"Do you play any instruments?"

I shook my head. "But I wish I could."

"If you're into music, I've got some stuff you might like. I make musical instruments. You wanna come and take a look sometime?"

"Sure. When?"

"What are you doing right now?"

"I have no plans," I said.

"I don't live far. Let's walk."

I hesitated for a moment, not sure if I should accompany a man I'd just met, but no one like him had ever been inter-ested in me. And there was something about Jeanun that made me want to follow him anywhere.

He took my elbow and guided me gently out the doors of the Kiegal Fine Arts building, across the street and through the university district.

As we walked, I asked, "What instruments do you play?"

"Lots of things: guitar, bass, keyboard, drums."

We walked a few blocks and then I followed him down a flight of stairs that led to a basement apartment.

A cobweb hung in the corner of the door frame. A big black spider clung to the center of the web.

Jeanun unlocked the door and I ducked inside.

The large room was filled with strange instruments formed like exotic animals, creatures not of this world. Resting on a stand was a guitar with the head and neck of a peacock and the body of a sea serpent, composed of bright colors, feathers and scales. A saxophone shaped like an ostrich's neck with an alligator's head, and a keyboard that was part horse and part dolphin sat beside the guitar. Such instruments could look tacky, like something you'd find at a discount mall, but these were lovely and magical.

"What do you think?" Jeanun asked.

"They're beautiful," I said. That's all I knew to say. I had no other words.

"This is what I do with my time," he said. "When I'm not creating instruments, I play. I started taking music classes at the university so I can be a better musician. It's my life."

I looked around at the musical creatures and understood why.

"They work?" I asked.

"Of course they work. Why wouldn't they work?" He went to the keyboard and played some chords. The keyboard made the loveliest sound I'd ever heard.

"Well, they're so unusually shaped. I thought it would affect the sound."

"Normally, maybe. But these are special. Which one do you want to learn?"

"I'm sorry?"

"Which instrument?"

I went over to the peacock/sea serpent guitar. "This one."

"Good," Jeanun said, smiling. "I know how to play that one best."

On that first day, he taught me a few chords and then showed me how to turn them into a song. And that's how my life found its focus.

Every day I ended up at Jeanun's, playing the guitar. At first it was because I really liked Jeanun. I liked looking at him; I liked how I felt when he touched me to help me find a chord or guide me through a door, his hand placed gently on the base of my spine. I liked talking to him, and I sensed he liked me, too. But as time went on, it became more about the music. At the end of October he said, "Amalie, you're a natural." I felt myself glowing; I knew he was right.

When I played, I felt as if I'd suddenly left my body, as if something greater had taken control. Maybe it was the music, maybe a higher power. Whatever it was, it was intense—like a drug, I suppose—though I'd never tried anything stronger than a decongestant.

And even though the peacock-and-sea serpent guitar drew me and held me as if it would never let go, I fulfilled my responsibilities. I went to class and was passing every subject, but whatever time I could spare I spent at Jeanun's.

Then it was Christmas break, and instead of going home I decided to stay at school so I'd have more time with my music. Instead of playing, though, I asked Jeanun to teach me how to make my own instruments. He agreed on one condition—that we form a band.

We found a drummer named Kanen and a keyboardist who called himself Babi. Jeanun played bass guitar and I played lead. We called ourselves Jeanun's Groove, and we were magic. Occasionally, Jeanun invited others to accompany us on his other instruments: the saxophone, the flute, the trumpets—whatever he thought a song needed.

When I wasn't making music, I was at Jeanun's working on a flute in the shape of a winged snake. I found that crafting the instruments consumed me more than making music did. I wanted nothing else but to carve and chisel away the wood to uncover the snake hiding beneath, to stain its body with scales and form its wings with feathers.

January came quickly, and school would soon start again. I was heading out the door to Jeanun's when my mother called.

"What classes are you taking this semester?" Her voice was weak, but I could tell she was still smiling. It seemed she was always smiling when she spoke to me, and I felt guilty for it.

"More generals," I lied. I hadn't signed up for any classes. I was planning to spend my time creating more instruments—my snake-flute had turned out beautifully—and making music in my free time.

"I told your Aunt Gwenda you made straight A's last semester. She was so proud. I'm still so proud myself," she said.

I'd lied about my report card, too. I'd barely passed my classes with C's.

"All those hours in the library were worth it, weren't they, honey?"

"You bet," I said.

"I just want to tell you, Amalie, I understand why you're spending so much time at school, why you couldn't come home for Christmas. But I want you to know that I miss you."

"I miss you, too," I lied again. I'd hardly thought about my mother or her cancer in the past few months except for when I came home to a phone message. I felt bad about that, but I couldn't turn my heart from the instruments, from the music.

"I'll send another check for your rent and whatever this afternoon."

"Thanks, Mom." It was all I could think of to say, though I should have said more. Maybe something like, "I love you," but it wasn't in me.

Over the next month I made a set of cymbals, two horns, and another flute. Though they were simple in design, creating them was pure ecstasy. But Jeanun was concerned.

"You've got to slow down," he said. He frowned at the spots of blood seeping through the bandages on my fingers. "You're working too much. If you let them heal, your fingers will develop calluses, and then you can play more often. But you've got to let them heal."

"They're fine," I said.

"And you're too thin. When was the last time you ate?"

I couldn't remember. I was drinking lots of water, but I wasn't eating. I couldn't eat. Since January, every time I ate something I threw it up. Not on purpose, but my body was rejecting food. I wasn't worried, though, because I wasn't really hungry.

"This morning," I said. "I'm fine, Jeanun."

"No, you're not. Look, Amalie, I really care about you. Please..." He reached for my hand and put it to his lips. "Don't do this to yourself."

I smiled and shook my head. It had never occurred to me that Jeanun could be melodramatic. He leaned in to kiss me, and I laughed.

He pulled back. "I thought you liked me, too," he said. His voice was tinged with hurt.

I thought I did, too. I had once, a lot. But now? "I have to focus on this, Jeanun. It's my chance at a great life."

"I thought I could be your chance," he said and walked away.

Though he once had said making music and creating the instruments was his life, he just didn't understand.

So I created my instruments and played the guitar, and the more I felt as if I were on fire, the more I improved. I knew soon my instruments could be as good as Jeanun's, or even better.

Somewhere in my mind I knew that what was happening wasn't logical. No matter how naturally gifted and talented, no woman could suddenly start making beautiful, functional instruments in just months. No one could turn into such a fine guitar player in mere months. But I didn't think about that. I concentrated on my music and what musical creature I would form next.

April came, strong and promising. And though they had sores on them that wouldn't heal, my fingers flew, creating gorgeous creatures that surpassed Jeanun's in beauty, sound, and quality. And we landed our first gig as a band.

Because of my hands, Jeanun threatened to keep me from performing unless I slowed down.

I said, "Who else can you get that's as good as I am? Who knows the music?"

He just walked away. I was his best shot.

I dressed for our first performance with care, putting on a bright red dress that looked like it was formed from thin, sheer scarves. I wove ribbons into my hair and went into Jeanun's bathroom to paint my face—pale skin and dark features.

That's when I first noticed it. As I watched myself in the mirror, my eyes grew dark like holes, and I grinned garishly. My face was gaunt, and it was like looking at a skull that housed something ancient and haunting.

I carefully powdered my cheeks and forehead and applied dark makeup to the stark palate of my face. I was no longer the inexperienced, directionless girl from a year ago. I knew who I was: master musician, master creator.

I barely remember our first performance at the club. But I knew we were good. The owner offered us a contract to play through the summer. He wanted us to perform through the fall and winter, too, but I declined. Who knew where I'd be then? Hopefully someplace better than some no-name club in a nowhere college town.

Two weeks later we returned to play. I looked different because I'd had to shave my head. I'd contracted a bad case of head lice, and no matter what I did, I couldn't get rid of them, their itch, the way they gnawed my scalp.

And still my fingers bled. But when I played, I was on fire, and when I made my instruments, my fingers did not hurt.

Each performance brought more people from the university district until the club had to turn them away. Those who couldn't get in didn't leave; they waited outside as we played. While the people inside danced and swayed to our music, the people outside danced, too. Or so they told me as they tried to touch us when we left.

The students started to buy our instruments, too—our magical instruments made in the image of fantastical creatures, instruments that, somehow, anyone could play, whether they were seasoned musicians or had never picked up an instrument before.

August brought our last performance.

I hated to see it come.

I had forgotten to pay my bills in March and April, so I finally had them sent directly to my mother—my rent, my utilities, that sort of thing. She hadn't seen me in a year, and coupled with receiving my bills because I was "too busy with school to pay them," she'd bought me a plane ticket home before school started again.

If I went home there would be no guitar to play, nor any instruments to create.

And then I realized that going home could be a very good thing—home was California, where I might find opportunities that a small midwest college town couldn't offer. The music and the instruments had to be shared with the world. I couldn't do that if I stayed. I had no choice—I would have to move.

I was supposed to meet the band at Jeanun's house so we could all ride to the last performance together. I also wanted to work on my bongos before the gig, and I was running late. I grabbed my clothes and makeup that I planned to wear for the show. As I was going out the door, the phone rang. I paused but let the answering machine pick it up. It was Helen, my mother's neighbor.

"Amalie, your mom's had a relapse and she's back in the hospital. Call me when you get this. I'll help you get an earlier flight out."

"I don't have time for this," I said and slammed the door.

At Jeanun's, I put the finishing touches on my owl/bear/ crab bongos. I tried for the hundredth time to scrub the lice off my bald, scabbed scalp. Then I wrapped my swollen, crusty fingers in purple-dyed bandages. As always, I applied my makeup carefully while I admired my deep, dark eyes that stared back at me from the mirror, as if trying to see through me. I slipped on my sheer purple dress that matched my bandages.

Jeanun stood in the living room, his head shaved. "Lice," was all he said. I understood.

Our final performance went well. I came back to myself at the end, and the audience screamed, waving their hands in the air, gyrating and jumping to the closing chords of the last song.

I ran to Jeanun to hug him, and as he turned to me I saw the same look I'd seen in the mirror just a few hours before.

"We're good," he said. "This is only the beginning."

As I gazed into his bottomless eyes, I knew he was right. But I would begin again, without them.

Afterward, we had a party in our dressing room, eating and drinking and laughing, talking about what would come next.

"When will you be back from California?" Babi asked.

I hesitated. I was afraid to tell them I wasn't coming back.

"She won't be gone long," Jeanun said, laughing. "She can't leave her instruments. She'll be back in three days, tops."

I swallowed hard. "I'm not coming back."

"What do you mean you're not coming back?" Jeanun's voice had gained an edge.

"I'm moving home."

"To California? What are you thinking?" Jeanun's hands clenched into fists.

"There's nothing for me here."

"How can you say there's *nothing* for you here? I'm here, the band's here. Or were you planning for us to come with you?" His voice had risen.

Babi and Kanen backed away from us.

"I'm going alone," I said. Jeanun's face flushed. My heart pounded against my chest.

"We're not good enough for you anymore?" Jeanun was pacing the room now, eyeing me.

"I'm ready to move beyond Jeanun's Groove. I can go all the way with this, but not here, not with you. You'll hold me back. You'll hold the music back."

"I don't believe this. I did everything for you!" He was in my face now, his eyes feverish. "*I* made that guitar you prize so much. *I* taught you to play! *I* taught you to make your *precious* instruments. *I* looked out for you when you became so obsessed with your music you couldn't even take care of yourself!"

Babi and Kanen were beside Jeanun now. Kanen tried to pull Jeanun back from me. "Calm down, man," Babi said, "It's no big deal."

"Was I talking to you?" Jeanun shoved Babi against the wall. Then he picked up his guitar, tramped toward the exit, and pounded his fist into the metal security door, leaving a dent. "Go ahead and throw me away—it's not going to work out for you, not the way you've planned. I promise you that." Jeanun slammed the door behind him.

Babi examined the dent in the door, a slow whistle escaping his teeth. "He's completely unhinged."

Kanen led me to the couch. "It's okay, Amalie. Here, have a drink."

Babi and Kanen fell asleep, maybe an hour ago.

I think I fell asleep, too. I drooled on the couch cushion, and my eyes are bleary.

The lights flicker and then go out.

"Kanen? Babi?"

"Hmmm?" Babi says.

"The power's gone out and I smell smoke."

"What?"

"I smell smoke."

"Hold on." I hear Babi get up and knock into something.

Kanen asks, "What's going on?"

"Smoke," I say. "I smell smoke."

"Can you hear them?" Babi asks. His voice squeaks.

"What?" I ask.

"They're still out there. They're screaming." A pause. "The door's hot."

"Go!" Kanen says. "Out the back door."

I stop to feel for my guitar that I know is near. I grab it and run for the back exit.

I trip on something, and a shock runs up my leg. I cry out.

"You okay?" Babi says.

"Yeah."

We follow Kanen out the door. Sirens are wailing in the distance.

Outside the streets and trees and cars are covered with ash. At first, I think it must be a trick—the moon's reflection, the early hour, maybe it's all a dream.

Smoke invades my nostrils.

On the sidewalk, I place my foot in the ash. I look into the sky. Flakes of gray drift to the ground.

We cross the street to get a better look at the building.

"Oh," Babi says.

The club is on fire, filled with flames. I can hear the screams now, coming from inside. They are soon drowned out by the approaching fire engines.

And somehow I know, though I don't know how, that I must get my instruments from Jeanun's.

"Where are you going?" Babi yells.

I just keep running, my guitar heavy on my back.

My heart pumps in my chest and stomach acid burns my throat.

Panting, I race through the empty streets of the university district. The rocks beneath the ashes cut through my sandals. For a few blocks the only light is the moon reflecting off the ashes, which cover the ground like a dusting of snow.

And then there is light. Orange flames leap into the sky. They are coming from Jeanun's neighborhood. I run faster, the guitar drumming against my back.

Then I find the source of the flames: the house where Jeanun has his basement apartment. There are no fire engines; there are no police. They are all at the club. There is no one, save me and the street, the night and the ashes, Jeanun's apartment and the fire.

I think only of my instruments.

I have no choice. I charge down the stairs into the apartment and the flames—I must rescue my creations, my instruments. Without them I am nothing.

Protocols of the Elders of Al-Quds

Simcha Laib Kuritzky

"Ms. Lapinsky, will you marry me?" Kreg opened the ring box as he knelt on the restaurant's plush carpet.

"Why, yes, Mr. Stonefield," Gloria said, then flashed a grin as she hugged him. They kissed, and then Gloria admired the ring.

"It was my grandmother's," Kreg said. "If you want, we can buy a new one instead, with a bigger diamond."

"Oh, don't you dare," she said. "I love antique jewelry, and this ring is gorgeous." She put it on and held it to the candlelight.

Kreg returned to his filet mignon. "So, was it a surprise?"

"I knew something was up when those Secret Service agents interviewed my boss and neighbors," Gloria said.

"They were from the Office of Personnel Management." Kreg cut into his steak. "They have to be certain you're not a spy or terrorist using me to get to someone important."

"*Da, tovarich*," Gloria said in a passable Russian accent. "So now you can tell me what you *really* do."

"You know what I do—I market goods from small companies to the federal government. In Washington, it's not what you know, but who knows what you know that really counts. The clearance is so you can attend fancy parties with other Washington insiders."

Gloria's face brightened. "Like that dinner this Friday with President Bush?"

Despite himself, Kreg smiled. She sounded like a child who had just discovered a toy store. "Sure, I couldn't take my girlfriend, but I can bring my fiancée."

"You're certain you can arrange it in only two days?"

"No problem."

"There's no special security to go through?"

"You've passed the background check." Gloria was about to speak again when Kreg cut her off. "Look, I swear to God that you'll be at that dinner." He relaxed when her expression of concern gave way to relief.

"Which deal is the dinner celebrating?"

"The World Bank and Saudis are funding the Palestinian Authority's purchase of equipment from Farmwest Irrigation. It's the first sale under the Oslo Accords, so Bush is making a big deal of it. Hopefully, it will lead to a peace treaty and lots of American contracts."

The champagne arrived, and they spent the rest of the evening talking about plans for the future: the wedding, moving in together, and where their children might go to school.

The next morning, Kreg called the White House social secretary and added Gloria to the invitation list. Lea Berman even congratulated him on his engagement. It felt good now that all the pieces were fitting together—a few years out of school, his firm was doing well, and he'd soon be settling down and raising a family with the woman he loved.

The trouble started on Friday, showing up as an unexpected visitor. A short, brown man in a dark tailored suit was ushered into Kreg's office by his assistant. The visitor's hair was gray except for a thick black mustache of the Middle Eastern fashion.

"Ibrahim Suleyman," he said with a crisp British accent. "Protocol Officer for the Palestinian Authority."

They shook hands, and Ibrahim handed Kreg a business card. It was in Arabic. Kreg turned it over, but the other side was in Hebrew.

"What can I do for you?" Kreg asked.

"We have some concerns about tonight's dinner," Ibrahim said.

"If it's because I'm left-handed, I can assure you I've learned to eat with my right." Kreg's attempt at humor failed to make any impression on his visitor.

"I reviewed the guest list this morning and noticed your fiancée's family name is Lapinsky. That's a Jewish name, no?"

"We've had Jewish staff members meet with Saudis and Palestinians without a problem before," Kreg said, concerned.

"Yes, but the PA now has a coalition government, and the new Minister of Agriculture who will be at the dinner tonight is from Hamas, not Fatah. Surely you can understand how someone devoted to freeing his land from the Zionist occupation would be uncomfortable to break bread with an enemy. After all, why do you think we're buying American irrigation equipment when Israel can produce the same more cheaply?"

The last time Kreg's church had featured a speaker on Palestine, the stories of Israel's brutality to Arab civilians had made him sick to his stomach. He mentally reviewed the guest list and realized Gloria wasn't the only Jew. "I thought the World Bank was sending Paul Wolfowitz to the dinner."

"The World Bank suddenly found something more important for Mr. Wolfowitz to do tonight," Ibrahim said.

"Well, I can understand the Minister's concerns, but I promised my future wife that I would take her to meet the President tonight."

"Tell her the deal fell through at the last minute, and you must work late tonight to patch it up. She'll never know the difference. If you're going to be happily married, you'll have to learn how to finesse promises." Ibrahim smiled diabolically.

"I just proposed to her. I don't want to start off our new life with a lie!"

"Do you want her first dinner at the White House to be an unpleasant one? There are only a dozen guests at this dinner. Surely she doesn't want to sit with a Palestinian any more than he wants to sit with her."

Kreg realized the truth of Mr. Suleyman's words. He couldn't shield Gloria from the nastiness of politics all the time, but Jews and Arabs were bitter enemies, and he should do what he could to ensure her first experience as a Washington insider was a good one. "I'll see what I can do," he said weakly. The Protocol Officer bowed and left.

Kreg called Ms. Berman at the White House and asked about the Agriculture Minister. She verified that Musa Ibn Abdualla had been elected on the Hamas list, but had resigned from that party to take his cabinet position. She still showed Wolfowitz as the World Bank's representative, so Kreg called him. The Director was unavailable, and his assistant was uncertain if Wolfowitz was going to the dinner or not.

"Jesus Christ!" Kreg said to himself. "Why couldn't her background check have finished next week?" He rubbed his temples and decided the World Bank would probably make any change in plans appear to be last minute, since it was illegal to exclude Jewish employees from working with Arab governments. However, that law did not extend to Jewish spouses or spouses-to-be attending dinner parties. Kreg called the White House again to give his fiancée's regrets. When Kreg called Gloria, he was grateful to get her voicemail. He told her there was a problem with the dinner and he would explain when he saw her that night.

The afternoon meetings had their tense and difficult moments, but probably nothing like when he would break the news to Gloria. He half wished the meetings would run late, but Kreg knew he should explain in person, and the last of the obstacles were overcome right at five o'clock. Kreg suspected this was part of the Saudi bargaining style.

When he got to his fiancée's townhouse in the Maryland suburbs, she was waiting for him. They kissed, and then she asked, "What's wrong?"

"I have bad news. I found out that the PA Agriculture Minister will be there, and he's a member of Hamas." Kreg tried to aspirate the "H" the way Ibrahim had done, but it made him cough.

Gloria looked puzzled. "So?"

"You wouldn't want to attend a dinner with a sworn enemy," he said.

"Hamas is an enemy of the United States, yet you're going. Besides, I have Arab coworkers—one's even a Palestinian—and we get along fine. We'll just avoid discussing politics."

Kreg sighed. "I spoke with his Protocol Officer this morning, and he asked that there be no Jews at the dinner."

Gloria looked as if he had punched her in the stomach. Then the shocked expression melted away, and she said, "You're not responsible for what other people do. I guess we can have our own intimate party here tonight."

It had never occurred to Kreg to stay home with her. Could he afford to miss dinner tonight? No, this was too important to Farmwest Irrigation, and the others knew he wasn't sick. "I *have* to be there tonight. It's my job."

Anger flashed across her face. "You're going to let those anti-Semites kick me out just because I was born Jewish? Is this how you're going to treat me when we're married?"

"Look, we can't solve the problems of the Middle East in one night. There'll be other dinners, with more congenial company."

"So, you're just going to abandon me."

"Sweetie..." Kreg put his arms around her. Gloria twisted out of his embrace. Then she pulled off her engagement ring and dropped it in his jacket pocket.

"You promised me—you swore to God—that you would take me tonight. A wedding is nothing more than a celebration of a promise. If this is how you keep your promises, I don't want any more of them."

Now it was Kreg's turn to be shocked. When he finally found his voice, he said, "Aren't you overreacting? Sure, this is a bad situation, but we can work it out."

"Go," she said quietly but firmly. "Go to your special dinner without me. Just don't expect to see me again."

Kreg must leave now or risk being delayed by rush-hour traffic. He walked unsteadily to his Lexus and drove off.

If Gloria was going to overreact every time there was a political situation, maybe this was all for the best. Even though she hadn't attended temple since her Bar Mitzvah, she was still a Jew and they were all so paranoid, quick to label anyone who disagreed with them an anti-Semite. But Kreg realized he wanted her, to marry her and spend the rest of his life with her. He was certain she loved him too. How could she throw all this away, over a few words and a broken dinner date? He would let her cool off over the weekend, that's what he'd do. Then he would find some romantic way to make it up to her, and she'd have to forgive him. After all, there weren't that many eligible Washington insiders, and who else could get her regular visits with the President?

Kreg managed to calm himself and get to the White House on time. That calm was shattered when he saw Ibn Abdualla speaking animatedly with Wolfowitz and Riza, Wolfowitz's Tunisian girlfriend. What was Wolfowitz doing here? Before Kreg could work his way into the conversation, the President was announced, and the guests formed a receiving line.

George and Laura Bush greeted each one in turn. "Good to see you again, Kreg," the President said.

"And you, Mr. President."

"Where is your fiancée, Miss Lapinsky? I was looking forward to meeting her."

"I'm afraid she's under the weather tonight."

"Oh, that's a shame—a real shame." As Kreg was escorted to the table, the President's last words, complete with Texas drawl, kept running through his head. What had he meant by that? His concern seemed to be more than mere politeness.

At dinner, Kreg was seated too far from Wolfowitz to speak with him discreetly, but he managed to lose himself for a while in conversation with his immediate neighbors. If peace prevailed and PA government reforms continued, this could be the first of a string of new deals, some financed by American aid. The PA needed houses, sewers, power lines, and more, and Kreg knew several companies that could use his assistance in getting those contracts.

Halfway through his prime rib, Kreg spied Ibrahim Suleyman standing in the antechamber to the dining room. He excused himself and went over. "What is Wolfowitz doing here? I thought you said he wasn't coming." Kreg spoke quietly, trying to keep from sounding desperate.

The Protocol Officer smiled and said, "I'm sorry, but we haven't been formally introduced. I'm Ephraim Shashoua, covering the negotiations for the *Washington Jewish Week*."

Kreg noticed the press pass hanging from the man's jacket pocket. His face flushed hot. Could he have the wrong man? They looked so much alike! Almost dumb-struck, all he could say was, "You look like an Arab."

"My grandfather fled Baghdad when the Ba'ath party came to power in 1934. My family speaks Arabic at home." Then he added, "We Jews come in all shapes and colors."

Kreg finally summoned the courage to ask, "Didn't you meet with me this morning?"

"Yes," Ephraim said. "That was for an article on official Washington anti-Semitism. I haven't sold it yet."

Kreg's hands started shaking. Was his fight with Gloria all over a stupid trick? "You spoke to me under false pretenses! You made me—" Kreg cut himself off. It was best to not admit anything to the press.

"I didn't *make* you do anything," the reporter said. For a moment it looked as if his eyes glinted red. "The assistant at the World Bank explained it was both immoral and illegal to comply with Ibn Abdualla's wishes. Lea Berman told me that the attendees were Americans, and that was all I should concern myself with. But you were eager to assist him with his prejudices, even accepting his claim of a Zionist occupation, when ninety-eight percent of the Palestinians have lived under PA control for years."

Kreg forced himself to remain calm, refusing to rise to Ephraim's bait—after all, Jews often lied in defense of Israel. If he stuck to his original plan, he could get Gloria back, as long as he kept his name out of the papers. "I never signed a release form. You can't publish my name."

"You will merely be a statistic. However, when I told President Bush about my research, he asked to see a more detailed description of my results. No names, but he is well aware of whose Jewish fiancée suddenly cancelled tonight."

Kreg said, "The law only prohibits complying with the Arab boycott of Israel!"

"There is an executive order sanctioning employees—and contractors—who comply with their client's ethnic prejudices. You'll never work in this town again."

"There must be some misunderstanding," Kreg said, now desperate as he saw his livelihood and only chance to win back Gloria fading away. "Gloria decided she didn't want to come."

"You said you promised to bring her." Ephraim's diabolical smile returned. "Just an hour ago, I phoned your fiancée, or should I say ex-fiancée, and she said she made you swear by God Himself that you would bring her tonight. Bad business this, breaking an oath—brings forth *ayin hara*, the evil eye."

As Kreg stood frozen in place, Ephraim turned and started chatting in Arabic to one of the other reporters. Kreg hung his head and rubbed his temples. Then he jumped back in shock. He must be having a nervous breakdown—Ephraim's shadow looked as if wings were growing out of his back! He staggered to the table, sat down, and wiped his face with the linen napkin.

Now he knew why Bush had said "that's a shame." The shame was that Kreg's career was now in the toilet. He stared at his steak knife and wondered if he had the courage to slit his wrists.

Seventy-two Virgins

Derwin Mak

Say to those who reject the Faith: "Soon, you will be vanquished and gathered together in Hell, an evil bed to lie on!"
—*The Koran*, Surah 3 (Al-'Imran), verse 12

In them [two gardens in Paradise] will be maidens, chaste, bashful, whom no man or Jinnee has touched before; then which of Our Lord's favors will you deny? Virgins like rubies and coral.
—*The Koran*, Surah 55 (Most Gracious), verses 56–58

When Qabeel arrived at his father's apartment building, he saw Farouk and Faisal leaving a small house across the street. The two young men had moved into the house after Faisal's uncle had died. For some reason, the uncle had left the house not to his children but to Faisal. To add to the intrigue, Farouk and Faisal had initially said that they were cousins, and later, that they were friends, but local gossips suspected that they were more than friends.

Farouk and Faisal were buying suitcases from one of the vendors who pushed his cart along the streets. Why did they need luggage? Certainly they could not be on a martyrdom mission.

After Farouk and Faisal paid the vendor, Qabeel crossed the street and looked at the luggage. "Are you traveling?"

Faisal nodded. "We are going to Canada. My uncle left me some money. We can go on vacation overseas."

"It is better than spending our free time here," Farouk said. "Nothing but bombs and bullets."

"So you flee, leaving others to do the fighting," Qabeel said, sneering. "I hear that marriage between man and man is legal in Canada now. Leave, go to Canada, get married. Then go to San Francisco for your honeymoon. But do not come back. If the Americans and Crusaders are good for anything, it is that they will house perverts like you."

"We are merely going on vacation," Farouk said.

Faisal motioned for Farouk to stay silent, but Farouk continued. "You are a disturbed individual."

"Not as disturbed as you," Qabeel said. "You two will soon go to the fires of hell, an evil bed to lie on! God wills it!"

Qabeel accepted the coffee from Al Majuj, leader of the Al Ghazu Jihad Brigade. He sipped the bitter drink and admired the decorations on the wall: a large gilt-framed photo of the Dome of the Rock; a Palestinian flag; a portrait of Saddam Hussein in military uniform; a caricature of an Israeli soldier as a rampaging monster; and a dartboard made from a photo of Yasser Arafat.

Al Majuj said, "Cursed be the traitors of the Palestinian Authority who conspire with the Zionists and the Americans to build a casino on our sacred soil! May they all go to hell, an evil bed to lie on!"

Qabeel set the coffee on the table. "Uh, great leader, is the merchandise designed yet?"

"Ah, yes, my friend, yes!" Al Majuj opened a bag and poured a smattering of objects on the table. "You will be famous, my friend!"

Qabeel's eyes lit up when he saw the merchandise: keychains, postcards, stickers, and buttons printed with his face and the word Martyr. He was most impressed by a poster showing him, grinning and holding a rifle, superimposed over the Dome of the Rock. This was how he wanted to be remembered, as a brave fighter laughing at death as he fought for his people.

"There is also a video of your farewell speech," Al Majuj said. "All proceeds from its sale will go to your family, of course."

Qabeel nodded. "My father will appreciate the proceeds. He has been unable to work since the Zionists ruined his leg in the *intifada*. Who needs a carpenter who cannot get around a construction site?"

"Cursed be the Zionists," Al Majuj said.

"What about the Saudis?" Qabeel said. "Did you ask them again? Will they give anything for my family?"

Al Majuj shook his head. "I asked the Saudi Interior Ministry, but it will not make an exception to its policy. It is unfortunate that you do not have a wife. Yes, the Saudis pay twenty thousand rials to the widow of each martyr, but they will pay only the widow."

A widow, Qabeel thought. If only I could leave a widow. All who would honor me would revere her too. Rich benefactors like Al Majuj and bin Laden—if anyone could find him—would shower her with gifts and money to compensate for her loss.

Areej had missed her chance. She would soon regret her rejection of him. She could have been the wife of a hero, widow of a martyr. But instead, she chose to be a harlot of the Zionists, the Americans, and their traitorous allies in the Palestinian Authority.

"But cheer up," Al Majuj said, "for you will be our first bomber martyr." He picked up a collector's card. "Look, my friend, here is your rookie card. Actually, all suicide martyr cards are rookie cards, but that only makes them more special."

Qabeel took the card and smiled. He was number one in the Al Ghazu Martyrs series. Unlike other organizations' martyr cards, Qabeel's was in full color, showing him raising his fist before a Palestinian flag.

He reached into his shirt pocket and pulled out another martyr card showing Mohammed Attah. It was a spectacular card, in color on brilliant white cardboard, with the words "Magnificent 19 Al Qaeda Aerial Combat Martyrs of New York and Washington" embossed in gold foil. Comparing his card to Mohammed Attah's, Qabeel suddenly felt sad.

"Great leader, why cannot I have a card like this with gold foil, maybe a hologram?"

Al Majuj smiled sympathetically. "Ah, my friend, do not be disappointed. Attah's card is part of a special edition made by friends of Al Qaeda. They had the money to print coated, gold-embossed cards. As for us, we must make do with a dwindling trust fund from Saddam Hussein. Mind you, the publishers of the Magnificent 19 set cannot get money from Al Qaeda anymore."

"Still, I would like to be remembered by a more attractive card," Qabeel said.

Al Majuj patted him on the back. "But your martyrdom mission against the casino will guarantee that our people will celebrate you as a hero. Then our youth will seek out and treasure your card, despite its lack of gold foil or a hologram."

"Yes, the martyrdom mission will give meaning to my life," Qabeel said. "All those people who sneered at me, what will they be? All those people who laughed at me, what will they be? All those people who called me a loser, what will they be? My uncle, who fired me from his company, what will he be? They are like swine, who simply eat and sleep and do nothing with their lives."

"Exactly! Better to fight and die like a lion than to cower and live like a pig," Al Majuj said. "For them will be the fires of hell, an evil bed to lie on. But for you awaits the gardens of paradise, place of flowing rivers, fruit trees, and seventy-two virgins to serve you."

Would they look like Areej? Qabeel hoped so.

Qabeel left Al Majuj's office. A young woman ran up beside him on the street.

"Qabeel, do not do anything stupid," she said.

"Areej," Qabeel said, "what is that dreadful costume you are wearing?"

Areej glared at him, straightened her red pantsuit and pointed at the button that proclaimed in Arabic and English, "CASINO TRAINEE: Ask me about the Slot Club Bonus Points."

"I am training to be a hostess," Areej said. "It will bring much needed employment and revenues to our town."

"You lie with the traitors," Qabeel said. "You are an affront to your own people."

Areej's brown eyes burned with anger as she put her hands on her hips. "And what about you? How are you helping our people by joining a terrorist group?"

"Al Ghazu is not a terrorist group. It is a freedom fighter brigade."

"Hah, I have heard that before," Areej said, smiling sardonically. "You are correct, how can it be a terrorist group? How can anyone be terrorized by a group whose own people drowned while training dolphins to attach bombs to Israeli boats?"

Qabeel forced himself to stay calm. "Perhaps we should have gotten dolphin trainers who knew how to swim. How were we to know that the dolphins would head for the deep end of the pool? But you must admit that Al Majuj's concept was brilliant. Only the execution was flawed."

"You are a loser," Areej said, "a bum who wastes his day loitering in the streets, spending what is left of his father's money.

"Look around you." She pointed at the dilapidated apartments, the rotting pavement, and the forlorn people shuffling through the street. "Look at the unemployment and poverty.

"But your family, among all others in Ramallah, does not live in this trap. Your father found a good school for you, one that offered you a scholarship, but it expelled you for truancy. Your uncle gave you a good job, but he fired you for laziness. How can your own uncle fire you from the only successful computer company in the area? All you ever wanted is money and girls, and you got neither. Now you are consorting with Al Majuj's gang of morons. Do not mess up your life any further!"

Qabeel pulled Areej into an alley and shook his finger at her. "Do not insult the great leader and Al Ghazu! I am finally doing something right with my life, and I will not mess it up!"

"Al Majuj's people mess everything up!"

"You who refused me, you who would lie with the Zionists and Americans, you who would help corrupt Saudi princes and Jews gamble, you will go to hell, an evil bed to lie on! God wills it!"

Areej laughed. "I rejected you after dating you for three months, and you ask God to send me to hell. Go ahead. At least I am helping our so-called country. I admit that a casino is not the most stable basis for an economy, but we must start somewhere. How are you helping? You loser, when will you realize that it is you who will go to hell?"

"When the time comes, God willing, I will not go to hell," Qabeel said. "I will enter paradise and be served by seventy-two virgins."

Areej laughed scornfully.

"All more beautiful than you," Qabeel added.

"Like hell you will find a girl more beautiful than me." Areej ran her hand through her wavy, black hair. Then she took a deep breath, and the anger faded from her eyes.

"Listen, Qabeel, our families come from the same village. My father fought alongside yours in the *intifada*. I do not want harm to come to you. Do not do anything stupid with Al Majuj's group."

She looked at her watch and gasped. "Oh, today is the day to switch to Daylight Savings Time! I forgot to turn my watch ahead one hour. It is 17:30 already. I am late for my training!"

"Bah, Zionist time! It is only 16:30 Palestinian time," Qabeel said.

"Live in whatever time zone you wish, but the casino is in the Zionist time zone, and I get paid according to the clock there," Areej called as she ran off. "Remember, Qabeel, do not do anything stupid."

As he watched Areej run down the street, Qabeel stared at her svelte body and gentle curves, beauty that the pant-suit could not hide. Seventy-two virgins awaited him in paradise. They would all look like Areej, and they would squeal in pain and ecstasy as he forced them into positions he had briefly glimpsed when a friend had found a discarded American magazine called *Hustler*....

I will be a hero, I will be a hero, I will be a hero, Qabeel chanted to himself as he walked away, admiring a key chain showing his face.

Jalut, the explosives expert, handed the time bomb to Qabeel. Among the wires and plastic explosive, a digital clock counted off the time.

"The clock is set to explode at 18:00," Jalut said.

"18:00," Qabeel repeated.

Al Majuj nodded and handed a set of car keys to Qabeel. "Take the blue car parked outside. Run the car through the front door of the casino, and the blast will wipe it off the face of the earth, God willing."

Qabeel held the bomb. It felt so light, so easy to carry. How could something so little carry a blast so big? That mass destruction could come in such a small package impressed him.

Jalut took the bomb from Qabeel and put it into a black briefcase. "Place it in the trunk so that no one can see it," Jalut said.

"May you have a successful mission," Al Majuj said, "and may the gates of paradise open to you."

Qabeel nodded, picked up the briefcase, and walked toward the door. Before he left, he turned and said, "Glory to God, and glory to Al Ghazu Jihad Brigade!"

Al Majuj and Jalut raised their fists to salute Qabeel, and Qabeel left the office, smiling.

"Ah, there goes another fine young fighter," Al Majuj said, "our first martyr. I feel so proud of him." He looked at his watch. "It is only 16:00. I still have time to catch the end of the Lebanon-Syria football match on TV."

Qabeel parked the car in front of his family's apartment. He checked his watch: 16:45. Well over an hour—plenty of time to leave a suicide note for his father and Areej.

Farouk and Faisal were hauling their suitcases onto the street. Qabeel could not resist the urge to insult them one last time.

He got out of the car and yelled, "Faisal, did you remember to pack a white dress to wear at your wedding?"

Farouk shouted back, "You are a disturbed individual!"

Qabeel laughed. "At least when I die, I will go to paradise, a place of sparkling rivers and nubile virgins. But God has a different fate for you. For you will be the fires of hell, an evil bed to lie on. And when you lie with the demons, it is you who will take the female position."

Farouk grunted with the luggage. "Be silent, swine. Our airplane does not leave for several hours, and we have plenty of time to beat the goat cheese out of you." Clenching his fists, he stalked toward Qabeel's car.

"Farouk, please do not," Faisal said.

Farouk looked rather scrawny to Qabeel. "You think you can fight me and win?"

Farouk swung his fist at Qabeel. Qabeel ducked, dodging the blow.

"You are a useless, lazy swine who cannot even make falafels for a living!" Farouk said.

Faisal shouted, "Farouk, please stop!"

"Take this, pervert!" Qabeel punched Farouk on the nose.

Stunned, Farouk reeled backwards. Faisal wailed.

"Ah, this is what is important in life, to hear the cries and lamentations of his woman," Qabeel said, paraphrasing an American movie he had seen years ago.

Farouk stood up sluggishly and raised his fists. Then Qabeel remembered his mission. He looked at his watch. 16:59. Did he have time to beat up the pervert?

Yes, plenty of time.

Rushing forward, he raised his fist again and smashed it into Farouk's eye.

The last thing he heard was the bomb exploding.

The angel had white, feathery wings like a dove's, and he wore a white robe, a gold belt, and a white turban. He sported a long beard the same black color as his eyes.

Behind the angel lay acres of green grass and shrubs; flowing rivers of sparkling white water; large, shady palm and pomegranate trees; a brilliant blue sky; and sunlight, bright yet cool instead of blistering.

Qabeel gazed at the angel and the scenery beyond. As he smelled the fragrance of roses, jasmine, and spices, he realized that he was not in Ramallah anymore.

"Praise be to God, I am in paradise!"

"That is what they all say when they arrive here," the angel said. He smiled and bowed. "Welcome, Qabeel, most honored martyr. We have been expecting you."

"How many Americans and Zionists were killed?" Qabeel asked with excitement.

The angel shrugged, making both his shoulders and wings move. "I do not know. Perhaps they went to the other place."

"Of course, of course."

"You must be eager to see the rest of the grounds," the angel said. "Will you follow me, please?"

The angel led Qabeel to a bed lined with rich red and gold brocade. Beside the bed stood a pomegranate tree surrounded by its own spring.

Qabeel knelt, put his hands into the spring, and lifted some water to his mouth. He had never tasted water as cool, clean, and refreshing as this. He certainly was no longer in Ramallah.

"Make yourself comfortable on the bed," the angel said. "I will fetch the *houris* for you."

Qabeel said, "Praise be to God, I will finally have my seventy-two virgins!"

The angel clapped his hands, and dozens of young men appeared from nowhere and paraded in front of the bed.

They were incredibly handsome, with oil glistening on their strong, muscular bodies and hairless chests. They wore only loincloths that barely covered their male parts. As they passed Qabeel, the men gazed at him and smirked and flexed their muscles, showing off their bodies.

The fragrance of flowers and spices gave way to the musky stink of male sweat. Qabeel squirmed, unnerved by the sight of half-naked men displaying themselves to him.

"Are these my servants?" Qabeel asked.

"No, these are the *houris*," the angel said. "Your seventy-two virgins."

But they did not look like Areej! Indeed, some of them looked like suicide bombers who had martyred themselves before Qabeel had. Others looked like local ruffians who had died in brawls.

Two men stepped forward from the crowd. Qabeel gasped. Farouk and Faisal.

Qabeel shrank back into the bed and looked furtively at them. "How can these be the virgins of paradise?"

"It is true. I am a virgin, thanks to you," Farouk said, scowling. "No man or woman had ever used me before your bomb killed me."

"Not even Faisal?"

Faisal shook his head sadly. "We never got to Canada."

A chill shot through Qabeel. "What are you doing here?"

"I should not have falsified my uncle's will," Faisal confessed. "The house was not intended for me."

"Or for me," Farouk said.

The angel smiled and put his hand on Faisal's shoulder. "Make our latest arrival comfortable, beautiful *houri*."

Faisal knelt on the bed and began to rub Qabeel's shoulders. Qabeel stiffened in fear as the dead man's hands caressed him.

"Your muscles are very tense," Faisal said. "Just relax, Qabeel. Soon, none of us will be virgins. But we will be gentle with you. You will be sore only for the first eighty days."

The virgins laughed, their voices filled with bitterness and sarcasm rather than humor and joy. Qabeel looked up and saw Farouk frowning at him.

Qabeel tried to get off the bed, but Faisal pushed him down on his back and began unbuttoning Qabeel's shirt.

"Just relax," Faisal said as he ran his hands over Qabeel's chest.

Qabeel bolted up again, but the virgins crowded around, held him down, and stripped him naked. He yelled as the young men forced him onto his knees and elbows.

Farouk climbed onto the bed and crouched behind Qabeel. With a long, mournful sigh, Farouk said, "How awful that I should lose my virginity to a disturbed individual like Qabeel!"

Farouk tore off his loincloth and flung it on Qabeel's head.

"No, no, no!" Qabeel shrieked as he struggled against the virgins.

The angel bowed. "Excuse me, but I must check on Mohammed Attah and his friends. I left them in the same room with Meir Kahane."

"Merciful God, is this how paradise should be?"

The angel said, "Paradise? Who said you are in paradise?"

Qabeel screamed when Farouk's rough hands caressed his buttocks. "Merciful God, save me from this evil bed to lie on!"

The angel shrugged. "The Americans have a saying: you made your bed, now lie on it."

Blasphemebus

Michael A. Arnzen

If God is your co-pilot—swap seats!

Charlie McGee parked in front of the First Church of the Prophecy so the headlights of his Chevy pickup would shine on the cheap letterboard sign. He sat behind the wheel, slurping bad coffee and tapping his thumbs on the steering wheel as he contemplated the message.

He didn't really get why the First Church of the Prophecy was advocating car accidents, but it didn't matter. He'd already worked out the word puzzle in his head the second he pulled in. It only took him a few minutes to fetch his ladder and climb to the lighted board by the roadside. He rearranged the plastic letters in their aluminum sliders and felt like a kid juggling tiles in a Scrabble tray. The ones he didn't need he tossed in the back of his truck, next to his ladder.

Back behind the wheel, he studied his revision:

God eats wops!

Not his most clever work. And he had nothing against Italians. But he laughed anyway, and laughed again as he circled around and drove past the sign a second and third time.

Charlie swished the sludge in the bottom of his travel mug, raised it to toast his reflection in the rearview, and then tossed it back.

He never tired of seeing his work up in lights. There were maybe twenty-five churches spread across Fremont

County, and he'd been sporadically messing with their signage for about five years now. Charlie used to be an on-again, off-again churchgoer, but ever since he lost his wife to cancer—and his child to a car wreck on the way to the hospital to visit her on the day she died—he hated the very idea of God.

God made him drink. God made him sloppy. God crashed into his car and killed his little boy.

For Charlie, religion was thereafter something like that cruel joke that Lucy always played on Charlie Brown, pulling the football from him just as he swung to kick. People who practiced the faith were destined, like both Charlies, to fall flat on their back.

When God stole his family, he had sent Charlie a message. He'd played a trick on him. Charlie could still hear him laughing. His play with the signs along the road was a way of playing the joke right back.

And he'd be damned if he hadn't invented some pretty good ones. *If you think it's hot here, imagine hell!* was cute, but he preferred his own teaser: *hello u hotties!* His jokes ranged from gross-outs to name-calling, but he enjoyed his smuttier renditions quite a bit, because he knew they drove the holy rollers crazy.

The way Charlie figured it, these church road signs—from the stupid puns to the self-righteous slogans—were so trite and uncreative that they represented just how boring and meaningless the church had become. They seemed clever at first glance, but most of them were regurgitated propaganda, lifted right out of some "how to lure the masses" manual; he knew this because he'd seen the same messages repeated from time to time, even across different denominations.

He was creative. The church was not. Some signs were easy targets, like the death threat that read *Don't make me come down there!*—God—which he quickly turned into a simple declarative response: *Eat me God!* Sometimes he had to sacrifice spelling to make a sign work (changing *God allows u-turns* into *Go suallow turds*). At other times he'd just go for the most bizarre thing he could think of. (The best he could do with *When God Ordains, He Sustains!* was *God Stains WHOres!*) But no matter how forced or convoluted the jokes, the defacement of the church's messages thrilled him. They were random stops, but the act had become so ritualized for him, that he approached every roadside sign the way some folks muse over a crossword puzzle during breakfast. And he prided himself on solving them before driving home.

His vandalism had become so well known in town that it even made the papers. Some churches went digital in response, but among those who hadn't, many were now picking their words carefully, trying to avoid his puns. They were fooling themselves as much as their flocks, if that were the case, because Charlie could make a blasphemous rebus (which he thought of as a "blasphemebus") out of anything. He could easily turn letters and numbers upside down, and even break off a piece if he needed a spot of punctuation or a line to fashion his own letters. Besides, he kept plenty of spare letters in his garage at home, pilfered from the leftovers. But he never did. He always beat them at their own game.

And sometimes he got justice. One of his favorites was the First Southern Baptist's lame attempt at making the church seem hip—*God answers Knee Mail*—which he used to spell out *God is a Kanser*. It probably didn't make sense to anyone but him, but Charlie didn't really care. He'd made his point.

Sometimes the church made its own point for him. One of his favorites was a sign he spotted once that read *Don't let stress kill you! The church can help!* He laughed all the way home when he saw that one.

Charlie pulled into the 24-hour Sunoco by the interstate ramp. He liked the way its lights flashed bright as Vegas, even though the rest of the town went dark after midnight. Few travelers bothered to stop for gas at that hour. He parked the Chevy and when he stepped out, he thought he could smell all the dead bugs fizzling in the streetlamps. He headed inside the shop for his usual coffee break with Marcy. Messing with church boards every week or two might have been routine for Charlie, but grabbing a donut and swapping gossip with the bored clerk working the graveyard shift was a nightly ritual. And he loved her nutty hot coffee.

Charlie entered the door and winked at Marcy, who was chatting on a phone behind the counter. She palmed the handset and said "Howdy Chuck," then dropped her voice to a whisper: "Coffee's just finished brewing." She turned around and continued talking.

He helped himself to the orange-ringed pot on the hot-plate, filled his aluminum travel mug, and nabbed three sugar packets. He took his usual seat at one of the three picnic-styled tables beside the register and tamped a filterless Camel from its pack. He lit up and studied the warning label while he waited for Marcy to join him for a smoke break, as she always did when the store was empty.

He mentally began twisting the "Surgeon General's Warning" letters around: *Gangrene nurse, Swagger Gal, large Surge in Wang…*

"Didja catch them Broncos?" Marcy asked as she sat down, breaking his concentration with a flick of her lighter. She always wore too much perfume—something pungent he associated with New Year's Eve for some reason—and while he enjoyed it, he wondered how flammable she was as she set fire to the tip of her generic cigarette. She blew a smoke ring. "Whatta game." She puffed and looked into his eyes. "They lost, of course, but they put on a good show."

Charlie watched the muscles in her neck move as she smoked. He liked the way the tiny gold cross that dangled on her too-tight necklace lifted its leg off the valley of her throat when she sucked. Charlie found Marcy attractive, but he never let on that he fancied her. He supposed hanging out at the store was the closest thing he did to dating since God took his Ginger away, and he wouldn't dare chance a rejection. Besides, apart from a few buddies at the Sportsman's Bar, she was one of the only people in town he might call a friend.

He lit up another smoke. "Damned Broncos... I knew they'd screw it up by the third quarter. They looked ill to me. Like they came down with a case of Bronchoitis or something."

Marcy snickered as she pulled a small pad from her uniform, licked her finger—which sort of grossed Charlie out because she'd been handling filthy dollar bills all day—and paged to a makeshift chart. She put what appeared to be the game score down on it. "You and your puns. You'd make a good sportswriter, Charlie." She looked up at him. "Bronchoitis.... Seriously, how do you come up with these things?"

He smiled and slurped coffee, looking at the jewelry on her neck again. "I work in mysterious ways," he said.

She wrote "Bronchoitis" in the margin of her notepad beside that week's score.

Charlie leaned back. "Speaking of which—have you seen the sign outside that church over on Chapel Hill Lane?"

"First Prophecy?"

"I guess."

"Sure, what about it?"

"It says 'God eats wops,' of all things." He swallowed coffee to drown the pride he heard in his own voice. "What do you make of that?"

Marcy shook her head. "Silly teenagers. Up to no good again. Must be the fifth time this month. Ain't they got nothing better to do than messing up other people's hard work?" She smoked. "I swear."

They'd talked about this before. Charlie enjoyed sharing his work with her on the sly, telling her what he "saw" on the road and gauging his success by her reactions.

"Oh, come now. It don't hurt nobody, and it could be worse," Charlie said. "I'd rather have that than graffiti all over downtown. And there's not much else to do in this town, anyway, so I don't blame 'em." He slid out of the booth and headed toward a crackly glazed donut he'd been eyeing. "Besides, I, for one, appreciate the entertainment. Some of them signs are pretty damned funny."

"But these are churches, Charlie. Holy ground. If they want to mess around with messages, why don't they pick on someone who deserves it, like the liquor stores or something." She blew smoke. "It's all kind of perverted, if you ask me."

Charlie frowned.

"I mean—take that sign they changed over at the First Southern Baptist, for example."

Charlie sat down and swallowed dry donut. "That the one on Hogback Road?"

"Yeah." She snuffed her butt in the ashtray with several taps, like she was telegraphing something in Morse code. "How could they do such a thing?"

Charlie squinted his right eye and sucked glaze from his teeth. "Do what? What are you talking about?"

She leaned toward him, surprised. "Haven't you seen it? It's right down the road. What a nasty piece of sacrilege. Just saw it myself today, coming to work. I was so shocked I nearly had an accident." Her eyes bugged out a bit. "Right there on the hill overlooking the highway, in bright lights for the whole world to see. Sheesh, I know it's just kids joking around, but vandalism like that makes our whole community look bad!"

Charlie felt his leg shaking beneath the table. He hadn't changed the Southern Baptist's sign for months. And he didn't like the idea of someone copycatting his crime. "Interesting! So what's it say?"

A customer came in the door, and Marcy pocketed her notepad. "See for yourself, Charlie. I wouldn't repeat those words, anyway." She made her way behind the counter and watched as the man in hunter's attire made his way to the coolers.

"I just might do that," he said, getting up. "See ya next time, Marcy."

She flashed him her customary farewell grin. "You bet."

Charlie nearly ran to his truck. He wanted to see his competitor's handiwork right away. And if he didn't like it, he knew just what to do: change it to something better.

As he pulled out of the parking lot, he realized he'd left Marcy alone in the store with a stranger in the middle of the night. He knew she'd been working graveyard for a long time, which proved she was capable of handling herself, but he didn't like abandoning her in haste. Usually they waved goodbye through the window as he pulled away, but this time she didn't pay heed. Instead, she was on the phone while she served the guy, the handset slipping off her shoulder as she tried to count coins. Smart tactic. Being on the line would make someone think twice about acting funny.

He stomped the gas pedal and raced toward Hogback Road, chugging coffee. When he crested the hill that led to the church, he noticed that the sign was completely dark. It was usually bright as a beacon on the hill above the highway, but tonight the whole churchyard was murky in shadow. It reminded Charlie of his house the first night he drove home after losing his wife and child. Creepy in its emptiness. Throbbing with silence. The angular tombstones in the graveyard on his left weren't helping matters. He popped on the high beams and twisted the truck to face the sign, pulling up to its bricked base.

God Knows, it read in the headlight gleam. Beneath that: *Psalm 139*.

He slapped the steering wheel. "Goddamn it! Too late." The Baptists must have been so offended or embarrassed by whatever his competition had written that they changed it on a weekday. He gripped the wheel and cooled down. He was upset that he couldn't get to see what had bothered Marcy so much, but that didn't mean he couldn't rectify the situation with his own little message.

He smoked another Camel and played with the words in his mind, rearranging the letters and testing different possibilities: *no God... Go now...*

Not much else came to mind. He'd have to dip into his own letter collection. He still had some leftovers in the bed of his truck. He got out of the Chevy and circled it to pop the tailgate.

As he rooted around, a little stone hit his aluminum ladder and tumbled below with a rattle.

He turned and realized that people were gathering around him. Silhouettes moved from behind the church, bodies crested the hillside that led down to the interstate, and shadows made their way among the tombstones like zombies. They all surged toward him, and he knew, deep inside, they were corralling him for a reason. Like hidden soldiers, they stepped from behind trees and rolled from beneath bushes.

They were silent, save for the scrape of shoes against gravel. He couldn't make out their faces—the group was a black mass in the shadow, a tightening dark circle. Children walked among them. They were the ones throwing rocks. Their parents didn't scold them. They just kept coming closer.

Charlie chuckled nervously and smacked away a pebble that someone lobbed from behind the front line of on-comers. "Just what the hell is all this about?" he asked, but there was no single leader to appeal to. They tightened their perimeter and moved closer.

His mind scrambled for excuses, but he felt in his gut that this mob wasn't here to talk or forgive. He quickly surmised that there were more men here than there were Baptists in town, and the mob was bigger than one church's flock. This was a collective attack.

"I'm sorry," Marcy said, slipping out from the crowd. Her face glared, pale and gaunt in the dust swirling near his headlights. Her gold cross shimmered as she clutched a softball-sized stone. "This must be done."

A pebble stung his ear.

He clambered into the truck and turned the key, but they pulled him from the cab and pinned his limbs to the ground. Their faces were monstrous in the light, and although he recognized none of his assailants, he counted old women and feeble men among them.

"Stop!" He wrestled against their hold. "Why are you—?"

They answered with rocks. The pain came sharp, and the horrifying grit of stones grinding flesh against his bones made him scream and flail as if ablaze.

A rock the size of a billiard ball landed against his temple, and light flared in his skull. He withdrew into a pool of darkness behind his eyelids as they beat him beyond repair, but the pain faded from his concern. He was going someplace else now. It felt like falling. Somewhere in the dim dark center of his pain, he recalled reading stories of stoning—Old Testament punishments that he'd always believed were the stuff of fairy tales and primitive cultures. He vomited and briefly came back to consciousness, realizing that he was now in some kind of pit, surrounded by walls of musty earth. He couldn't see anyone above, but a stone struck his chest, tossed inside the hole, so he knew they were still there. He couldn't move, not even his chin, so he wasn't sure if they'd crushed his spine or if his limbs had been entirely beaten off his body.

But he could see, and his vision was improving between the throbs of lancing agony behind his eyes. A bright light flickered above—probably the road sign, judging from its color—and he knew he lay in a freshly-dug grave in the churchyard. A monument was illuminated overhead, too, its polished surface glinting in the night.

He heard a collective prayer murmuring above. Then a deep grunt.

And as he looked up from the pit of earth, Charlie McGee clearly saw the message chiseled deep into the marble before the stone tipped over and tumbled toward his face.

He could read it but he did not understand it.

And he could not change it.

THOU SHALT NOT...

Violate the Day of Rest

Button's and Bo's

John M. Floyd

"He struck again last night," Button said.

Ray Woodson turned to look at her as he zipped his coat. His eyes were dark, his jaw set. "I heard."

Button just nodded. Everyone in town had heard by now about the killings—one every Sunday night for the past four weeks. Whoever it was, he was stealthy and quick and always left behind messages scrawled in pink lipstick, four different versions of the fourth commandment: OBSERVE THE SAB-BATH; SIX DAYS SHALL YE LABOR; HONOR GOD'S DAY OF REST; ONLY SINNERS WORK ON SUNDAY. The press was calling him the Sabbath Slayer.

And every single victim—three women and one man, so far—had been a convenience store clerk.

Like Button McKenna.

Ray's face softened a bit. "You'll be okay," he said.

And she believed him. Never mind that today was a Sunday, and that she would go on duty at eight P.M., and that all the murders had been between eight and nine, and that she always worked alone. That didn't matter. Button believed him. She thought she *would* be okay.

Because Ray was the killer.

She wasn't positive; there was no hard evidence. But she was pretty sure. Every Sunday night for the past month—almost as long as they'd been dating—Ray had told her he had to go somewhere. On one hand, that seemed

129

reasonable: Button was on duty every weekend night, and had made it clear to Ray that she didn't need him babysitting her at the store during work hours.

Last night she had phoned Eddie's Bar and Grill, where Ray had told her he was going, to finish writing his newspaper column. He wasn't there.

And there were other factors. Like the pistol he'd kept hidden in his waistband lately, and the scratches she'd noticed on the shoulder of his old leather jacket. A whole row of scratches—like the kind fingernails might make.

This morning she'd found an old tube of her lipstick—like her late mother, Button had always favored pink—that she'd left in her glove compartment weeks ago. Ray could easily have been using it, then putting it back.

Button sighed. Was Ray actually a religious fanatic? Had he kept it hidden, like his gun? More important, did she have enough evidence to call the police? She didn't know. *Would* she call the police, even if she did? She didn't know that either.

What she did know was that she loved Ray Woodson. She loved him completely and desperately, in a way that she never could have imagined before she met him. And she knew he loved her too.

They'd both had hard lives—he was a smalltime writer, she a struggling divorcee—but their unlikely meeting and growing relationship seemed, to Button, a beacon of hope. A promising future.

And then the killings had started.

Maybe she was wrong. Maybe he was innocent, and the only fault was her overactive imagination. She hoped so. With all her heart she hoped so.

And at that instant, as she stood there in the hallway of her apartment watching him leave, Button had an idea. She knew how she could find out, once and for all.

"I need a favor, Ray," she blurted.

He stopped and turned, his hand on the doorknob.

"My dad called a few minutes ago," she said, "while you were in the bathroom." The call had actually been one of those telemarketing surveys, but Ray wouldn't know that—he would only remember hearing the phone ring. "He's sick and needs me to drive over. Could you fill in for me tonight at the store?"

Ray hesitated. Button held her breath.

Her reasoning, she thought, was sound. If Ray was tending the store, he couldn't go wherever it was that he was going. And if nine o'clock came and went, and no one was murdered...

Button swallowed. At least she would *know.*

But Ray was no fool. He'd never met her father, but she knew Ray was aware of their problems. Button's dad, even though he lived near here, had never known her ex-husband Bo either, and didn't even know where she worked. Button hadn't spoken to her dad in months. A week ago, when she'd taken him a package of clothes for his birthday—mostly things Bo had left behind—her dad hadn't even answered the door. She left the box on his porch.

Button's father, a former church deacon, was now a Lost Cause. Alcoholic, abusive, violent—none of the adjectives were pretty. He'd always told her he would become famous someday. But all he ever became was a failure, at just about everything he tried.

Button knew she would be the last person her dad would call if he were sick. Ray probably knew that too.

Even so, after a long pause, he smiled. "Sure. The poker game can make it without me, I guess." He pushed the door shut, held out his arms, and Button stepped into them, pressing the side of her head against his broad chest as he hugged her.

But she could feel, through his coat, the handle of the gun in his belt.

An hour later Button knelt at the edge of the woods, fifty yards from the parking lot of the convenience store where she worked. Mosquitoes buzzed around her face, and needle-sharp blackberry vines pricked her hands when she pushed aside the undergrowth so she could see.

The Button's and Bo's Mini-Mart, a cinderblock building containing everything from pocketknives to Hostess Cupcakes, was the last in a row of small businesses lining the frontage road of I-55, on the south edge of the city. She had received the store as her part of the settlement when Bo McKenna divorced her six months ago, and despite its seedy location she'd decided to keep it, along with its name. Now, from her vantage point here on the hill, Button could see only one side of the building and some of the front, but the parking lot was brightly lit. She would have a clear view of anyone coming or going.

At the moment, Ray was inside, and Button wanted to make sure he stayed there.

She glanced down at her luminous wristwatch. 8:07. She decided to wait until nine, then trudge back through the woods to her car and drive over to relieve him. And if tonight's ten o'clock news reported no further victims, she would know.

She'd also know if they *did* report another victim.

God forgive me, Button thought, that would be even better.

She sat down crosslegged in the damp leaves of the hillside and watched.

At 8:45 she jerked awake. She rubbed her eyes with her knuckles, furious with herself, then focused on the scene below. Nothing seemed to have changed, except for the cars outside Button's and Bo's. Ttwo of them were there now, a late model Lexus and Ray's white Toyota.

Then, so suddenly it made her yelp, she heard a gunshot.

A longhaired young man burst through the front door and out into the parking lot. He stood there a moment, as if dazed, then broke into a run, heading north up the now deserted frontage road.

Oh my God, Button thought. *What have I done?*

For a full ten seconds she watched the building, hands over her mouth and tears stinging her eyes. No one else came out.

Finally she snapped out of it. *Maybe he's not dead....*

Button rose, trembling, and tried to run—but one of her legs was asleep. She fell heavily, slid sideways, and tumbled down a muddy embankment onto a mound of rocks. Her left leg and hip took the brunt of the fall, sending a blinding jolt of pain through her body.

For a few minutes she lay stunned at the bottom of the ravine, out of sight from the rest of the world. She was vaguely aware of the sound of approaching sirens. Then she spotted a broken tree limb several yards away and crawled toward it.

Ten minutes later, using the branch as a crutch, little Button McKenna limped into the parking lot of the mini-mart.

Police cars were everywhere, lights blinking and flashing. Off to one side, an attractive middle-aged blonde was shouting at a policeman about something.

For a moment Button just stood there, tears washing down her cheeks. She had already glimpsed the body being loaded into an ambulance—at least the bottom fourth of a body, wearing jeans and hiking boots.

Ray's hiking boots.

She drew a ragged breath.

The man on the stretcher was Ray Woodson. She knew it. It was Ray, and he was dead, and she was the reason he was dead.

And then she heard someone behind her. She flinched, turned, stared—and threw herself into his arms.

"You're alive," she whispered, her voice muffled by his soft leather jacket. "I can't believe it. I thought—"

Ray hugged her, then held her away long enough to see that she was hurt. Before he could speak, she saw again the scratches on his jacket, and this time she knew what had made them.

"Blackberry bushes," she murmured. Their eyes locked. "That's where you were, those nights. Up there in the woods, watching out for me."

He shrugged. "Good thing I wasn't up there tonight, and you down here. I'd've probably got us both killed."

"What do you mean?" Through a haze of tears she looked at the ambulance. "Didn't you shoot the guy?"

"I was too slow. He pulled his gun and made me hand mine over."

"Then how—"

"A lady customer was about to check out. He pushed her away from the counter, and when he did I hit him over the head with an orange juice bottle. He's not dead, he's just unconscious."

Button gaped at him. "But I heard a shot—"

"His gun went off when he fell. Your Coke machine was mortally wounded."

Her thoughts whirled. This was too much to take in all at once. "Is he… is he the one, Ray?"

"Yeah. Positive ID, according to the cops—video and audio. Last week's victim had a security camera."

"Audio?"

"He repeated himself," Ray said. "He told me, before I beaned him, that he'd been sent by God."

"Did he say why?"

"To teach sinners to respect the Sabbath."

Ray added, "I have some bad news too—"

"Mr. Woodson?" a voice said. Button turned to see a blonde woman standing there, with a teenaged girl in tow. The woman was the one Button had noticed earlier, arguing with the cop. The girl looked as if she'd been crying.

"Button, this is Ms. Farrell," Ray said. "She and her kids were here when it happened."

And suddenly Button understood. The Lexus parked beside Ray's car belonged to this woman; the killer must've come on foot, planning to escape into the woods afterward. And the young man Button had seen dash out of the store—

"Her son ran to a pay phone down the street to call 911," Ray said. "Our line was cut."

"And for once I'd left my cell phone at home," Ms. Farrell said.

"My God," Button murmured. "You must be the lady he pushed, just before Ray hit him."

Ms. Farrell grinned. "It was my orange juice bottle."

"No charge," Ray said.

Then Button remembered his earlier comment. "What did you mean, about bad news?"

Ray sighed. "My gun. It's not licensed. It's not even mine—I borrowed it from a friend when all this started, a few weeks ago."

"And?"

"And the city cops and I go way back."

Button's eyes widened. "You have a record?"

"Not that kind. But I used to be a reporter. The police brutality cases got a lot of coverage."

"Don't worry," Farrell said. "That's been taken care of."

Ray looked at her. "It's what?"

"I had a little talk with our boys in blue." To Button Ms. Farrell said, "This man"—she nodded to Ray—"saved our lives. That's what I explained to the cops. In about an hour I'll explain it to the rest of the city. By tomorrow, he can run for mayor if he wants."

Button's mouth dropped open. "Of course. Melissa Farrell.... You're Channel 5 News."

"I'm the anchor," Farrell agreed, smiling, "but believe me, your husband is the news." She left with one arm around her daughter. On the other side of the lot, past the milling crowd and the policemen and the flashing lights, the TV crews were beginning to arrive.

"Come on," Ray said. "Let's get you to a doc."

Only then did the Farrell woman's last words register. "My God, Ray," Button said. "She thinks I'm your wife! What if she says that on TV?"

With his fingertip he brushed a muddy lock of hair from her forehead. "Then I guess I'll have to correct the situation."

"Tell her the truth, you mean?"

"No," he said and grinned. "That's not what I mean."

And for the first time in days, Button smiled too. Only hours ago, she'd been convinced that Ray was a killer, that he was the religious zealot who punished Sunday workers. Now he was a hero. And, apparently, her fiance.

Then she thought of something. "Ray," she said, solemn again, "I lied to you. I didn't go to my father's tonight."

"I know."

"You know?"

"I called his house," Ray said. "His number was on your bulletin board, beside the counter. No one was home."

She nodded. "He's probably dead drunk. Or in jail." She drew a shaky breath and let it out. "I can't believe I didn't trust you. A few minutes ago, when I saw that guy's hiking-boots—I thought it was you, that you'd been shot."

"His boots?"

"They looked like the ones you bought a few weeks ago."

"But I didn't keep them, remember?" he said. "They didn't fit."

She blinked. "What?"

"I put them in the box you took to your dad's. I thought maybe he could use—"

He never finished the sentence. Button turned away to look at the retreating ambulance. As the truth hit her, as she remembered her fundamentalist upbringing, as she remembered leaving her mother's cosmetics packed in boxes at her parents' house, as she gasped and clapped her hands over her mouth, she had another thought. A crazy but somehow logical thought:

Her father had become famous after all....

Curtain Call

Jacqueline West

"Everybody decent?"

Jock tapped twice on the dressing room door, then turned the knob without waiting for an answer. Inside, nine girls sat on folding chairs along a low Formica counter, busy with makeup pencils and brushes, their faces illuminated by a long row of fly-blotched light bulbs. Over each chair back and piled in every cinderblock corner lay skeins of battered gold lamé and brightly dyed feather boas, a few aging acrylic wigs and broken strings of Mardi Gras beads.

Jock kicked aside a pair of high heels and planted his bulk in the middle of the room. "We've got word on tomorrow night's show," he announced.

Nine heads swiveled to look at him, nine elaborate hairstyles appearing suddenly in the mirror.

"The box office took some reservations today, which will bring us up to nine. So we *will* be doing the show."

"Nine?" wailed several voices at once.

"For only nine people—are you serious?"

"There'll be as many of us on stage as in the house!" protested Janie.

"Eight's the cut-off, and we've got more than eight. So, that's that. Sorry." Jock shrugged, glancing down the row of disappointed, gaudily painted faces. "Have a good show tonight."

139

"Damn it," Jock heard one of the girls whisper as he pulled the dressing room door shut. Through the narrowing gap he caught a glimpse of Lydia, looking as tragic as a little girl who has been told that she can't stay up for another hour.

Lydia had come to him a week ago, an hour before the evening show, as he stood tinkering at the control board. Without her makeup, Lydia was nothing special. With it, she could have passed for a Vegas showgirl. She was just a blank canvas, Jock realized, skinny legs, clear skin, big empty eyes.

"Hey, Jock," she had stammered, toying with an extension cord, "Do you know yet whether we're going to be off on Easter? Because my family in Hayward is having a big party, kind of a reunion, and if we're off, I could leave after the Saturday show and be back in time for Tuesday matinee."

Jock directed his gaze on Lydia, and she turned away.

"I don't know for sure, but let's plan on being here on Sunday. Like they say, the show must go on, right?" Jock cracked a wide smile. "Right?"

Lydia gave a little nod.

Jock had patted her shoulder with his meaty palm. "Right."

Oh, well, thought Jock, that's what these girls sign on for when they decide to be performers. They get Mondays off and can sleep late every morning. Not a bad life for a girl without real education. Maybe Catholic grade school, in Lydia's case.

Jock had been running the Mifflin Street Theatre for almost twenty years. He was director, producer, and stage manager—"Jock-of-all-trades" as he liked to joke—and in his opinion, the only person keeping the theatre afloat. It needed every twelve-dollar ticket, every matinee tour group, and every corner that Jock could cut.

The Mifflin stood on a dingy block of Milwaukee's warehouse district, where former beer company holdings had devolved into cheap apartments and third-shift bars. It was the kind of venue frequented by men too cowardly for real strip clubs and groups of elderly women with fond memories of vaudeville. It was also known for allowing patrons to bring drinks from the bar into the theatre. Until the curtain opened, rail drinks were half price.

The *Silver Spangles Revue*, a mishmash of songs with low licensing fees, had been running for three months at Mifflin Street and had barely recouped production costs. These girls, thought Jock, just because they get paid by the week and not by the show, they don't care if the theatre's making anything at all. Eight shows a week and no sick days: they knew what they were getting into.

At 7:45 on Sunday night, Jock made the fifteen minutes call through the intercom. One by one the girls straggled up from the basement. The wings of the Mifflin were high, narrow, and drafty, made of old brick covered with a thin shield of black-painted plywood. The girls shivered in their jeweled leotards, rubbing their bare arms, huddling close to each other like a flock of lost flamingos.

Michelle put her eye to the gap in the red velour curtains.

"Can you see anyone? *Is* there anyone?" whispered Tracy over Michelle's shoulder.

"I see a few people moving around, I think, but they're all way in the back."

"God, it's totally silent out there," said Jess to Liz, who was knitting a giant afghan in the prop corner.

"Well, who wants to go to a show on Easter?" Liz said bitterly.

"I know." Jess rearranged a bobby pin. "I wish I was at home right now."

"Five minutes, ladies," Jock whispered, poking his head around the backdrop.

At 8:00 sharp, the canned music blasted from the cheap box speakers at each side of the stage. Tinny trumpets played a short fanfare before the violins swept in, rising to a schmaltzy peak just as the girls popped through the curtains in their glittering white costumes.

The first number was a peppy medley smattered with can-can kicks and pirouettes. The girls' waxy red smiles beamed into the empty house, over the rows of unused seats folded up neatly as clams, toward the spot in the back where the darkness thickened. When the stage lights shifted, sending one bright spot to the middle of the stage, something glistened from the back rows—the reflection of light on someone's glasses, or a wristwatch, or a pair of eyes.

The other girls rushed offstage as the music segued into Michelle's solo number.

Michelle finished two verses in her low, coppery voice, then zipped around the stage with a row of tap-turns, her patent leather shoes sparkling like wet teeth. A few strands of dark hair fell out of her bun and wavered like tentacles around her face. She froze on the last booming chord, out of breath, posing triumphantly at center stage.

Nothing.

No clapping, no whistling.

Not even the creaking hinge of a chair, or an uncomfortable, throat-clearing cough. Nothing but silence.

The smile on Michelle's face began to melt.

Her eyes flicked toward the scrim where Jock watched from the light board. For a moment she stared into the empty house toward that clot of darkness at the back, and for a split second she saw the reflected flicker of stage lights in nine pairs of eyes.

Then Michelle turned to her left and walked off the stage.

The girls clustered around her at the edge of the curtain, exclaiming in sympathetic whispers.

"Oh, you poor thing!"

"Sweetie, don't worry about it..."

"Oh, my God," said Michelle quietly. "They really hated me."

"No, no," answered Janie quickly. "It's not you, it's them. They're a tiny crowd, they're self-conscious. You were great."

Michelle didn't answer. She walked shakily to the prop table, poured a cup of water, and leaned against the wall in rattled silence.

Liz, Janie, and Lydia had the next number.

They belted out the chorus, flouncing the feather boas on their shoulders, and finished with the forward splits, long bare legs evenly spaced along the lip of the stage.

Again, there was only silence.

Liz barely waited for the recorded tone to finish its reverberation before getting up and stalking off the stage.

In the wings, Jock called an impromptu huddle. "Okay," he said as Liz, Lydia and Janie joined the cluster, "Don't expect any applause. At the end of each song, just smile, pose for three beats, and get off."

"Are you sure that there's even anyone out there?" said Betsy skeptically.

"Couldn't you see their eyes?" asked Lydia.

"Yeah, they're out there," Jock assured them. "They move around now and then. They're just quiet. Don't let it bother you, just give them the best show that you can."

The next three songs flew by with no response. Backstage, the girls told each other that it felt like they were having a dress rehearsal three months into the run. To some of them, the situation became hilarious. Jess, Janie, and Emmy were shaking with ironic laughter when the whole troupe ran out for the act one finale, the title number from *Applause*.

When the curtain slid shut between them and the house's resounding silence, the girls sank down on the gritty stage floor, muffling their laughter with their hands, mascara smearing their teary eyes.

Whispered cursing erupted from the direction of the light board. The girls looked up, quieting, as Jock strode angrily across the stage and through the curtain onto the thrust.

"Folks, folks," they heard him announce, standing in the dusty spotlight. "We apologize, but we seem to have blown a fuse, so the house lights are temporarily out of commission. Please feel free to get up and leave the theatre, enjoy a drink at the bar, and we will try to get the lights up again as soon as possible. Thanks for your patience, folks."

"Damn it," Jock muttered, dropping his formal voice as he burst back through the curtains. "I'll be downstairs."

Jock thundered down to the basement. The girls milled impatiently backstage, touching up their lipstick, pulling on sweaters. Michelle had returned to the gap in the curtains. Lydia approached her quietly.

"I still don't hear anything. Did they leave?" she asked.

Michelle made room for Lydia to peek into the house.

"They haven't moved," Michelle answered.

For a few seconds they watched in silence.

Michelle glanced at Lydia out of the corner of her eye. "I think there's something strange about them. Don't you?"

"Maybe they're deaf," suggested Lydia.

"Why would deaf people go to a musical?"

"I don't know. We had that group of hearing-impaired people from the nursing home last month..."

"No, I mean something stranger than that," Michelle said, turning back to the curtain gap. "Look—can you see the outline of their silhouettes?"

The doors between the theatre lobby and the house were open for intermission. A faint light filtered from without, settling like gold dust along the outlines of empty seats, touching the black shapes at the back of the house with a pale halo, thin as a hair.

"Don't they look kind of funny? Like they're a little smoother, or maybe just bigger... I don't know. Something."

Nine pairs of eyes glittered suddenly through the dark.

Michelle and Lydia took a startled step backward.

"I think they can see us," said Lydia.

"There's no way anyone can see from that far away, through that tiny hole in the curtain," said Michelle, but both of them scurried around the end of the backdrop and joined the other girls.

Jock thudded back up the stairs. "It's not the fuse," he declared from the landing. "It must be a problem with the wiring itself. Who knows, in this crummy old place. Everything's falling apart."

Jock retreated to the light board, sulking, and the girls, clumped together around the prop table, listened to him mumbling over the switches and knobs.

"Um, Jock?" ventured Lydia, peeping into his corner. "What are we going to do for the curtain call? Because it seems kind of funny for us to all go out there and bow when no one is clapping."

"Same as always," Jock snapped. "It's timed to the music. Just go out, bow, get off the stage."

Jock bumped Lydia out of the way with his shoulder, and craned around the backdrop.

"Five minutes, ladies," he called. "And we'll be doing curtain call same as always. You take your bows, and I'll close the curtain right after."

Lydia flattened herself against the wall as Jock squeezed past her, returning to the light board.

A few minutes later the music boomed on. On the stage, the girls spun and sang and mugged by rote, red smiles plastered to their faces. None of them felt like laughing anymore. The stage lights were high and blinding; the shadows that branched from their twirling bodies split into pink, blue, and gold petals. The girls could barely see beyond the edge of the stage, but each sensed the darkness pressing closer, encroaching on that insubstantial boundary of light.

Betsy and Tracy plodded through their solos like mannequins, transfixed by the glistening cluster in the darkness. By the last verse, their frothy Broadway ballads had trailed away to an inaudible pianissimo. Sara and Emmy's comic duet was hollow as a balloon. There was no laughter, no applause, not even the low sound of breath. The silence in the house was no longer passive. It was malevolent, ravenous, solid as a fist. It waited in the darkness with eyes like shards of a mirror.

The finale blasted on at last, crescendos rattling the speakers. The girls jitterbugged while glancing over their shoulders, fear spread thick as greasepaint on their faces. Only Liz managed to maintain a smile—a tight, sneering smile that twisted her blood-colored lips like a rag.

The final song ended, the curtain call music blared, and the girls fluttered into a line. Lydia, Michelle, Tracy, and the others bowed quickly, keeping their eyes fixed on the back wall. Janie made a lavish curtsy, sweeping her arms to the floor like a sarcastic swan. Liz strutted languidly to the front of the stage for her bow with a defiant grin welded to her face.

The last chord trailed to an end. The girls stood frozen in their final poses. The speakers hissed the dead tone of static.

Still, the curtain did not close. The stage gaped at the empty house, at the silence that had become a roar. Nine pairs of eyes flickered through the black.

Lydia and Michelle looked over at Jock's place behind the scrim. The others craned their heads, trying to catch some glimpse of motion, of Jock jerking, startled, from a doze and yanking on the ropes.

There was nothing.

In the darkness, eighteen glittering points grew brighter. Nine dark shapes were moving at last, drawing closer to the stage.

"Jock!" hissed Janie through her teeth.

No answer.

"Jock!" shouted Liz.

Nothing followed but a soft dripping sound, thick liquid hitting the wooden floor.

The stage lights were blinding. Rhinestones flared like fireworks. The girls didn't move, staring into the darkness like moths from a fire.

Nine pairs of eyes, sharp as needles, came closer. A clump of black forms reached the lip of the stage.

And then there was no more silence.

Like waves, the sound spread from the theatre, blasting the bricks, shrieking through windows. But in all of the empty Mifflin Street bars, the locked consignment shops, the restaurants with "Closed for the Holiday" signs on their doors, there was no one to hear.

Flashback

Lawrence C. Connolly

She always slept through the night and awoke just before dawn. It was a routine that drove Harold nuts, but this morning he wasn't there to notice. The space beside her was empty. She touched it. It felt cool. He hadn't returned in the night.

She sat up, looking toward the closed door that she had left open before coming to bed. If Harold hadn't returned, who had closed the door?

A lamp stood beside the bed. She reached for it, feeling along its base until she found the switch.

Click!

Light struck her arm.

"Sweet Jesus!"

She drew back from the lamp, turning her hand in the light, trying to understand what she was seeing. And as she raised her other arm to verify that it was as filthy as the first, she became aware of the pungent smell of dead matter: wood, peat, leaves, and grass. The room reeked of compost, and her hands and arms were covered with loam.

What have I been doing?

The answer was obvious. The condition that Auntie Ariel had helped her overcome nine years ago was out of remission and back with a vengeance.

She stood. Clumps of dirt fell from her nightgown. Her feet were clean, but her shoes (lying on their sides at the foot of the bed) were as filthy as her arms. She recognized the signs. She had been sleepwalking again.

Fully awake now, she hurried toward the door, following the tracks of her muddy shoes, stopping abruptly when she reached the far side of the bed.

A pile of wood lay between bed and door. The pieces were familiar: twelve three-foot slats, two fifteen-foot stringers—the remains of the rickety basement stairs that she had ripped out and dumped in the landfill behind the tool shed.

I brought them back.

She had done such things before, in her early teens, when she would awake to find her room full of garbage: pizza boxes, milk cartons, coffee filters, all retrieved from alley Dumpsters and arranged into patterns that defied reason. Sometimes the piles came with notes, the writing always as cryptic as the garbage.

But that had been long ago. Auntie had cured her. But now Auntie was gone.

And the condition was back.

A long strip of decorative wood sat atop one of the stringers. And there were other things, too: a power drill with a Philips-head bit, a box of screws, a crowbar....

Don't ask what it means! Auntie's voice came back to her as she stared at the pile. *Knowing what it means isn't as important as knowing how to stop it.*

Rachel turned and faced the door. She had evidently closed it herself after bringing the wood and tools into the room, and now, as she gripped the knob, she realized she had done something else, too.

The door was locked.

She had two keys that could open the door. One was a master that opened everything in the house. She kept that one in the kitchen. The second worked the bedroom door alone, and that key she kept in the top drawer of the nightstand. She turned, retraced her steps, and opened the drawer. The key was gone. In its place lay a dirt-smeared note:

THE KEY IS IN THE CROWN.
GET TO WORK!

Unlike the cryptic notes she had left herself in the past, this one seemed to mean something.

The bedroom occupied the top floor of a pentagonal tower on the house's northeast corner. High overhead, plaster gave way to a peaked ceiling of galvanized tin, and between the two, softening the transition, ran five strips of wood molding—*crown* molding.

THE KEY IS IN THE CROWN.

High overhead, she saw the key jammed into the molding, shoved so deep that only its handle was visible. *The trim,* she thought, realizing how she had placed the key. She looked down at the long piece of decorative wood lying atop the disassembled stairs. A notch had been cut into one of its ends, perfect for holding a key and pushing it into place, useless for pulling it free. "You want me to work," she said, speaking to her compulsion. "It's Sunday morning, and you want me to build something."

She looked at the long planks of roughhewn pine, each tooled with a succession of right-angle cuts. Placed parallel, the stringers would support the planks, transforming them into a series of treads that would almost reach the crown molding. She stepped back, trying to estimate the distance. With one end of each stringer wedged against the foot of the bed, and the other elevated and pressed high against the plaster wall, the structure would get her close enough to hook the crowbar against the section of wooden molding that held the key. She had no doubt that she could pry away the molding with a few well-placed tugs. But why had her sleeping mind felt a need to goad her into working on the Sabbath?

She sat on the bed, trying to understand, and it was then that she became aware of something new inside the room. It was silent, invisible, but definitely there—becoming more noticeable with each breath.

Somewhere in the house, something was burning.

She returned to the door, dropped to her knees, and peered through the keyhole. The lamp was on in the hall, illuminating plumes of rising smoke.

Panicking now, she left the door and crossed to the window. It opened grudgingly, groaning as she forced it upward. There was no screen. Could she tie sheets together and make a ladder?

She leaned out, looked down along the tower's wall, and realized she couldn't risk falling to the ground below. Down there, lying right where Harold had left it, was a lethal menagerie of garden tools: hoe, shovel, pick, pitchfork, rake. She had asked him to clear the weeds from around the foundation, and that simple request had set him off— started him shouting about the same things he'd been on her about since she had inherited Auntie's house. He didn't care that Auntie's memory was important to her. He couldn't understand why she didn't want to sell the place, and he was tired of watching her put effort and money into a renovation project that would never be finished.

"And besides," he had said, storming toward the house, "I'm tired. I'll clear the weeds tomorrow."

Perhaps, if she had been able to leave it at that, he would never have stormed out of her life, but instead she chased him, catching him on the porch where she explained that there would be no working on the house tomorrow. "Auntie's rule," she explained. "No work on Sundays." That was the last straw. He went ballistic. Five minutes later he was gone.

The smell of smoke grew stronger after she shut the window and returned to the center of the room. She understood that the fire was her doing. After lighting it somewhere on the first floor, she had returned to bed, leaving her conscious self to wake and contend with it. And now it completed the message, combining with the wood, tools, and note to convey the fears of her unconscious mind: her commitment to Auntie's memory was destroying her life. The old woman's house was not worth keeping, and her rules no longer applied.

But the message missed a crucial point. It was as if her unconscious failed to grasp that the rule wasn't Auntie's alone. It predated her by over three thousand years, and its importance had as much to do with Rachel's mental health as it did with Auntie's religious devotion.

Rachel remembered how Auntie had explained it.

"You sleepwalk because you don't know how to rest. You collect garbage because you don't know how to work. Rest and work need to be purposeful, with times set aside for each. Do you understand, Rachel? Are you listening?" Auntie took Rachel's hand, pulling it down against the table. Only then did Rachel realize that she had been using that hand to pull her hair, plucking out individual strands and wrapping them around her fingers.

"The work you do should always be purposeful, never compulsive." Auntie leaned closer. "Six days for purposeful activity. One day for contemplative rest. Learn these things, Rachel. Learn them and understand that your problem extends far beyond sleepwalking."

Rachel's hand jerked in Auntie's grip. The fingers wanted to go back to pulling hair.

But Auntie was strong. She held firm a moment longer. "Do you understand, Rachel?"

"Yeah. You're like saying it's Sunday. I can't do stuff because it's Sunday." She slipped her hand from Auntie's grip, but she did not go back to pulling her hair. "You're saying I can't do nothing on Sunday."

Auntie frowned. "You can. Sometimes emergencies arise. Some things can't be put off. That's where sound judgment comes in. Not only on Sunday, but every day. Your actions must always serve a greater good." Again, she took Rachel's hand, this time to stop it from drumming the table. "Do you understand me, Rachel?"

"What's a greater good?"

Auntie leaned close, looking deep into Rachel's eyes. "For the moment," she said, "it's your health."

"We gonna work on that?"

"That's right."

"That why Mom brought me here to live with you?"

"Yes."

"So when do we start?"

Auntie gripped Rachel's hand, squeezing tight. "We've already started."

But even if her unconscious didn't grasp it, and even if her long overdue breakup with Harold had caused a return of her sleepwalking, Rachel still understood what Auntie had told her about the greater good. Auntie would not want her to sit in the house and burn. *Sometimes emergencies arise....*

Rachel rose from the bed, lifted one of the fifteen-foot stringers, and wedged it between bed and wall. She did the same with the other, positioning it parallel to the first. When the two were aligned, she secured them by screwing a single tread into position about five feet from the floor. Then she hung on the tread, testing it. The stringers groaned. The left one shifted, angling outward. She let go and grabbed another tread, but this one she positioned beneath the first, creating a brace. The drill whirred, anchoring the wood. Then, again, she tested the structure with her weight. It held.

She threw down the drill and picked up an armload of treads. There was neither time nor need to secure them. She simply laid them down as needed, sliding them into every other position as she climbed. Then she returned to the floor, grabbed the crowbar, and hurried back up the creaking stairs.

The height looked much more precarious from the top and, as she stood on the top step, the left stringer shifted again, skidding out of alignment and digging into the plaster wall. But she couldn't stop to secure it. The smell of smoke was stronger than ever. She had to act now, get the key, get out of the room.

She swung the crowbar, driving it hard against the molding. She pulled. Nails groaned. Mahogany shattered. The key dropped, pinging against the hardwood floor.

The left stringer shifted again as she descended, the top planks falling away as she reached the secured tread in the middle position. From there she jumped, landed on the bed, and bounded down to the floor to retrieve the key.

She crossed the room, disengaged the lock, and opened the door.

Smoke poured in, breaking over her like a soundless wave. She raced forward. Three strides brought her to the balustrade. She gripped it and turned, stumbling down into thickening smoke.

She lost balance near the bottom, falling backward to crack her head against the chair rail that extended along the front hall and into the foyer. She started to pull herself up, but stopped when she realized that the air was clearer near the floor. She could see the length of the hall, past the door that led to the living room, all the way to the foyer and the closed front door. Smoke billowed from the living room arch. Dark smoke. No hint of flame. What kind of fire was this, anyway?

She hurried forward, crawling beneath the smoke, keeping her head low. And then something stepped in front of her. She saw it through the smoke, a creature with the face of a pig and the body of...

He reached for her. She recognized his hand.

"See!" he said. "You don't have to follow her rules!" He grabbed her and pulled her down the hall.

She leaned against him, blinking back the stinging smoke as she saw Harold's eyes peering through the Plexiglas goggles of a pig-nose gasmask. And behind him, barely visible as they passed the living room, she glimpsed the fireplace piled high with smoldering peat. He had ignited the stuff and closed the flue. Then he had donned a breathing mask and waited for her to work herself out of the bedroom.

"I did this for you," he said, pulling her to the foyer. "Teach you a lesson!" His voice came muffled through the gasmask, adding to the strangeness of the moment. She felt confused, disoriented, as if the churning smoke had entered her head, and yet now she understood that she'd been too quick to blame herself, too willing to believe that her old compulsions had returned. The mind game had been Harold's, not hers. And as was often the case, his game was all about blaming her.

She looked into his crazy eyes as he headed for the door. She wanted to scream at him, but suddenly a shape in the smoke struck her dumb. A face had formed behind Harold: gaunt cheeks, sunken temples, strong eyes. It was Auntie, her features advancing as Harold entered the foyer.

Am I dreaming this?

Auntie extended a smoky arm, reaching out as Harold opened the front door. Rachel felt a gust of inrushing air. Cool and sweet with misting rain, it broke against her shoulders, tousling her hair and stirring the smoke. Auntie became a whirlwind, a soot-black cyclone with an extended arm that touched Harold's neck, brightened, started to crackle, and then ignited....

BLAM!

The wind was no longer at Rachel's back. It slammed hot against her face, throwing her out of the house, through the door and onto the porch... and all the while her eyes remained open and staring as Harold and the whirlwind melded into a fiery tongue that split against the ceiling. And then, as suddenly as it flared, the flame died, falling in on itself as Rachel scrambled off the porch and into the mist of a sweet-smelling rain.

The house went dark. But the rain was brightening.

She turned, looking east to see a sliver of sun clearing the slope behind the shed.

She found Harold's remains stretched across the front hall. There wasn't much, just ashes on the carpet, the charred shadow of a man in flight that scattered with the wind as she reentered the house.

The fire marshal talked about flashbacks as he inspected the damage. "You had the flue closed," he said, looking at the fireplace. "That starved the fire, but didn't put it out." He stirred the peat ashes with a blackened poker. "That's why your house filled with smoke. And that's why you got that flash when you opened the door. You was lucky."

"Guess I could've been incinerated."

He looked at her. "Not likely. Not if you was opening the door. The flash you saw was back here, in the fireplace. When I said you was lucky, I meant on account of the smoke. Smoke kills more people than fire. You was lucky you made it to the door."

"But the flash was in the hall," she said.

"No." He grinned. "It might've looked that way. A flash in a darkened house can seem closer than it is. But it was back here." He pointed at the fireplace. "So what the hell kind of fire were you trying to build here, anyway?"

The police helped her put the rest of it together.

Harold had waited until she was asleep before reentering the house. He carted the wood to her room, sprinkled her with dirt, and jammed the key into place. Then he locked her door with the master key, lit the fireplace, and closed the flue when he heard her footsteps on the floor above.

It all made sense, but naturally she didn't tell them about the part where Auntie came out of the smoke and set Harold aflame. As far as they were concerned he had fled the scene. "We'll find him," they said, but she knew otherwise. After all, it had been Harold who had violated the commandment by engaging in malicious work on the Sabbath.

And Auntie had always understood the importance of working for the greater good.

The Wiggly People

Eugie Foster

Mama and I were supposed to go to the zoo today. I like the monkeys best. When they make faces, Mama laughs, and her eyes crinkle at the corners. I once told her the monkeys reminded me of Uncle Karl. She smiled so bright I felt like another sun had come out.

But she told me, "Donny, you mustn't say that again. You don't want to get Uncle Karl angry."

Uncle Karl shouts when he's mad, and sometimes he smacks Mama. That always makes the sharp things hurt me and the wiggly people come out.

Today I had my good pants on, and Mama picked out a clean shirt for me to button, all by myself. But when the phone rang, I stopped buttoning. Mama doesn't allow me on the phone, not anymore, not since the police came. Now, whenever the phone rings, I get scared. Sometimes the screaming-jangle brings the wiggly people. Then I need to take a pill.

My pills are nice. They're green and white, shiny on the outside like candy. If I crunch them, they taste bad, and they leave my tongue prickly. If I swallow them, they put a cushion around the sharp things in my head, and the wiggly people leave.

One time, the sharp things got so bad I threw up. I sicked up the pill along with the hot dog I'd had for lunch. I thought my head was going to pop. A wiggly person came and told me he would make it better if I let him hold my hand. As soon as I touched him, it was like floating in a swimming pool. No more sharp things. I had a dream of people screaming and running. But Mama says no, I wasn't asleep.

When I woke up, I was in a room that smelled like pee. It was dark, and I was alone. I cried until my eyes dried up. Mama came and got me, and ever since, I've never let the wiggly people touch me.

It was Uncle Karl on the phone, shouting.

"I been out every night this week," Mama shouted back.

"It's Sunday! Johns don't come out on church nights."

The sharp things in my head burst. The wiggly people came, first with their shadows in the dark places, flickering and hazy.

"I just want to take Donny to the zoo." Mama stopped shouting. "I promised. And it's Sunday... No. I didn't... No, I'm sorry. I'm sorry!"

There was a click and Mama put down the phone.

"Are we going to the zoo now?" I asked.

"I don't think so, baby. Uncle Karl wants me to work."

Mama works at night. The zoo is far away; we have to take a train there. She never takes me to the zoo when she has to work.

The wiggly people beckoned to me with their eyes all black and their fingers like needles.

"I'm sorry," she said. "You know how much Mama loves our zoo trips."

Another flash of burning in my head. I reached into my pocket for my pills.

"Your head hurt again?"

I nodded, because I didn't think I should talk. Sometimes the wiggly people made me say bad things.

Mama hugged me. She smelled so good, like springtime flowers. It softened the sharp things, and the wiggly people turned their faces away.

"I did promise the zoo, didn't I?"

I nodded again. The wiggly people drifted away, like the smoke on birthday candles after you blow them out.

"What about Uncle Karl?" I asked.

"Never mind him. Finish your buttons and we'll go." Mama smiled, although her eyes didn't crinkle.

I like buttons. Sometimes it takes me a while because they're so little and my fingers are so big, but when I push them through the hole the right way, it makes me proud.

Mama made herself up pretty and had her purse out. I wasn't done yet, but she didn't rush me.

I only had one last button to go when the door burst open. It was Uncle Karl. He didn't talk, just stomped up to Mama and smacked her, hard.

"You don't sass back to me, whore! You work when I say you work. If I say I want you ass up and legs spread twenty-four seven, you say, 'yes, sir'!" He hit her again.

Mama fell down, and the sharp things in my head exploded. A wiggly person slithered past, grinning. Its teeth were red and wet, like angry blood.

"You're working tonight, you hear me?" Each word Uncle Karl shouted was like someone stabbing my eyes with nails. It hurt so bad I wet myself, messing my good pants.

Uncle Karl wrinkled his nose at the stink. "If you think you can dick me around, you're just as retarded as your pants-pissing boy. Hell, he's smarter than you. He knows you're good for nothing but whoring."

He dragged me to where Mama lay, crying on the floor.

"Tell your mama! Tell her she's a whore!"

The red-toothed wiggly person held out his hand. It was blackened, like burned meat, the fingertips pointed.

"Tell your mama she's a whore, boy. Say it!"

The wiggly person was so close, close enough to touch.

"Leave him alone," Mama sobbed.

Uncle Karl kicked Mama in the belly. White fire filled my head. I screamed and grabbed the wiggly person's hand.

It felt so good not to hurt. Even when the wiggly person poured into my mouth, filling me up, I didn't care.

We sank our red teeth into Uncle Karl's neck, and it was like biting into a juicy hamburger. We shoved our pointy fingernails into his face, and his eyeballs popped like raw eggs.

Mama screamed, and I was sad we'd made her unhappy.

Uncle Karl made wet noises as we ate his face.

Mama and I weren't going to the zoo, but at least she wouldn't have to work tonight.

Michael's Grave

Dave Raines

If the dead were to sit up on some great morning, they would be rewarded with a gorgeous view of the sun rising over the Cascade Mountains. If the season were right, they could see acres of strawberries, marionberries, and blueberries. They would see their property, their livelihood.

Four generations of Arends were buried in the old family cemetery located at the end of the road that ran through the woods and past the farmworker housing. Last year's addition to the collection of Arend headstones read:

Michael S. Arend
1929–1953

Michael's father Stan sometimes stood in the road and watched the *campesinos* climb the hill, pause in the shade of the maple tree that loomed over Michael's grave, perhaps enjoy a cool breeze. Most of them were fond of the Arends. Now and then, they reminisced about Michael during their breaks. They had considered "Mr. Michael" a polite young man, respectful to them as few growers were, and a hard worker. They remembered how he picked with them, bending over the bushes, racing to see who could finish a row fastest. Sometimes he won, sometimes he didn't; always, he laughed. Now, the *campesinos* shook their heads in regret. "Mr. Michael—dead so young!" Juan, the field boss, often visited the grave alone.

Today, Stan sat under the maple tree, looking down the hill at the vines heavy with marionberries, hybrid blackberries, ripe for the picking. It was four in the afternoon, and he had been up twelve hours, working to get the berries in. He knew he needed a break if he was going to work the rest of the day. He scooped a handful of dirt from the grave and let it sift through his fingers. Nothing grew on Michael's grave. Stan had planted grass, then wildflowers, but nothing took. He accepted the mystery as if it were some kind of tribute to his son, as if the grass refused to grow out of respect for Michael.

The field boss approached. "Mr. Stan, what are you going to do?"

"I dunno, Juan. Tomorrow's the Sabbath. You know I don't work you on the Sabbath—"

"But there's a storm coming." Juan finished his sentence for him.

A storm coming on the Sabbath, Stan thought bitterly. "How are you coming, Johnny?"

Juan shrugged. "We'll be done with the south field by midnight, if we pick fast."

"But not the field by the house."

"No. And boss, if it's a hard rain, or even hail, you'll lose those berries."

Just like last year. Another year like last year, and he'd lose the farm.

Lord, he prayed, I'm a faithful guy. Why do you do this to me?

"Well," said Juan, "we'll pick for you."

"I can't ask you to."

"We'll pick for you. You pay top dollar and now we pay you back. We'll pick till three, four in the morning, and get it done. We sleep all day tomorrow, when the storm comes! See, we'll only break the Sabbath a little bit."

It's a test, ain't it, Lord?

Stan looked at Juan. The stocky little man had brought his crew back to the farm for fifteen straight years now. The field boss could be secretive, could be cruel; and his unchristian boasts about ancient Aztec rites and mysteries grew tiresome. But he was utterly reliable, even charismatic, and bossed an excellent crew.

Of course Stan paid well. He was an Old Testament kind of guy, and he read there, "Thou shalt not muzzle the ox when he treadeth out the corn." Don't stiff your workers, was Stan's translation. But his relationship with Juan was based on something more than money. Stan had come to rely on the man, and by now, the field boss knew Stan's word was gold. And nobody had been sadder than Juan when Michael died.

"Okay," said Stan. "Okay. I appreciate it. I'll drive the wagons."

"Oh no, boss. It's the Sabbath! You got to stay home." Juan paused and then said with a peculiar urgency, "We don't work on the Sabbath, not much. On the Sabbath, the crew gotta be together, *all* of us."

Stan was confused. "What do you mean, 'all of us'?"

Juan ignored him. "It's part of our, our culture. The boys get kind of—out of hand, on the Sabbath, sometimes. It's a holy day for you, but we're not holy people, ha! You got to stay inside. Promise me you'll stay home." Then he added, "Or the deal's off."

Stan bristled. He didn't tolerate disrespect. And he'd never asked his workers to do something he wouldn't do. On the other hand, Juan knew him pretty well, knew he had never worked on the Sabbath, never in his life. Maybe the field boss was giving him a way out.

"Okay," he said. "And thanks."

After dark, Stan stood outside, watching the *campesinos* labor, amazed at their stamina. Picking was hard work, back-breaking work, but the fieldhands were still as fast and efficient as ever after, what—fifteen hours of picking? Now and then one paused long enough to stretch, and then plunged his hands back into the bushes. A little after eleven, they finished the south field and moved to the field by the house.

Just before midnight Juan came over and chucked him on the arm, a little too affectionately. "Okay, boss. Go home, get inside!"

"Okay, Johnny, okay." Stan bristled, but after all, he'd agreed to it. He turned and trudged home. His feet scuffled dirt and gravel with every step, not simply from fatigue, but because he didn't want to go.

At 1:00 A.M. Stan sat at his kitchen table. Michael used to sit at this same table, drawing ice-water pictures on the Formica. Now and then Stan's eyes slowly closed; then his head fell forward until suddenly he jerked himself alert. He was too tired to sleep and too restless to stay inside, though he had agreed to. When he felt the sudden breeze blow through the open windows and heard the rumble of thunder in the distance, he got up and peered through the kitchen window.

Thunder? In the Valley? This storm was going to be bad.

He couldn't stand it. But he had promised to stay home.

But there was a balcony off his bedroom.

He took the servants' stairway from the kitchen to the second floor and stepped onto the balcony. Sure enough, he could see the workers out in the field, stark black-and-white shadows in the headlights of the old farm pickup. The pickers seemed to be working by feel as much as by sight. He watched for a while, uneasy at bending the spirit of his promise.

One picker stood taller than the rest, seemed a little clumsy. Stan didn't remember seeing him before and certainly didn't recognize him. That was odd: Stan prided himself on knowing the names of his crew members. He strained to see, but the distance and the bad lighting made it impossible to discern features. The tall man looked familiar though.

There was a pair of binoculars with his camping equipment. He ran to get them. By the time he returned he felt light-headed. He was too old for all-nighters. He breathed deep to steady himself and put the binoculars to his eyes.

Between the spots still dancing in his vision, he saw that the man looked like Michael. But the light was too bad, it was casting illusions.

Angrily, Stan flicked a tear from the corner of his eye. He was just tired, that's all.

The last time Stan had seen him, Michael was dying. The boy's throat had been cut. Michael had been working on repairs for the farmworker housing. A sheet of plate glass had slid off the truck where it had been carelessly stacked. Michael had reached out to stop it, but it slipped past his fingers and made a clean cut across his throat. Juan was holding him and crying, pressing on the artery, trying to stanch the bleeding. Jets of blood escaped Juan's fingers, spurting across the dirt. By the time Stan reached Michael, the blood had almost stopped flowing.

Stan looked again through the binoculars at the man who resembled Michael.

I'm over it. A year has passed, and it's high time I stopped this foolishness.

Without binoculars, Stan scanned the distant workers. It seemed as if there were others. Other strangers. His conversation with Juan came back to him and he grew uneasy. Who in the world did "all of us" include?

Stan stood still, agonized. For a moment, his promise held him. Then, half-conscious that he was breaking it, reckless enough not to care, he stumbled down the back stairs and outside. The rising wind slapped his face. He lurched down the rutted access road and plunged into the field, calling, "Juan! Juan!"

Suddenly he was in the midst of the fieldworkers, brushing shoulders. The crew stopped their labor and gathered around him. But he didn't care. He was looking for Juan, and found him.

In the glare of the headlights the field boss's eyes glittered with unholy power, and his mouth was twisted in— anger? Fear?

"Boss, boss," said Juan. "You shoulda stayed home." The *campesinos* surrounded Stan, drawing much closer than they should have. Usually they smelled of honest sweat or lye soap. Tonight they smelled like a cat after a couple of hot days dead.

"Juan," Stan said. "I saw a new guy out here. Who the hell have you got working tonight?"

"I loved Michael," Juan said softly. "A kind man, a hard worker. I made him part of my crew. Michael, come here." A tall figure stepped from the shadows beside the truck into the light. Stan would have known Michael anywhere, even at two in the morning, even backlit, even impossibly alive.

Even with cheekbone showing through his skin.

Even with a dark gash in his pallid throat.

Stan glanced around nervously. Juan looked solid, human. And so Stan knew it wasn't a trick of the light when one of the pickers reached for him with fingers like gnawed chicken bones, and when another's frayed shirt split to reveal the backbone underneath, and when another's gut literally flopped over his belt.

"The Sabbath is not a good day for us, my friend," said Juan. "I wish you had stayed inside."

"The seventh day is a Sabbath to the LORD your God. On it you shall not do any work, neither you... nor the alien within your gates..."

THOU
SHALT
NOT...

Dishonor
Your
Parents

The Day the Radio Did Most of the Talking

Marc Paoletti

Paul waved to the schoolbus driver to show he was in the house, then closed the front door against wind that had numbed his face and made his eyes water.

He heard a choking cough from the bedroom. Matthew was sick. Again. It seemed like Matthew had been sick with bad croup or fever every day since he was born three years ago. And if he was sick, Paul knew Mom was with him.

It wasn't fair.

Matthew being sick all the time made Mom quiet and sad. It made her yell for no reason. Paul didn't like to bother Mom when she was taking care of Matthew, but today he had no choice.

Today was the last episode of *Captain Midnight*.

Today Captain Midnight would show Ivan Shark and his daughter Fury (who had the same name as Straight Arrow's horse!) who was boss. This time for sure.

He looked through the kitchen into the family room where the polished brown Silvertone radio sat invitingly on an end table. It was a tombstone model, Dad had told him once, with eight tubes and lots of stations. The Silvertone was better than anything, even a mountain of Smarties.

But there wasn't time to think about all that now. The wall clock above the radio told him it was nearly Children's Hour. He had to hurry.

He stomped snow from his red galoshes onto the door-mat before slipping out of them and placing them aside. He pulled off his red hat and mittens next, wriggled free from his red wool jacket, and tossed the whole lump onto a kitchen chair.

Paul took a deep breath for courage, then tiptoed through the living room and down the short hallway until he reached his brother's bedroom. The shades were drawn. The dancing clown lamp on the dresser was lit, the one with the shaded bulb for a head. It didn't give off much light. The air smelled stale and sour. Paul wrinkled his nose.

Matthew lay in bed, buried under wooly gray surplus blankets. His face was the color of hardboiled egg yolk and his eyes were yucky with white crust. Mom was there, all right, whispering to Matthew with her forehead pressed against his cheek. Matthew saw Paul and stuck out his tongue. Paul stuck out his tongue in return and Matthew's cracked lips squirmed into a smile.

What a twerp! Paul stood quietly at the foot of the bed and waited for Mom to notice him. After a few moments, he couldn't wait any longer. *Captain Midnight* was close to starting.

"Mom?" he said. Her body jerked like he'd surprised her. She didn't look up. "Mom, can you help me tune the radio to *Captain Midnight*?"

Still not looking at him, she said in a low voice, "I'm busy with your brother now."

"It's the last episode."

"In a few minutes."

"The *very* last episode."

She glared at him. Her eyes were angry and had dark circles. "In a few minutes, I said."

Paul knew it wouldn't be a few minutes. He knew she would stay here for hours like she always did when Matthew was sick.

"But in a few minutes I'll miss it," he said quietly.

"Paul!"

He took a step back. When Mom raised her voice like that, his stomach squeezed itself into a tight lump.

"Your little brother is very ill," she said. "He can't take care of himself. You should understand that. You need to be a big boy."

That stopped him. That always stopped him. More than anything, he wanted to prove that he was a big boy. He was six years old now! Not a baby like Matthew. He stared at the floor.

"Don't stand there moping," she said. "Go fetch me the Nyall."

Paul padded down the hall and into the bathroom. There, he closed the toilet lid and climbed on top, taking care not to slip. He reached over the sink and opened the mirrored medicine cabinet. He dug past bottles labeled Epsom and Ipecac and Watkins Liniment and Vicks until he spotted Nyall Croup Ointment. He grabbed it.

He closed the door and caught his reflection. He frowned. He still had a little-boy face, not at all rough and hairy like Dad's.

Mom's words floated back to him. *Be a big boy.*

He was already trying. Like the time last Christmas when he'd bumped the Silvertone by accident and a show called *The Shadow* came on. He was alone in the room. There weren't any flying captains on that show, only scary laughter that gave him nightmares for a week. But he kept his bad dreams to himself so Mom and Dad wouldn't worry.

Paul wanted to ask about other ways he could be grown up, but Mom and Dad didn't talk so much anymore. It seemed like the radio had done most of the talking at home since Matthew was born.

At dinnertime, Dad used to talk about his job at GM and Powerglide transmissions and the good honest work of the UAW. Paul didn't understand these grown-up things, but he liked very much the sound of Dad telling them.

Now when Dad came home, he turned on the Silvertone and yelled for quiet. Most nights the show was about a man named Fibber McGee who opened a closet door and made stuff crash out. The crashing noises made Paul giggle, but Dad listened without making a sound.

And Mom, she never asked him about school anymore. When she wasn't with Matthew, she hushed Paul and listened to a show about Helen Trent, a girl who wanted to get married but couldn't. Sometimes Mom cried while listening to the show. Other times she went into her room and closed the door.

Paul jumped off the toilet and headed back down the hall. He'd gotten so used to Mom and Dad not talking that he felt sort of empty and alone when they did.

Be a big boy.

Paul thought about Matthew smiling at him before, like he was playing a mean dirty trick. Smiling like he knew today was the last episode of *Captain Midnight*. Paul wanted to get back at Matthew, but how could he with Mom in the room?

Paul cleared his throat, and then opened the Nyall bottle. Slowly, carefully, he spat a thin rope of mucus into the creamy ointment. That would show the little twerp. He replaced the lid and returned to the bedroom.

Mom took the Nyall from him without saying a word. She pulled down Matthew's quilts. Matthew wasn't wearing a nightshirt. His chest was pale yellow like his face and his arms were thin as broomsticks. Mom opened the Nyall and poured a large dollop onto her palm. Paul watched as she rubbed the snotty ointment across his brother's chest and then under his nose.

Satisfied, Paul hurried into the kitchen to fetch his Captain Midnight Orange Shake-Up Mug from its place beneath the sink. He filled it just below the rim with cold milk from the refrigerator. Two teaspoons of Ovaltine powder went in next, and then he closed the mug and shook it hard while counting to ten. Finally, he dug the secret decoder ring from the front pocket of his bluejeans and slipped it firmly onto his index finger.

Paul padded into the living room and looked intently at the Silvertone. It sat on a shiny black table, its numbered dial eye level with him. A big boy should be able to turn on and tune a radio. But would he hear something as scary as *The Shadow* again?

He took a deep breath for courage, and set the Shake-Up Mug on the green velvet rug, careful to steady it so it wouldn't spill. He studied the two knobs on either side of the numbered dial and the six square buttons along the bottom. He decided to start with the buttons and move left to right, like he was learning to write in school.

Paul laid his first finger on the leftmost button and pushed timidly. It wouldn't budge. He pressed a little harder until the tip of his finger bent back and turned red, but still the button stayed stuck. Then he pressed with all his strength, using his entire arm this time, and the button slid in with a hollow *sshuk*, which made the tuning needle dart from left to right across the dial.

He flushed with pride until he realized there wasn't any sound coming from the speaker. He pushed all the buttons in the same purposeful way, causing the needle to dart this way and that, but the speaker stayed quiet.

Paul moved on to the knobs. He turned the upper right knob both ways. Still no sound. Next, he twisted the lower right knob and the numbered dial lit up suddenly, making him jump back. A faint murmur issued from the speaker, and a wide smile broke across his face. He'd done it!

The murmur was so soft that the volume must be on low. He reached for the same knob and then stopped, not wanting to accidentally undo what he just did. Instead, he pressed his ear against the rough fabric speaker and listened hard like when Mom used to read to him.

He heard light, happy music like one of Dad's old jazz records that disappeared every few seconds beneath a crackling hiss. He knew this wasn't the right station because *Captain Midnight* had music that was more thumpy and serious.

Keeping his ear pressed against the speaker, he twisted the upper left knob this time, which he guessed might move the needle to a different band. The music was replaced by a high-pitched whine that grew louder and softer as he turned the knob. He kept twisting, face pinched in concentration, until the whine evened out and became a man's voice.

But the voice didn't belong to Captain Midnight or Ivan Shark. This was a man he'd never heard before, speaking in a deep and even voice without exciting music or the sound of airplanes swooping.

This was a grown-up discussing grown-up things. The man reminded him of the way Mom and Dad used to talk to him before Matthew came along.

Soon, he became lulled by the steady monotone.

Listening closely, Paul made out strange bits like "Korea" and "thirty-eighth parallel" and "Security Council." Then he heard a longer bit that went, "...the U.S. condemns the Communist aggression and insists that it will not stand."

Paul drew back and stared at the dial. It occurred to him for the first time that if he memorized its place, he would never have to rely on Mom again. He could find the radio show on his own like a big boy.

He also decided if Mom and Dad wouldn't talk to him after school, then he would listen to this new show in secret when they were out of the room. Even though a few of the strange words made his stomach tighten for some reason, at least they weren't scary like *The Shadow.*

He replaced his ear against the speaker and heard, "...development of the hydrogen bomb is the only way to ensure national security..."

Paul kept listening, and it wasn't long before he forgot about his sick, twerpy brother and about missing the last episode of *Captain Midnight.* Over the next few weeks, he also forgot what he missed about talking to Mom and Dad, preferring instead to listen to the radio and absorbing the grown-up ideas that it had to teach him.

180   *THE DAY THE RADIO DID MOST OF THE TALKING*
~ Marc Paoletti

Clink Clank

Derryl Murphy

Clink. Clank.

Sounds from the basement.

Ken looked at his mom as she stirred the scrambled eggs—a rare treat—but she kept her eyes down, never looked toward the basement or to the table where Ken and his dad sat, Ken blowing bubbles in his OJ and his dad reading the paper and drinking coffee. Before he could say anything, she grabbed his plate, threw on a thick clump of eggs, added bacon and gave it to him.

"Eat." Mom's gaze drifted over to his dad, hidden behind the paper, fingers white and slowly crumpling the newsprint. Her hand rested on Ken's shoulder, hard and firm. "You have to get to school."

After she served Dad and herself, she filled another plate and slipped it into the oven. Ken tried to ask, but one look from his dad forced the curiosity back down his throat.

Clink. Clank.

When Ken came home from school that afternoon, his mom looked pale and nervous and tired. She took Ken to his room and had him sit at the old desk, had him do his homework there instead of at the kitchen table. She brought him a snack and shut the door when she left.

Clink. Clank.

Ken got up from the desk and walked quietly over to the window, looked outside, just in case.

Clink. Clank.

Below his feet. He looked down, saw the vent. Was it the furnace? Some piece of it rolling around inside, banging against another piece of metal? He crouched and put his ear to the vent, waited.

Clink. Clank.

It didn't sound like the furnace. He strained to hear more.

Cough.

His dad walked in. "What are you doing?"

Guilty but not sure why, Ken jumped to his feet. "I dropped a toy dinosaur. I think it went down there." He pointed to the vent.

His dad's eyes were a hard squint, lines of worry on his face. For the first time that Ken could ever remember in his eight years, Dad looked old. He said, "You listen to me. Your mom and I need you to know that right now the basement is off limits. Okay?"

"But—"

"But nothing. I haven't been getting much work this past year, but your mom found something that'll help us. We haven't received all the money for it, though. Until we do, stay upstairs. Understand?"

Ken nodded. "Yes, sir."

His dad ruffled Ken's hair. "Good boy."

Clink. Clank.

His dad closed the door, mouth a hard line, ignoring the noise.

Clink. Clank.

At supper Ken's mom and dad were quiet. His mom said how lovely the hamburgers were, especially after nothing but mac and cheese for the past week, but she couldn't hold the thought, it seemed, and her words vanished into the air.

Sitting on the counter beside the fridge was another plate, two burgers, fries, and carrot sticks on it. Again he tried to ask, and again was warned with a look, so Ken excused himself to use the toilet. When he returned the plate was gone. Mom's face was red, and she made to brush away imaginary crumbs from her blouse.

Clink. Clank.

In bed that night, Ken turned on his side and watched the vent, barely acknowledged his mom and dad as they came in to kiss him good night. His mom ran her nervous, sweaty fingers through his hair, and his dad clapped him on the shoulder and, after a kiss on the forehead, reminded him to stay upstairs.

Door shut, dull glow of a distant streetlight seeping through the window, Ken tried to keep his eyes open, but eventually he drifted off to sleep. He dreamed of ogres and treasures and aliens, sometimes all at once.

Clink. Clank.

Scrape.

His eyes popped open. Had he dreamed the new sound?

Ken looked at his door and saw that the lights in the house were out. His parents were asleep. He climbed out of bed and scooted over to the floor vent, and after a fidgety few seconds of indecision, ran his fingernail across the metal slats of the vent.

TICK-tack-tack-tack-tacktacktacktacktack.

Clink. Clank.

Scrape.

Then: "*Come down here.*"

Just a whisper, really, so distant Ken wondered if it had come from his own head. He jumped up, his dad's order all but forgotten, and found a flashlight in his toy box.

He sneaked down the hall, past his parents' bedroom and his dad's snores, and turned on the flashlight once he got to the top of the basement stairs.

Clink. Clank.

One step down, he stopped and listened. Again. He watched the light dance wildly on the wall at the bottom, his hands shaking. Finally he reached the cold concrete floor of the basement and raised the light to see.

Clink. Clank.

No longer distant. At the edge of the light, a chain scraped slowly across the floor. Ken followed the movement with the flashlight to a cuff clamped on a man's ankle. He tracked the light up and into the eyes of a strange man, sitting on a cot.

The man shaded his eyes with one hand and smiled, a broad toothy grin that looked ready to devour anything in its path. "Heya kid." His voice was low, throaty, a rumble that scraped Ken's ears.

Ken hung back, lowered the flashlight to the gulf of the floor between them. "Hey."

"Can you get me a drink of water?" He pointed to a plastic cup beside him.

Ken didn't move. "Who are you? Why are you here?"

"The government pays citizens to host prisoners now," the man said. He frowned as he reached down to scratch around the cuff on his leg. "Cheaper than building new prisons."

"What'd you do?"

The man gave another toothy, hungry smile, held out the cup like he was offering a reward. "Get me that drink of water and I'll tell you."

Clink. Clank.

Scrape.

Close of Play

B. M. Freman

First Inning (Tuesday)

The school bus stopped beside the walkway leading to the Close. The grating squeak of its doors echoed around the bush and the surrounding gardens followed by a rumbling echo as it moved off. None of this made any impression inside the silent house. Here the only sound was a mouse-ish rustle of paper. In the laundry the dog shivered her tail but made no other move. She knew she wasn't in the game yet.

The children walked in at the usual time, dropping their bags in the hall before going into the lounge room where they found the baby happily playing in a nest of torn newspapers. The mother lay quietly in her big chair, makeup perfect as always, but her everyday frilled robe grubby.

The boy nodded to the two girls who picked up the baby and wrinkled their noses at the urine smell. Yet they smiled at the child and accepted her welcoming kisses.

After they left the room the boy turned to the mother. "We're home now. Why don't you go and have a rest."

The mother moved her head slowly. "Oh yes, good idea, think I will, thank you."

The boy watched her go before turning his blank, arrived-home face toward the window. He listened as she shuffled along the hall and stumbled by the study door on the first of the three small steps that led to the bedroom hall.

At one time he would have blinked back tears, imagining her hands trying to grip the stains they had tracked along the walls over the years, but he did neither of those things anymore.

The boy went into the hall to collect the heavy school bags, then carried them to the far end of the lounge room, where he opened the sliding doors into the family room and closed them tightly behind him as the girls returned with the baby.

A baby dish sat on the big table in the center of the room. The area around it was covered with dried food stains, and the elder girl took away the dish and cleaned the table as the boy and the younger girl dragged a box of books and toys from the corner where it sat between a big dollhouse and the breakfast bar. While the baby crawled over to her box, the girls emptied the dishwasher and the boy studied a list stuck on the door of the fridge before taking packages out of the freezer. He put these in the fridge, then poured fruit juice into three plastic mugs and one baby bottle. He placed these on the family room side of the breakfast bar, set the kitchen timer to thirty minutes, and placed it beside the drinks.

The two older children took out their schoolwork and settled around the table with their juice. The younger girl set out her work before she took some small dolls from the toy box and played with the baby, moving the dolls in and out of the dollhouse, its front now opened wide to show the tiny furniture they never allowed the baby to handle on her own.

After thirty minutes, the kitchen timer rang and the two girls changed places. The elder girl reset the timer before taking big, brightly colored books out of the box and reading to the baby, who pointed to the pictures on the page with her grubby fingers.

After the second thirty minutes the elder girl and the boy changed places. The boy took out a box of big plastic bricks and showed the baby how to pile them up and knock them down. At the end of the third half hour the boy closed up the dollhouse, put away the paper books and settled the baby with her bottle of fruit juice, the bricks, and a few cloth books. Then he joined his sisters at the table after setting the timer to forty-five minutes.

The family's built-in garage bordered the lounge, family room, kitchen and laundry. The door from the garage to the house led to a small passageway where another external door, complete with doggy flap, opened onto a paved patio. The laundry also opened off this passageway, and the clunky golden retriever Bess rested there under the bench—when she wasn't lying on the patio—until the father came home, when she joined in the game.

Just before the timer rang its forty-five-minute summons, the children began to pack up their books. They heard their father's key click in the garage door and they heard him greet Bess. They turned to welcome them both as Bess charged ahead, her claws clattering on her way to the kitchen.

The father passed through the kitchen into the family room and dropped his briefcase beside the school bags before looking around. The four smiled at each other, the baby gurgled, and Bess wiped the floor with her plumed tail: unspoken congratulations all round for another milestone achieved, another day, another game.

The elder girl began the evening's proceedings. "Hi Dad, how's your day?"

"Good, good. Pretty busy, but it all got done. How about you lot?"

"I got an A for my homework."

The father ruffled the younger girl's hair in congratulations.

"I've got a new piece to practice for my flute." The elder girl offered her father a sheet of music she had pulled from her bag. She smiled shyly as she received her hair-ruffling praise.

"Clever girl. How about you, Son?"

"Oh, we had a routine day but I think my end-of-year results will be good enough for senior level."

Father and son exchanged some imaginary boxing moves before the man bent down to ask the baby what she had been doing. She spat out the dummy pinned to her shoulder and offered him a sample of her bricks and cloth books. The father jiggled her nose with his finger and then ruffled her hair. "I think you are going to be the cleverest of us all."

The family moved wordlessly into their evening game as the father hung his jacket on back of the one of the chairs and the younger girl began to set the table for the evening meal.

The microwave timer pinged, and the father took another baby dish and four plates from the cupboard. He withdrew a fifth plate and raised his eyebrows at the elder girl. She shrugged and went into the hall, where she stood by the three steps outside the study for a moment before going back into the kitchen and saying that the mother didn't want anything to eat at the moment. The father put the fifth plate back into the cupboard and they continued to make their calming moves.

When the meal was finished and the table cleared, the children picked up their school bags and, saying a general goodnight, went to their rooms. The father put the baby to bed, organized a few clothes into the washing machine and stacked the dishwasher to wait for tomorrow's breakfast dishes. Then he went into the study. There he poured his one evening whisky and opened his briefcase, spreading the papers under the desk lamp that glowed over the stained desk.

Second Inning (Wednesday)

The games moved as usual through their carefully written programs. Although the boy thought that the father's evening routine was less well performed than usual, he said nothing. He watched the man over his glasses throughout the evening.

The father finally sat back in his desk chair and sipped his daily whisky. The phone rang.

"Hello Max. Yes, I've tried to explain it to her. She just doesn't seem to understand. She really thinks it's me trying to get away without her." ——

"No, she really doesn't believe, she doesn't *want* to believe, that the company would refuse to accept wives on business trips." ——

"But it's not going to be that easy. She's saying that if she can't come she'll leave." ——

"I know it wouldn't be a bad thing, but she's talking of taking the baby with her." ——

"True, but she scrubs up perfect, you know that, maybe eventually we could get the baby back, but what would happen to her before then. What would happen to the poor little thing in the meantime?" ——

"I can't risk that." ——

"I know that, you know that, everybody I work with knows that, although they pretend they don't: the boss's wife is a drunk. But a court isn't going to know that." ——

"Yeah, maybe we could, maybe everyone who knows her could, but what would all the kids suffer in the meantime? How would the baby cope if she was dragged away?" ——

"I don't know. I don't know what we're going to do." ——

"Of course I can't take her overseas, even if I paid for her myself, which I can't afford. That last clinic cost more than a year's salary. The company would hear about it and they would not be pleased." ——

"No, no, they might decide that I'm not a reliable general manager. Anyway, we'll see." ——

"OK. G'night Max."

As the father put the phone down and picked up his evening glass again, the boy crept backwards up the three steps and slipped silently along the bedroom hall.

End Game (Friday)

The children arrived home from school at the usual time and began their routines while the older children talked about the washing and the chance of rain. As the mother was leaving the lounge room the boy spoke to her wavering back, as if thinking aloud.

"Hm, we really ought to think of bringing the washing in. Dad thinks it might rain before he gets home, but I don't know if I have time to do it."

The mother gripped the doorframe and half turned back. "Does the washing need to be brought in? I can do that, I *can* do that. Where's the basket."

"In the laundry."

"I will do it. I'll do it now, before I have a rest."

"Thanks, Mum. Oh, and Dad says we must be careful and keep the gate to the swimming pool closed 'cause Bess is getting old and he doesn't want her falling in."

Bess gave her tail a wiggle at the sound of her name, then put her nose back down on her paws: not time to join in.

"That's a very good idea. I'll make sure."

The mother shuffled out to the clothesline and hummed tunelessly to herself as she tossed all the clothes toward the basket. When she turned to go back to the house she trampled on the things that had fallen on the grass, taking no notice of them other than to kick them off her feet.

As she slithered across the lawn she noticed that the swimming pool gate was open. She remembered her responsibility and went to the pool. There was something blocking the gate on the inside and she went in to move it.

She turned back, half pulling the gate behind her and half leaning on it. The two older children were there, standing in its place, with their hands behind their backs—watching her.

They moved toward her silently and she backed away. They continued to move toward her. She continued to back away.

Eventually she lost her footing and rolled gently into the water. The children watched the grubby frills float momentarily, then sink. The boy kicked the basket of clothes into the water after her.

On their way back to the house the boy said, "We mustn't forget to close the patio gate, we don't want Bess falling into the water."

When the father came home, the evening games began as usual.

Then—after the elder girl had given her day's report— she remembered something.

"Oh, I was supposed to bring in the washing, but it's dark now."

The father was about to hang his jacket on the back of the chair but he shrugged it on again. "I'll do it. You keep Bess here and think of a nice dessert."

Sins of the Mother

Eugie Foster

Rose gazed at the crags and creases of her mother's face. Where once eyes had blazed from a countenance strong and fierce, now there was only a wreckage of pain and exhaustion. Rose contemplated the dying woman who had borne and raised her, fed and housed her.

She'd prayed for Mother to die, fantasized about being freed from her. It had been a day of rejoicing when the doctors told her that Mother's cancer was inoperable. But she'd exceeded their longest estimates, clung to each minute, every second of life.

Nevertheless, even Mother couldn't win against death.

The doctors were gone, the nurses retreating in their wake. There was nothing for them to do but leave daughter and mother to their destinies—one to die and one to grieve.

Rose and her mother were alone now, alone with the humming machines, the tubes and pumps that kept life in Mother's devastated body. Those insufferable machines had sustained her for so long. Too long. They gave her rest and peaceful surcease from the sickness devouring her. It was more than she deserved.

"I prayed you would die in agony," Rose whispered. "Screaming like I screamed when your lash tore me and your cigarettes burned me. Or die, strangled in your own filth. Remember when you wouldn't let me use the bathroom? It was my eighth birthday. I held it for as long as I

195

could. I begged you. But you wanted to teach me a lesson, you said."

Rose glanced at the catheter that governed her mother's bladder functions. "What lesson have *you* learned?"

She glared at the morphine drip. How easy it would be to kink the feed.

"I considered letting you die alone. You lied to Greg. I loved him, and you drove him away, like you drove Father away. Everything that ever mattered to me, you spoiled. I want to watch you die. You owe me that much."

Mother's eyes twitched open, rheumy blue and unfocused.

"Rose?" Her voice was frail and reedy, such a contrast to the shrill klaxon it used to be, reducing a young girl to tears. "Rose? Are you there?"

"I'm here."

"I thought you'd left me. You're so much like your father."

"I'm here," she repeated. Father had escaped one night, when Mother chased him from the house, hurling china and shrieking obscenities. Rose had been three. How she'd wished he'd taken her with him.

When Rose was older, he had sent conciliatory letters, birthday cards, and left the occasional message on her answering machine. She never replied, never called him back. How could she forgive him for forsaking her to Mother's mercy? She hated him too.

Rose watched the talon of her mother's hand grope the air. A ruby ring hung loose on that once powerful hand, the gem like a drop of blood. It was Mother's favorite. It gave Rose a glow of pleasure, the thought of stripping that ring off her mother's lifeless hand. She'd sell it, that cherished possession of her mother's, and buy herself something pretty with the money. Maybe a red dress with a high hem and thin straps. Mother had never let her wear pretty clothes.

"You look like a tramp," she'd sneered. Or, "You're too fat for those outfits."

"Rose?"

"Yes."

Her mother's hand drooped to the sheet. "I had a dream. I dreamed of heaven, so clean, white. St. Peter was there. He wasn't happy with me."

"No. I can't imagine he would be."

"I haven't been the best mother to you."

Rose's eyes were hot embers, burning in her skull. They were dry. No tears now. Not today.

"There's a weight on my soul, Rosie. You can lighten it. Tell me you forgive me. Give me your blessing."

Rose pursed her lips.

"I'm dying, Rose. Say you forgive me."

Rose leaned close. Her mother's breath smelled like ashes and corruption. "I *don't* forgive you." She spat out each word, clear and crisp. "I hope you burn in hell."

Her mother's mouth curled down; spittle dripped from the corners. "Ungrateful brat," she rasped. "I should have aborted you like I wanted to. You were an accident, damn you."

"You first, Mother." Rose straightened.

Her mother's chest rose, a labored gasp. Rose waited for her next breath. And waited.

Mother's eyes glared, sightless and glassy. Her body had become a husk, void of all vitality. She was dead, her last words as full of spite as her life had been.

Rose waited for the triumph, the euphoria to wash over her. She felt nothing at all. The shell before her was just a corpse in a world overflowing with death and pain and sickness.

With mechanical precision, Rose tugged the ruby from Mother's hand. It was a hollow gesture, devoid of significance. The red stone with its bloody facets glinted in the fluorescent light. The band had clacked like teeth snapping when her mother drummed it against the arm of her chair. It had bitten Rose, this ring. Rose touched the scar on her cheek—a backhanded blow that had opened a gash, spilling more rubies. Like calling to like.

That's my ring.

Rose gasped and spun around. Mother's voice reverberated in the room, as fierce and bitter as when she'd been well, before the cancer stole her strength. But Mother hadn't moved, not her lips, not her face. She was still as death.

Rose scowled. She needed to rest, that was all. She slipped the ring over her thumb.

Slut! What did I just tell you?

The ring clattered to the floor. It glittered at her, malevolent and hard, like her mother had been.

"You're dead, Mother," Rose said. "You can't hurt me anymore."

Dead I may be, but I can still hurt you. You should have absolved me, Rosie. You should have forgiven me.

Rose screamed. Outside, in the hospital corridor, the doctors exchanged somber glances. They'd heard it before, the ragged sounds of a daughter's grief.

Hungry Ghosts

Sarah Brandel

Children who lingered at dusk during the Ghost Month risked possession by wandering spirits. The only wraiths Lian saw when she stepped off the city bus from the university were the twining plumes of incense rising from family shrines.

Joss incense scented the air like autumn wood smoke come early. The smell was tempered by the fading sauna heat of the day. Once outside the air conditioning of the bus, Lian's blouse clung to her like wet laundry.

Her empty suitcase banged against her right leg as she walked. Her parents' house was eight blocks from the bus stop. Maybe, by the time she arrived, she would think of what to say to them.

She dug out her lighter and lit a wilting cigarette. "I've come for my things," wasn't right. Neither was, "I'm sorry you're giving up on the house." Or, "*Zufu* and *Zumu* would be so ashamed of you."

Maybe, when she reached her parents' house, all she'd want was a shower.

After dark, Chinatown had the same lurid neon glow as the Strip in Las Vegas. The gutters were clogged with gaudy trash tonight; she must have missed a parade earlier in the evening. A half-burned piece of paper crunched under her foot. Hell money. Lian looked from the twenty-dollar Hell Bank Note to the full moon, cursing silently. Why were her parents moving now? Moving during the Ghost Month was doubly unlucky, and tonight was the Hungry Ghost Festival. Her fist clenched tighter on the hard plastic handle of the suitcase. Her parents couldn't have chosen a worse time to call her home.

She forced herself to keep walking. Eventually, the apartments and restaurants gave way to low houses that sloped from the city down to the river. Lian's grandparents had settled in this neighborhood over fifty years ago. She hadn't called this home in a long time, and when her parents moved, it would sever her ties to this place completely.

On the cracked sidewalk near the gate to her parents' yard sat a low wooden altar. The neighborhood shrine was decorated with a forest of photographs. Chrysanthemums, peonies, and lotus flowers sprouted among the frozen faces. Plates of candied ginger and rice-flour noodles overflowed onto the sidewalk. A pot of sand held the smoldering remains of twenty or thirty red sticks of joss. The word "joss" also meant "luck," and hungry ghosts needed as much luck as they could get.

When she bowed to the altar, Lian knew without looking that her grandparents' photographs were missing. This year was no different from any other.

Each step she took toward the house was a step closer to memory, a step closer to disappointment. The gray roof was bowed, as if tired of the weight it bore. Paint and shingles had sloughed off the house like dead skin. The cracks in the stucco had widened with time, and even the window frames seemed skewed. Memory smoothed over some of the details if she didn't look too carefully. Lian unlatched the rusted gate and let herself into the overgrown yard. Though she hadn't been home since she moved out after high school, she was still surprised when the key stuck in the lock to the front door.

"C'mon," she said, twisting harder. Then she relaxed and stepped back from the door. Maybe she should just leave, check into the nearest motel. She'd call Nick and tell him that she'd be coming back to the university early. When she was younger, her parents had treated her as if she were invisible, a ghost. They'd claimed their neglect protected her from the family curse. Maybe it was time to return the favor.

A wisp of incense from the street brushed her chin as if enticing her to turn. Lian peered at the altar through the fence, trying to see any of the hungry ghosts that supposedly feasted there. When she was younger, it would have been easier to pretend, but now she couldn't spare the energy. All of her strength would be needed for this last visit, even if it was just to pack up her things and be gone. She twisted the key in the lock once more, and the door opened reluctantly.

The smell of spices wafting from inside displaced the joss outside. Lian hadn't noticed she was hungry until the aroma surrounded her, thick as gravy. There hadn't been much to eat on the way down from the university. Now, her memories fed her morsels of moon festival cakes and new years' feasts.

Lian's mother met her at the door in a blue work shirt with the sleeves rolled up. Her black hair was tied back in a ponytail. Apparently, Lian had caught her in the middle of packing.

"Where is Nick?" her mother said, before Lian had a chance to say hello. She peered over Lian's shoulder to see if he'd followed her in.

"He had exams, and he couldn't take any time off work." Lian used her suitcase to push past her mother and into the house. "I tried to call, but the phone was already disconnected." That had made it easier, really—no explanations needed. In truth, she hadn't invited Nick because she didn't want her parents to treat him with the same indifference they showed to her.

Her mother bustled past her in an attempt to tidy up, but she might as well have tried to sweep back the tide. The house had rotted all the way from the outside to the core. Black mold sprouted from the carpet and window ledges, and the glass in several windows had cracked. The wallpaper was half stripped from the walls. The curls that remained hanging couldn't cover the chunks missing from the plaster. Even the ceiling had fallen in patches. The familiar bones of the house were there, but the walls and floors were decaying and dropping off them. The clutter of moving boxes hid some of the wreckage, but this was not a home. Her parents weren't moving, they were fleeing.

Lian swallowed, her throat tight with horror and revulsion. "Where's—" Then she realized she didn't need to ask. Her father's corner of the living room looked exactly as it had when Lian left for college, down to the last half-empty bottle of Tsingtao. Only now the area seemed tented, as if the walls were leaning in toward him.

He would have seen it that way, she thought. He'd always felt overshadowed by malign spirits, ill luck, and accidents. An injury had forced him into early retirement last spring, but prevented him from being able to fix the house. They'd deteriorated together.

"Hello, *Baba*," she said to the balding spot on the back of his head.

He didn't bother to look at her. "Why isn't my future son-in-law here?"

"He was too busy to meet us," her mother replied for her.

Lian said, "I'll be in my room," and made her escape. They wouldn't miss her.

Her old room was no more comforting. Dark stains leaked from the windows, and the wallpaper had peeled away near the ceiling, but she thought it would hold together for her brief visit. Pushing aside the folded guest sheets, she set her secondhand suitcase on the mattress. Even before she'd unzipped the top, she knew that most of her abandoned belongings wouldn't fit inside. The folding screen she'd painted in high school, the three-panel mirror on her dresser, her grandfather's ceremonial swords—none of these things would be going back with her.

The clothing she'd left behind in her closet was formal, dated: a long cherry blossom *qipao* she'd worn at her sixteenth birthday, and the red silk *tangzhuang* jacket her grandparents had bought her when she was ten. Both had been worn until the shine had come off, like a battered childhood memory.

One memory that still shone lay in the bottom drawer of her scratched brown dresser—unless her mother had found it when she'd taken out the guest sheets. Lian carefully unfolded the sheets and lifted out what she'd hidden before she'd left for school. Her grandparents' portraits were a weathered diptych in steely blue and faded rose. Their faces seemed idealized, like the portraits of European aristocrats. Somehow, her grandfather always managed to look like Mao. Their personalities shone through mostly in the corners of their eyes and the curl of their lips. The silent images spoke to her in this language of glimpses, even though the photographs had outlived their subjects.

Lian's *zufu* and *zumu* had drowned in the river during a boating accident when she was twelve. She'd worn the blue ribbon tied around their photographs on her sleeve, long past the hundred-day mourning period. Seven days after her grandparents' deaths, the *shen*—their spirits—were supposed to return home. They hadn't come the seventh day, or the next day, but she'd kept hoping. After waiting four months, she'd known her parents had kept them away.

Her parents were supposed to set a red card outside the house after the funeral so the *shen* didn't get lost on their way home. Her parents had argued about it the day before, her mother protesting when her father refused to set out the card. As their son, it was his duty, but now his word was law. He had quarreled with his parents before they left for the river cruise, and now there would be no forgiveness on either side.

"My father is no longer head of this household," her father had said, rebellious and resolute. "I will honor him no more." When her *mama* had spilled flour on the floor that day, it wasn't to check for the footsteps of returning ancestors. Instead, she'd fallen when Lian's father had struck her for disobeying him.

So it was Lian who had kept vigil for her grandparents every year at the Hungry Ghost Festival, burning hell money and incense, setting out orchids and peaches. It was her secret rebellion. A wax-wrapped packet of stale joss incense had been tucked in the sheets under the portraits. She examined the incense, wondering whether it was still good, or if it would fizzle like an old firecracker.

Someone knocked on her door like popping fireworks. "Lian," her mother called. "You want dinner?"

Lian was more startled by the question than by the pounding. "No, *Mama*," she lied, hastily shoving a stuffed panda and some of her old Chinese grammar books into her suitcase. "I ate on the bus." Despite her rush to look busy, the door stayed closed. Heavy silence suffused the hallway, and Lian cringed. Even unintended, this was a per-sonal blow: junk food had been good enough for dinner, but her mother's cooking wasn't. She quickly added, "Maybe I can take something home tomorrow?"

"You want take-out, you go to a restaurant," her mother replied, and her footsteps withdrew to the kitchen.

Lian regretted the lost opportunity but let it go. There wasn't time to patch things up with her family. She only planned to stay until she finished going through her belongings.

In the bottom drawer of her dresser, she found a stack of postcards her grandparents had brought back from their home city of Chengdu in the Sichuan province. There were also a few disastrous examples of her grandparents' attempt to teach her calligraphy. The ink-stained brush and brick of ink were in a box beneath the practice pages. She used a silk scarf to gather the items from the drawer before setting them in the suitcase. The suitcase dwarfed the small bundle.

What else should she take with her? She'd run out of ideas. Despite her lie, Lian was ravenous, and food might clear her head. She slid her wallet and the remaining joss into her back pocket and left her bedroom.

"Lian," her father called. "Didn't want to say hello, eh?"

Why was he addressing her now? "I'm just taking a walk, *Baba*. I'll be back."

"Get me a beer on your way out."

She fetched him a bottle of beer and he settled back on the couch. She waited nearby, but he had nothing else to say to her. He'd only spoken to her because he'd wanted something.

Lian clenched her teeth and restrained her anger until she was out of the yard. Then she whirled and slammed the gate. It shrieked on its hinges, and Lian looked up at the house. Someone drifted past the curtains, watching her as if from behind a veil.

The impact of the gate jostled the portraits on their shaky altar. Kneeling down, she righted the tumbled frames and scattered flowers. Then she pulled the incense from her back pocket and lit all the sticks at once with a flick of her lighter. As they smoldered between her palms, she raised the sticks to the sky and back down to her heart. This was for her grandparents, and for her: the forgotten ones, the ghosts. The concrete of the sidewalk was rough where it pressed against her forehead and arms as she bowed, hands outstretched.

When she finally sat up, she felt calmer, and gently planted the sticks of joss in the pot of sand. Ribbons of smoke tangled in her black hair. Lian bowed to the altar one last time out of respect, and raised her head.

Vague faces peered down at her, outlined in smoke and illuminated by the full moon. Their features were wavering, indistinct, but she knew them by their mouths and eyes.

She breathed in fear and wonder with the smoke. "*Zufu?*" She extended a trembling hand to the figure nearest to her. The evening was sweltering, but when her fingers passed into the cobweb outlines of his body, they went numb with cold.

Lian cried in pain and stumbled backward. Where she'd touched the smoky face, her fingertips were waxy and gray-white, the color of frostbite.

As she watched, her grandparents' shimmering outlines began to solidify. Their gourd-shaped bodies were swollen, with necks too thin to feed their distended bellies. She rubbed her smarting fingers. Had her slight touch given them definition? They drifted closer, and she saw hunger in their softly glowing eyes. Recognition and yearning—they knew her by her taste, and wanted more.

She feinted toward the house, then dashed past them down the empty street. They brushed her as she passed, slashing at her left side like a blade of ice. When she grabbed her arm to check for damage, a jagged streak of white showed against her silk blouse like a band in onyx.

Gravity kept her running toward the river and away from the creatures gliding after her. She wondered what Nick would say when she told him this story. She clung to that thought. As a *guai lo*, a foreign devil, he was not born to this world and its traditions. He wouldn't believe her. Now, she wished she did not believe.

Then memories of her grandparents calmed her. Their lives had been one long exercise in *tai chi*, a harmonious garland woven of tradition and belief. Nothing she'd known them to do would damn them to live as *kui*, hungry ghosts. Seeing them... like this...

It was Lian's father who had cut the thread that bound him to the past, shirking his duty as eldest son. He'd blamed his vengeful parents for his ill luck, but he was the root of it. Now her grandparents had taken away the house, the last thing they'd left him. There was nothing for jealous spirits to envy in such a broken man. Lian had the most to lose, now—last in the family line, the first to attend college and graduate school. She was easy prey. With no husband or children to properly mourn them, unmarried daughters also became *kui*.

Offerings were made outside the home to prevent spirits from coming inside. That had been her first mistake tonight. Her second was misinterpreting the ceremony as a game. There were consequences to both action and inaction, and she'd neglected her veneration of all her ancestors.

The *kui* with her grandparents' faces moved silently on the wind. She tried to quiet herself, holding her breath and making her steps as light as possible. Then a shriek, like an *erhu* torturously bowed, cut through her. They were nearby, still stalking her.

The interstate ran overhead, and beyond that, she could taste the cold, foul breath of the river. Lian tried to reign in her frantic thoughts as momentum carried her under the bridge and toward the warehouses. Did running water stop *kui*, or was water their element? Her tutelage in tradition had stopped when her *zufu* and *zumu* had died. They were no help to her now.

The brick steps down to the river were slimed with mud. Lian ran her fingers over spray-painted tags as if they were Braille telling her how to save herself. A block behind her, the spirits of her grandparents drifted closer, deceptively delicate on the wind.

Escape into the river seemed her only choice. Maybe she could wade along the bank. Perhaps the bottom would remain level along the brick wall and the current wouldn't sweep her away. After her grandparents' accident, Lian had never learned to swim, but one step into the river told her it wouldn't have helped her. The current ripped at her jeans with soggy black fingers. Curling up on the bottom step, she faced the water. She didn't want to see them when they came for her.

Lights danced on the river, shining as they swept past her. One came close enough to touch, but it was gone before she could reach it. The luminous boats were paper lanterns carrying votive candles. Each lantern resembled a flower, its petals cradling the candle as a lotus blossom had once cradled the Buddha.

The lanterns had been released at the end of the Hungry Ghost parade. Each was a light to guide home the souls of the drowned. Two had washed up at the bottom of the steps. One held a burnt-out votive and a second had caught fire and partially sunk. Lian looked up and saw the two forms settling over her like a cobweb net.

Desperately, she yanked the lighter from her back pocket and transferred the candle to the seaworthy boat. She flicked the wheel, and the candle sputtered, its wick

drowned in warm wax. She dug the wick out with a fingernail, sparked the lighter again, and held the flame to the
wick until the wax melted away. It caught and flared. She
urged the boat into the current.

A hand brushed her head like a spider descending, then
lifted away. As her grandparents followed the boat out over
the river, she watched their bodies disintegrate like ashes.

Crouched against the dank brick of the stairs, Lian
finally let herself panic. What else had they taken from her
with that touch? They'd taken her father's health and his
career, in retaliation. By association, they'd taken her
mother's home. They'd driven her from her parents
through neglect. Lian followed the chain of events to its
final link, and realized what they'd left her. She, too, was a
hungry ghost. Unlike them, she was still alive.

When Lian returned to the house, her mother met her at
the door with wide eyes. "What did you do to your hair?"
She dragged Lian into the guest bathroom and tilted her
head down. In the cracked mirror Lian saw what had caused
her mother's shock. On the crown of her head was a skull-
cap of white as large as a cupped hand. The color matched
the streak along her left sleeve.

Lian looked at her right hand, where the numbed skin of
her fingers had begun to turn black. Part of her was already
dead. What else would her ancestors take before they were
through?

Close up, she could see that her mother was crumbling,
like the house. Her skin seemed fragile, riddled with cracks,
and silver threaded her hair. She hadn't always looked like
this. The curse on the house had blighted her, like the
ghosts' touch had withered Lian's skin.

"Have you learned your lesson yet?" Her mother twisted
her hand tighter in Lian's hair.

Lian's scalp stung as she tried to look up. Her mother's expression, fractured in the mirror, was suddenly fierce with fear and rage. "Have you, girl?" Her voice cracked like the walls of the house. "You've seen what happens when children neglect their ancestors, when they are not venerated, not honored, after death."

Tears sprang to Lian's eyes. "How do you..." Her voice died away. Her mother had taken out the guest sheets for her, but Lian was not a guest—her old sheets should have been good enough for one night. She must have known what was folded away in the sheets, and how Lian would react to finding the photographs there. Her mother hadn't been completely blind to her games.

Digging her fingers deeper into Lian's hair, she hauled her daughter up by force of pain. "You didn't think it would take you this long to see them again, did you?" She must have been the figure Lian had seen at the window, just before her grandparents had materialized.

Lian finally wrenched her head out of her mother's grasp. Wisps of her black hair still ringed her mother's fingers.

"I want you to think about what is going to happen when your father and I die." The woman stood between Lian and the bathroom door. Lian was too exhausted by the evening's events to try rushing her. "We will be lost as well, without someone to honor us after our passing."

Lian laughed in dry gasps. "Am I supposed to mourn you when you're gone?"

"You won't need to." Her mother leaned against the door, shutting them in together. "We won't be going anywhere."

As the last few minutes of the Hungry Ghost Festival ticked away, Lian could feel the invisible presence of spirits lift from the house. Without their silent company, she was completely alone with her parents.

They sat down for a farce of a family meal, a midnight picnic with all of her favorite dishes: spicy *ma po* tofu, dry-fried green beans, and *gong bao* chicken. Perhaps they'd meant to bribe her with food earlier in the evening, but old animosity had prevented it. Now she touched nothing, and starved before the feast laid out for her.

"It's unfortunate Nick was unable to come," her father said as he stared at the flickering TV screen. "He may not have felt welcome in this house, but he will be welcome in our new one." He turned too quickly, and caught Lian's gaze before she could turn away. "Love and duty, Lian. I learned too late, but you still have time."

Even when duty was loathsome, it remained a responsibility. Lian didn't need to love her parents to perform it. But what of those she did love? Would denying her parents bring their wrath down on Nick as well?

When she left that morning, her suitcase was empty of keepsakes, but full of fears for the future.

THOU
SHALT
NOT...

Murder

Lord Torquiere

Barry Hollander

I sipped coffee that evening at an outdoor café. Word had been sent to a wealthy and curious man, a figure of consequence in court and a fellow no doubt unused to such a summons as mine. The message read:

> Lord Torquiere:
> Meet me at the Café Thibodeaux at 11.
> I drink coffee, and will not smile.
> Yours, A Friend

That his lordship would appear I had no doubt, for Felix had arranged the meeting. An artist with a knife, our Felix, and yet he went too far when he revealed our secret existence to an outsider.

"He asked," was all Felix mustered in his defense. "So I told him."

A black carriage rattled down the cobblestone street, its horse snorting clouds of warm breath. Through my feet I felt the hum of steam as it spewed from the orange glow of the central district out to a hungry city.

Nearby, a man and woman shared a table. She wore black nails and hard eyes while he had the look of a visiting provincial businessman puffed up with importance, a face full of whiskers and a stomach full of wine.

The carriage rolled to a stop. From it stepped Lord Torquiere in a cape so dark its red might easily be mistaken for black. After scanning the few occupied tables, his pale gaze fell on me. He smiled in greeting.

I did not.

Again he studied the wet tables, the sullen waiter standing nearby with towel draped over an arm. Then he stepped closer.

"A friend, I presume?"

I sipped my coffee. He was a large, fleshy man living well off the starving peasants of some distant province. Understand this: I did not fault the man his means of economic support; I merely add this information to paint a portrait for what was to come.

"Indeed," I said. "A friend."

"Good. Very good. May I sit?"

I motioned agreement and the waiter lurched from his state of indifference to one of servitude. Torquiere ordered wine and waited.

"I am Arnaud," I said. "I believe you met an acquaintance of mine, and made a certain inquiry."

"Yes, an inquiry. I wish to join you and," here he hesitated, seeking the right phrase, "your friends." As if I belonged to some common club.

Voices rose from my left, the provincial businessman demanding more wine as the woman attempted to hush his loutish outburst. He pulled her close, groped a breast and buried his face in her neck. She moaned a whimper of pleasure that sounded false to my ear and then slipped a hand into his coat pocket. From its hiding place came his wallet. With deft fingers she removed most of the bills and slid the wallet back to its home. I watched as she eased the paper into a place so private even he would not discover it at a café table. Her eyes met mine and she offered a small, vulgar twitch of a lip, so I returned to the matter at hand.

Felix had met this lord in some gambling hall and had boasted of his membership even as money slipped through his fingers. Torquiere had covered his bets, wrangled more details over gambling and drinks. Felix is a marvel with a knife but less expert when he holds a glass of wine. We all have our weaknesses. I sat my cup on its saucer.

"My lord, exactly what is it you wish to join? A man of your stature certainly must find his name among the rolls of the most important clubs: The Che Seqouex, The Melau, even The Happenchance." Of course I knew he belonged to all three. My puffery failed to have its anticipated effect; he waved a hand as if dispensing with a troublesome gnat.

"Nothing. Those mean nothing." He lowered his voice to a whisper. "I know what you are about. I have worked in the same discipline, though quietly. Not so sophisticated as yourself, perhaps, yet I believe I bring something to the table, some small skill and delicacy." At this, he rolled his tongue as if savoring a fine vintage. "That is the word," he continued. "Delicacy. That is what I offer. And of course, I wish to learn from a master such as you."

I smiled. Not because of his flattery, though certainly it played a part, but from the possibility we might add to our small company. An artist's life can be a lonely one.

"Perhaps you shall," I heard myself say. "Perhaps you shall."

We meet in a large but unremarkable estate south of the canal, beyond the bright lights and busy boulevards. Dim carriages rolled through an unlit gate, its guard an ancient fellow so long in our employ he might as well be one of us, except that he had no tongue with which to speak and his rheumy eyes, while still present in a wrinkled skull, saw little of consequence. Of ears he had two, and both worked exceptionally well. A whistle signaled our approach, a tune that changed from week to week. If he heard other things, he could not speak of them.

Coded messages had passed among us. So rare was my proposal to consider a new member that it required additional messages to confirm the earlier ones. Many of my companions suspected some trick, for I had a reputation for an occasional jest, though never over something as serious as membership. My efforts tended toward the more subtle at our few social gatherings: a hand jutting up from a punch bowl and grasping a piece of fruit, a woman's breasts turned inside out, within them a holiday pudding of raisins and nuts. Our members, I regret to report, suffer from a lack of humor.

We took my carriage, the curtains pulled tight as we traveled a circuitous route to cause confusion. I offered him wine.

"A red," he said, inspecting the burgundy. "Appropriate." A small leather case rested at his side. I carried one of my own.

I swept him into the house. If he expected a greeting, he revealed no disappointment. Down dark halls where lanterns burned low, we came to the stone stairway that led deeper into the earth and to the room where our membership stood, faces hidden behind masks of simple black. Strapped in a chair sat the woman from the café.

I cleared my throat. "I submit for your consideration, Lord Torquiere." Grave eyes and solemn nods greeted my announcement. A figure separated from the group.

"Is he worthy?"

"Of the test, I judge him worthy." Indeed, conversation with Torquiere made it obvious he knew his art, that his observations were keen. Even the most imaginative cannot invent the particulars of the sweet science—the way blood oozes from a deep puncture, the sound of a scream muffled by silk, how the smell of sour sweat contrasts with an emptied bladder, or the simple physical reaction to certain probes and prods. A dabbler? Not this man. He struck me as not only knowledgeable, but enthusiastic.

The members parted, offering a path to the woman.

If he recognized those hard eyes from the café, he showed no reaction. In her own eyes, I saw that she knew and yet could not place me. An old lover? A man robbed and discarded?

"Your lordship," I said. "Your canvas awaits."

She strained at her bonds, pleaded for release in a voice no doubt hoarse since being taken the evening before. Torquiere ignored her pleadings, the threats, her offers of her body and that of others, her promise of riches she could not possibly possess and treasures she could not possibly acquire. I will not detail the exquisite nature of his concert except to note that the members were impressed to the point of applause when, at the end, she succumbed to a series of inventive stabs of tiny needles into her face.

Our leader stepped forth, put a hand on Torquiere's shoulder.

"Worthy indeed," he said, lifting his mask. Others did the same.

His lordship bowed.

"You are too kind," he whispered. "Far too kind."

Three months later in a café, the night air grew heavy with the promise of rain. My oyster soup was excellent, the bread fresh and the beer as cold as winter's snow. This was a rough meal far from the pretence of the boulevards, not the kind of place I expected to run into a companion from my small society.

He sat in a rush. "Arnaud, have you heard?" He wore red eyes and a pale complexion.

"Only an hour past," I said.

Another of our members murdered, and yet this was no simple death, no brutish crime of passion. Phillipe had been tortured, his body found in an abandoned abbey, arms and legs positioned in such a way as to appear in the act of prayer. More important, he was the third of our membership to be killed within the week.

The first had been found in a less-than-fashionable inn sharing a room with a common slattern, their bodies coupled in the act of fornication, wires cobbling their arms and legs and private parts together in a deathly embrace. A special poison had been used, one that forces a steady flow of blood from the orifices and which left their bodies held together not only by wires but their own sticky fluids. The second had been discovered alone in his carriage, a glass of wine held in his hand by a set of clever thin metal strips forced through the flesh and then out again. Another metal strip pierced his cheek and his hand, keeping him in an everlasting drink. To me, all spoke of more than mere slaughter. To murder alone is a crime, but to do so as art— ah, that is something altogether different.

I dabbed a piece of bread into my stew and put the sop into my mouth, waiting for him to continue.

"How can you sit and eat?" he asked. "Especially here in this vile place?"

I sipped my beer. "I agree we appear to be losing members at an alarming rate, but I disagree with your assessment of this establishment. The oyster stew is excellent."

"Damn the stew and damn you, Arnaud. We might well be next."

True enough. That our members had become prey struck me as worthy of concern, but the public display of their deaths I found both vulgar and fascinating. Art is best reserved for those who can appreciate it, but this open exhibition provided new and interesting possibilities.

I saw him staring at me, apparently waiting for some response.

"What do you suggest?" I asked. "Flee the city? I have no such plan."

He looked at me then with different eyes. A suspicious man can be read as easily as a newspaper column.

"Stay, then," he said. "Drink in your dingy cafés." He stood and tromped toward his carriage. Two men sat above it, both armed.

As he left, I signaled for another beer and contemplated the turn of events. Three men dead: one in an act of prayer, a man who had not seen the inside of a cathedral in decades; another in the act of fornication with a prostitute, a man noted for his preference for young boys; and the third drinking wine, a fellow who to the best of my knowledge avoided all drink due to a medical condition. After the second death, members whispered a single name—Lord Torquiere—a man recent to our circle, a man with demonstrable talent and enthusiasm, yet a man so coarse as to pursue membership rather than await our attention. It hardly required a great detective to reach that conclusion, and yet I found the conclusion unsatisfying.

Now I sat, wondering over my oyster stew whether Torquiere was the killer—and whether I cared.

My meal complete and cane in hand, I signaled my carriage to proceed without me.

Clearly Torquiere had waited for just such an occurrence.

A smudge of shadow emerged from an alley and I smelled fear in the air, the sweet stench of sweat and the potential for death. He clung to the alley like a rodent avoiding a prowling cat.

"Arnaud?"

I stopped but my heart sped on, in my mind a sudden stream of frames in how I might appear. Murdered, yes, but the aftermath, the art—that sent my head spinning. How would I be found? What did I most avoid or love, what contortions would he force upon my limbs to create an artistic effect?

"Your lordship?" I said, clearing my thoughts. "You are oddly met."

His head swiveled like that of a turtle taking care to remain safe within its dark shell.

"Not so odd, *friend*. Death stalks the city. I fear it hungers to kill again."

Strange words from my chief suspect, perhaps using a ruse to win my trust. I motioned for him to join me as I walked, but he held back, head shaking.

"Come with me," he said, and then disappeared into the alley.

A cautious man would have refused the invitation, but caution makes for a plain sauce.

We shared no words on our trek through the city's underbelly, where children fight over scraps of bread and adults kill for a hunk of fatty meat. A mean existence to be sure, and yet an improvement over the great fires of the central district, a hellish place where human life is as cheap as the black coal that feeds the city's great steam engines. They flee the center when possible and carve a life of sorts on the fringe, and yet certain rules are obeyed even among them. None dared molest us, and none did, though several times I expected just such an obvious attack.

He stopped at a building the gray of cold ash, a piss pot resting near a heavy door of peeling green paint.

"Here we may speak privately," he said.

I am no fool, however I might be judged. Within my cane was a sword of finest steel, and inside my coat nestled a small yet efficient pistol. I followed him within. If the outside of the building was unremarkable, the inside boasted just the opposite, a place of fine furniture in a cramped but comfortable setting, the windows bricked shut, luxurious drapes and thick carpet used to soften the appearance. A cheery fire dried the air, the burning wood from some fruit tree: apple or pear. He directed me to a chair near the warming blaze. His hand shook as he poured two snifters of brandy, the clink of crystal on crystal as unmistakable as a church bell on a peaceful Sunday morning.

He sat and we studied one another.

"I keep this place for obvious reasons. If I take someone from a boulevard, questions might be asked. Here?" He shrugged. "I have a room below, appropriate given my interests. The rest I reserve for simple living space. No servants, mind you, though I spend a few coins to keep the building watched and guarded."

I sniffed the brandy, watched him drink his in a single gulp.

"My lord," I said. "You favor me with such hospitality."

He stood, stalked the room, then poured himself another brandy and drank it down. He poured a third and returned to his chair.

"I am not guilty," he said.

"Have I accused you of a crime?" I sniffed the brandy, fine stuff that deserved to be savored, not swilled. "I can hardly accuse any man of a crime."

He snorted. "You know what I mean—the deaths, man, the three recent deaths. Mind you, the taking of life has never bothered me, but as the newest member I am no doubt their chief suspect. That is why I am here, hiding in my humblest of homes." He leaned forward and brandy sloshed from his glass, staining the carpet. "Tell me, Arnaud. Am I suspected? Will they come for me?"

"Perhaps." I swirled the glass, then took the smallest of sips. Fine stuff indeed.

"I am innocent. What can I do? Will they listen to me?" His face brightened. "You. They will listen to you."

I chuckled. "Innocent? A virtue I have never claimed and one, I am sure, hardly attaches itself to any of our members who are above mortal laws and rules. No, *friend*, I will not vouch for you, or for any man. Not even for myself."

My words wormed their way into his alcohol-fuddled mind.

"You?" he whispered.

I shrugged and took another sip. Let him believe it, let them all believe it. If I claimed the role, perhaps the true artist would emerge in a fit of jealousy to lay claim to his works of art. I must admit I admired this daring artist who sculpted with such special clay: the very people who preyed on others. Superb.

"I suspected as much," he said. "I have something to show you."

Careful to take my cane, I followed him out of the sitting room and into a dark hallway. We followed a set of narrow stone steps down to a well-lit chamber.

Strapped to an iron chair, a gag in his mouth, sat my old friend Felix.

What the room lacked in size it made up for in efficiency, with clever rotating shelves and swiveled lights playing on a chair that could shift into a table as the need arose. Torquiere saw my admiring smile and sighed in relief.

"So, you are satisfied?" he asked, like some breathless youth in hopes of springtime love. "We are in agreement?"

"Eh?"

"Him." He pointed to Felix, who needed only an apple in his mouth to play the part of a doomed swine ready for the roasting pit. "I know you are the one. Who else? I have provided you another victim as a peace offering, as a partnership." Sweat beaded on his lip. "You and I, partners. The possibilities are endless."

I strolled to the table and fingered a few of the devices, as yet unused.

"Good evening, Felix," I said. "You are well?"

He shook his head and attempted to speak through his gag. I patted his shoulder. "Be at ease."

I lifted a silver probe from the table, let the light reflect into his eyes. "I should have been a doctor, though admittedly such a profession is beneath my station." I meandered across the room, talking as I went of this and that, my family and my background. Felix watched in despair, Lord Torquiere in growing comfort. For too long I had been bored with my own art and that of others. These killings offered something new, something exciting—a fresh sauce for the tasting.

And though I had not been the original chef, I knew now that neither had Lord Torquiere.

In a smooth motion I stepped behind his lordship and whipped my sword from its cane. With its point pressed against the base of his neck, I used my other hand to withdraw my small gun.

"What's this? We had an understanding." His own hand inched toward a pocket. I nudged the blade, drawing a sweet bead of blood, and directed him to a second, more traditional chair than the one Felix occupied. He sat and I ordered him to wrap leather straps around his legs and ankles, then his waist, all the time ignoring his offers of assistance and wealth. From behind I tightened his bindings and added more of my own.

"I knew it," he spat. "You are the killer."

"No." I stepped to where he could see my smiling face. "At least, I was not until now."

"Who then?"

I slid my sword back into its cane. "Perhaps you have the killer here," I said, nodding toward Felix. "I suspect so. He had grown ever the fool of late in matters both small and large. Now I believe it a mask he wore to bring someone new into our fold, to provide the perfect stooge." I stepped closer to Felix and gave a deep bow. "You have my admiration, sir, for what you accomplished. Well done, Felix. Well done indeed."

He nodded acceptance.

"And now, to the task at hand." I set aside my cane, searched the room until I found a bottle of passable cognac and a glass. I pulled a chair close to Lord Torquiere, sat, and savored the drink.

I put a hand on his knee, felt him tremble like a girl at her first bedding.

"Tell me, *friend*, of the desires that most consume your life." I sipped the cognac, set it aside and found a scrap of paper and pen. "And tell me also of those matters that you cannot abide."

His mouth moved, but no sound emerged.

"I can be patient, but please be specific." I tested the pen, scratching a line across the paper. "Remember, this is no mere death. It is for the sake of art."

From behind his gag, I saw Felix smile.

Eyes Watching

Barbara Stanley

The toy store was packed, worse than usual for a Saturday. Kids careened down the aisles, firing plastic lasers, yanking talking babies and bears off the shelves, screeching for Mom in a horrid din. Claire looked around and shook her head. What was she doing here?

Claire had no kids and wanted none, but "Aunt Claire's" best friend had a daughter almost ten, so here she was, trapped in the jungle, looking for just the right birthday gift for a young girl. Her dollhouse was minus some essential items for kitchen and bath, and Claire's job was to find a tiny porcelain tub and sink.

This toy store had a pre-fab dollhouse, flashier than those in Claire's day, complete with housewares and furniture. A family of dolls occupied the house, frozen in the motions of living: baby in the crib, brother and sister playing cards, Mom at the stove in the kitchen. But where was Dad in this pre-fab idyll? Claire peeked through the kitchen window and laughed. Dad was out mowing the lawn, of course, with a custom mini power mower. But as she continued to look out the window, the damnedest thing happened. It was weird, but that little guy appeared to be staring back at Claire.

Just a stupid doll, of course, but something about the doll was... familiar. A hot flush crept up Claire's neck. She seemed unable to pull herself from the window. Her back ached from crouching. Her mind raced forward with forgotten thoughts and questions: Why is he watching me? Why won't he stop?

Mommy—Mommy, help me.

From a dark corner of her mind came a face and a word, a name from years past.

Ralph.

The man who had watched her from the kitchen window when she was ten years old.

Claire closed her eyes, instantly transported to her mom's kitchen where she sat at the table, head down, pretending to study. The radio played low, a song about love-ins and flower children. Nearby was the kitchen window, which Claire would *not* look through, because Ralph was outside, and she knew he was watching her.

He was supposed to be doing yardwork as partial rent payment to her mom, but Claire heard no sounds of clippers or rake. Mom had not yet returned from her part-time job and, although Claire was a grown-up ten, she felt very young and small. Except for the radio the house was quiet, hushed like outside, where no dogs barked or birds sang on this warm Saturday afternoon. All the world was waiting, silent, for the moment when Claire would look up and face Ralph.

She turned back from the window and looked around the kitchen. Dust motes drifted through a beam of sunlight that highlighted the geometric pattern of the dirty floor. A rag rug was bunched up below the sink; it hadn't been washed in ages. A fly zoomed nearby then landed for a moment on her knuckle, challenging Claire to look up.

Look up, look up, look up, the silence cried. Her heart beat in the same rhythm, bouncing along at a Super Ball pace. Oh, where was Mom? Why did Dad have to go and die on them? Why did Claire have to be by herself on this sunny day, feeling weird, like something *not nice* was going on?

She decided to stay in the kitchen and wait for her mom to come home. She would count all the diamonds in the geometric floor pattern. She would sing along with the radio. She would spell and re-spell *camouflage*, a new word for her. She would do everything in the world but look out the kitchen window.

Claire let out a deep sigh. Jeez, she'd been holding her breath all this time. I sure can get myself worked up in a hurry, she thought. "Too much imagination," her mom would say.

Mom would be home soon to start dinner, bringing goodies and stories from work. Fresh gossip was always coming into the grocery store, regular as produce or baked goods delivered. The two of them would eat chicken pot pie or hamburgers, have ice cream for dessert. Mom might bring home mint chocolate chip, Claire's favorite.

This will be a good night, Claire promised herself. This will be a six P.M. night for Mom, not a one A.M. morning. Everything will be okay.

Ralph might talk to her mom later, reporting on yard-work, but he wouldn't be able to stare at Claire. She could go to her room to study or read. She could watch TV in the living room. Ralph would go downstairs to his basement apartment, and Claire could pretend he was miles away, that it was just Claire and her mom and her dad, together again.

Claire let herself relax. The scent of cut grass and roses wafted in through the window. A crow gave a big loud caw, breaking the silence outside. She wondered if it was the big one that flew sometimes close to her. He was a shiny blue-black with smooth feathers that looked like silk. Claire stole a glance upward, out the kitchen window. Curious eyes stared back, meeting her gaze. The crow preened itself and cawed once more. But Ralph was nowhere to be seen.

Claire blinked her eyes a couple of times, back in the din of the toy store. She steadied herself against the edge of a countertop, trying to figure out what had just happened.

Was it a flashback? Some distant memory? She had so few of her tenth year. But the images, the sounds and smells of those moments were so sharp and vivid. Claire combed through past memory fragments, retrieving the small set that had been her only ones all these years: a moustached smile; dark eyes; Mom saying, "It never happened"; hands reaching towards her; a thin red snake...

A tear rolled down her cheek, startling her. She wasn't aware of feeling sadness or grief. She seemed to be inhabiting a different body, one that reacted on it's own to the sudden flood of images. Claire wanted to leave the store, get up and run out, but her body would not move, and she remained against the countertop. Stop it, she thought. *No no no.* Against her will, new memories came.

She was sitting in her fourth grade classroom, her classmates so quiet she could hear their breathing. The school movie they'd just watched was over. Except for one terrible picture, Claire had missed the police photos shown afterward. Claire knew she would suffer for that one though. The image was burned into her brain. If she closed her eyes she could see the two little bodies clearly. Today, tonight, and forever.

The film was a warning to the kids in Claire's school because a pervert was loose in the neighborhood. He'd plucked one victim already just two blocks from the playground. The police decided to scare kids into attention with the movie. The first part of the movie was a corny drama about the risks of trusting strangers. The second part was bad. Photos of actual victims were displayed in graphic detail. Claire's mom, bleary-eyed, had signed the permission slip that morning allowing her to see the second half. But Claire kept her eyes shut tight after the first part ended. Except for one tiny glance.

A black and white photo. Two little girls lying face down on pavement. Both wearing dresses, both dresses ripped apart from the waist up. Darkness around them. A dark pool of—

"Mama! Mama! No!" Toy store noises again. A little boy near the dollhouse shrieked, clutching a plastic laser gun. He looked to be about four—a beautiful child, olive skin, big almond eyes and a shock of brown hair. His mother spoke to him in Spanish, gently urging the toy gun away from him. His superhero T-shirt twisted fiercely, resisting her grasp. "No—no!" he said again.

No, Claire echoed. But the force of her resistance was as fragile as a bubble, ready to pop. She felt that bubble encircle her heart; when it burst she understood that the thin film of darkness had been pierced at last, the memories were pouring through, and she was powerless to stop them. Her fingers brushed the dollhouse front door, and she heard it click shut, like her mother's front door had on that long ago Saturday. But it was not her mother who had entered the house.

Ralph had come in through the front door. How had Claire missed that—the sound of him opening the door? The crow answered with three loud caws. I hate you, Claire thought.

Familiar footsteps clumped through the living room. Hesitant footsteps that stopped once, waited, then continued on more decisively. Moving toward the kitchen. Moving toward Claire.

"Mom not home yet, huh?" Ralph towered in the doorway. He was a big, awkward man, with a pear-shaped body, carrying all his weight in his hips and his bottom, like a woman did.

"She'll be here soon." Claire hoped. Otherwise her mom would stagger in past midnight, throw up in the bathroom, sleep off her hangover until noon.

Claire watched Ralph cross the kitchen to pour himself a glass of water from the sink. His hands were huge. They were freshly scrubbed, Claire noticed.

Ralph plopped onto a chair, right across the kitchen table from Claire. She caught a pungent whiff of cigarettes, earth, and sweat, and pulled back. Ralph smiled, showing crooked white teeth beneath a sparse moustache. He had never sat and talked with her before.

I could run, Claire thought. But Ralph was so big. Why had she never noticed that before?

"Your mom tells me you're something of an artist." His eyes were dark, watching her. His fingertips made little clouds of moisture on the drinking glass. "Thought you might be able to help me."

What was this all about?

"Been working on something, thought you might like to see it." He blinked, twice. "It's in the basement."

Claire couldn't answer, could hardly breathe.

"It'll just take a minute, honest," Ralph said. He was smiling again.

If I screamed, he could smother me with one hand. She knew this was true.

Ralph—the nicest man in the world—a handyman who could fix anything, who worked around the house a lot. The man who watched Claire at odd times, a funny look on his face. Nobody seemed to notice that the "pervert" had struck just two months after Ralph came to live in their house.

Her mom had told her, "It's only temporary honey, and he's a real nice man." She had met him in a bar.

Now this nice man was taking her to the basement.

No no no! Claire's brain screamed as her body stood up from her chair. *I don't want to!* she cried inside as she followed Ralph to the basement door. Her brain continued to shout, but her body moved toward the stairs, afraid of Ralph's size and his dark smile—and what he might do if he got mad.

The stair light spilled into the dark below. Claire could make out the lines of a table, a square shape on top. She could hear the drip of a distant sink as she dragged her feet down the stairs.

Mommy—Mommy, help me.

Ralph turned, two steps below Claire. His Adam's apple bobbed with a noisy swallow. His hands reached toward her.

"Now close your eyes Claire," he whispered.

Two little girls appeared before Claire. She saw tiny harlequin glasses, folded, lying near a lifeless body. The images vanished, and she reached out toward Ralph.

I want my daddy.

And pushed.

Ralph stumbled, grabbed at air. His eyebrows shot up in confusion. Then he fell backward, tumbling down the steps, and landed on the cement with an ugly smack.

Claire's teeth chattered as her eyes squeezed shut. Very slowly, she opened them.

Ralph lay at the bottom of the stairs, head bent to the left. His mouth formed an O, as if he were surprised to be dead. His eyes were open, staring. This time, they looked at nothing.

Claire watched a thin red snake ooze from behind his ear and wander across the floor.

Outside, dogs barked, birds sang, a power mower hummed in the distance. Inside, the sink dripped, the stair creaked, and the two little girls appeared again, floating in front of Claire. One girl turned to face the stairway light. Her dark hair, plastered with blood, lay smeared across her face. She looked at Claire and smiled. Then both girls vanished, for good.

Camouflage: to disguise in order to conceal.

Conceal: to keep a secret deep inside, safe from the outside. Ralph was dead and Claire had killed him.

It didn't feel bad.

It felt good.

It turned out to be a six P.M. night for Claire's mom after all.

"Oh God, my God!" she cried when she found Claire sitting on the steps, looking at the body lying below.

Ralph's accident was the talk of the neighborhood for weeks afterward.

Things changed. Claire's mom stopped drinking, and Mom's sister came to live with them. Aunt Pat cleaned the house, cooked yummy dinners, taught Claire how to sew. She tucked Claire in on the nights Claire's mom fell off the wagon.

The pervert was caught and turned out to be a teenaged boy who was new to the neighborhood. Neighbors went back to leaving their doors unlocked, and kids played outside until dark.

Claire agreed to put it all behind her.

"Just pretend it didn't happen, honey—it never happened," her mom said.

Better to forget…

How long Claire had sat in the toy store, she didn't know. She stared at the dollhouse, but she saw a different one now. This one had carpeting, glass windows and electric lights in every room. Wood doors swung open on brass hinges, a curved staircase wound up to the second floor. It was beautiful in every aspect, and Claire could see each detail, as clearly as the first time she had seen that dollhouse, thirty-nine years ago. Aunt Pat had found it on a table near the bottom of the basement steps, when she'd gone down to clean out Ralph's room.

Claire stood up and took a quick look around. Her tears were gone, her head clear. She scooped up the dad doll, power mower and all, and stuffed him in her pocket. The store was not so noisy now. While walking out of the building she snapped off the little man's head and rolled it around with her fingers.

C-a-m-o-u-f-l-a-g-e.

I can still spell that word, Claire thought. And then she stepped into the harsh brightness of the sunny afternoon.

The Agonies

Lisa Silverthorne

Anthony Dugan curled into a fetal position on a cot in a Chicago shelter. Coughs and moans echoed around him in the half darkness, people dreaming of better days and better places, but Anthony couldn't sleep, let alone dream. He just wanted to hide away a few hours. The threadbare blanket, pulled over his head, let in the October chill. But it was better than the streets. The blanket smelled musty, rough against his shaking arms.

He huddled deeper into the thin mattress, sour sweat mixing with the gritty stink of dirty clothes from days of running. And when he closed his eyes, it all flooded back and his stomach lurched.

He'd killed someone.

"Hey, buddy, you okay?" asked a raspy voice from the next cot over. "Got the agonies?"

Anthony wanted to laugh. He had the agonies all right, but not something he could chase away with a shot of tequila. He ignored the man, squeezing his eyelids shut, trying to force himself to sleep. If he could just stay here a couple of days, rest and get his bearings. Everything was so tangled. And he couldn't remember everything.

A blanket rustled. Quiet footsteps tapped against cracked linoleum; the clean scent of soap wafted over him. A hand gently gripped his shoulder and he jumped.

"I said you got the agonies?"

Anthony eased the blanket off his head, letting it slide to his chin. An old man with bristly gray hair and humped shoulders stood beside him. Rough, ruddy skin with deeply carved lines and a thick nose might have made the man look angry, but his pale blue eyes brightened his whole face. He looked like somebody's grandpa, somebody who'd pat you on the head, hand you a five-dollar bill, and tell you funny stories. But it didn't ease Anthony's wariness.

"No. No drugs, old timer."

"Nice shiner," the man said, pointing at his left eye. His smile remained as he let go of Anthony's shoulder. "With all that shakin' and quiverin', I thought you was in bad need of a fix."

He was, desperate beyond anything he could even describe, but no one could help him now. Chicago wasn't so far from the small town where... he struggled to remember... remembered the gun in his hand—then what? He clenched his eyes closed, sucking in a breath. He'd killed someone. He couldn't go back there and face it.

"Well, you got somethin' bad wrong to make you shake like that." He pinched his nose between thumb and forefinger. "And stink like that. How long you been on the run?"

Anthony's eyes widened. God, was he that transparent? No one at the shelter had even spoken to him when he slipped inside from the cold streets. But if this old codger figured that out, the cops would spot him right away. He was so screwed. By tomorrow night, he'd probably be in custody and on his way back to Hadleyville, Indiana.

He struggled to sit up, propping a thin pillow behind his back. His hiking boots stuck out from beneath the blanket. In two hours, he'd go back to the streets and head north toward Wisconsin.

"What makes you think I'm on the run?" He rubbed the lock of dark hair out of his eyes, his blue coat rasping against the mattress. He didn't dare leave anything beside the cot and risk it walking off if he fell asleep.

The man chuckled, backing up to the cot beside Anthony and easing himself onto the edge. His humped shoulders looked out of proportion to the rest of his body. His worn yellow cardigan was stretched tight over his shoulders, bunched around his thick middle.

The old man pointed at Anthony's shoes. "Don't know if it's the law, a bride you left at the altar, or some final exam, but son, you're runnin' from somethin'. Somethin' bad."

Anthony sighed, staring at his hands as he clutched the blanket. "What if I am? What's it to you?" He nodded toward the half-open doorway where dim light melted into the bunk room. "You gonna call somebody?"

The man held up a meaty hand. "Relax, Hiking Boots, I'm just askin' because you're new here." He gestured at the rows of cots in the long, high-ceilinged room. "I heard a lot of cryin' and moanin' in this place. I seen all the signs. You's pretty bad off to me. You need some help."

Despite his apprehension, Anthony appreciated anyone taking an interest. His younger brothers got all the attention and Anthony felt invisible. His brothers were smarter and better at sports. He usually did something wrong during games: a dropped fly ball, a bad pass, or any number of stupid mistakes.

Dad made fun of him for it, too, a lot of times at the soccer or baseball fields. Dad was always knocking him around, blaming him when things went wrong. The more he tried to be like his brothers, the more annoyed and critical Dad became until finally Anthony gave up. And he started hating the man.

To Mom, he'd always been the good kid, the one she didn't have to worry about. The invisible one. He swallowed hard. What did she think of him now?

"I said you need some help," the old man said, his voice rising beyond the hoarse whisper. "A doctor or somethin'."

"Heard you the first time," said Anthony, turning over. He hugged the musty blanket against his chest and squeezed his eyes shut.

He thought he'd fallen asleep when voices rumbled around him. Cots squeaked. Footsteps skittered.

Scalding light snapped on.

Hand over his eyes, Anthony jolted awake and tossed the blanket aside. Bleary-eyed, he slid to his feet, glancing around the room at the tangle of fleeing people. The stale smell of alcohol and body odor rose.

"Cops!"

"Shit, get out the way!" someone shouted, running for the doorway.

"Hide that! C'mon, move!"

Cops! Anthony's heart pounded against his ribs, sweat threading his upper lip. He ran through the tangle of dazed, half-dressed people toward the doorway. A thin black woman with wild hair shoved past him. Two men in army jackets, flannel shirts and torn jeans squeezed around a confused man drinking a bottle of vodka and a pregnant woman hitting a crack pipe.

"Hey, Hiking Boots, wait up!" the old man called from somewhere behind Anthony.

Anthony ignored the old man, pressed past the confused guy, and followed the army jackets into the dining area. Three uniformed cops rushed at the fleeing people who flowed around the lunch tables and old green couches along the wall toward the glass front doors leading to the street.

"You, there!" A cop pointed in Anthony's direction. "Stop!"

One officer rushed forward as Anthony bolted, heart in his throat. He lurched out of the swinging glass door as the cop grabbed the man behind him.

Cold air burned his throat. He staggered onto the sidewalk and sprinted across the street as people poured out of the shelter. Sirens squawked. Red and blue lights strobed the dark streets. The L rattled above him, cars surging through green lights as he ran several blocks.

He stopped at Michigan Avenue. His side ached, lungs burning from the cold air. He turned east, heading for Grant Park and Lake Michigan. It was only three blocks from here. He knew the park well. He headed toward the huge bronze statue of Columbus and the Union Central railroad below the street.

Ahead, a distant light winked on the edge of the dark lake. The lighthouse on the breakwall.

When he was a kid, his folks brought the family to Grant Park. He remembered the scent of fresh-mown grass rising above the smell of gas and hot pavement. At dusk that night, when the lightning bugs winked at each other and buildings cast their tall shadows over the trees, Anthony saw the lighthouse blink back at him. He'd wanted to walk out on the breakwall, but it had been too far away. Like now.

Shouts and the clatter of footfalls echoed behind him.

Anthony bolted across still busy Michigan Avenue toward Grant Park and the railroad yard. He ran across the dark grass and past the swings toward Roosevelt. He stopped, leaning on the railing and stared at the dizzying spin of train tracks below. He reached out a hand toward the endless track and the silent boxcars. They looked like they hadn't moved in decades. Suddenly, the old man was beside him.

"You keep runnin' that way and you'll fall into the lake, Hiking Boots."

"Man, don't do that!"

Anthony turned away from the tracks, his chest still heaving from the run. He rubbed his hand across his hot, sweaty face, the wind cooling it.

The old man sniffed the air, wrinkling his nose. "For you, a swim in the lake might not be so bad."

Finally, his huffing got softer. "Why'd you follow me?"

The man crossed his arms, looking all hunched over, those blue eyes piercing. Beneath the cardigan, his shoulders twitched. Crazy old fool didn't have on a coat. He wasn't even out of breath, but he didn't have cops chasing him either.

"I told you, you need help."

Anthony held out his arms. Why didn't this guy leave him alone? "Everybody in that shelter needs help! Like that pregnant crack-head or the guy sucking down vodka like it's a Slurpee." He waved the guy away. "Go help them... it's too late for me."

The man smiled, his shoulders twitching again. "It's never too late to ask."

Anthony's eyes welled with tears and he bit his lip, trying to will away this show of emotion. Kids cried, not adults. He was nineteen—the oldest.

Suck it up, Anthony. Can't you at least do one thing right? Can't even outrun an old man. You run like a girl! What's your problem? Even your little brothers run faster.

"Look, I killed somebody, okay!" He gripped his hair, tugging it between his fingers, squinching his eyes as some of the memory spilled back.

Rifle's smooth balance. Snap of cartridges into the barrel. Pounding of his pulse at his temples. Cold terror gouged him. He knew this time, he had what it took to fire it. No turning back now. Fluid squeeze of the trigger. Blam!

Afterward. Sudden, icy silence. Final.

He'd killed someone. But who? He winced. He couldn't remember.

He hid his face in his hands, sickness rising in his throat. If only he'd known what it'd be like afterward. If only he'd thought it through first.

He turned away and leaned over the railing, the criss-cross of tracks spinning off into darkness. If he could just take it all back and follow them out of here.

The old man laid his hand on Anthony's shoulder and squeezed.

"No matter what, you gotta know what happened. You gotta go back. It's the only way."

Anthony turned his gaze to the railing then back to the old man.

"I can't go back," he said, shaking his head.

For a moment, Anthony stared at the man then threw himself over the railing.

Something gray—a shadow—fluttered around him, blotting out the railroad tracks rushing up at him. Scent of burnt oil and sweat, cold air sharp against his skin as the gray shadow enfolded him. He clenched his eyes shut, bracing for pain and blackness. But it did not come. Instead, he was rising.

Indigo sky spilled white with stars, a sliver of moon rising above Lake Michigan. He tried to ask what was happening, tried to work his mouth, but his lips and tongue felt frozen. At his back, the harbor lighthouse receded, its light winking softer and softer into the distance like a lightning bug. The air felt warm, smelling of fresh rain, clean. Moisture beaded his face as the gray shadow beat at the night. Flying south.

Then he knew. Toward Hadleyville.

"What's happening?" His voice echoed across the dark clouds that drifted slowly below him. But no one answered him. The great gray shadow fluttered on, the sound of wings beating the air.

"What's happening! Tell me!"

No response. Just the steady beat of wings.

In what seemed like forever and only moments at the same time, smokestacks appeared on the horizon. An endless city of factories below him stretched into the distance. Lines of smokestacks streamed smoke into the air, the dark factories stacked like bricks on the flat terrain. The gray shadow began to descend into the wasteland of burned out neighborhoods and dirty streets. The air smelled like rubber and old paper. Gritty against Anthony's face.

"Not back here—no!"

The gray shadow descended into a neighborhood of Craftsman houses and quiet desperation. Ocala Street. Sickness rose in his stomach. The beige bungalow where he'd killed a man.

He blinked and was standing in front of the door. His parents' home. He swallowed a lump in his throat. He couldn't go inside. Anthony turned away.

And the door was in front of him again.

"Stop it! I'm not going in there."

"You've gotta face it," the old man's voice rasped in his ear.

Two more times, Anthony turned away from the door and each time, the door appeared in front of him again. And the final time, it opened.

Dark wood floors. End tables, a fireplace, a thirty-six-inch television, a burgundy sectional. His two brothers sat motionless on the sectional, staring at the cartoons droning in the background. Kevin and Cole looked dazed, their faces stained with tears, eyes rimmed red.

Anthony's flesh chilled. He knew now. He'd killed his father.

Wincing, Anthony took a step inside, looking closer at his younger brothers. Cole, a Cubs baseball cap on his head, wore a first baseman's mitt on his left hand and he snapped a dirty baseball in and out of the pocket. Anthony had given him the hat and mitt for his birthday last month. At thirteen, Cole was already an excellent first baseman.

Three years older, Kevin sank back into the sofa cushions, face drawn, arms crossed. He was wearing Anthony's Hadleyville High School jacket.

From one of the bedrooms, someone cried. His heart smashed into pieces at the sound of his mother weeping. He walked slowly down the hallway that smelled like blood and Febreze and stopped at the bathroom. To his right, his mother lay on his bed sobbing, her face swollen with tears, her blonde hair flat against her head.

Unable to face her, he turned away, feeling sick, and moved past his brothers' bedroom on the left to stand before his parent's bedroom. The door was closed, a sliver of yellow police tape still stuck to it. Slowly, he gripped the doorknob, his breath coming in gasps now. His face burned.

A muffled voice inside made him pause. He didn't care anymore. It was time to end this. He had to look.

He opened the door and the stark white tape outline of the body stared back him. The blue comforter had been stripped from the bed. Propped against the dresser was his dad's rifle.

Dad sat on the unmade bed, his arms wrapped around his middle, eyes red, mouth quivering. A newspaper lay on the bed and Anthony stared at the headline.

Hadleyville Man Holds Dad Hostage Then Commits Suicide

Anthony stumbled backward. He remembered putting the barrel to his dad's head. And he remembered pulling the trigger.

The rest flooded back.

He'd burst into his parents' bedroom with the rifle and pointed it at Dad's head, wanting to hurt him, to pay him back for all the mean things he'd said, for knocking him around all the time. For not loving him like Kevin and Cole. He'd pressed the barrel to Dad's head, but after a few minutes, he knew the only way to fix it was his own final exit.

"Dad?" he called. "Dad?"

His dad didn't turn. Instead, he picked up Anthony's framed picture from the nightstand and held it against his chest, tears squeezing from his eyes.

"Oh, God, Anthony—why? Why!"

"I told you, you needed help!" The old man was beside him, wearing only a faded white shirt, the cardigan draped over one meaty arm. The outline of furled gray wings were at his back.

Anthony's eyes widened. "What are you?" His voice quavered.

"One of the lesser angels—nobody important. I just separate the soul from the body. That's what I was supposed to do ta you." He bowed his head. "But you had the agonies so bad, thought I'd try to help—give you another chance at all this." He shook his head. "But you never asked."

A chill washed over Anthony. "If I'd have asked?"

The old man looked up. "Ask and find out."

All his life, Anthony had tried to do it all himself, not needing or wanting anyone's help. He'd tried to show his dad he could do it, but even that hadn't been enough. His gaze met the old man's.

"You had another choice that night. What if it'd been your dad, like you'd been fearin' all along?"

Anthony asked in a quiet, shaky voice: "Will you help me?"

The old man unfurled his gray wings and enfolded Anthony.

Anger burned like a blowtorch, simmering into a full blown rage inside Anthony. He sat on his bed, loading the rifle while his father took a nap in the next room. His left eye, blackened, had puffed up. His chest was so tight he could barely breathe. Gritting his teeth, he held the rifle in both hands. Dad would never hit him again.

Rifle's smooth balance. Snap of cartridges into the barrel. Pounding of his pulse at his temples. Cold terror gouged him. He knew this time, he had what it took to fire it. No turning back now.

It's him or me, Anthony thought.

He rushed into his parents' bedroom. Dad stared at him in wide-eyed terror as Anthony raised the rifle to his chin. His own picture stared back at him from the nightstand and his breath caught.

Only then did he realize he had a third choice.

Our Souls Abide on This Ocean's Tide

M. Stephen Lukac

The sun and moon share the same sky, yet they are strangers. Like you and me, they travel the same path but never meet. They inhabit the same realm but never share the same sky, although sometimes, the afterglow of one remains as the other arrives.

Just like you and me.

The moon generates no light. There is no fusion at its core, no atomic fire to light the surrounding darkness, no fuel to warm the encompassing gloom. The moon reflects what the sun provides, its cold, dead surface visible only because of solar generosity, a generosity born of circumstance, not benevolence.

You are the sun; I am the moon.

The moon casts no shadows tonight. There's nothing on the beach to interrupt the lunar light, no structures or trees to create pockets of darkness on the soft, wet sand beyond my position. From horizon to horizon, my refuge is a continuous carpet of undisturbed loam; barren except for Laurel and me, and still, save for the gentle lapping of the ocean against its boundaries and the small sobs that pass through my lips.

Doubt assails me as I sit cradled by the cooling sand. My resolve, which seemed so firm in the warm light of afternoon, wavers beneath the cold glow of midnight. Intermixed with the sounds of the surf's incursion come noises of feeding as multi-legged and winged scavengers dine at the buffet I've provided, every bite and tear weakening my determination.

I shake my head, casting scarlet droplets from the point of my chin. I recall the day's heat, and with its memory, dispel the frosty uncertainty that threatens to consume me. I've had my feast; who am I to deny them theirs?

It's too late for doubt, too late to reconsider the path I chose, a path proved correct by virtue of my arrival here. Clarity returns as I review the mileposts along my route, every marker appearing just as I had predicted.

Laurel's trusting smile as we drove up the coast road, the convertible top down and the stereo volume up. The adoration in her eyes as I promised an end to the triangle, a resolution to the heartache caused by my indecision. "I know what to do now," I told her as I parked the car.

And I did.

The reactions washing across your face as Laurel and I emerged from the line of trees separating the road from the beach. Recognition first, then confusion. Shock, then anger, and ultimately resignation as your eyes finally saw the truth you should have sensed months ago.

Laurel moved closer to me; I felt her arm wind through mine and I watched your eyes widen at the unspoken challenge. You stepped back as we approached, distancing yourself from me yet again, the physical separation mirroring the emotional miles that had kept us apart for so long.

Just as I had expected.

Then the tears came, moisture and mascara mingling and cascading down your face. I hoped for the unexpected, a deviation from my carefully scripted scenario. Confronted with a glimpse of your heart, I began to close the gap between us, pulling against Laurel's grip on my arm.

Your eyes narrowed, Laurel tightened her hand and events veered back upon their predetermined course. I sighed and shook my head. Your walls ensured our path, funneled our destinies along the only route left to us.

Beside me, the sounds of the banquet continue. I flick my hand to dislodge something from my leg, a diner looking to sample a different dish. Discouraged, the creature returns to his brethren. I am neither for him nor for his fellow revelers.

I am only for you.

That's all I ever wanted; all I ever asked from you. To slip into your arms and feel warmed by the fire of your passion, not trapped in the circle of your cold embrace. Recitation of Hallmark verses could not nourish me, the rote monologues delivered in a monotone, the right words lacking the appropriate actions. When thought and deed collided, deed triumphed and negated the word, leaving me starving amidst a cornucopia of hollow sentiment.

If there's no food in the house, won't a man look elsewhere to eat?

I found my sustenance in the heart of another. I discovered the light of emotion in the eyes of a stranger, Laurel's passion so abundant I could swim in it, dousing myself in the heat of her desire. Physical distance meant nothing to us; her adoration surrounded me from miles away. We circled each other in ever-widening orbits of secrecy, never severing the ethereal connection that kept us anchored, one to the other.

We shouted our love in silence and the soundless declaration threatened to shake the heavens.

Yet, all I wanted was you.

My detachment matched your own and you never noticed. I copied your apathy and you found nothing amiss in your reflection from my eyes. I concocted elaborate explanations I never used because the questions never came.

Until it was too late.

The surf moves closer to my toes as the tide rolls in. There's a hint of red in the foam, but I realize it's only a trick of the light, filtered through the splatter caked in my eyelashes—crimson highlights matching the stain on my lips.

Clear crystal blue washes dense grainy gold, every pulse erasing your presence from the sand, but not from my mind. My stomach growls in time with the rhythm of the tide, but I ignore the call to feed. I've had my final meal, swallowed my last morsels and left the remains to the sand and the surf.

My heart pulled me forward. Laurel pulled me back. I was willing to break her heart to gain yours, and reclaim my own, but your response made this desperate gambit my only hope. I locked my eyes onto yours, our teary gazes identical, and pulled Laurel closer. She opened her mouth to celebrate her triumph, but her voice failed.

No words could travel past the fountain of blood and bile that erupted from her lips as I ripped the blade across her torso. The serrated edge sawed through flesh and muscle; bone splintered against hardened steel as I made my ultimate sacrifice on the altar of your indifference. Your eyes danced in time to Laurel's spasms, the revulsion in them contradicted by a small curl of victory at the corner of your mouth.

The usurper was vanquished.

You ran to me. I dropped Laurel onto the beach, her still-twitching body marring the sand in scarlet sculptures of blood. I opened my arms to you, but you stopped, pausing to spit on Laurel before slapping my face. Then came the screams, gurgling accusations of betrayal as the object of your contempt died at your feet.

Allegations of infidelity, but no mention of murder. Misplaced priorities in the face of what mattered.

I, on the other hand, prioritize quite well and even after Laurel, the knife was still sharp enough to finish my task.

I don't like leaving Laurel on the sand. She deserves better. I console myself with what rests in my stomach, gastric juices speeding our final communion throughout my veins.

No matter what happens to the shell I leave for the scavengers, Laurel's heart will be with me. She offered it to me, I accepted it and now I've kept that promise. The seat of her soul—if it truly exists—is safe in my care and I will care for it well.

Moonshine sparkles beyond the waves. Whitecaps create a line of demarcation, separating what is from what might be. I wonder how far you've traveled, what miles the tides have put between us as you begin your cleansing and I anticipate mine.

The sea scours. What lies beneath the blue horizon is abraded, polished and born anew. What devours is soon devoured, blurring origin and resolution until what remains is an amalgamation of what began.

I will find you again. Your spark will endure and call mine to it. In the depths, carried by current and chance, we will be one again. What kept us apart sloughed away in an onslaught of rock and coral, what drew us together buffed by the elements and made fresh.

I rise and walk toward the surf. Salt stings my skin as I stand at the threshold of rebirth. I look back at Laurel one last time, mentally erasing the damage I've inflicted, remembering her whole and alive, to carry that image into the ocean as I cross over from what is to what will be.

I walk. The weight belt slides against my hips as I force my way into the surf. Water slaps against my thighs, turning my legs to ice, but I continue my steps. My body's numbness fuels my resolve and soon the waves roll over my shoulders. My only warmth is the remnant of Laurel, but the ocean overwhelms that too.

Bouncing on my toes to delay my submersion, I fill my lungs with night air and scream your name. My voice skips across the surface, swallowed by oceanic surges, but at least you'll know I'm coming.

When my feet no longer scrape the bottom, I swim. When the weight drags me below, I'll walk again. When my lungs burst, I'll resign myself to the kindness of the sea, trusting it to bring me to you.

I'm coming.

I'm com...

I'm...

Between Sisters

Kevin Anderson

Agatha knew death was at her door. She had sensed the dark angel's visits for almost a year, but in the past few months death seemed to be keeping vigil over her, observing her suffering, watching her wither into nothing. So many times she wished the darkness would just take her, relieve her of the pain and of this illness that teams of doctors could not diagnose. If it hadn't been for her sister Margaret urging her to continue to fight and endure the pain, Agatha would have given in to death's invitation long ago.

It was her sister's selfless dedication that made Agatha's decision so hard, knowing that the last thing she had left to do, her final act, would be to break her baby sister's heart.

"You've been such a godsend to me this past year, Margy. Being my steward, quitting your job to stay home with me during these final days." A tear slipped down her wrinkled cheek.

Margaret sat on Agatha's bed, took her sister's withered hand in hers. "Don't talk like that. I want you to hang in there."

Agatha squeezed her sister's hand with waning strength. "Dear Margy, it pains me to think what you have given up in the last year, and it makes what I have to do even more difficult."

Margaret stroked Agatha's silver hair. "And what is that?"

"I must tell you something I did many years ago. It is the single regret of my life, and I cannot take the guilt with me to heaven."

"Hush... none of that matters now."

Agatha tried to sit up in her bed, but the effort was thwarted by internal anguish. She settled back down. "I must." She moistened her lips, stared into her sister's eyes and said, "It happened more than thirty years ago, when both our husbands were still alive."

Margaret shook her head. "It doesn't matter."

"When you and Aaron separated for a few months and my Bernie was in St. Louis at a convention... I visited Aaron at his hotel. I went there with the intention of talking him into coming back to you—really I did."

Margaret closed her eyes and sighed. "Never mind. You needn't do this—"

"No, I must. It happened just the one time and never again. We both swore to take it to the grave but—"

"Enough." Margaret's eyes narrowed into slits. "I know all about it, dear sister."

"What, how—"

"Why do you think I've been encouraging you to fight the good fight, endure the pain for just one more day?"

"I don't understand."

Margaret leaned forward, just inches from Agatha's ear. "Who do you think has been poisoning you this past year?"

Perfect Crystal

Heather Wardell

The doorbell rang, and Anthony jumped. She was here.

His wife was away, visiting her parents. He wasn't welcome there; they'd never forgiven him for what had happened a few years before he and Denise had married.

Denise hadn't really forgiven him either, and their sex life had become virtually non-existent. Which was why he'd called the escort service.

And here she was.

Anthony opened the front door and let in the tall stunning blonde. She reminded him a bit of how Denise had looked, before twenty-five years of marriage and three children had dulled her inside and out.

She smiled sweetly. "I'm Crystal," she said, handing him her coat. The strong floral scent of her perfume enveloped him, and he shivered as he hung her coat in the closet. He was so ready for this. Their eyes met. She smiled again, and said, "Where would you like me?"

He pointed wordlessly up the stairs, and she took his hand. He guided her up the stairs to his bedroom, where he'd slept alone for the last ten years, and closed the door firmly behind them.

Two hours later, he paid Crystal her standard fee plus a three-hundred-dollar tip, and led her back down the stairs. After she left, he collapsed on the living room couch, exhausted yet unable to keep the silly grin from his face.

Why had he waited so long? He'd gone for years without being with a woman, and now he couldn't understand why he'd let it happen. When a woman like Crystal was just a phone call away, why not make that call? She was perfect.

Denise returned home five days later. Anthony had called Crystal twice more during that time, and was so relaxed and happy that he greeted Denise with a rare enthusiasm. She looked at him suspiciously.

"What have you been up to?"

"Nothing much. You?"

"My parents had some interesting news."

"Oh?"

"Yes. They... they have a surprise for us."

"Really?" Anthony tried to keep the sneer out of his voice, but apparently he was unsuccessful.

"Yes, really. We're having dinner with them on Friday. Try to be polite, please."

Denise turned and walked away. She didn't speak to him again until they arrived at the restaurant on Friday, where they managed to put on a fairly decent "happy family" act for Denise's parents. They sipped wine and made awkward small talk. After ten minutes, Anthony, bored and annoyed as he always was when in the company of Denise's parents, excused himself on the pretext of needing to use the washroom.

On his return, a woman was sitting at their table with her back to him. Denise immediately launched into excited introductions and explanations. Anthony sat and listened, frozen in shock.

"I didn't know they'd done it," Denise said, "but my *darling* parents registered my name with the adoption group, just in case our baby ever wanted to know about her biological parents. And she did! Her name's Crystal now and she's twenty-seven. Isn't she perfect?"

Of course she was.

Savoir-Faire

Lee Allen Howard

Wyatt Bell hadn't been with a woman in over a year, but Natalie Trattoriano was well worth the wait. He met her at the fall E-Commerce Services Fair while he was staffing his company's booth. She sashayed to the table in a blood-red suit and leaned over the sales literature.

"I wonder if you could... help me," she said, and he no longer cared what he sold that day, so long as he sold himself to her. He managed to make a date for a drink in the hotel lounge that evening.

After a bottle of Cabernet Sauvignon and some stimulating conversation, she raked her glistening nails across his palm and smiled salaciously.

Sooner than he thought possible, they were up in his room, peeling off each other's clothes. Their sex was hot, savage, ravenous. Afterward, she caressed his navel while he drew his fingers through her jet-black hair. He was waiting for her to answer this question: "Stay the night?"

"I'd love to," she said. "There's just one problem."

"What's that?" Right then, he could imagine no such thing as a problem.

Natalie stroked his navel and said: "I'm... married, Wyatt. Married."

That was the first time Natalie mentioned her husband to Wyatt, but it wasn't the last. In fact, every time they were together—even in bed—she mentioned Vince. Hers weren't venomous, hate-filled words about a man who cared less about her. Vince sounded like a nice, sensitive guy who was fond of her but who had a few problems.

Vince worked nights, so Natalie rarely saw him. When she was up, he was asleep, and when she was tired, he was getting ready for work. They never enjoyed a meal together. Worse yet, they never slept together. For someone as sexually voracious as she, Wyatt could understand her frustration.

However, their issues weren't what Wyatt wanted to discuss when Natalie was writhing beneath him in his bed after work. It was time to concentrate on the task at hand.

She gasped and he grinned, panting.

"Ohh, Wyatt... Vince could never have done it twice."

Wyatt's smile faded, and he threw back the sheet.

"What's wrong?" she said, drawing the covers over her breasts.

"Must you always compare me with him?"

"Who, Vince?"

"Who else?" He yanked up his boxers. "We can't even make love without you bringing him into bed with us."

Natalie sat up. "I'm sorry, Wyatt. I didn't know you were so sensitive about him."

"Sensitive?" He huffed. "Why do you go on about him? Did you ever think if he really loved you, he'd want to satisfy you sexually?"

She glanced out the door, down the hall.

He stood at the end of the bed, his arms crossed over his chest. "If you love him so much, why are you having an affair?"

"I don't know. He's such a wonderful man, and he's really good to me, and I wish things were different between us. I know if you met him, you'd really like—"

"*Meet* him?" Wyatt snapped. "I don't want to meet him for God's sake, I can't stand him! I don't ever want to hear his name again. I wish we were rid of him, and it was just you and me."

"Wyatt!" She flung back the covers and reached for her black bra. "Unless you want this to be the last time, don't talk about Vince that way again."

Wyatt grumbled, pulling on an old Penn State sweatshirt. He looked squarely into her coal-black eyes. "And unless *you* want this to be the last time, don't mention Vince in my bed again."

She frowned but said nothing more. When she finished dressing, she left Wyatt's apartment to go home to Vince.

The following evening, Wyatt glanced out his office window at Symplex Systems and straightened the contracts on his desk. It was after the fall time change and already getting dark.

He studied the appointment column of his planner and then glanced at his watch. One more meeting and he would be done for the day. New business with a guy named Levesque from some company with an acronym he couldn't interpret.

He started a fresh pot of coffee and carried his presentation materials to the front conference room. David the receptionist was shrugging on his coat.

"Wyatt, I'm gone for the day. I set the phones on night-ring. I know you've got a late appointment, so listen for the door."

"All right, good night."

David pushed through the front doors and disappeared into the parking lot.

Wyatt prepared the laptop for the multimedia demo. He retrieved the coffee and two clean Symplex mugs. He was arranging the tray on the conference table when someone knocked on the reception desk. Wyatt straightened his tie before entering the foyer. A slender man over six feet with short, dark hair and finely sculpted features stood holding his overcoat.

"Mr. Levesque? Wyatt Bell. Welcome to Symplex Systems."

Levesque shook firmly with a large, strong hand.

"Let me take your coat." Wyatt hung the heavy wool wrap in the hall closet.

"Won't you step into the conference room? I've got everything set up." Wyatt followed Levesque into the room.

"Coffee?" Wyatt asked.

"No thank you, but you go ahead." Levesque's voice was deep and soft with a vague European accent, and when he smiled, his dark eyes sparkled.

Wyatt poured coffee in his mug and stationed himself beside the laptop.

Levesque described the current operations of Ex Libris Corporation, a large book chain, and explained why their Data Services Division was interested in a Symplex solution. Wyatt listened attentively, commenting and asking for clarification when necessary.

He dimmed the overhead lights and started the presentation. As the familiar sounds and images about scaleable servers played on the slim screen, Wyatt daydreamed about Natalie, how her hair cascaded across the pillows, the way she bit her lower lip, the long, sharp nails she dug into his back....

"I can see you're preoccupied," Levesque said.

Wyatt snapped to attention. The presentation had ended and he hadn't noticed.

"I'm sorry, Mr. Levesque. It's been a long day."

"Then you've had no dinner." Nothing in Levesque's tone or expression betrayed annoyance. "Tell you what. I need this information by tomorrow, but why don't you relax for a while, have something to eat and then meet me for a drink, say, around eight."

Wyatt was grateful for Levesque's understanding. He found himself saying, "That sounds like a great idea. You know Brochere's?"

"Fine place. I'll see you there."

Wyatt stood with Levesque, helped him with his coat, and watched him disappear into the darkness outside.

What a nice guy, he thought, gathering his materials for their evening meeting. He would try harder to win his business.

After shutting down the laptop and flicking off the lights, Wyatt locked the front doors and headed for his car.

The lights were dim inside the lounge, where a few stragglers remained from happy hour. Wyatt was glad he wouldn't have to shout to make himself heard. He found a secluded table big enough to spread some literature.

A minute later, Levesque strode past the bar, heading toward the table. He smiled warmly, and Wyatt stood to greet him.

"Feeling refreshed?" Levesque shed his overcoat. He was still wearing the same fine wool suit, but had taken off his tie.

My kinda guy, Wyatt thought. "Yes. I apologize again."

"No need. I enjoyed the break myself." Levesque sat down.

Wyatt waved the waiter over. He ordered drinks and they got down to business. Ex Libris was looking for an Internet commerce firm to build a business-to-consumer website to sell books, CDs, and DVDs. Wyatt rambled through his spiel as if the Symplex solution was designed expressly for Levesque and Ex Libris.

As Wyatt sipped his Tanqueray and tonic, an approaching figure caught his eye.

Natalie was slinking through the lobby in a black suede miniskirt, red blouse, and beaver stole. Her lissome thighs flexed beneath black hose and, with each long stride, she thrust a patent leather stiletto into the carpet.

Levesque swiveled his chair to see what Wyatt was gaping at.

Tugging off her black leather gloves, Natalie headed straight for their table. Wyatt no longer cared whether he won Ex Libris' business; he had talked with Levesque long enough. It was time for pleasure.

Wyatt smiled, but it felt more like leering. He caught Natalie's eye and, as she swept her gaze to Levesque, he noticed panic in her eyes. Levesque took her white hand, and her features softened.

Turning to Wyatt, Levesque smiled and said, "Mr. Bell, I'd like you meet Natalie Trattoriano… my beautiful wife."

Natalie extended her hand demurely. After hesitating a moment, Wyatt accepted it. Her fingers were like icicles.

"And please," Levesque said, "call me Vincien."

"Or Vince," Natalie added.

They all sat down. Wyatt remained speechless, staring into Natalie's impenetrable black eyes as Vincien Levesque ordered another round of drinks.

"I hope you don't mind Natalie dropping by," Vincien said. He gazed at her affectionately, and she touched his handsome face.

"No, not at all," Wyatt said and choked on his own spit.

"Mr. Bell is with Symplex Systems, darling. They're going to build us an Internet ordering system."

Natalie looked insincerely impressed.

"Is there someone you can call?" Vincien asked him. "To join us for drinks, I mean."

Wyatt's heart ticked like a stopwatch. "Ah, no, unfortunately, there isn't."

Vincien appeared genuinely pained. "I'm sorry to hear that. You're welcome to stay and chat with us. We'd love to have you, wouldn't we, darling?" Vincien slipped his arm around her.

Natalie pursed her lips sweetly.

"It's just as well," Wyatt said, collecting his literature. "I need to get right on this to come up with the best solution for Sex Libris."

"Sex?" Natalie said, arching her eyebrows.

"What!" Wyatt said.

"Sex," Vincien said. "You said *Sex* Libris."

Wyatt felt burning shame creep up his neck and flood his face. "Did I?" He struggled into his jacket.

"You most certainly did," Natalie said, smirking.

"Slip of the tongue," he rasped, averting his eyes.

"Why, Mr. Bell, you *are* preoccupied." Vincien grinned like an alligator, stretching out his hand.

He didn't want to, but Wyatt shook it, braying his goodbyes.

"Call me when your proposal's ready," Vincien said.

Wyatt nodded and hurried out of Brochere's.

"He's not what you think." Natalie was pleading in that tone she always used.

"Here we go again!" Wyatt sprang out of bed and began dressing. After meeting Vincien that night two months ago, Wyatt thought Natalie would never mention him again. At least not in bed.

Wyatt was amazed she'd called him afterward—other than to say so long. She had shrugged it off, saying Vince was clever that way and, yes, he probably knew, but she didn't think it bothered him. She said Vince genuinely liked Wyatt and hoped Ex Libris' business with Symplex would succeed.

Wyatt found it hard to believe a man as powerful and sophisticated as Vincien Levesque would knowingly be cuckolded, allowing his gorgeous wife to sleep around. She said he let her do what she wanted so long as she managed his affairs.

"I have to take care of him," she said, nearly pouting. That was her new catch-phrase about Vincien.

"He's no invalid," Wyatt said. "He likes hang-gliding. Does he have some disease?"

"No… no," She tried pulling Wyatt's clothes back off.

Wyatt moved away from her groping hands. "He doesn't seem the type you wait on, cook him dinner, bring his slippers, that type."

"Definitely not. Besides, do I look like I cook?"

Wyatt didn't answer. He buttoned his white oxford, slipped into his slacks. "Then what do you mean you have to take care of him?"

She looked momentarily forlorn, shrugged her milk-white shoulders. "He's different. I just…"

"What? You never have sex."

She arched her back, changing the subject, and Wyatt found himself taking off his clothes again.

Alone in bed that night, Wyatt sipped at an inch of Canadian Club and stared out the window at the clear night sky.

He wondered if he was a fool for continuing his relationship with Natalie. He truly liked her, but she talked about Vincien all the time. For some reason, she wouldn't leave him. Was it his money? His looks, his charm? Why would she stay with a man who didn't satisfy her?

Wyatt couldn't match Vincien's savoir-faire, but he was just as successful, just as good looking. And man, could he perform.

Natalie admitted there'd been other men, but said she wanted to keep Wyatt around. She said she loved him. He was beginning to think they were meant to be together.

He took another smoldering sip.

Since the rendezvous at Brochere's, he had contacted Vincien numerous times concerning the Ex Libris project, and he detected no hostility, jealousy, or ill will. Vincien really was a kind man, an understanding man, a good-natured man, and what frustrated Wyatt most was that Vincien actually liked him. Wyatt wanted to mock him, despise him, rub his nose in the fact he was bedding Natalie three nights a week. But he couldn't. Natalie was right: "If you meet him, I know you'll like him." Well, he had, he did, and he hated himself for it.

The only way he could break free from this self-loathing was to end the relationship with Natalie. Inside, he whined like a little boy. Even if he called it quits with her, he would have to sabotage the Ex Libris project, pass it off to someone else, or quit his job.

Wyatt drained the glass, still feeling trapped.

Where did Vincien get his power of attraction? He was reasonable, well spoken, intelligent. He was witty, urbane, yet down to earth. And yes, he was graceful, handsome, sexy. That last one caught Wyatt off guard. He set the glass on the nightstand, snapped off the lamp and squirmed under the sheets, striving to pinpoint the answer. Vincien Levesque was all those things, but none of them—nor their collection—explained his appeal.

Maybe Wyatt was looking at it the wrong way. Perhaps all of those attributes were emanations or expressions of Vince's essential power. Because of this elementary endowment, he seemed reasonable, well spoken, intelligent; he seemed witty, urbane, down to earth; he seemed graceful, handsome, and yes, even sexy. Wyatt had fallen under his spell. But for what purpose?

He rolled over. It was bad enough with Natalie in tryst, but here he was alone in bed, thinking about that damned Vincien. Disgusting.

After a while, Wyatt drifted off and dreamed of Vincien presenting Natalie to him, of Natalie smirking, then rolling her pink tongue over red, red lips.

The phone rang, and he jolted upright.

"Mm, hello?"

"Wyatt? Vincien. I'm sorry if I woke you."

"Just lying here."

"Say, I'd like to move the Ex Libris deal into production as soon as possible. Are you doing anything this weekend?"

"Nothing special planned." *Except nailing your wife.*

"You can think about it for a day or two, but how about if we spend the weekend at Big Rock Lake? Just you and me. We could work on the project, watch the hang-gliders—"

"I'm no hang-glider."

Vincien chuckled. "We can just watch. I want to finish the design specs so we can begin phase one development of Ex Libris Online."

Wyatt rubbed his eyes. "I'll think about it."

"Could you let me know by Wednesday?"

"Wednesday? Sure, Vince."

"Go back to sleep now."

Wyatt cradled the phone and nestled back under the covers. Was he still dreaming? The weekend alone with Vincien…. The situation was absurd.

Muttering complaints, Wyatt slid into sleep, envisioning Natalie in a dominatrix outfit, whip in hand, beckoning, beckoning.

Approaching the second hour in Vincien's Acura, Wyatt's dread dissolved into a pulpy resignation. He'd debated whether to make the trip to Big Rock Lake and had asked Natalie what she thought her dear husband was up to. "He wants to get going on Sex Libris Online." Every possible chance, she fondly referred to Ex Libris by Wyatt's Freudian slip. It irked him.

"You sure he's not secretly plotting to lure me into the mountains and kill me in a freak hang-gliding accident?"

"Secretly? No. We planned it all out the other night. Want to see the PowerPoint presentation?" She smiled wickedly with those straight, white teeth of hers. "Give it a rest, Wyatt. Why are you always trying to pin some kind of underhanded motive on him? Can't you tell? Vince likes you. He wants to get the project underway. You don't have to go."

Wyatt pouted, staring into the bath suds.

"*Wy*-att..." She drove her slender hand into the bubbles on an exploratory undersea diving mission.

He shivered and grabbed her arm. "Stop that. You've already exhausted me."

"Aw, poor baby's all tuckered out." She made pouty lips, withdrew her hand, and massaged the clinging suds into his chest hair. "You should at least get away for a couple days to catch up on your rest."

He narrowed his eyes as she went snorkeling. "Natalie, you're going to kill me."

She hadn't replied; she had just blown bubbles in the water.

Vincien's pulling off the interstate curtailed his fantasy, and Wyatt was relieved to see the green sign at the end of the exit ramp: BIG ROCK LAKE, 15 MI.

Vincien turned onto the two-lane road and asked, "Thinking about work?"

"No, just thinking I could use some rest."

Vincien said, "I promise I won't work you too hard this weekend. The cabin's really the place to relax, get some fresh air. Let's knock off tonight, wind down. Tomorrow morning, we can maybe go for a hike, watch the gliders. If we finish work in the afternoon, we'll have the evening for dinner, whatever."

Wyatt thought about it for a moment. His resignation was forming itself into something more appealing.

"Sounds great." He offered Vincien a smile.

Vincien wet his lips, and his face worked subtly, as if he were carefully choosing his words.

"Something on your mind?"

Vincien laughed softly. "I was going to ask whether you had second thoughts about accepting my offer to spend the weekend up here."

As the car penetrated the dusk, Wyatt watched the lines on the road emerge in the headlights and zip under the hood. He considered dismissing the query, but dared being frank.

"Truthfully, I didn't know what to expect. I enjoy doing business with you, spending time with you, but I wasn't sure what your motives were."

"I understand how you feel," Vincien said. "You already know how much I want to complete the design specs. I thought it might be nice to get away from the everyday grind, get to know you better as a person, not just a business associate. Frankly, I weary spending all my time putting food on the table."

Wyatt thought it dubious that Vincien and Natalie were struggling to make ends meet. Then again, maybe they did have financial pressures. The more you make, the more you spend.

"I hope I'm not bringing you here against your will." For the first time, Vincien sounded insecure.

Maybe Vincien wasn't as devious as Wyatt supposed. After all, Wyatt *was* having an affair with the man's wife. Who was he to judge who was being crafty?

"Of course not," Wyatt said. "I make my own decisions. I had my reservations, but if I didn't want to come, I would've declined and made other arrangements to get our work done."

Vincien seemed relieved. He smiled again, his eyes glistening in the dashboard's glow. "I'm glad we're being honest," he said. "And I'm glad you decided to come. The cabin, the lake.... It's a special place, and I think it'll give you a new perspective on who I am."

Vincien was, if nothing else, a reasonable guy. Maybe joining him on a weekend getaway was a good idea after all.

Later at Big Rock Lake, they sat with their feet propped up, holding a couple of icy Grolsches that sweated in the heat from the fireplace. Wyatt took another deep swig and watched as reflected firelight danced over the Shaker settle between the two far windows. The cabin reminded him of his grandparents' farmhouse.

The beer was kicking in, and so far their conversation was pleasant. Vincien leaned forward.

"I've been meaning to bring this up for some time now."

Wyatt shifted in the recliner, suddenly feeling uneasy.

"The night we met at Brochere's and Natalie dropped by, it seems I put you on the spot. I apologize for embarrassing you."

"Oh. No problem. I'd forgotten all about it." Embarrassed again, he wondered how to steer the conversation to some other subject. At all costs, Wyatt wanted to avoid any confrontation concerning Natalie.

"My wife's a beautiful woman," Vincien said, "so I'm used to how men react when they set eyes on her. I only wish things were different."

Wyatt knew he shouldn't pursue it. He should just let it go and say nothing. Except Vincien sounded concerned, and Wyatt didn't want to snub him.

"What do you mean?"

Vincien sighed, looking worn as he stared into the fire. "I wish I could... satisfy her."

Wyatt's heart sank. Playing sexual counselor to his lover's husband was the last thing he wanted to do. He was getting in too deep, but there seemed to be no turning back.

Wyatt said, "It looks like you and Natalie have a wonderful relationship." He almost said, *She talks about you all the time*, but managed to curb his tongue.

"It's not what it seems."

"How so?"

Vincien smiled sadly, folding his hands over one knee. "Our relationship is—how can I say it? Platonic? Perhaps. More of a business partnership, than a true marriage. It's not how I wish it were, but with the way I am, it's how we've fallen into things."

Wyatt didn't know how to respond.

"I'm not saying we don't get along. We do. I know she wants more, but some things I just can't provide. I have some special needs she helps fulfill. I guess it works out, but..."

"What's wrong with that? If it works for you, why should you care you're not like everybody else?"

Vincien stood and paced behind the chair. Turmoil brewed beneath his features; he clenched his long hands into fists. "Oh—I don't know. It seems dishonest. I've deceived so many people. If they found out, they wouldn't believe it, wouldn't understand. I..."

It finally dawned on Wyatt what the problem was. No wonder Vincien hadn't been jealous. It wasn't impotence—

"I like you a great deal, Wyatt."

Wyatt sat up, grasping his Grolsch.

Vincien moved between him and the fireplace. "Ever since Natalie told me about you."

"You mean—"

"Yes. I know all about you and her."

Wyatt hung his head. "I'm sorry, Vince."

"Don't be. Please."

They were still for a moment, the only sounds being the creak of the dying fire and the tick of sleet on the dark pane windows.

Wyatt wondered how they would ever get any work done with this between them. "I don't know what to say."

"You don't have to say anything, Wyatt. I just wanted you to know."

Wyatt nodded, and Vincien retired for the night, leaving him staring into the dying embers.

The following morning was cold, spitting snow and sleet from a lowering sky. They both slept late, but Wyatt rose first. He stacked logs on the grate and started a fire, then carried last night's beer bottles into the kitchen.

"Morning."

Wyatt turned to see Vincien planted in the doorway. In the tank-top undershirt, his shoulders were pale and muscular. His hands were balled in the pockets of his slate-colored sweatpants, which were cuffed at the ankles, revealing long, white feet.

"Good morning." Wyatt tried to smile as Vincien went to the refrigerator.

"There's some cranberry juice in here. Are you hungry?"

"I could eat," Wyatt said.

"How about if I cook you breakfast?"

"That'd be terrific."

Vincien looked grateful for Wyatt's gesture of acceptance. "You can eat healthy—bran bagels. Or tasty—bacon and eggs."

"If it makes no difference to you, I'm all for tasty."

While Vincien busied himself breaking eggs and slicing bacon, Wyatt poured them juice and sat down at the table, pondering what a strange weekend this had turned out to be. To think he had hated this man and wanted to hurt him, stooping so low as to believe his good will was only a ruse. Thinking Vince had lured him to the hinterland to give him what for or, worse yet, to kill him. For a moment, Wyatt was ashamed of himself. Then he let it go, realizing Vince had already forgiven him, held nothing against him. It should have made him feel better. Instead, he felt incredibly sad.

As Vincien moved about the kitchen, Wyatt noticed how emaciated he looked, and it worried him. Vincien set the steaming plate before him.

"Thank you. This looks delicious." Wyatt picked up his fork.

Vincien slid into the chair across from him and reached for his juice glass. Wyatt was self-conscious with Vincien watching him eat.

"Piece of bacon?" He slid his plate toward Vincien.

Vincien held up his hand. "Thank you, no."

He finished eating and Vincien made coffee.

Wyatt couldn't bear to continue with such tension between them. It was finally time to break the ice and offer some grace. It would be a fitting response to Vincien's savoir-faire, a way to prove—at least to himself—that he had learned something from such a noble man.

"Look, Vince. I know you're not holding my involvement with Natalie against me. But I want to apologize. I hope I haven't damaged anything between you two."

Vincien nodded somberly. He looked old.

"I'm sorry your situation troubles you," Wyatt continued, "and I can't say I understand what it's like for you, but I'm humbled that you trusted me enough to share it with me. I guess I had the wrong idea about you. You're a better man than I. A very special man." Wyatt reached over and touched Vince's hand. "I understand."

Vincien replied with a melancholy smile. "Thanks, Wyatt. I only wish you did."

Because the weather was bad, they stayed inside and tackled the Ex Libris Online spec. They covered their business perfunctorily, wrapping up as night fell. The atmosphere between them had thawed some, but there was still an unease, some wound, Wyatt realized, that might never heal.

Vincien returned from the kitchen, carrying an open beer. He handed it to Wyatt and sat on the other chair by the fireplace.

"What's on your mind?"

Vincien worked his fingers nervously before the fire. "Before you answer, think. And please take me seriously."

Wyatt nodded with apprehension.

"What would you say if I invited you to... continue your relationship with Natalie?"

Wyatt raised his eyebrows. This wasn't the proposition he'd expected.

"I, well—"

"Please. Seriously *think* about it." Vincien launched himself from the chair and paced about the room.

Wyatt sat back, trying to remain composed. Could he do it? It sounded too good to be true. It was one thing to sleep with another man's wife when you thought you were being sneaky, when you believed you had bested him. But to do it openly, with her husband's approval.... It just wasn't the same.

He recalled rocking with his grandmother on her porch swing, tucked under her soft arm as she warned him about the dangers of the world. What had she told him? "There's a price to pay for committing adultery, Wyatt: 'Whoso committeth adultery lacketh understanding: he that doeth it destroyeth his own soul.'" But that was long ago. His grandmother was dead and, along with her sayings, only a memory.

Wyatt looked at Vincien, but Vincien was gazing out the window at the night. Wyatt thought he glimpsed Natalie standing outside in the cold, but it was only the reflection of Vincien's gaunt face.

Wyatt took a long draught of beer before he spoke.

"That's tempting. Natalie is a beautiful woman."

"She says you satisfy her."

Mortified, Wyatt shut his eyes. He never dreamed Natalie had shared any details. For a moment, he wondered if Vincien wanted a threesome. No, he refused to go there.

"Believe me," Vincien said, "I'm not doing this for you. I'm doing it for her."

Wyatt thought again before he replied. "I don't doubt the honor of your sacrifice. But how long could this arrangement last? I'm a single guy. I'd like to get married one day. Natalie's a treasure, yet if I couldn't have her for myself...."

Vincien's eyes glowed in the firelight. "I see."

For all Vincien's selflessness, Wyatt thought he looked relieved. More than that. Thrilled. Wyatt felt he'd made the right decision.

Vincien left the room.

Wyatt's mouth had gone dry. He finished his beer, set the empty bottle on the floor beside his chair, leaned back and closed his eyes. He would have to break it off completely with Natalie now. He would miss her, but he felt relieved also. He drifted off to sleep to the soft hiss of the fire.

When he roused, he expected to see dying embers but, opening his eyes, it wasn't the fireplace he saw. He was staring, bleary-eyed, at the cabin's rough-timbered ceiling.

Where am I? Did I pass out?

He realized he was lying on the kitchen table. Naked. His crotch was wet as if he'd just had sex. He tried to lift his head, but it only rolled to one side. He felt sluggish, drugged.

Natalie stood there in a red teddy, sobbing, mascara bleeding down her swollen cheeks. Her lacquered nails flashed like rubies as she tortured her shining sable hair.

He lolled his head to the other side. Tall and raw-boned, Vincien stooped over him, a sallow grimness in his features.

Wyatt's heart raced. Blood thundered in his head.

Natalie gasped and clawed Wyatt's shoulder. "He's not what you think, Wyatt. I have to take care of him! I'm sorry I couldn't save you."

A large, cold hand pressed down on Wyatt's chest. He groaned from deep within.

Thin lips parting, Vincien's white face drew nearer.

Wyatt pinched his mouth shut, tried to twist his head away. Vincien's rancid panting moved lower.

When Wyatt glimpsed the lustrous teeth, he realized Vincien wasn't sex-hungry. Never had been.

Writhing under the torrid slavering, Wyatt bucked as the fangs sunk in.

5

Marked

Mark Tullius

Olsen was too good to be true. The old man hadn't learned his lesson. He still flaunted his wealth, kept the same exact routines, and never watched his back. It was like the fat slob wanted to get robbed again.

When Nick first got out of the joint, he'd promised himself he'd never do this sort of thing again, but Olsen was the perfect victim and the money was too good. Three hundred thousand would solve a lot of problems. It'd also make up a little for the time locked up. Hell, a payday like that would equal close to fifty thousand for each of his seven years in the pen.

Nick turned the page on the newspaper and sneaked another glance at the jewelry store directly across from the mall's food court. From his seat outside of the McDonald's Express he could keep a close eye on the old man while looking like just another fool reading the help wanted ads. Not that he would ever lower himself to take one of those jobs. Just for the hell of it he ran through the list. The only positions he qualified for were below him. And the other ninety percent of the jobs wouldn't be worth taking even if the manager had no hang-up with hiring an uneducated ex-con. Who wants to wear a monkey suit and take orders from some college dork just to make thirty thousand a year? To hell with that.

It was nearing seven o'clock and Suzanne, his inside, was pleasantly escorting the last couple out of the jewelry store. Before she headed back in, Suzanne made eye contact with Nick and gave him a discreet thumbs-up sign. When he set down the paper to acknowledge her, she flashed four fingers. This was going to be sweeter than he had imagined. Olsen was taking home more work than usual.

Nick grabbed his coffee and headed for the exit. He didn't have to hurry; Olsen wouldn't be done closing up shop for another half hour, but he was too excited to stay still. Four hundred thousand. A hundred thousand for each of the months he'd been out on parole, unable to find a decent job.

Olsen's car wasn't in its spot. The black BMW had been there when Nick arrived two hours before and it should still be there. Olsen hadn't left his sight for more than five minutes. No way he could have come out and moved it.

Nick was tempted to race back inside to find Suzanne, but that would be foolish. It wouldn't look good for a tattooed thug to be seen with her. Someone might get the wrong idea and put things together. Especially if he went ahead with the robbery. He couldn't bring her into it. Not because he liked her, but because he didn't trust her. Just like everyone else on the planet, if it was her ass or his, she would sell him out in a second. Just like the backstabbing bastard that had put him away in the first place.

Not sure what to do, Nick did a one-eighty and headed for his beater Ford. He felt like a fool when he spotted Olsen's 745i in the next row, wedged between two SUVs. He had to get a grip if he was going to pull this thing off. How could he not know where the car was parked? He was acting like a damn fish straight out of the tank.

Easing into his lowered front seat, Nick concentrated on the BMW's driver door, trying not to think about how nervous he was. He had nothing to worry about. Olsen was an easy target. He'd been an easy target for Bear and hadn't changed his ways since.

Bear... now that was one untrustworthy sonofabitch. After sharing a three-by-six concrete cell for two years you'd think you'd get to know someone. They'd sworn allegiance to each other, become blood brothers, beaten down punks together. All that, and Bear had still ditched him when it counted. Three months ago, Bear had called Nick to tell him about this mark. They were supposed to do it together and split the profit, but Bear must've got greedy because, after a week of staking out and planning, he went ahead and did it on his own.

The only decent thing Bear had done was give Suzanne Nick's name and number so she could call a week later and tell him that Bear had taken her boss for close to two hundred thousand. The good news was that their plan had worked and the old man continued his reckless ways. The bad news was that Bear had split town without saying a word, which seemed pretty risky considering he was on paper for the next three years. Probably went to Mexico where he wouldn't have to worry about some parole officer making housecalls.

Nick knew all about that headache. As far as pigs went, his P.O. was pretty cool, but the guy was still a pain in the butt. He held Nick's parole papers over his head, constantly reminding him that the smallest screw-up would send him back in to finish his last two years. And the home invasion he had planned was more than a little mistake. It would earn him an additional five-to-ten on top of the two. That was not an option. Nick would never go back.

He considered calling the whole thing off. Maybe it wasn't worth the risk. Nick had missed the first seven years of his only son's childhood, precious years he would never get back, and he wasn't going to miss anymore. In the past four months he'd seen glimpses of the father he could be, if only he stayed out of prison. How could he risk missing another seven? Nicky deserved better than that. But getting a crappy, low-paying, idiotic job wasn't much of an option either. What kind of role model would he be if he could barely afford to take his son out for a Happy Meal? He needed money and he needed it now. He would just have to be extra careful.

The dashboard clock read 7:40. Olsen was late. He should have been out of the parking lot ten minutes ago. Instead of getting worked up about the delay, Nick counted his blessings. The sun had set and it would be difficult for the old man to spot him.

Nick didn't have to wait much longer. Without checking his surroundings, Olsen unlocked his Beemer and slid his leather overcoat across the backseat. After stroking his bushy gray goatee, he plopped into the driver's seat, briefcase and all.

Just the sight of the treasured briefcase made Nick's imagination run wild. There was no question whether or not he would do this. An easy target with a huge payoff. What more could he ask for?

Not wanting to spook him, Nick gave Olsen a few seconds head start. It was okay if he lost him for a moment or two. Nick knew the route Olsen would take and knew he wouldn't deviate from it. All that mattered was that Nick arrived at the house either before, or exactly when, the fat man pulled in.

Nick was stopped three cars behind Olsen's when they reached the traffic signal marking the halfway point. After slipping on his black leather gloves, Nick opened the glovebox and pulled out his gun. The thirty-eight wasn't in the best condition, and possession of it could land him back in the pen, but the reassuring feel of the hard metal in his hand gave him the confidence he was lacking. For this kind of job he should really have a partner, but he had to do it alone. As an ex-con on parole, he couldn't risk trusting anyone. He'd made that mistake with Bear and wouldn't make it again. And if that idiot had been able to do this on his own, then there was no reason for Nick to doubt his own ability to pull it off.

Without fail, Olsen drove three blocks down and pulled into the McDonald's drive-thru. Nick knew the slob would order three Big Macs, two large fries, a large strawberry shake, an apple pie, and a caramel sundae. He also knew that, judging by the cars ahead of Olsen, it would take six to eight minutes for him to get his food and reenter traffic. Plenty of time for Nick to get to the house and decide what course of action to take.

As he made his way through Olsen's sparsely populated neighborhood, Nick hoped he wouldn't have to use the gun. He didn't want to hurt, let alone kill, anyone. It wasn't his style, but prison had taught him an important lesson in life: Sometimes you have to be violent to survive. If it came down to him or Olsen, he wouldn't hesitate to pull the trigger.

The original plan had called for Bear to hide in the garage and have Nick tail the Beemer. Once it pulled into the driveway and then the garage, where the fat man parked it every night, Nick would race onto the property and block the garage so Olsen couldn't pull out. Now that Nick was flying solo, he would have to improvise.

He wished he knew which route Bear had taken, but wishing would get him nowhere. He had to act soon. If he tried driving in behind the Beemer, Olsen would be sure to spot him and could easily close the garage door before Nick could slip inside. If Nick hid in the garage, he would be without a quick escape and he'd have to worry about the guy jumping back into his car and driving away if he smelled something fishy. And that was only if he could get inside the garage. Suzanne said the code still worked, but who knew how accurate that info was.

Before another minute ticked off, Nick made his decision. He pulled onto Olsen's street, passed the house, did a U-turn, and parked directly across from the driveway that divided the eight-foot-high wall surrounding the property. Although the neighborhood was definitely upper class, the houses were so spread out that Nick didn't have to worry about any nosy neighbors wondering what his beater was doing there.

With five minutes left to get into position, Nick tucked the pistol into the waistband of his jeans and eased out of the car. Acting as if he had business being there, he sauntered across the street and entered Olsen's lushly landscaped property. The house was to his right, and directly before him stood the attached three-car garage. He hurried over and slid open the small remote on the wall. Punching in Suzanne's code, knowing in his heart that it wouldn't work, Nick was shocked when the door rumbled open. Before it rose halfway, he slipped inside, knocked loose the automatic light, and hit the switch that lowered the door.

Having forgotten a flashlight and not wanting to turn on the garage's fluorescent lights, Nick waited for his eyes to adjust to the darkness. When he heard the unmistakable sound of a car pulling into the driveway, Nick backed against the side wall and ducked behind some barrels. He remembered to slip on his black ski mask just as the garage door began to rise.

The piercing headlights illuminated the garage, allowing Nick to see he was hiding behind two plastic trashcans. Peering through the small opening between the blue cans and the wall, Nick saw the tail end of the BMW pulling in. He also noticed the electric gate sliding shut, something he had never noticed before. In all the days he had staked out the house, with Bear and without him, he had never once seen the gate closed. He hadn't even realized there was a gate, but thinking back he did remember walking across its track. Why Olsen decided to close it now was beyond him, but Nick guessed it was a good thing. Instead of fretting about having to jump over it when he left, he thought about how much more secure and isolated it made the house from the outside. Now, he needn't worry about some Good Samaritan spotting him and calling the cops.

When the car's engine and headlights turned off, Nick pulled out the thirty-eight. Nick gathered his nerves as the garage door closed, further cutting them off from the rest of the world. Now was the crucial moment. As soon as that car door opened and closed again, he would spring up and take control of the situation. No more hiding, no more waiting.

The old man seemed to be taking a long time getting out of the car. Was he on his cell phone? That would be no good. If Olsen got out of the car while still on the phone, Nick was screwed. He couldn't make a move unless he knew a phone wasn't in play, but at the same time he couldn't risk being seen just to see what the delay was.

Five torturous seconds ticked away before the car door creaked open. Nick strained his ears but he heard nothing. Although Olsen wasn't talking on the phone, he could be listening to someone else. The fat man's dress shoes clicked on the cold concrete and then the door slammed shut. Still no talking. Nick had to act. If the old man was on the phone, he'd signal for him to turn it off, and if the guy tried something squirrelly, Nick would deal with him, snag that briefcase and run like hell.

Before Olsen took another step, Nick popped up. He had worried for nothing. The briefcase was in hand, but no phone.

Nick pointed the gun at Olsen's head, trying to still his jumping nerves. "Hold it right there."

The guy didn't even flinch. He slowly turned to face Nick, the Beemer between them. Olsen was smiling.

"Hold it right there."

"I heard you the first time."

If the car hadn't been in the way, Nick would have slapped the smug bastard. "Put the briefcase on the hood and slide it over."

"But the paint. Surely you wouldn't want me to scratch it."

"Are you serious? Put the goddamn briefcase on the car!"

"Calm down, Son. You don't want to use that."

"I will."

"No, you won't."

"Yes, I will!"

A soft voice from the opposite corner startled Nick. "Not if you want to live."

Without taking the gun off the old man, Nick glanced to his right. Dressed in black, barely recognizable in the dark, Suzanne was crouching behind Olsen's other car, a pistol pointed at his head.

Nick was so frustrated and upset he could barely speak. "What the hell are you doing?"

"What does it look like?"

"It looks like you're pointing that thing at me. Put it down."

"Now why would she want to do that?"

Nick turned his attention back to Olsen. The smile was maddening. "I'll shoot you."

"No you won't, Nicholas. You'll put down your gun and realize you made a very bad mistake coming here."

The old man knew his name. Knew Nick was in the garage. Suzanne had been waiting for him. She had set him up.

When he turned his gun on Suzanne, he heard Olsen move. He looked over at the fat man, who now had another gun trained on him.

Unwilling to give up his only chance at salvation, Nick fiercely held the gun, moving it from Olsen to Suzanne and back again. "What is this crap? You were helping me. What happened? Did he find out? Make you do this?"

"Are you really that stupid?" She stood and walked around the trunk of the Jag. "Not even Bear was that stupid. Now put down your gun."

"Do as she says. Shooting you will give me little pleasure, and it will make quite a mess, which I really have no interest in cleaning."

Nick couldn't speak, but he continued moving the gun from one target to the other.

"Come on, Nick," Suzanne said. "Put it down. You really think I'd give you a working gun?"

Nick looked at the piece and then back at her. She was heading toward Olsen with her gun lowered. Nick had never used the gun. When Bear had given it to him, he hid it away, automatically assuming that it functioned. He never once thought about trying it, and it wasn't as if he could take it to the firing range.

Unable to lower the gun, Nick continued to aim at Olsen. "I'll put mine down when he puts his down."

"Now that's not very smart, Nicholas."

"Quit calling me that, you fat bastard."

"That's not very nice. Set the gun down and, while you're at it, why don't you take off your mask and get comfortable."

Suzanne switched on the overhead light. Nick was sickened when she slid her slight frame against the man's bulging side. Nick couldn't imagine what an attractive girl like her would want with a man twice her age and three times her weight. Must be his money. But that still didn't explain why she had tricked him. Had Bear's departure upset her and sent her into the arms of this guy?

"Okay, this is getting very tedious. If you insist on forcing me to shoot you, I'd better use this one," Olsen said, switching guns with Suzanne.

If Nick was to act, now was his chance. With the guns exchanging hands, Nick took aim at the side of Olsen's head and pulled the trigger. He squeezed it again. And again. And again. Nothing happened.

"Now will you put it down?" Olsen raised the silenced pistol. "I really didn't invite you here just to shoot you."

Nick dropped the worthless gun and pulled off his mask. "Let me go. I didn't do anything. This is entrapment."

Suzanne smiled as she ran her hand over Olsen's protruding belly. "We're not cops, so entrapment doesn't mean all that much to us. If you'd like to call the police and tell them about it, I'd be more than happy to let you use my phone." She dug through her purse and pulled out a cell phone. She held it out to him. "I'm sure they'd agree with you and lock us up. They wouldn't question why you were on another's man property without his permission. They also wouldn't wonder what an ex-felon is doing with a firearm."

Nick shook his head at the phone and asked them what they wanted.

"We merely desire your presence," Olsen said, "and we didn't think you'd accept our request."

"But why? What do you want?"

"To show you something. Come with us. Go ahead, Nicholas. Follow Suzanne."

With no option but to do as he was told, Nick trailed Suzanne through the laundry room and into the kitchen. He considered trying to grab her and use her as a shield, but he could feel Olsen's cannon pressing against his back.

"You still haven't told me why. I didn't do anything to you. I don't even know you." Nick watched Suzanne's hips sway as she led them down a long hallway.

"Nicholas, my boy, you are really in no position to demand an explanation."

"Or anything else for that matter," Suzanne added.

"But I'm feeling generous. The truth is that I'm a big reality TV buff. Problem is, the quality of shows they give us. Go ahead," Olsen said, urging Nick into the room Suzanne had entered.

The guy wasn't lying. From the looks of it, he had himself his own little movie studio. Nick counted over twenty screens and a wall full of recording equipment in this room alone.

"The mindless programs they call entertainment are insulting to my intelligence. Shows about love, infatuation, infidelity, sex. Shows about cliques, pacts, alliances, betrayals. Garbage. All garbage."

Suzanne hit a switch that blanked out all the screens.

Nick asked, "So what's your brilliant idea? What do you have that Hollywood hasn't thought of?"

"A glimpse into man's true spirit."

"What do I have to do?"

"Spend the next three months in my guestroom, just on the other side of that door." Olsen pointed at the metal door Suzanne stood next to.

"What's the catch?"

"There is none."

"And if I refuse?"

"What do you think the gun's for, Nicholas?"

Nick searched their faces for some clue. He knew there was more to the story but he had no idea what it was. "Three months? And then you just let me go? No cops?"

"You have my word. Now if you would be so kind to give Suzanne your car keys, we'll park your car in the garage so you don't get towed."

"How thoughtful." Nick threw his keys at Suzanne.

"Now, now, Nicholas. Be a sport."

Nick wouldn't look at him.

"That's fine. I've had enough of your uncivil company." Olsen motioned toward the door. "Go ahead, Suze."

The door swung open, revealing a long corridor with another metal door at the end of it. Nick walked the hallway, not surprised when the door slammed shut behind him. When he came to the far end of the hallway, he called out in frustration, "And how exactly am I supposed to get in?"

A loud click answered his question. Nick pushed open the door and stepped into the dark chamber. The second he was clear of the door, it slammed shut behind him, the lock loudly snapping into place.

Assuming the cameras were equipped with audio, Nick said, "So you're going to see if I'm scared of the dark. 'Fraid not, big guy. You'll have to do better than that."

The lights turned on, momentarily blinding him. Nick squinted and saw he was in a rather large, but otherwise ordinary, guestroom. There was no dungeonmaster with whips and chains, no rabid dog, no bed of roaches. Just a large, windowless room with a single bed against one wall, a couch across from it, and a toilet and sink in the far corner. If Olsen got his jollies watching grown men taking a crap on camera, then maybe this wasn't going to be as bad as he thought.

Nick heard a low moan coming from the couch. With his eyes now adjusted to the light, he saw that someone was sitting there looking at him. The unclothed man rose to his feet, his emaciated body tottering on spindly legs.

Over a loudspeaker, Olsen said, "You're not being very polite, Nicholas. You could at least say hello."

Nick wasn't sure which development he detested more: sharing the room with some freak or being subjected to Olsen's smug comments. "Didn't know I was getting a roommate."

"I thought you'd be happy. You haven't seen each other in quite some time."

Nick stared across the room. Olsen couldn't be serious. Nick had never seen this person before. Bear was a solid two hundred pounds. This poor soul with his protruding ribs and bloated stomach couldn't weigh more than a hundred.

"True, he looks a little worse for wear, but that's no reason to ignore him."

The bearded man inched closer. He held something shiny in his hand. His right hand. His bony right hand with the shamrock and swastika tattooed across its back. The same exact tattoo Nick had spent hours working on between count times.

"I know Bear is happy to see you. He hasn't had a thing to eat in over—what is it?—seven days. And that doesn't include the eighty days prior in which he was given a mere thousand calories."

Eighty-seven days. A couple shy of Olsen's deadline. "Stop right there," Nick ordered his old cellmate.

Bear didn't stop. There was only five feet between them. He pointed the knife at Nick's chest.

"What's it going to be, fellows? Who's going to make it to see tomorrow? Bear, you'll finally get to eat and in a few days have your freedom. Nicholas, you'll have three months to wonder who your final meal will be. Have at it, boys, tape is rolling."

The Thief

Jennifer Busick

Excuse me. Yeah, I have the window. Hah, yeah, and the emergency exit door. Lucky me, right? Guess that's what I get for arriving late.

You seem pretty intent on that legal pad. May I ask what it is you're doing? Really? That's fascinating! Writing what? Oh, well, I don't mean to pry. But tell me, why won't you discuss it?

I see. Now that—that is really interesting. In fact, I should have guessed that, because I've known others who have had that very experience. No, oh no, not other writers. Really, you'd be surprised.

It could happen to anyone.

"Morale is in the toilet," the man behind the desk said, from the comfort and security of his high-backed leather chair. "I've had to cut the work force by forty percent. Bottom line, see? Do you have any idea what kind of return venture capitalists expect? I produce, or it's my head. Same goes for the people who work for me. Sure, the hours are long—mandatory overtime and double-backs, all at straight time, with no shift differential. That's all I can afford. If they don't like it, they can find another job. Or try to. Blamed good thing I was able to keep the union out!

"Look, this has been going on for a year. Production is suffering. Quality is suffering. Clients are howling. And nothing I do seems to make any difference. The workers just

299

don't know what I'm going through. If I can't show a profit, I'm sunk."

He kept talking, and I let him. After all, that's what I do.

"Anyway," he said, "I talked to my buddy Dwight over at CallaCo, and he recommended you. Said last year he was really in a fix, same way, tried everything, and nothing helped—until he talked to you. Said within six months, everything was better. Workers quit complaining, quit calling in sick. Quality didn't get any better, but then, it didn't get any worse. Dwight said he just upped quotas, so he could throw out the bad product. He gave me your number. Said you're a, what is it? Motivator, facilitator, something like that?"

I shrugged. "Something like that."

"So what is it exactly that you do?"

"My work is deeply personal. I'll get to know each of your employees. Every last one. I'll find out what really motivates them, what they really care about, and I'll channel their motivations so that they become better workers." A vague description, but corporate types are always more interested in results than methods.

He nodded. "Sounds good. So you can make them happier about their jobs?"

I shrugged. "When I'm finished, they'll be willing workers."

His head was still nodding, like a bouncing rubber ball. "Good, good. How long will it take?"

"CallaCo had three hundred workers, and took me fifteen months. You have a hundred and fifty—"

"Sixty-two. Hundred and sixty-two."

"So let's say eight months."

"Good. Good." His pen was in his hand, a fat black fountain pen with gold trim. A man's pen. "Here's your copy of the contract." He scratched the pen across the bottom of it and pushed it toward me.

"And my fee," I said.

"What is it? Half now, half in eight months?"

"Yes."

The pen scratched again, signing the check, which he also handed to me.

Plagiarism? No, that's not what I'm talking about. Plagiarism is just misrepresented authorship. I'm talking about actually taking something.

Well, it's like this. You said you don't like to talk about stories you're working on, because you might lose them somehow, the inspiration, the intensity, the power—that is what you said?

I know exactly how that is.

I hadn't had a girl in a while, so I sat in my car and watched when second shift let out, until I saw one I liked. Not obese, but carrying a little too much in the hips, perhaps. Not ugly, but obviously no genius with makeup or hair. No rings. No baby seat in her car. Very, very likely.

She went straight to a bar. Jackpot! I sat outside for fifteen minutes, and followed her in.

The place was a real dive—early garage sale decor, no two chairs that matched. Some dude with an overactive appetite and an underactive thyroid sprawled in front of a video poker machine with his fat hams spilling over two bar stools. Cheap paneling covered half the walls; the rest were chalky plaster under a layer of Bud advertisements and curling green paint.

It took me a minute to find the girl. She slouched at the bar, shoving chips in her mouth between alternate draws on a cigarette and a long-necked beer bottle, intent on the TV in the corner. I sat down three seats away from her and studied the television. Some banal sitcom. Man, I hate sitcoms. They drive me berserk.

She laughed, so I laughed. I ordered a beer and sipped it. And then she made my job a *whole* lot easier.

"I like Molson's, too," she said, so softly I wasn't sure I heard her. Had I ordered a Molson? I had picked a name from the chalkboard over the bar, pretty much at random. I'm really not a drinker; have to keep my wits.

I smiled at her. "Well, let me buy you one," I said. I motioned to the bartender, and moved over next to her.

"You're new," she said.

"Not really," I replied. "I was on third shift over at Calla-Co, but then I got on second. So now I'm off work, and I can't go home to sleep!"

She laughed. "You'll get over it. You know, I had a friend at CallaCo."

"Really? Who?"

"Pam Trainor. You know her?"

"Yeah, she works in the QC lab."

"Yeah, she does! I haven't talked to her in forever. How's she doing?"

"Oh, fine, I guess," I said. "We're not close."

"Oh."

"I'm Adam," I said. I always start with "A," and go straight through the alphabet. That way, I don't repeat myself right off, and people don't get wise.

"Becky," she said.

I smiled. Becky turned out to be a real talker. Easy—in more ways than one.

Speaking of talking—you know, I would think a writer would talk more. You're a tough nut to crack. Most people are so glad to have anybody take an interest in them, so happy to have someone listen, that they just spill their guts right off. I would think a storyteller would have plenty to say. You're the first person I've ever met who insisted that I keep talking. Really, you should tell me a little about yourself.

It's just not the same, is it? Telling all your stories on paper, I mean. In a way, it's almost like telling them to yourself. Don't you ever just talk about things? I mean, what does a writer do all day? Come on, tell me something. What's the best story you ever wrote?

I've never heard of that magazine. So what was the story about? What do you mean, you can't really explain it? No, thanks—there's no need to send me a copy. I'm really not much of a reader. I just never got a thrill out of reading, the way I do out of hearing a story told by the person it matters to.

What was that? Oh, my experience. Yeah, that.

Well, it works this way.

The other thing I never do is two women in a row. Sometimes that's tricky, depending on the male/female ratio, but in this case I had a good balance, heavily favoring men. Women talk, see, they get concerned about other women, they start asking questions and linking things together. With men you're less likely to run into that.

The guy I visited the second day was Gary. After work, Gary went home, argued with his wife, and went off to his shed out back, where he had a wood shop. I ambled over from a neighbor's yard, said I was a visiting relative named Bob, and struck up a conversation. Pretty soon we were sharing a couple of beers, sitting in these really nice chairs Gary had made there in his shop. Once again, Gary was easy.

"My dad taught me woodworking," he said. He gestured around the shop at his ongoing projects and the tools hung on pegboard. "Most of these tools were his. Taught me hunting, fishing. I had six older sisters, so Dad and I went off together a lot by ourselves, to get away from all that nagging."

I laughed.

Gary started on his second beer. "I took my wife hunting once. That was before we got married. She said she wanted to go. I dunno why, some girl thing. Anyway, she doesn't have a gun, she's not interested in shooting anything, just wants to sit up in the deer stand with me. I said okay. Just the once. So we're up there in the deer stand, everything's quiet, and what do you think she does?"

I shrugged. "What?" I was starting to get that buzz—not from the beer, I told you, I really don't drink much—but that feeling, that excitement, when people are telling me their stories.

"Oh, take a wild guess."

"She wants to make out?"

"No! Not even that. She takes out a *Bride* magazine! *Bride* magazine, can you believe it? Starts riffling through the pages. *Bride* magazine!"

I laughed, loud and hard and long. Why *Bride* magazine is a bad thing to have in a deer stand, I have no idea, but Gary seems to find it appalling. Inside I'm high, my heart is really racing, I feel like the king of the world. "So did you ever take her hunting again?"

"Did I what?" he asks, and I know I've done my job. That was one of Gary's best stories, and it's mine now. He barely remembers it, barely remembers that his dad taught him hunting and fishing and woodworking. What was a great story, the stuff and substance of Gary's life, the thing that made him a whole man and not some kind of robot, belongs to me. But not all, not yet, so I keep him talking.

He tells me stories about his kids, his cousins, his sisters. He talks to me until the only thing we haven't talked about is his job, and television. That's all I leave to folks, see, when

I do that kind of work. I mean, when all you have to look forward to is an endless stream of insipid sitcoms—you know those things are all alike? I mean, they recycle the scripts, have been since *I Love Lucy.* Why would you want to leave work?

I don't know, exactly. I just know I've always been able to do it. Took a while to figure out, but I love to listen to people. I live on other people's stories, I always have.

People used to tell me things, and I'd get excited, and want to try it too. They would tell me how much they enjoyed this or that—like hunting. And I'd say, "I'd like to do that sometime!" and they'd say, "Sure," and then it would never happen. We'd never do it. And I would ask later, and they had completely forgotten about enjoying it, had never done it again.

So I would ask what they did instead. What new thing they were interested in. And they didn't have anything new. They had stuff they'd done all along, but it was like a piece had been taken out of their lives. So they'd say, "Oh, I haven't gone to a monster truck rally in ages. But I have tickets for the WWF on Friday!" And they'd tell me about that, and I'd find out later they didn't even go.

That's how I figured it out. It's like your stories. All the excitement, the intensity, the thrill—I've got that. I don't hunt. I don't actually do any of this stuff. I never have to. I know how exciting it is to be on a roller coaster, or finish a triathlon, or do volunteer work. It's all in the stories.

So where are you headed? Where's home? Indy, hey? Home of the 500. I talked to a guy once who bought tickets every year. He was there when Foyt won his fourth. What a story that was! May was his boss's busy season, though, so he needed to give it up to keep his job. So I guess you could say I did him a favor.

What are you, taking notes? Gonna write some of this down? Might as well. I never will.

One of my best jobs, that I'm really proud of, was this older lady. They don't take to me, somehow, so they're always a challenge. I think they have a natural suspicion about young men who take an interest in them. So it's best if I can get them to take an interest in me somehow, or if I can find a way in with them that's not suspicious.

I'd been watching this old woman—she was maybe sixty—for a month. Finally, she took a day off work. She was waiting on a plumber, and he came and left, so maybe an hour later I walked up to her door and rang the bell. Told her I was polling the precinct for the Democrats. Good move! She was *so* thrilled to see a young person taking an interest in politics. And that canvassing gig—it's great! People agree up front to answer your questions. So I don't use it too much, but I always keep some of those little forms handy, just in case. Anyway, she invites me in and serves me cookies and soda, and we sit down to talk a little politics.

She answered all the questions—how did you vote in the last election, all that. And then she says:

"You know, it's been probably two months since I talked to Lee. What did he end up doing about that poor girl who worked for him?"

That caught me off guard. Obviously I'm supposed to know who Lee is, and what the problem was with that poor girl. And the question was so specific—nothing I could say yes or no to, nothing I could wave off and say, "Oh, you know." I actually had to think for a minute. She must have caught my hesitation. "I'm not sure," I said.

"Well, who gave you the forms?"

I realized Lee must be with the Democrats some way, probably precinct committeeman. Man, I should've known she'd know the precinct committeeman! Who gave me the forms? "Lee did," I said. "I didn't see any girl."

"Ah," she says, but I can see she doesn't trust me now. "Where did you say you live?"

She probably knows everybody for blocks around, so I'm trying to think of a street far enough away, but not too far. "Over on Queen Street."

"Which house is it?"

"The brick one nearest the park," I say, hoping desperately that there *is* a brick house on Queen Street, somewhere near a park.

"Sims Park, or Sarah Douglas Park?"

"Sims."

"Well, now, I don't see how any house on Queen Street is going to be closer to Sims Park than it is to Sarah Douglas Park. Are you north or south of the middle school?"

"I'm not exactly sure," I said. "I haven't lived around here long." I laughed. "I thought polling the precinct would help me get to know the place a little better."

She stood up, and I could see she was about to wish me good day, and I hadn't got a single thing out of her yet, except some voting information that most people can live without anyway. I was really sweating. I looked around her living room in desperation. It was super formal, no television, flocked wallpaper, religious pictures on the walls. Nothing personal at all, not even a family portrait. But next to an armchair was this really bizarre looking ashtray made out of horseshoes welded together. "That is quite an ashtray," I said, and acted like I was going to stand up.

"Why yes," she said. "My husband made that when he was in high school. Doesn't really go with the decor, but I've always been partial to it."

She sat back down, and I had her.

Me? I'm going on to Detroit. Company there wants me to head off a strike.

Well, it was nice meeting you. Nice to meet a kindred spirit like—what? Well, same to you, buddy! Think you're better than me, do you? "I give people's stories back." Well, ain't you something?

Waitaminute. Let me see that pad. There was some stuff in what I told you that I wanted to keep. Seems like I'm having trouble remembering… I mean it, give it here! Hey! Those are my *stories!*

We Wish You a Merry Christmas

Mary Aldrin

Jim donned his uniform, then hitched his belt around his waist, noting that he had to fasten it one notch looser these days. He was going to have to start exercising. His leisurely security patrols through the department store bore no resemblance to the activity level he'd maintained on the force. And tonight would be no different—just another ho-hum evening.

Lydia's pale face appeared in the mirror beside him. Even after eighteen years of marriage, she was still the pretty blonde slip of a girl he'd married. The only difference was that the gentle curve of her smiling mouth had gradually become a straight line of resignation.

"I didn't know you were working tonight," she said.

"I thought I told you. Guess it slipped my mind," he said with a shrug. "I'm covering swing shift for Cooper. He has a wedding to go to."

Lydia sighed. "So do we."

"Is that today?"

"Yes." Another sigh.

"Sorry, babe. I know you hate to go alone, but the kids'll be there, and I won't be missed. Not by Bart anyway." Her holier-than-thou brother, father of the bride, was on the force, and knew why Jim and three fellow officers had hastily taken early retirement. Bart hadn't been touched by the scandal, but Jim didn't believe he was pure as the proverbial driven snow. Nobody was. Everybody was on the take in one way or another.

Jim turned and rubbed Lydia's upper arms. She looked down, undoubtedly to hide tears. "People will probably think you were ashamed to come," she said.

An expletive came to mind, but instead, he said, "Nonsense," and hugged her. "You'll tell them I had to work. And it's true. I can't afford to pass up overtime."

He felt her sigh again. "If only…" She mumbled into his chest.

Those two little words spoke volumes. If only he'd fought back when he was caught up in the investigation rather than resigning, he wouldn't have ended up with a substantially reduced pension and no medical insurance. They wouldn't have had to sell their nice, big house in the heights and move into this tiny bungalow. The kids wouldn't have had to change school systems. He wouldn't have to work as a lousy security guard at not much more than minimum wage, and work swing and night shifts in order to get a damn twenty-five cent shift differential. If only…

Of course, Lydia didn't know that he *couldn't* have fought it. He could never admit that to her, though. He wouldn't be able to stand the hurt and disappointment in her eyes. He'd seen too much of that over the years. But she just didn't understand the ways of the world.

"I know, I know," he said in reply to her unspoken lament. "But things'll be okay again, you'll see. As for tonight, you and the kids'll have a great time. And I promise, on my honor, I'll go to Bart's New Year's party with you this year."

She nodded and pulled away. "I'd better let you go," she said as she reached up to straighten his tie. "It's after 3:30 and you don't want to be late."

He smiled and kissed her.

Jim went to his daughter's room to say goodbye and tell her to stick by her mom tonight. If Katie wasn't out with friends, she was usually in her room. But she wasn't there. And she wasn't downstairs either. Neither were the two boys. Out making mischief of some kind, no doubt, he thought with a smile. Lydia worried about them and their teenage pranks, and she thought all three kids were insolent. But they just had spunk like him, that's all. And a lucky thing they *were* more like him than like their mother. Much as he loved Lydia, he wouldn't want his kids to be soft and sentimental, or overly moral. It just didn't pay in today's world.

When he got to the mall, Jim parked outside the shipping/receiving area behind the store, then let himself in the back door. He punched the time clock and headed to the security office. It was a small, windowless room, distinguished only by a scrawny silver Christmas tree and a dozen TV monitors linked to the various security cameras. Each monitor rotated among three or four different cameras, the images on the screens changing automatically every ten seconds. The guard could manually override the system if he spotted something that needed a closer look. One of the younger guards was sitting at the console.

"Hey, Vinny," Jim said.

"Hey, Jim," the young man said, leaning back in his chair and stretching. "Wanna take over here so I can do a walk-through? I been sittin' on my ass for over two hours. I need to stretch my legs."

"Sure, go ahead," Jim said.

Vinny vacated his seat in the leather chair on wheels, and Jim settled in, giving the monitors a quick scan. He saw that Vinny had altered the position of the camera in the Ladies Lingerie dressing room. That camera was in a stationary position, trained on the corridor between the cubicles. But if you altered the angle a little, the camera caught part of the mirror in the farthest cubicle. And if the woman inside was standing in just the right place, and if she was trying on bras, you might get a nice knocker shot. Jim used the little lever to readjust the camera to its intended position. He was no prude, but there was a big difference between appreciating *Playboy* or *Hustler* and playing peeping Tom. He'd never rat on the guys who did it; after all, he might have done the same in his younger days. But now, the thought of some horny little bastard getting an eyeful of Lydia or Katie pissed him off. One of these days, he'd see if he could remount or do something else to the camera to prevent the angle from being changed.

Beginning after the dinner hour, the other security guards started leaving. By ten o'clock, everything was locked up and everybody was gone except Jim. He smiled. It was now his favorite time of swing shift—the two hours he spent alone in the store prior to the night guard's arrival, and the time he did his "shopping." Not long after he'd started the job, he'd realized there was an additional perk to working the back turns. The pay scale became $8.50 an hour and all you could steal.

The store only did inventory twice a year, and there was always what was referred to as "shrinkage," merchandise lost to shoplifters... mostly. If Jim didn't go overboard, he could take whatever he wanted, as long as it could be carried out in a double-handled shopping bag. Management would look askance at shrinkage that involved big items a customer couldn't have gotten out of the store unnoticed. But anything else was fair game.

The first time Jim had done it, he'd taken a classy coat for Lydia and top-of-the-line CD players for the kids. He'd always spoiled them with gifts, so he'd been taken by surprise when Lydia questioned the cost. He should have thought of that since his income was way less than it used to be. He'd quickly recovered and explained that the items were all clearance sale priced, and with his twenty percent employee discount, he just couldn't pass up the bargains.

This satisfied Lydia, but after that, Jim was more careful, and mostly took things for himself. He'd already greatly supplemented his home workshop with new power tools. When he brought them home, though, he'd get rid of the box and rub a little grease on the tools so they'd look used. And he'd gotten himself new fishing and camping equipment, which Lydia would never notice mixed in with his other stuff. There were plenty of other things Jim had his eye on, but he'd take his time collecting them. Wouldn't want to take too much too quickly and raise suspicions at the store or at home.

Today he planned to do his Christmas shopping. He waited until 10:30 to be sure no one returned for some forgotten item. He put the cameras in the departments he'd be visiting on pause to avoid capturing his actions on tape, then strutted out of the security office.

The dimmed security lighting in the store didn't make it gloomy. In fact, it seemed to make the artistically hung garland and towering decorated trees sparkle all the more. It put Jim in a festive mood, and he whistled *We Wish You a Merry Christmas* as he made his way to his first stop, Leather Goods.

His son Mark had been hankering for a particular pair of black leather cowboy boots. Jim, who had the same shoe size, tried on half a dozen different pairs before deciding for sure on the boots. He put the box containing Mark's gift into a black plastic garbage bag he'd lifted from Janitorial Services, then checked out the belts. Wide belts with big, gaudy buckles were all the rage among Katie's friends. He selected one in soft beige leather that had a fancy gold buckle, and slipped that into the garbage bag as well.

He was about to leave Leather Goods when he noticed a rack of new arrivals. One section had leather vests, and he decided to get himself a gift, too. He picked a snazzy tan number. He turned back and forth in front of the mirror. This was the one for Jim. If he sucked in his stomach, the vest made his pecs look bigger and more solid than they really were. The vest was actually too small and felt tight around his chest, but it was the only one like it on the rack, and it would spur him to lose weight after the holidays, so he took it.

After the vest was tucked into the bag, Jim went to Fine Jewelry. He'd been anxious to shop there, but hadn't been able to so far. The glass display cases and cabinets were kept locked after closing, and Security didn't have keys to them. He'd been waiting for the clerk to slip up and fail to lock them, and today might just be the day. As always, Jim had kept an eye on that department's video image at closing time. The cute little clerk had been distracted because she was bantering with Vinny. It looked to Jim like she'd forgotten to lock a case.

Jim went behind the counter and pushed on one of the sliding doors under the register. Sure enough, it slid right open. It contained the better watches. The cabinet next to it had women's gold chains. He'd only take one watch and one chain. He wasn't greedy.

He left the department and went back to Janitorial Services to borrow a pair of rubber gloves. Highly unlikely there'd ever be a criminal investigation of the missing items, but no sense leaving his fingerprints inside the cupboard. He went back to Jewelry and looked through the watches, selecting one of the best for his oldest son. It was no Rolex—the department store didn't carry high-end merchandise. But a five-hundred-dollar sports watch was nothing to sneeze at either. It was a far nicer gift than Stevie would ever have asked for.

He tossed the watch into the black trash bag, then examined the gold chains. For Lydia, he picked out a thick, expensive one in tri-colored gold with tiny diamond chips along its length. When she asked him how he could afford such a gift, he'd give her the "on sale plus employee discount" line, and add that he'd wanted to do something special for her for Christmas, and that's why he'd been working so much overtime. In a way, it was true, he thought with a chuckle.

He admired the necklace one last time before closing its box and placing it in the bag with the other gifts. It would look great around Lydia's slim neck.

Jim closed the cases, then grabbed tissue from a box on the counter to wipe the area on the doors that he'd touched when testing them. He returned the gloves to the janitor's closet and went to the security office, where he took the cameras he'd messed with off of pause. He looked at the monitor which covered the back parking lot. Not a car in the area other than his own, and not a soul in sight.

He paused the outdoor camera, then strutted through Shipping and Receiving and opened the service door. He looked around to be sure no one had shown up, then carried the garbage bag containing the booty to his car and placed it in the trunk.

As he reentered the service door, he heard a phone ringing. "Damn!" The only phone that rang at night was in the security office. All other calls were diverted to a recording which informed the caller that the store was closed and gave the store hours. Not many people had the number of the outside line that went directly to security, and it had only rung once after hours in all the time Jim had worked here.

That had been right after he'd taken the job. It had been his boss calling to be sure everything was going okay.

When Jim had first started his shopping excursions, he'd left a walkie-talkie with an open mike next to the phone so he could hear if it rang. But other than that one time, it had never rung again, so Jim had stopped bothering to do that. He shouldn't have gotten so lax.

Maybe it's a wrong number, he thought as he sprinted toward the office. But if it was his boss calling, he'd say he had heard noises out by the shipping/receiving dock and had gone to check it out. It would be the only reason to leave his post. After hours he was supposed to stay put and keep an eye on the monitors. There was no reason to patrol since there was no one in the store and he could see almost everything he needed to on one camera or another. He couldn't even say he'd gone to the restroom since there was a toilet right off the security office.

It wasn't a wrong number, and it wasn't his boss. It was the police. It took Jim a minute to realize that, and comprehend what the officer was saying. "Could you say that again? I... I'm not sure I heard you right."

"There's been a car accident, and we got this number from your wife's wallet. Your family is at Metropolitan Hospital."

"Are they okay?"

The man hesitated briefly. "I wasn't on the scene. I just know they were taken to the hospital for treatment."

"Is it bad? Should I go there now? I mean, I'm the only one on the job here for the next half hour."

"I wouldn't wait," the cop said.

Jim felt an intense tightness in his chest as he scribbled a quick note to leave on the console for the night shift guard. He then raced out of the building and sped to the hospital.

The emergency room smelled of disinfectant and the coppery scent of blood. There were only a handful of people inside. Most of the patients were kids—a sniffling baby, a little boy holding his arm as though it was broken, a teenager pressing a dish towel to his bloody head. And as in most places during the season, soft, piped-in Christmas music permeated the room. It irritated Jim since he now felt anything but festive.

He checked in with the receptionist, who told him she'd let the nurses know he was here. He sat down in one of the orange plastic chairs to wait for what seemed like forever, but was actually less than ten minutes.

A woman who looked too young to be a nurse came out of the double doors marked "Authorized Personnel Only" and called his name. He stood, just a little unsteadily, and followed her into the trauma area. Before they reached the treatment bays, she opened a wooden door. The sign next to the door indicated it was a consultation room.

"Have a seat. The doctor will be with you in a moment."

"Can't I see my wife and kids? I want to be with them."

"The doctor would like to update you on their conditions first."

The room was small. The only furniture consisted of a sofa, a little desk with a chair in front of it and an identical chair next to it. There was no overhead lighting, just the soft glow coming from a shaded lamp on the desk.

Jim sat down next to the desk and immediately started drumming his fingers in impatience, then tapping his foot. After a little while, he felt that if he had to listen to one more minute of *Jingle Bells* or *Silent Night*, he'd lose it. He was just about to leave the room and demand to see his family, when the door opened.

A tall, sallow-faced man with a receding hairline entered. Jim stood and shook hands when the doctor introduced himself. "I'm Dr. Culver, the Trauma Center attending physician."

Jim nodded. "How are they? And when can I see them?"

"Please have a seat," the doctor said and sat down in front of the desk, giving Jim no other choice than to sit down, too.

"Are they okay?" Jim demanded.

The doctor set a small sheaf of papers on the desk. "Let me explain the accident and go over their conditions one at a time."

Jim didn't like the sound of that, but he said nothing else. He concentrated on breathing slowly to ease the increased tightness in his chest.

Dr. Culver cleared his throat. "The police will be able to give you more details, but from what I understand, the accident happened on the interstate. Your son..." The doctor paused and glanced at the top page of the papers on the desk. "Steven was driving. They were behind a truck that was carrying scrap metal. A sheet of metal came loose and fell off the back. It struck your car. It caused Steven to swerve and hit the median. The car behind him couldn't stop and ran in to the back of your vehicle."

Jim shook his head. Poor Stevie would feel like hell about this. But even though he hadn't been driving that long, from what it sounded like, he wasn't at fault. Lydia would blame herself, of course, for letting him drive. He probably begged to, and she had trouble driving in the dark because her night vision wasn't that great. But she'd feel guilty.

Jim snapped back to attention. The doctor continued. "Steven apparently had his arm out the window, his fingers touching the roof of the car. When the metal hit the car, it sliced through his forearm, just above the wrist, completely severing it."

"Jesus," Jim said, feeling queasy. "But... but it can be reattached, can't it? I mean... I know they can do that kind of stuff nowadays."

Dr. Culver nodded slowly. "Yes, that kind of thing is normally possible, provided the appendage isn't too badly damaged and the procedure is done quickly enough, but..."

Jim glanced at his watch to see the time. "Did they get him here quick enough? What time was the accident?"

"His hand was crushed, run over by the vehicle behind, is what the police think. So it isn't possible to reattach it. But let me assure you that there are very fine prosthetic devices available."

"Christ," Jim said, looking again at his watch, but thinking about the sports watch in his trunk and the fact that Stevie no longer had a wrist to wear it on. Jim felt sick to his stomach, and an ache started in his left shoulder and then spread up into his jaw.

He took a deep breath and said, "What about Lydia and Katie and Mark?"

"Mark and your daughter were on the passenger side, the side hit by the trailing vehicle. The back end of that side of the car was accordioned. Mark was in the back seat and I'm afraid the bones in his lower legs were... to use a lay term... shattered. We have our best orthopedic surgeons evaluating him, but with the extent of the injuries, it's unlikely that they'll be able to do much."

"What... what are you saying?"

"They'll probably have to amputate both legs below the knee."

Jim gasped as a picture of Mark formed in his head— Mark in a wheelchair with his legs ending in stumps. And Mark was watching Jim as he strutted in front of a mirror in the Leather Goods department, showing off the pair of shiny new cowboy boots. Jim shook his head to dislodge the image. It was coincidence. That's all it was.

"What... what else?" he asked in a pained voice.

"I am so sorry to deliver this news," Dr. Culver said, reaching over to touch Jim's left arm.

Jim jerked the arm away, then started rubbing it to ease the numbness that had crept into it. "What else?"

The doctor sighed. "Your daughter was in the front seat. Her seat belt prevented her from going through the windshield, but as occasionally happens in a violent collision, the seat belt itself caused internal abdominal injuries."

Jim's stomach turned again and he put his hand against his abdomen. He felt his belt buckle under his palm and thought about the beige leather belt with the gold buckle. Maybe it wasn't coincidence, he thought, and almost vomited. "How bad is she?" he asked through clenched teeth.

"Very bad," the doctor said softly. "Her internal injuries were severe and she lost an excessive amount of blood. She's in surgery right now, but her chances are very slim."

"Oh God, oh Christ," Jim moaned. He was afraid to ask about Lydia. He reached up and touched the base of his neck and thought about the gold necklace. He was afraid he knew what was coming. Her neck was broken and she was paralyzed. He didn't want to hear that, but he forced himself to say, "My wife?"

He learned that Lydia wasn't paralyzed. It was worse than that.

Dr. Culver cleared his throat again. "The sheet metal that hit the car and injured your son... sliced right into the car, and the angle it was at... I'm sorry, but... but be assured it was instantaneous and painless."

Jim's eyes widened. Before him he saw an image of Lydia's head rolling on the ground with the necklace still around her neck. This time, he did vomit. Sweat started pouring off of him, and the tightness inside became an unbearable pressure. It felt like a steel band was tightening around his chest and he knew, even hoped, that his heart was giving out. His last thought before he collapsed on the floor was that he was glad he had taken the vest, too. And the last sound he heard was the piped-in strains of *We Wish You a Merry Christmas*.

THOU SHALT NOT...

Bear False Testimony

Tattletale

Christopher Fisher

"Where are your children, Mr. Sparks?"

The officer stares down at the chair where I sit. But I don't answer him. When he and three sheriff's deputies kicked in the front door just two minutes ago, I didn't even get up from my chair. I haven't said a word since. The officer must think I'm waiting for an attorney, but that's not it. That's not it at all.

"*Where* are your children, Mr. Sparks?" he repeats in a typical East Texas drawl.

I turn away, silent, and watch as two of the deputies start to rearrange the barricade blocking the entrance to the boys' room. The couch and sofa. The dining room table and chairs. The bed, desk, and dresser from my bedroom, even the refrigerator. Everything but this chair. It's all packed tightly in the hallway from wall to wall, from floor to ceiling like an overstuffed storage locker.

The third deputy guards the front door, either to keep me from getting away or to keep Anne from coming in. I see her through the window that overlooks the porch. She's alternating between chewing her hands and sobbing on Stan's shoulder. She called the cops, I guess, after I didn't answer the door when she came to pick up the boys. I'm sure Stan had something to do with it, though. Stan is fond of calling the police.

Anne turns to me, sneering as our eyes meet. Then she screams, her voice muffled by the glass like it's coming from the big Tudor across the street.

"What did you do? What did you do with my children?"

I turn away, thinking her choice of words is rather funny. Six months ago they were *our* kids. But not anymore. Now they don't belong to either of us.

The deputies in the hall work quickly, like rescue workers, but it still takes them a good ten minutes to get through my barricade. They carry the smaller items into the living room and shove the heavier pieces against the walls, opening a narrow, jagged path to the boarded up door of the boys' room

One of them starts working at the boards with a pry bar. I hear the crack of splintering wood, the screech of buried nails being yanked from the oak doorframe. I nailed another layer of board beneath that one. But at the pace they're working they'll be through it in no time. They continue prying and ripping. I can see most of the door now. One of them snaps off the last board with a stiff kick and knocks the door open with his shoulder. I don't even blink as they go inside. I know what they will find.

After a brief moment, they come back out. The officer in front of me puts his hand on his gun before turning to look at them. They both shrug, and one of them says, "Empty. There's no one in there."

The officer returns to me. "Do you *know* where your children are, Mr. Sparks?"

This time I pause. Yes, I can answer that one. I give a careful nod.

"Did someone take your children?"

Tears sting my eyes, and my breath comes in short gasps. I nod again.

"Did you see who it was? Do you know who took your kids?"

I feel a tremor in my top lip, and the words begin to rise. Then my jaw closes tight as I'm hit with the terror that merely thinking the answer is enough. But the name is still there, floating at the back of my throat. Because I want to tell. God, how I want to tell.

I never liked old man Sipes. He never gave me a reason to. The first time we spoke was over the phone, the time he called at 4:30 in the morning to complain about my barking dog. This was before Anne left, and the small yard where we kept the dog was right outside our bedroom window. We hadn't heard a thing all night, so I couldn't understand how the barking—if there was any—could be bothering Sipes, who lived five houses down.

"Go back to bed or go to hell," I told him. "I don't care which."

Ten minutes after I hung up, I heard someone beating on the front door. Then the boys started crying in their room at the other end of the house. I stomped through the living room, ready to throw open the door and strangle the old man with my bare hands. But when I looked through the blinds, I saw two police officers.

Sipes had called the cops on me. Over a dog. He did it again the next night. And the night after that. And though no one else on Sycamore Street ever complained, the police threatened me with a two-hundred-dollar fine for disturbing the peace if I couldn't keep the dog quiet. I could have bought an expensive shock collar. Business was good at the shop back then. But what good is a dog that can't even bark? I gave the dog to my brother Dan.

For two years after that, I didn't hear a peep out of Sipes. Occasionally I'd see him walking his little yipping poodle down the sidewalk, sometimes passing by, sometimes stopping to let the thing crap in my yard. But I never spoke to him.

Not until that afternoon with the boys, just last week.

Sparks Automotive had folded six months before, and Anne had moved out and shacked up with Stan, though our divorce hadn't gone through. Still hasn't, to this day. My sons—Jacob, six, and Tyler, four—were visiting me for the weekend. That Friday afternoon I was replacing the fuel pump in my Dodge while the boys rode their bikes on the sidewalk.

They got away from me for a minute. Happens to the best of us. When I looked up they were down the street in front of the Sipes house, off their bicycles and headed for his porch. I started down there to collect them, but Sipes beat me to it. He stepped out on the porch and yelled, "Git!" Then he chased the boys away with a broom like two stray cats.

It took everything I had to keep from breaking that broom handle over the old man's head. Instead, I gathered the boys and their bikes and said, plenty loud, "Boys, that's just a mean old man."

"And you're a bad father!" Sipes said. "I should call child protection on you for letting them roam around by themselves!"

That got me. I was trying to get custody—I loved my boys—and if Sipes called the authorities on me, it would be the second time in just a few months. Not long after Anne first moved herself and the kids into Stan's place, I went over there to take the boys fishing, and Anne wouldn't let me have them. When I refused to leave, Stan came to the door like he was going to settle it.

I poked two fingers in his chest. "Stan, I've reason enough not to like you. But if you try to keep me from my boys, you'll need a surgeon to put that pretty face back where it used to be."

He didn't step outside and square off with me. Like a *man*. He just deadbolted the door, called the police, and filed a formal complaint. A week later, Anne used that altercation to gain temporary custody of the boys until the hearing, leaving me with only a weekend visit, at her discretion.

Another visit from the police could destroy me in court, so I decided to beat Sipes to the punch, calling the police on *him* for assaulting my kids. All they did was take a report and talk to him, but at least I knew Anne couldn't use the incident against me. Still, Sipes had me fuming, which I guess had a lot to do with what happened later that night.

I always encouraged my boys to work out their problems between themselves, but living with "Stan the Sissy" had an influence. Jacob had started tattling on his younger brother over every little thing.

"Tyler tore a page in my book."

"Tyler opened my backpack."

"Tyler made a *face* at me!"

I'd heard this was normal, but I couldn't help thinking it was Stan rubbing off on him. I figured when Tyler got big enough, he'd get fed up and rattle Jacob's skull for it. But I was getting tired of waiting, sick of seeing the smirk of my wife's lover on the face of my son.

That night, just a few hours after Sipes swept my sons off his porch, Jacob came in the living room with that indignant look on his face. "Daddy, Tyler threw my Thunder Man at the *ceiling fan!*"

I don't know what came over me, or where the idea came from. I pulled Jacob close, held a finger to my lips, and whispered, "Shhh. I wouldn't be tattling if I were you."

Jacob paused, the fire over his abused toy quickly cooling. "Why?"

"You know what happens to tattletales."

He shifted his weight to one foot. "What?"

"That mean old Mr. Sipes might hear you, and you don't want *that*."

"Why not?"

"Because he'll come *get* you, is why not."

"No—he—*won't*! Because my Daddy will beat him up before he gets in the door."

I smiled. "But he doesn't come through the door. He comes in through the ground. Under your bed while you're asleep."

"How's he gonna do that? With a back hole?"

I struggled to keep a straight face. "Oh, no. He doesn't need a backhoe. Because he's really a *ghost*. He's the Devil's nightmare.

"He digs a tunnel from his grave in the cemetery, all the way across town if he has to, clawing at the dirt with his long, yellow nails, crawling through the worms and the maggots until he comes up underneath the bed of the tattle-tale. And then he snatches him and takes him away, back to his grave. And he keeps all the tattletales there with him. In the dark. Deep down in the dirt where no one above ground can hear them screaming."

The house was quiet. I felt a wicked smile melt from my face, hardly believing what I had just said to a six-year-old, wondering why I had enjoyed saying it, in spite of the way it set my neck hairs on end. Jacob gave me a blank look, and I didn't know if he would laugh or cry. Finally he smiled and pointed a tiny finger at me. "I *know* you're joking, Daddy!"

I started to laugh back, hoping that would break the spell for both of us, but from the corner of my eye, at the end of the hall, I saw the Thunder Man toy drop from Tyler's hand and hit the hardwood floor. I had no idea he'd been listen-ing. His little body trembled, and I'm sure that if I hadn't managed a smile right then, he would have wet his pants. But he saw the smile and ran to me, hugging me tight.

I tried to take it back. I laughed and told them it wasn't true. But the look in Tyler's eyes told me it wouldn't help. Some words you just can't take back. Tyler was a believer, and nothing I could say would change his mind. So I just kept laughing and hugging him, trying to lighten the mood. Hoping he'd forget about it in a day or two.

But later that night, the boys woke screaming in their bunk beds, and I had to let them sleep with me. Then the next night, the same thing. I didn't bring up the story again—not even to insist that I had made it all up. I wanted them to forget about it, and that would never happen if I kept reminding them. When Anne came to pick them up Sunday, I could still see the fear in Tyler's eyes. And even a little in Jacob's.

I expected that next week would be a normal five days of repairing cars and waiting for Friday, when I would see my boys again. I'd started working in my driveway, since the bank took my shop, and stayed pretty busy doing odd jobs. Tuesday morning, I started on a transmission that would pay just enough to cover the mortgage. A couple of hours into the job, I crawled out from under the car to stretch. Gazing down the street, along the double row of live oaks and sycamores, I saw Mr. Sipes standing on his manicured lawn, in front of his tidy yellow and white house, just staring at me.

I figured he didn't like me working in the driveway and was cursing under his breath about sinking property values. But as I stared back at him, it wasn't anger I saw. It was... nothing. Like his head was a dried up, hollow gourd with a few dead seeds rattling around inside. I couldn't be sure because of the distance, but I thought I saw a shiny string of saliva dripping from his chin to his white shirt. I huffed and went inside for a sandwich and a beer. When I came back out, Sipes had moved to a chair on his porch where he sat staring at the street until I finished for the day.

I came out the next morning to finish the transmission, half expecting him to still be sitting there on the porch drooling on himself. But he was hobbling past my house with his poodle, that same idiot stare fixed on his face. Ten minutes later he passed by on the way back. Then he came by again. He was trying to get a rise out of me, I figured, so I did my best to ignore him. But he kept walking up and down the sidewalk for almost three hours in the Texas heat, the little dog lagging behind on the leash, its tongue hanging out.

At lunchtime I stood and dusted myself off, watching him come down the sidewalk toward me. As he passed by I said, "Why don't you go inside before you have a stroke, you crazy old fart?" He didn't look at me, just kept walking.

About sunset, I finished and started cleaning up my tools. It occurred to me that I hadn't seen Sipes walk by for a while, and I thought he'd finally given up trying to annoy me. But when I looked at the sidewalk, he was standing there, just staring at the front of my house. The leash in his hand was limp. The dog lay on its side at the old man's feet. Dead. Flies buzzed in the air above it.

"You sick, twisted freak!" I started toward him. He slowly faced his house and hobbled away, dragging the dead dog along the sidewalk by its leash. I walked out to where he had stood, watching to make sure he went inside this time. He did, dragging the stinking dog through the door behind him. When I looked down at where Sipes had been standing, I saw a pile of fat, white maggots squirming on the sidewalk.

For the rest of the night I couldn't get the images of that afternoon out of my mind—especially the maggots. I'd said something in the Sipes story about maggots. And worms. Growing up in the South, it's nearly impossible to avoid going to church now and then. I remembered a preacher who spoke about the "faith of a child." How faith like that could pick up a mountain in Montana and set it down right next to Galveston Bay. Then I remembered the look on Tyler's face, how he had believed so *perfectly* in the Sipes story. And the image of those maggots returned.

Thursday morning the phone rang, and I thought it was my tranny customer asking about her car. I'd forgotten to tell her I was done. But when I picked up the phone, it was Anne.

"What have you been telling the boys?"

I knew what she was going to say. But I tried to play it off. "Come on, baby. Don't I even get a 'hello'?"

"Sure. Hello. What kind of crap have you been telling the boys?"

"Jeez, it was just a *story*. A joke, really."

"Well, it's not funny. They've been having nightmares since Sunday. And Tyler is so afraid of the dark he won't sleep without a flashlight."

That hurt—the thought of my boy huddled beneath his blankets, sweating in terror I had invented. I wanted to punch myself in the face. "I'm sorry, Anne. I didn't mean for him to hear. I only told Jacob to get him to stop tattling like a baby."

"That's another thing! I got a call from the school this morning. Jacob has been telling that story to his friends, and now the whole school is talking about the Sipes trial."

"Well, kids are gonna—" I stopped. "Did you say 'Sipes *trial*'?"

Anne's voice became a hot whisper. "Yes! That old story. What do you think I've been talking about?"

"I, I don't know. I thought—" What did she mean *old story?* I'd made it up just a few days before.

"You of all people should know better than to tell kids about that, if for no other reason than out of respect for Dan."

"Dan? My brother?"

"Yes, *Dan*. Are you drinking? Are you *drunk?*"

I couldn't answer. Everything she said seemed to destroy the laws of physics, sloping the floor of the house upward, slanting the walls toward each other. Or maybe away from each other.

"You'd better *believe* all this is coming up in the hearing!" she said. The phone clicked.

I dialed Dan's number. All I got was a recording, saying the number was no longer in service. That couldn't be right. I'd just talked to him a few days before. I felt those sloping walls closing in on me, and the house started to feel strange, like someone else's home. I grabbed my keys to go for a drive.

Outside, I felt it again. Everything in the yard was the same, but *different*. I heard a bark behind me and turned to the back gate. My dog, which hadn't been mine for two years, stood behind the fence, wagging its tail. I told myself that maybe I *had* been drinking too much. Maybe Dan had gone out of town and left the dog with me this morning, and I hadn't heard him knock. I sleep heavy on a few beers. But part of me felt I was just a shadow on a black and white screen, with an overdubbed Rod Serling talking about parallel universes.

I shook my head and climbed in the truck, glancing at Mr. Sipes' house. My joints locked up like rusted pistons. My arteries filled with Freon. It was his house, but it looked like it had aged a hundred years. I cruised past for a closer look. The perfectly clipped grass was now a foot high. The windows were broken, and the roof sagged. The white and yellow paint looked as if it had been sandblasted. The steps and railing around the porch were crumbling with termites and dry rot. A weathered sign on the door read CON-DEMNED. And there was no sign of Mr. Sipes.

I stomped on the gas and drove, having no idea where I was going or what I was looking for. I circled around town, up and down the business loop. When I saw the city library ahead, I realized what I needed was probably inside. I asked a woman behind the desk how I could read up on some local history. She showed me how to use a computer to search old newspapers. When she walked away, I typed in "Sipes" and hit Enter. Then I spent the next three hours reading about a local urban legend that went back more than thirty years.

The short version: Harold Sipes was a wealthy business-man back in the seventies who had a soft spot for fondling little boys. He'd molested dozens, threatening to torture and kill them if they ever told. "You know what happens to tattletales," the paper had quoted him as saying. Those were *my* words. Three boys finally came forward, my brother Dan one of them. There was a trial, and Sipes broke down in the courtroom, shouting that he'd kill the boys for telling. That nothing could stop him. *Nothing.* The judge gave him twenty years, but before they could transfer him upstate, he hung himself in the county jail and was buried in the local cemetery. The following week, one by one, all three of the witnesses, including ten-year-old Dan Sparks, who I remem-bered clearly as being my best man eighteen years later, sim-ply disappeared from their beds in the night. They were never seen again.

I left the library and drove home in a daze. The story I told the boys sounded like the CliffsNotes version of what I had just read. I imagined Jacob spreading my story around to his friends at school. I saw the lie growing, feeding like a living thing on each telling. I could see, how many? Fifty? A hundred? Maybe even two hundred kids out there, believing and believing, making it more real each day.

Worse, they were re-telling it, filling in the gaps. And kids can be very imaginative. They had added other details besides the trial. Like the legend that the hole under the bed where Sipes comes in can only be seen when the lights are out. And the waves of vanishings that crop up every seven or eight years (this was also documented in the paper, though I had no memory of it) were really the old man coming out again. And if your neighbor's kid, or the girl who sits behind you in math, or one of the boys in gym class should happen to disappear one day... say it was aliens. Say it was Santa Claus. Say anything but Sipes. Because you *know* what happens to tattletales.

The next day, I was surprised when Anne showed up at the door with the boys. I thought after our fight on the phone that she would keep them, out of spite. But there was no anger in her eyes, at least no more than usual. It was as if the argument had never happened. Even the boys were different. They were so quiet.

During dinner, I asked Jacob how things were at school. He shrugged and stirred a puddle of ketchup on his plate with a French fry. "Maggie Reece wasn't there."

Tyler's head popped up, his eyes wide. The comment made me a bit nervous, too, but I tried to keep things light. "Oh, is she sick?"

Jacob shook his head. "Been gone a week now."

Tyler looked antsy, like he had to pee.

"Oh," I said, thinking it best to leave it at that.

But Jacob continued. "Mrs. Fillmore says she must've gone to live with her daddy."

Just then, Tyler snapped his face toward me and said in his timid, four-year-old voice: "It was Mr. Sipes, Daddy. He *took* her."

Jacob's hand lashed out like a broken fan belt, hitting Tyler in the mouth. Tyler fell from his chair and hit the floor wailing. I rushed over to pick him up. Blood and slobber spilled over his bottom lip.

"Get in your room, Jacob!" I shouted over Tyler's screaming.

Jacob stood still, staring at Tyler.

"Go! Sit on your bed and wait for me!" This time he ran from the dining room while I held Tyler to my chest, rocking him.

After Tyler stopped crying, I sat him down in the living room and turned on a cartoon. Then I walked down the hall to deal with Jacob. He wasn't in bed when I opened the door. He sat glassy-eyed in the far corner, his legs spread open and his hands on his knees. I could see the fear in his eyes—not fear of punishment, but something else.

"Why did you do that?"

"He *told*, Daddy. Tyler tattled on Mr. S—" He cut the name short.

"That's just a story your... *stupid* father made up. It's not real. None of it!"

Jacob lowered his head and stared at the floor as if he hadn't heard me. I walked out and slammed the door.

I put them to bed at 9:30. Around midnight they ran into my room screaming. Jacob, who slept on the bottom bunk, said he heard scratching underneath him, like someone digging in the ground. I scolded him and told him to stop scaring his brother. But I let them sleep with me.

The next day I took the boys fishing. Out on Lake Caddo, the whole Sipes story seemed to evaporate in the sun. Tyler hooked a three-pound bass, though I had to help him reel it in. He was so proud, when we got back to the house he made me take a picture of it to show his mom before I cleaned it and fried it. After dinner, we watched cartoons on the living room floor. Aside from Jacob's occasional glance down the hallway, it seemed as if old man Sipes had never existed. I didn't make them sleep in their room. When they fell asleep on the couch, I turned out the lights and went to bed.

I dreamed of darkness.

And somewhere behind the darkness, a sound. A faint, rapid scraping, like a dog scratching at a door to be let in. The darkness took shape—a rough roundness, a tunnel. The sound grew louder, closer. There was light up ahead, and blocking the light, a figure. I drew closer, right behind it. Heard the frantic scratching, smelled the sour rottenness of dead fish. Ahead and above, I saw a pinpoint of light, a tiny hole, and something picking at it, scraping at it, covering and uncovering the light and creating a strobe effect in the darkness.

And the hole became bigger. Pieces of concrete came loose as bits of gravel, stones, then chunks, were followed by splintered planks of oak flooring. And light poured in, revealing withered hands. Rotten hands. Hands with skin like torn tissue paper draping the bones and tipped with long, yellow nails.

Through the widening hole appeared bed rails, slats, a mattress.

I sat up in bed. It wasn't the dream, but something else that woke me. A sound. I waited, and it came again, faint but distinct from the living room.

"Shhh."

"Daddy!" Jacob screamed. "Daddy, he's taking Tyler! Mr. Sipes is—"

Another voice cut him off, a dry, raspy voice like someone speaking through a mouthful of brake dust. But the word came through clearly enough.

"*Tattletale!*"

Jacob screamed again. The sound rattled my eardrums. I jumped from the bed and into the living room. At the end of the hall, I saw a flash of movement as Jacob's kicking legs disappeared into the boys' bedroom. I ran down the hall, hearing the door slam shut, feeling the wind as I reached it. I threw my shoulder into the door, but it didn't budge. From inside, I heard both the boys now. They were screaming one word over and over.

"Daddy! Daddy!"

I kicked the door. Punched it. Slammed into it with all my weight. But it didn't even rattle in the frame. It felt like a bulldozer was parked behind it. But I kept trying, screaming back at the boys, "It's not real! Oh, God, I made it up! I made it *all* up! It isn't real!"

The boys' screams began to fade, became distant, vanished completely.

I slid down the wall and collapsed on the floor, sobbing. After a moment, the door shook, seemed to loosen. I stood and tried the handle. It opened. Inside, I turned on the light and searched the room. The closet, the toy chest, the window—still locked from the inside. Then I looked under the bed. Nothing but a few worms and fat maggots writhing on the dusty oak floor.

I looked up at the light switch, wondering if a tunnel would appear in the dark, thinking maybe it wasn't too late. Then I tried to imagine climbing down into that dank hole and going after them, crawling in the earthy darkness through miles of worms and maggots. And finally coming to the tunnel's end. Coming to...

I didn't turn off the light. I shut the door and boarded it up from the outside with two-by-fours and nails. Then I walled it up again. After that, I stacked furniture against the boarded door, moving everything, until there was nothing else in the house I could cram into the hallway. Nothing but this chair, where I sat down to wait.

"Mr. Sparks, do you *know* who took your kids?"

I give the officer the only answer I can. Silence. And I see the sad, knowing look in his eyes. And I know the name that is on his tongue, caged by those thin lips.

"Mr. Sparks," he finally says. "I'm afraid you're under arrest." He starts to cuff me, reciting the lines I've heard on so many late night movies.

Apparently, I have the right to remain silent.

And silent I will be.

The attorneys, the interrogators, the head-shrinkers and medical examiners, the jury, and even the judge as he passes sentence will all get the same answer—not a single word.

That's right.

Mum's the word for me.

False Witness

Bev Vincent

Margaret wrapped the hammer in a tea towel. After making sure no one could see her across the backyard fence, she turned her head away from the back door window and swung. The first time she was too tentative, but on the second stroke the glass shattered inward—it had to go inward—without making much noise.

She reached through the opening to turn the deadbolt, being careful not to cut herself on the jagged shards. Scratches on her arm would look suspicious. Besides, at her age she didn't heal as quickly as she once had. *Good health is wasted on the young*, she thought.

Satisfied with her work, Margaret stepped gingerly around the glass shards and wiped off the deadbolt with her tea towel. In the kitchen, she put on a pair of disposable latex gloves and opened the grocery bag on the table. The paper cup she extracted had a few teaspoons of fluid sloshing around in the bottom. She gripped it by the semitransparent lid to avoid smearing any fingerprints or obliterating DNA evidence on the straw.

Where would a cup look out of place but not conspicuously so? She knew the answer to this question, but wasn't happy about it. With a deep sigh, she acknowledged that sometimes a person had to make sacrifices. She sprinkled a little water around the cup's base to complete the picture, but as she walked away from the house she couldn't help but shudder at the thought of what she had just done.

Downtown, she made herself known to several people who would remember her. She had her hair done at the salon—her regular weekly appointment—and found time to gossip about that horrible Noonan boy who had been making life miserable for everyone lately, with his squealing tires and booming car stereo.

"He tears up and down the street day and night," she told Mildred Jamieson. "It's only a matter of time before he hurts someone."

Having established a suitable alibi, Margaret returned home. She parked her car well away from the edge of the street. You never knew when some young hoodlum would take it into his head to throw eggs or break windows. A couple of streets over, nine people had awakened one recent morning to find their tires flattened by someone with an ice pick. Whatever was the world coming to? When she was a little girl... but that was a long time ago. The world was a far different—better—place then.

She slammed her car door extra loud, knowing it would draw the attention of Winnie Miller, who lived across the street and kept track of everyone's comings and goings. Winnie was the closest thing they had to a neighborhood watch, a self-appointed busybody and an integral cog in the rumor mill.

Margaret climbed her back steps and stopped with a gasp. She placed her right hand on her breastbone, in case anyone was watching.

"Oh, dear," she said, completely in her role now. "Oh, my."

She hesitated on the step for a few seconds, as if trying to work out what to do. Someone had broken in the back window of her house, and the door stood slightly ajar. Was the robber still inside? They always said that if you came home and found signs of a robbery, you should go somewhere safe and call the police.

Margaret looked across the street to Winnie's house. She hated to be a bother, but after all...

The police officers who came to investigate were very nice, but they turned down her offer of tea and cake. After making sure no one was still in the house, they asked her to look around to see if anything was missing. The box under the bed was empty, of course.

"How much did you keep in it?" the younger of the two policemen asked.

"Quite a lot, I'm afraid," Margaret said. "Nearly six thousand dollars."

The officer's eyes widened at this, and the two men suddenly seemed much more interested in their investigation. They made calls on their radios and used their little flashlights to look for clues.

"My, my, what is that doing there?" Margaret said, reaching for the waxed soft drink cup on her mahogany coffee table.

"Please don't touch that, ma'am," the older officer said. Margaret liked the way he called her ma'am. It was a touch of respect utterly lacking in the younger generation.

"But look," she said. "The water. It will leave a stain."

She pointed at the ring gathering around the cup's base in case the officer came from the type of home where people didn't use coasters.

"Yes, ma'am, but we might get fingerprints from that. You're sure it wasn't here before."

Margaret snorted. "I never drink from disposable cups, and I would never let anybody place one on my fine antique table. Are you sure we can't move it so I can wipe it off?" By this time she was feeling poorly about the whole situation. Sacrifices were sometimes required, but the table had been her mother's.

The officer seemed sympathetic. After snapping a few photographs, he took out a handkerchief and gripped the cup delicately by the rim and placed it in a plastic bag.

"Can I wipe that up, now? Please?"

The officer took more photographs and wrote something on his notepad. "Yes, ma'am. Be sure to make note of any damage for the report."

Margaret liked him. In spite of their earlier refusal, after she wiped up the mess with a tea towel—as she'd feared, the water had left a permanent mark in the finish—she went into the kitchen and made a pot of tea, which she served with a plate of her famous cupcakes.

The officers asked her a few more questions, but she resisted the temptation to implicate any specific person. From watching crime shows on television, she knew their forensic science would point fingers more convincingly than she could. The one thing she stressed was how traumatic she found the whole experience. How violated. It was the closest thing to a victim impact statement she might get to make.

The wheels of justice did not turn fast. Margaret knew she had to be patient. When you reached a certain age, your relationship to time changed. Though some things seemed more urgent, a lifetime of experience reminded you it was okay to wait for things to happen in their own good time.

Two weeks after the burglary, a police car stopped in front of the Noonan house up the street. Margaret's eyes would not be the only ones focused on the scene. Across the road, Winnie would be taking it all in, barely looking away from the window long enough to push the buttons on her mobile telephone as she spread the news up one side of the street and down the other.

Margaret sipped tea and treated herself to a second cupcake as she watched the drama unfold. After a scene at the front door, the police officers went inside and emerged a few minutes later with the Noonan brat jammed between them. His hands were cuffed behind him, and he argued all the way to the car.

She would have to testify against him if it came to a trial, but how often did these cases get that far? After reading her statement, the prosecutor would hopefully drive a hard bargain. Surely a good lawyer, seeing the evidence against his client, would strike a deal.

Of course, there would be an offer of restitution, even though there had never been any cash in the box under her bed, but no amount of money would fix the ugly stain on her antique coffee table. That bothered her more than anything else about the whole ordeal, but you don't win battles with half measures.

Later that week, she received a call from Winnie, telling her that the Noonan boy had pleaded no contest to the charges and had been sentenced to a year in the county jail.

A year, a glorious year without reckless driving and insufferable disruptions. She was sitting in her favorite chair in the living room when Winnie delivered the verdict, sipping tea.

"He claimed he didn't do it, but they had him dead to rights," Winnie said. "DNA and fingerprints both."

Of course they did, Margaret thought. She had watched the miscreant throw the fast food cup from his car window the day before the robbery. That infraction—the final straw, so to speak—was what had inspired her in the first place.

"But you didn't get to testify," Winnie continued, sounding disappointed. "Imagine, pointing your finger at someone and saying, 'It was him, your honor.'"

Margaret laughed at Winnie's dramatics. "I gave them my sworn statement," she said. "That was enough. The police did the rest."

No man had ever been granted access to Margaret's bedroom, not even when she had been younger and less wise. Men were an unnecessary complication. The source of most of the world's misery. She preferred a life of solitary pursuits to the complicated melodramas that many of her friends invited into their lives by having boyfriends and lovers and husbands.

Which was why it came as such a shock when she opened her eyes in the middle of the night to find a young man lurking at the foot of her bed. She blinked and squinted, trying to make sense out of what she was seeing. Was it a dream? A nightmare? A hallucination?

A burglar, was her next thought, and fear gripped her. However, the man-shaped form was doing nothing sinister or burglar-like. He just stood there, staring at her in the semidarkness. Did he have an aura about him, a dim glow that penetrated a few inches beyond his outline? Margaret thought perhaps he did, but she didn't have her glasses on and everyone knew—for she often told them as much—that she was blind as a mole without them.

She fumbled at the bedside table for her bifocals. By the time she got them affixed to her face, though, the figure had dissipated. She had the feeling that it pointed at her before vanishing, an accusatory gesture that made her think of old Marley and Ebenezer Scrooge.

Margaret was finishing her scones and strawberry preserves at the kitchen table the next morning when the phone rang. She considered letting the answering machine pick up, but two things fought this inclination. First, she was curious about who might be calling her. It could be something important and she'd hate to miss out on important details if the caller left a sketchy message. Second, if it was one of her neighbors, the caller would know she was home and wonder why she hadn't answered. If the neighbor was sufficiently concerned—or nosey—he or she would show up at the front door, inquiring if Margaret was all right.

In either case, it would be better if she answered.

"Shame about the boy, don't you think?"

"Hello, Winnie," Margaret responded.

"Don't you think?"

"I'm sure I don't know what you're talking about," Margaret said, but deep down inside she thought she did.

"That Noonan boy. The one you had arrested."

"I didn't have him arrested. That was the police. They did their tests and—"

"Anyway, he didn't deserve that."

"What? Going to jail for robbing my house?"

"To die, that's what I mean."

"What? What?"

"I thought for sure you'd have heard by now," Winnie said, though Margaret knew that Winnie would have been sorely disappointed if she wasn't the first to pass on the news.

"I haven't."

"Got himself stuck with a knife, he did. Right there in the jail."

"How is that possible?"

"Don't you watch television? Happens all the time. They make knives out of spoons or toothbrushes."

"But why?"

Winnie lowered her voice. "He probably wouldn't put out for some big burly brute of a man." She sounded excited by the idea.

Margaret had no intention of pursuing the conversation if it continued in this direction. Winnie apparently understood the significance of her prolonged silence.

"Anyhow, there's those that say he didn't deserve it, that's all."

"I would agree."

"And there are those who would say it's your fault, really."

Margaret almost shouted into the receiver before regaining her composure, although it took a few seconds. "Who'd say that?" Her voice trembled slightly, but perhaps not enough for Winnie to notice.

"You know how people are."

I know how you are, Margaret thought. She said, "It's not my fault that boy broke into my house and left his fingerprints all over the place."

"Pressed charges though, didn't you. No second chances for one of our own, a young boy we've known all his life."

By now Margaret was livid. She recalled numerous occasions when Winnie harped about how that rapscallion needed a stricter hand and would grow up to be no good. Tempted though she might have been, reminding Winnie would do no good. "I didn't press charges. The police did, and he pleaded guilty."

"No contest."

"Pardon?"

"He pleaded no contest, which isn't the same thing at all. He was trapped. If you'd've stepped in and said a good word on his behalf..." Winnie let the sentence dangle, its implication clear.

"What would I have said? I don't mind that he broke my window, invaded my house, stole my money and damaged a precious heirloom? That he's normally such a good boy and it was all a simple misunderstanding?"

Margaret could almost hear Winnie shrugging over the telephone wires. "It's not me, mind you. I'm just warning you what people might say."

Margaret extricated herself from the conversation as gracefully as possible. Winnie was no ally, but she would make a formidable enemy, so it was best to placate the woman and end on good terms. Though she nearly choked on the words, Margaret thanked Winnie for her concern and for warning her about what "people" might be saying, knowing full well that it would be Winnie doing most of the saying.

After they hung up, Margaret returned to the table, but all the joy had gone out of her morning. Remembering the vision she had experienced the night before, she wondered if it had been a premonition. She knew people who claimed to have been visited by loved ones in the night at the moment of their deaths, but it was something she'd never experienced before. Had her phantom guest been the spec-ter of young Noonan, accusing her of being responsible for his death?

She felt bad for the way things turned out, but it wasn't as if she had planned it this way. Without a doubt, no one on the street save for the lad's parents—and perhaps not even them—regretted seeing him going away for a year, unable to wreak havoc on the neighborhood. Through her actions, she had put a temporary stop to his reign of terror, and if that hiatus had turned into something more permanent, well, it probably would have happened to him eventually anyway. Did anyone doubt that the boy would end up behind bars in the long run?

She made herself a pot of tea, but her milk had turned sour and she couldn't bear drinking it black. After adding milk to her shopping list, she turned her attention to household chores, trying to push away images of what the boy's last moments on the earth must have been like. Did he hate her? Did he go to meet his maker—or the other—with evil thoughts clouding his mind?

If people talked, none of them said anything to Margaret, except for Winnie, who made a few pointed digs before moving on to something else. Eventually she seemed to tire of her gibes about the Noonan boy when she got no response from Margaret.

Was it a ghost or a dream that visited her at night? Margaret could never be sure. The figure seemed real enough, standing quietly at the end of her bed. Usually it did nothing more than stare, but its gaze was terrible. The young man's brow was furrowed, as if he were concentrating on something or trying to work out a difficult problem. He neither frowned nor smiled. If anything, he merely looked perplexed.

This usually occurred during the darkest hours, between three and four in the morning, when Margaret could never bring herself fully awake, no matter how hard she tried. She convinced herself that it was only a dream, the product of a vaguely guilty mind. The boy deserved to be in jail; just not for the crime he was accused of committing. This argument did little to placate her, though. She had been the instrument of his incarceration and had set into motion a chain of events that led inexorably to his death.

Half asleep—or in her dreams as she preferred to think of it—she started talking to the boy, who looked more like a

young man. How old had he been, after all? For some reason she had thought of him as barely a teenager, but in ret-
rospect, if they'd put him in jail with the other criminals, he
must have been older. Perhaps as much as seventeen or
eighteen. On the verge of adulthood.

On the verge of becoming a hardened criminal, she told
the boy, but he did not answer. And was that true? What had
he done beyond being a little rambunctious? Squealed his
tires, played his music loud, frightened the children and
pets? Annoyed crotchety old women like herself? Littered
her lawn?

All this she said to him, and much more, though it may
all have been a dream.

In the end, it was more than she could bear. Though her
nocturnal visitor said never a word, rarely did so much as
point at her—*j'accuse*—she felt the unspoken accusation all
the same. She pleaded her case with him night after night
and never received so much as a nod of acknowledgment in
return.

Would Winnie remember that she had picked up a prescription for her? Or that Margaret had insisted she take the
bottles from the bag—not in the drug store, where the phar-
macist might notice and wonder what she was doing—to
make sure the vials contained the correct number of pills?

"They cheat, you know. A pill here, a pill there, it adds
up. And it's our money they're stealing," Margaret had con-
fided, and Winnie had taken it all in. So willing to believe in
a massive pharmaceutical conspiracy that she unwittingly
left her fingerprints all over the vials.

Margaret baked one final batch of her famous cupcakes,
using a tin that Winnie had loaned her months earlier. It
had her initials, WM, etched in the bottom because people
had a habit of picking things up, you know. They would act

innocent if caught, but they really intended to steal your belongings, or so Winnie believed.

The final batch was heavily laced with prescription sedatives. It had taken her several hours at the library to reassure herself that they would maintain their potency when cooked in a 350-degree oven for eighteen minutes, or until done.

The empty prescription bottles she'd put in a paper bag and tossed in Winnie's trash can late the evening before. The garbage wasn't due to be collected for several days, and the police would surely look there eventually. Especially when they didn't find any pill bottles in Margaret's house and discovered one drug-laden cupcake remaining in Winnie's muffin tin on the coffee table, where it covered the hideous stain left by the sweating soda cup.

She sat in her favorite chair next to the living room window with a plate of cupcakes, and sipped tea. Outside, the street was peaceful. Children were playing and the cars drove past at a respectable speed.

When she could no longer fight off the growing drowsiness, she found a comfortable place on the floor where it might look as if she had collapsed. She lowered herself onto the carpet, rested her head against her arm and drifted off.

The index finger at the end of her outstretched arm pointed in unconscious accusation toward the coffee table.

Bitter Taste of Memory

Chris Stout

This story is about my brother Stevie. He was ten years old when I killed him.

Until he died Stevie was the oldest. He had two years on me, and I had seven-and-a-half on our sister Katrina. Mom and Dad always referred to her as their "happy little surprise." For me and Stevie, Katrina was one more bother in our lives.

We grew up in a simple house in the suburbs. Pick any small town in the Midwest and you've probably seen our home. Our parents were decent, hard-working folks who dragged us to church every Sunday. My father served on one church board or another for as long as I could remember, and my mother was always active with the Women's Circle. They were good folks. Stevie and I knew what was expected of us, and tried to follow the rules as best as two boys could. At eight and ten, the two biggest ones were: "Don't wake the baby," and "No cursing." We did well with the first; an education at public school significantly handicapped us for the second.

Summertime finally came and released us from the sacred halls of McKinley Elementary School. Stevie was especially thrilled because he wouldn't have to go back next year. He was headed for the awesome might of Howard Taft Middle School. I was insanely jealous. My friends had always held Stevie in high regard. Now that he was moving on to

Howard Taft, he was seen as a mythic hero. I, on the other hand, was still regarded by Stevie's friends as a pest. I would have given anything to trade places with him, even for a few hours, and bask in the glow of all that adoration.

With us two boys suddenly unleashed on the world, our father wisely began putting extra hours in at the office. Our mother shooed us out the door each morning with the admonition: "If you come in, don't wake your sister, and for heaven's sake watch your mouths!" We'd each experienced the foul taste of being cleansed with soap on account of the second part, so we at least made sure to do our swearing out of earshot. Generally that kept us from violating rule number one.

June 12 came on a Friday that year. That afternoon Stevie and I were outside riding our bikes together. We fancied ourselves to be real BMX racers. The street curbs and our neighbors' driveways served as the platforms where our simple wheelies became high-flying tabletops and other impossible stunts. By mid-afternoon it was steaming hot.

Stevie and I sat under the shade of the flowering cherry tree in our front yard, drinking lemonade Mom had given us before she put Katrina down for her nap. We saw some of the boys from Stevie's class hiking up the block with gloves and bats in hand. Since we lived on a cul-de-sac, it was an ideal location for an impromptu baseball game. But as soon as his classmates appeared, I ceased to exist. It simply wasn't cool for Stevie to be seen hanging out with his little brother. I resented that.

The boys had their teams set, and Stevie quickly joined the ranks of his chosen group. I stood under our tree in protest. "Hey! I wanna play too!"

"Aw, get lost, pipsqueak," one of the bigger boys said with a dismissive wave of his hand. "Don't you have a diaper to change?"

"Yeah," someone else said. "His own!"

This sent the boys into a fit of jeering laughter. To his credit, Stevie was gracious enough not to join them. Instead he came back over and said: "Look, Jesse, the teams'll be uneven. Why don't you be our batboy?"

My face was hot with shame, and this conciliatory gesture on his part seemed to be the ultimate embarrassment to me. So I fired back with the only threat I could make: "I'm telling Mom!"

I turned and ran into the house, slamming the front door, waking Katrina in the process. But I managed to hold back the tears until I was inside.

My storming entrance startled Katrina, who had been napping peacefully on the living room floor while my mom read her magazines.

"What in heaven's name is going on? Didn't I tell you not to wake your sister?" She shouted to make herself heard over the wailing baby.

I sniveled and looked down at my feet. I muttered something even I couldn't hear over Katrina's cries.

Mom swallowed back any further reprimand. "Hold on a minute, Jesse." Mom rocked the baby in her arms and cooed softly until she quieted down. She nestled Katrina with one arm and put the other on her hip as she stared me down. "Now. What happened?"

"Stevie won't let me play ball with him and the other boys." I sniffed and wiped my eye for effect, but I could already tell the excuse wasn't good enough.

"Well Jesse, he's a bit older than you. Sometimes you'll have to let him play with his friends. You've got enough of your own. Go visit one of them, instead of raising Cain in here."

It simply wasn't fair that I should be ignored and then scolded for it. I guess my own undeveloped sense of injustice determined the next words out of my mouth.

I squared my shoulders, looked Mom straight in the eye, and said, "But he used a bad word." I crossed my arms over my chest and rocked from side to side. "He used GD."

Mom's eyes went wide and then narrowed to slits.

"He used GD," I said again. Then, I added, "With the F-word."

I could hear small sounds in the quiet. The clock on the wall of the kitchen ticking. The house creaking in the heat of the day. An air conditioner humming in Katrina's room. The crack of a bat striking a ball followed by a chorus of cheers from outside. I remember it all.

"Hold your sister," Mom said.

I could feel a tremor in her arms as she passed the baby to me. My mom shook when she was truly mad. Some people mistook it as a sign of weakness. My brother and I knew better. Stevie was in for it.

Katrina cooed and giggled as she squirmed in my arms. She batted at my face with her tiny hands. Our mother pushed through the screen door and strode onto the lawn. Then she unleashed hell.

"Steven Alexander! Get in the house this instant!"

Her shout scattered all of my brother's friends like a tidal wave. Stevie stood frozen in the imaginary batter's box, not understanding what had ignited her fury.

Our mother marched toward him. "I said now, mister!" She grabbed Stevie by the arm and hauled him back to the house. Stevie stumbled and struggled to keep up.

They came through the front door. I stood still in the hall holding Katrina. Our mother jerked Stevie to a halt and pointed at me. "Tell me what you said to him."

Stevie's face was pure confusion. "What?" It was the wrong answer.

Mom swatted the back of his head, knocking his ball cap to the floor. "I said, tell me."

Stevie rubbed the point of impact. "Nothing, Mom, I swear. I told him the teams would be uneven and he could be our batboy. I swear!"

His assertions weren't good enough. Our mother had already passed judgment. She took him by the arm again. "Into the bathroom with you, young man." She nodded in my direction. "Jesse, put your sister in her crib."

In our house, punishment was usually swift and severe, but our parents did not believe in publicly humiliating the guilty party. I bowed my head and carried Katrina to her room. Stevie protested and pleaded, and then began to cry when the water started running. He gave one last cry, a final plea of innocence, and then it was quiet as the soap was administered. I knew the next sound would be flesh cracking against flesh for the spanking, so I left Katrina to amuse herself with her mobile. I went out of the house and sat down under the cherry tree.

I don't remember how long it was before Stevie came back outside. A while, I guess. He came out through the front door and let it slam behind him. He had retrieved his baseball cap. Beneath its brim, his face was a dark cloud, hidden.

Stevie stormed past me, picked up his bike from the lawn, and swung his leg over the frame. Then he turned to me.

"How could you do that?"

I swallowed a lump in my throat and stared hard at a fallen twig.

"I tried to let you play. Why'd you say that?"

A few dried and shriveled leaves still clung to the end of the twig.

"Mom says it's going to be even worse when Dad gets home." He scrunched his face up and spat a few times into the grass. That was the most he would do to clear the taste of soap from his mouth. Stevie was strong that way. I usually vomited shortly after such an ordeal. Stevie wiped his mouth. "You're nothing but a rotten little liar."

One of the leaves shivered in a breeze that blew across the yard. Bits of it flaked off and scattered away.

"You know what? If I'm going to get it, I might as well deserve it. God damn you, Jesse. God damn you!"

Even though I wasn't the one with the bitter taste of soap in my mouth, I still felt sick to my stomach.

Stevie mounted the pedals and pushed off toward the street. I jumped up and righted my bike. "Wait, Stevie. Wait!"

He was heading out of the cul-de-sac. By the time I got going, he had reached the intersection and was peeling into a wide left turn. He didn't look both ways, and he failed to see the pickup truck speeding from his right.

Stevie was only twenty yards from me when the truck hit him. The sound of the impact was spectacular. Stevie and his bike vanished beneath the big tires. The truck screeched to a halt. The scrap heap that was Stevie's bike sparked against the pavement beneath it. My brother was left behind.

I dropped my bike and raced into the street. Stevie lay facedown on the pavement. A smear of red trailed behind his body.

His head was crushed flat against the pavement. A pulpy mass had been mashed from his skull, and for some reason I remember thinking that this looked nothing like what we saw on TV when Stevie and I sneaked down at night to watch horror movies on the cable channels. Then a man shouted, "Oh Jesus! I never saw him! Sweet Jesus, I never saw him!"

And our mother ran from the house, screaming. "Oh God... Please God, no. Please God, no!"

And that's what happened the day I killed my brother.

It's been twenty years since that day. I never did tell my folks that it was my fault. Every night I lie awake and replay the events from start to finish, over and over. More bitter than the taste of any soap, my brother's last words to me echo across the years. And I wait for the day when they will finally come true.

THOU
SHALT
NOT...

Covet

The Seventh Reflection

K. Tempest Bradford

Clia stood before the large, oval mirror in her room and stared at the reflection. Bone-straight hair—long, shiny and black—a heart-shaped face, perfect button nose, sensual mouth, and wide green eyes. The skin held no blemish and no imperfection—not too dark, but not too light. An elegant neck; firm, round breasts; smooth, flat stomach; curvy hips; long, muscular legs tapering toward the floor and ending at the bottom of the mirror.

"Yes, this is what I want," Clia said. Her mouth moved. The reflection's did not.

Are you ready to gather what I need?

"Yes. It'll take a few days, though."

I have nothing but time. The reflection shimmered away, replaced by an image of what Clia looked like in every other mirror.

She did not often look at mirrors.

It took four days to find the mugwort. She combed the phone book for a Wiccan store near her tiny town. When she found one, the goth girl behind the counter didn't even look up when she told Clia to hunt for it out back.

"What, you have a garden or something?" Clia asked.

"No, a parking lot," the girl said. "There's some growing by the fence."

Clia didn't like the tone of her voice.

"What is that smell?" her mother asked.

"Tea," Clia replied.

"It's awfully strong. Are you sure it's okay to drink?"

Clia responded with an over-the-book, you're-persecuting-me-again glare.

Her mother tried to smile the tension away. "Is it one of those herbal teas that help you think better or something?"

Clia just shrugged and was silent. So silent that she drove her mother from the room.

She coated the mirror's surface with mugwort tea. It then instructed her to pry out the smaller mirrors, seven in number, set in the decorative wood framing it. She hoped her mother wouldn't barge in suddenly and see what she was doing.

The mirror had come to her father when great aunt May Ella passed on. Her mother suggested giving it to Clia because she was reaching "that age" and might want to "take more pride in her appearance." Five generations had gazed into this mirror before her. Clia wondered what they'd looked like before... and then after.

She tried to think of this instead of her reflection. She kept catching glimpses of herself in the glass. Her true self.

What a cruel gift, she thought. Even if it is magical.

As the bell rang on her first period class Clia decided that the time was right. She marched over to Jennie Garner's desk, which was surrounded by the *crème de la crème* of the Jackson High School social circle, and inserted herself into the scene.

"Hi Jennie," she said over the conversation. The other kids didn't even bother to taper off and glare at her in distaste. They just ignored her and kept talking. Jennie rolled her eyes before tearing them away from Scott Jackson to finally acknowledge her. Her look said volumes about her opinion of Clia and her interruption.

"Yeah?"

"Merry Christmas." Clia extended a small package.

"For me?" Jennie seemed genuinely surprised. "Thanks." She took the gift and tore into the paper.

"It's a mirror," Clia said. "I made it myself."

The other kids had stopped talking by then and watched this little exchange with interest. Jennie finally unwrapped the hand mirror and held it up to her face. Her fingers traced the decorations Clia had burned into the polished wood.

"You made this yourself? It's pretty." Jennie was absorbed in her own reflection.

"I knew you'd like it." Of course she liked it. Who could blame her for admiring any mirror that reflected a face like that? Perfect heart shape, perfect button nose, sensual mouth. She had great eyes, too. But they were blue. Clia had always wanted green eyes.

"You made that?" Rachel asked. "Will you make me one?"

Green eyes like Rachel had.

"I already did," Clia said, handing her a similar package. "For helping me with that geometry test."

Rachel hadn't actually helped. She'd stolen the answers and made Clia pay twenty dollars to share them.

"You're welcome."

Clia returned to her desk. She knew what the other kids were saying behind her back. They were probably calling her a suck-up or a lesbian. She didn't care. Soon it wouldn't matter.

Fourth period English. Clia's seat was right next to Chelsea's, yet the two had never spoken. The light-skinned girl barely knew she existed. But Clia was always aware of her neighbor. Chelsea never got pimples or pock marks. Her skin was always smooth and clear. Clia imagined that it was soft to the touch.

She set the gift on Chelsea's desk just before class ended.

"What's this?" Chelsea asked.

"A Christmas gift."

"For me?" She picked it up, a small frown on her face. "But I don't really know you."

"I know. I just thought you'd like it. Open it." Clia twisted the fringes of her sweater nervously.

"I can't accept this." Chelsea held it out to her. "I mean, I didn't get you anything."

Clia stood up quickly when the bell rang. "That's okay. Really. Please, take it." She joined the rest of the class filing out into the hall. When she looked back, Chelsea had unwrapped the mirror and was using it to check her lipstick.

At lunch Clia stopped by Christina Carter's table and gave her a mirror, too. She pretended that it was to repay Chris for showing her around on her first day back in October. While Clia talked to Christina, she dutifully averted her gaze from the senior's breasts.

In seventh period gym, after suffering through twenty push-ups and a game of dodgeball, Clia caught Miko before she left the locker room.

"Happy Holidays." Clia pressed the mirror into the exchange student's hand.

Miko's face lit up, her smile genuine and warm. "For me? Oh, thank you!" She reached into her gym bag and handed Clia a small tin of holiday chocolates. "Happy Christmas to you, too."

Clia didn't know what to say. She hadn't expected a gift from her. From anyone. She watched as Miko worked the wrapping off carefully so as to not tear it. Clia almost pulled the mirror away before she could look in it, the guilt making her slightly nauseated. But one look at Miko's long, beautiful hair stayed her hand.

After school, Clia waited by Mary's locker. Her own was just across the hall so she knew the star forward would pass by on her way to practice. A few minutes later Mary jogged down the hall and smiled at Clia as she dialed her combination.

"Last week's game... you were really great," Clia stammered, her eyes lingering on Mary's long legs.

"I got lucky on that last point," she said absently.

"This is for you." Clia held out the mirror.

"Thanks." Mary tossed it into her locker and closed the door. "See ya."

Clia's heart sped up. It wouldn't work if Mary didn't look in it. "Wait!"

Mary looked over and frowned. "What?"

"Aren't you going to unwrap it? It's a Christmas present."

"From you?"

She nodded.

Mary shrugged. "Can it wait? I'm gonna be late for practice."

She might unwrap it afterwards, but if she didn't...

"Just... that I made it myself."

"Oh, is it like the one you gave Jennie?" Mary opened her locker and ripped the wrapping off.

Clia's fingers were tangled in the fringes of her sweater. One look is all it took. She relaxed when Mary finally held it up, admiring herself.

"Thanks. This is really pretty." She dropped the mirror into her backpack and jogged off down the hall.

Clia was imagining how those legs would look in shorts when Mary turned back and called out to her. "Hey, we're having a winter break party at my house tomorrow night. You should come by."

Clia smiled. "Sure!" She leaned against a locker until the nausea passed.

She packed the remaining mugwort into one of her mother's silver ashtrays.

Light it on fire.

Clia did so. The pungent aroma filled the room.

Now begin.

Clia took the one small mirror she hadn't given away and popped it into the center notch of the frame above the big mirror. She'd moved the heavy thing in front of the window at sunset. Now the moon was reflected in both surfaces.

She hesitated.

Keep going.

The kitchen knife was sharp and cold and painful in her arm. She forced herself to cut deep enough. Dark red blood dribbled into a small bowl on her dresser. She filled it halfway and then stopped to wrap the cut with gauze.

"Now what?"

Draw the person you want to be.

"On the mirror?"

Yes.

Clia dipped her finger in the blood and brought it up to the glass. Her hand shook, but she drew.

At first she used her own outline as a guide, putting the face where it should be. Perfect shape. Perfect nose. Perfect mouth. One of the small mirrors appeared in its notch. Her own reflection faded away. She drew the eyes. The second mirror appeared. Next came the hair, long and straight. The third mirror. Upper body, curves, breasts, smooth lines. The fourth mirror. Long, muscular legs. The fifth mirror. Clia only saw six, including hers. There should have been seven. Then she remembered. She used the last of the blood to fill in the lines. The last mirror appeared.

Clia stepped back and waited.

The drawing blinked. The edges blurred. Clia blinked. The mirror was covered in blood.

Movement caught the corner of her eye. In one of the little mirrors she saw Jennie. Just her face, then her image pulled away, back into the glass, farther and farther, like she was falling, then gone. In the next she saw Rachel's green eyes. And again, the image pulled away until she became only a dot in the silverblack landscape of the glass. Miko's raven hair twirled and twirled and twirled into the background. Christina's heaving torso fell away. Mary's long legs kicked into nothingness. Chelsea's perfect skin filled her space then dissolved.

The blood seeped into the space between the glass and the wood, leaving a clean surface and a reflection behind— the perfect image Clia had seen only in this mirror and her most desperate daydreams. She reached toward it.

The reflection reached out, too.

Slowly, her hand abandoned its course and went instead to touch the hair—no longer kinky and coarse, but silky and straight. Clia and her reflection discovered her new self by touch. Perfect skin. Perfect nose. Perfect mouth. Firm breasts. Curvy hips. Legs that were long and...

Clia screamed.

Her reflection ended at her ankles. It had no feet. She had no feet. There was nothing below her legs.

"Where are my feet?"

You didn't ask for feet.

Clia crashed to the floor, the illusion no longer holding up, and screamed in pain. Her legs ended in bloody stumps, a dull ache, and the phantom feeling of feet that should have been there.

"I gave you six souls for this!" she shrieked. "I gave what you asked!"

If you want feet, you'll have to give me seven.

Someone pounded on her door.

"Clia!" Her mother. "What's wrong? Are you all right? Open the door!"

She looked from the door to the mirror, then down at the raw stumps.

"Clia! Are you hurt?"

The reflection was still standing. Now it held something in its hand. A pair of sandals. Her mother's beaded sandals. The sandals Clia coveted but could never borrow. Her own feet had always been too big.

"Clia!"

Her mother was trying to break in.

She strained and grunted, using her knees for leverage, and slid the mirror around to face the door.

She had no choice. She needed feet.

And the lock would give way any moment.

Mr. Rutherford's Journal

Leslie Brown

May 1

My therapist thinks keeping a journal will help me work through some of my difficulties, but I think I have bigger problems than can be solved by scribbling in a book that no one else will read. Dr. Petersen says that my depression stems from "gender identification issues." I'm a married man for crying out loud! My depression stems from not being able to hold down a job. Sharon's a trooper, says she makes more than enough to support our lifestyle. I just wish I could bring in some money and feel less of a parasite.

May 12

Today I had a close call but at least it gives me something to write about. Sharon bought a negligée yesterday. Not one of those skimpy teddies, but a full-length one with the ruffles and flounces. And a matching housecoat. I only had it on for a minute when she pulled into the driveway. I almost tore it taking it off. It's no big deal. Lots of guys like the feel of silk. I'll be more careful tomorrow and try it on in the middle of the day.

May 30

Oh, heady excitement! Who says nothing happens on this street? New neighbors moved in today. I watched them through the sheer curtains. No kids, thank God. They're a handsome couple. The wife has gorgeous blonde hair and, you know, except for our coloring, we could be brother and sister. She has great taste in clothes and they look like they might fit me. Sharon wants to bring them some tulips for their garden, a housewarming present that will come back every spring.

June 10

Elsa and Bill are the names of our new neighbors. Sharon and I tried for days before we found them at home to deliver our welcome-to-the-neighborhood present. The tulips had begun to wilt in the gift basket, but I think the bulbs can still be planted.

Elsa is my exact height. They seem happy together, married for five years but still act like newlyweds. It inspired me for later but I fizzled out. As usual. Sharon patted me on the thigh and said it was all right, she was too tired anyway.

June 14

We've had some beautiful weather lately. Everyone was barbecuing and the air held the aroma of steaks cooking. Elsa and Bill put out the good crystal and china on their glass patio table. I watched them from our bedroom window. They had steak and wine with a tossed salad. Bill took Elsa's hand and kissed all her fingers. They put some music on the stereo and opened a window so they could hear it. They danced on their patio all evening.

June 18

I can't believe my nerve. Elsa left her patio door open a foot or so when she went to her pilates class. I went over as soon as I saw her pull out of the driveway. Her clothes are lovely and most of them fit me perfectly. She has tasteful jewelry, presents from Bill, no doubt. They have a lot of pictures on their mantel. They look happy in all of them. It appears that they travel a lot. I've never been out of state. Bill looks a lot younger than forty-five—I bet he'll age well.

I took their extra house key. They'll never notice that it's gone. I also took a photo of Bill from a pile of holiday pictures waiting to be put in an album. Oh yeah, and I sprayed on some of Elsa's perfume, but I remembered to wash it off before Sharon got home.

June 29

Sharon left on a business trip the same weekend Bill and Elsa went to Martha's Vineyard. I did it! I slept in their bed. I made sure I was on Elsa's side: I could smell her perfume on the pillow. Then I held Bill's pillow in my arms. Next morning I set two places, pretended Bill and I were having breakfast.

I'm not gay. I just think he'd be great to be with.

July 12

God, I don't know what to do. Sharon asked me for a divorce. Turns out all those business meetings evenings and weekends were held in motels. She says she loves me but she needs the physical part of a marriage. I lost it. I called her some names and then hit her on the back of the head with a fry pan when she was leaving. It's been hours; she's gone stiff. I put her in the bed, in case she wakes up, but it doesn't seem likely.

Elsa's home. I just heard her pull into the driveway. I have an idea.

July 12 again

The house next door was on fire when Bill got home and he went over to see if there was anything he could do while I sprayed the side of our house with the garden hose to keep blowing sparks from taking hold. It was dark when he came back.

They found two bodies burned beyond recognition, he told me through the smoke. It looks like it was the Rutherfords. How terrible, I said softly. I felt Elsa's hair slip a bit and eased it back into place without Bill noticing. I went upstairs first to get ready for bed. (This hair won't keep forever. I'll have to find a wig of similar color at the mall.)

I hear Bill coming up to bed. I'm sure he'll be surprised at first, but he's always seemed to like me. I'll empty the savings account tomorrow. There should be enough to pay for the operation. That will show him that I can pull my own weight in this relationship.

This will be my last entry. I'm starting a new life. My therapist was right. Keeping a journal does help you work through your issues!

The Method Coach

Alison J. Littlewood

Her hair was new, soft blonde waves, and she was thinner, lithe. Looked every inch the Hollywood starlet, like she'd had surgery and BOTOX and a thousand-dollar hairdresser and a colorist and probably a therapist too, to iron out the creases you don't see.

Stella. My friend, Stella. We came out here to grasp the dream, to catch life by the neck. We came here together, this land of dreams. Land of nightmares.

She flexed, all perfect curves. Her hair glistened. I compared it to my dull red curls, out of control, my blue pinafore. A waitress's uniform. Out of control was right.

Stella laughed, ran a hand through those perfect waves, and leaned in close. "I'm not sure I should tell you this," she said, "but I have a secret weapon."

She opened a red leather handbag, Chanel, the latest style. She caught me looking. "Got it for free." She rummaged. "They want me to take it to the *Catch All* promos next week. Course, I agreed." Stella winked as she handed me a small, crumpled card.

I held it in both hands. Carlos Myers – Method Acting Coach. There was an address from a fashionable part of the city.

"Give him a try," Stella said, and gave a last flash of freshly capped teeth. "You won't regret it."

She looked at me over her shoulder as she left. "Course, there's a price. But it's sure as hell worth it!"

Back in my tiny flat, I put the card next to the letter home that I had written but not posted.

Guess what. I have an audition. A small part, but it's opposite Steve Redheugh. They want someone English. And there's even a love scene, can you imagine?

The letter had lain there for months, gathering dust. A letter just for me now, a reminder of how Stella, my friend Stella, had swept in and got the part. Stella, who was going to premiers, who was clutching Chanel, who was seen all around town with Steve Redheugh himself. She could pass me in the street without noticing.

What the hell was her secret? Could some acting coach really have done all this? And I heard her again: "Of course, there's a price." Would have to be, wouldn't there? But I remembered the Gucci dress and Chanel bag and that to-die-for hair, and thought, isn't it worth it? Aren't I?

Carlos Myers opened the door of his clean white villa himself, something I wasn't prepared for. But I knew it was him, even though the image I had (tall, Mediterranean, handsome, pony-tailed) didn't fit.

Carlos was tall but spindly, spidery. As he emerged from a blue doorway in a white wall, he looked dusty in comparison, fragile even. But the eyes, sharp blue eyes in a mask of deep lines and fissures, were clean and strong. Pure. Like they could peer into your soul.

"Come in, dear girl," he said. The accent, like mine, was English, but a little aristocratic. Maybe he put it on for the Hollywood starlets.

Soon I found myself sitting with him, sipping tea, telling him everything. How I came to be here. How lonely I was. How I knew, I knew my friend was going to be a success, and how I fell short each time of being happy for her. About how she was living my dream.

How she was beautiful. How she looked golden like some goddess, and outshone my drab skin, my dull red hair.

Carlos grabbed hold of my seat, spinning me.

I gasped and found myself facing a mirror. Carlos snapped out a hand, flicking on a row of lightbulbs. A film star's mirror.

I stared at his reflection. I stared at mine.

Carlos waved a hand in front of my face. Suddenly, my hair changed, straightened, grew lighter. The corkscrews were unraveling, becoming sleek. I was a platinum blonde with a washed-out complexion. I looked jaded, a washed-up waitress, not an actress-waiting-to-happen.

He waved his hand again.

My hair was gold. My hair was brown. My hair was a severe, black bob.

My hair was red again and suddenly my skin didn't look so pale; it had a soft gold sheen, a healthy glow. My hair was not red, it never had been. My hair was auburn.

He settled back, satisfied, taking me in.

"Your hair," he said, "is not the problem."

He got up, looked at me. "You," he said, "are the problem."

A thousand questions rose to my lips and stopped there. How? Who was he? Who was I? And if I was the problem, what in hell was I supposed to do about it?

"Don't worry," he said. "We'll take it one step at a time." And he smiled, the wrinkles retreating into deep hollows.

"Tomorrow," he said.

"But how much...?"

"Tomorrow."

The next day, there were no pleasantries. He just beckoned me through into a large, white studio with one mirrored wall.

He bent, suddenly and shockingly lithe, picked up a script and threw. I caught it. Lady Macbeth, the soliloquy. On every training actor's repertoire. I must have done this a thousand times.

"But not how you will do it again, Miss Davenport," he said, reading my thoughts. "Now. Read!"

And I read.

"No."

I looked up, startled. I had barely begun.

"You see," he said, "with you, it isn't a matter of your looks. Your skin, your hair, those things will take care of themselves."

He leaned in, and although he was across the room, I could feel his breath on my face.

"You have to feel it. Breathe it. You must do more than act each part, Miss Davenport. You have to *be* each part. More work for me, of course..."

Aah. Here it was. The price. A price that might just be too much.

"Ten percent, Miss Davenport," he snapped, suddenly all business. "That's all. If you ever land a role and feel it is in any way because of me, that's all you pay."

He moved across the room, swift, and thrust something at me. A contract. "If you don't, of course, if you don't bene-fit in some way, then nothing."

He leaned in close. "Put yourself in my hands. Bend the way I bend. Breathe the way I breathe. You will laugh, you will cry, and sometimes, it will hurt. But, Miss Davenport, you will learn."

I somehow felt the price had nothing to do with nickels and dimes, his ten percent. But I remembered Stella's unbounded confidence, heard her breezy laughter, and I nodded my agreement to his terms.

Then, he acted the part for me. Carlos, tall, straight, became hunched. His face grew set, as though the musculature beneath had solidified. His eyes intensified, burned.

> "Thou wouldst be great;
> Art not without ambition, but without
> The illness should attend it. What thou wouldst highly,
> That wouldst thou holily; wouldst not play false,
> And yet wouldst wrongly win."

And he breathed Lady Macbeth, every fiber expressed her, was her. And when he finished, as his face resolved into the Carlos I knew, I still stared.

"Spellbound, Miss Davenport?" He smiled. "Think. That is how your audiences will look. One day. When you are finished."

And he taught me how to breathe, how to look, how to be. How to become.

"I called someone," he said as he opened the door.

I was used to this now, the no preliminaries style.

"Bateman. He's casting for a film, wants someone for a part. A small part, but you get in with Bateman..."

Yes, I knew. The start of something. Bigger things. A step on the ladder, a foot in the door.

"The audition's tomorrow. You're on last." He threw some papers at me and we started to practice.

I was better at this now. I could sense this person who loomed out of the white page, the black ink. She was bold. Brassy. She presented a confident face to the world, but she was hiding something. A vulnerable edge, a hidden past maybe. Inside, she hurt. Carlos made me stand like her, walk like her. Then he put his hands on me.

And something happened. "Feel it," he kept saying. "Feel it."

And I did, it was starting inside, a small pain, but lodged there. I could feel it, feel her hurts inside my own. He showed me. He showed me how to feel like her, how to think like her. The pain moved. And twisted. He showed me how to be her.

Carlos smiled as he showed me to the door.

Outside, I could feel it still. It was there when I walked, and I tried to shake it off like an ache. But it wasn't an ache, it wasn't physical. It wasn't even really there. It was as though he'd planted it in my head, a strange seed, and it was growing.

I wondered how he did it. Had it been like this for Stella? The wondering grew with the pain, that tight pain, and so I called her.

We exchanged pleasantries. Yes, it was too hot. Yes, it must be great to be working. She had just landed a part in a new movie, hotly tipped as the summer's biggest slasher, and I just knew it would be a success. I could hear it in her voice. This time she was to be the star, not play some bit part. I tried to feel glad.

"I was just calling about Carlos." I paused. What to say? Why would she believe? But then, she had been there. Worked with him. "Was there anything different about your sessions with him? Anything strange?"

She laughed, but it was a new laugh for her, one I had forgotten. It took me a moment to get it. It was a nervous laugh, unsure.

"Well, there was the hairdresser, of course. He knows everyone. I mean, everyone. And the colorist..."

There was something more, more than this. "What else?"

She paused. "You know, I wouldn't tell you this if you weren't my friend. If I didn't think..."

"What?"

"Well, I had a problem, you see. The film I was up for, there was a sex scene. And you know what I was like, back in college."

I did. She could never relax, always looked wooden. If she had to kiss, she'd bump teeth, bite the guy's lip. If she had to get naked, she'd collapse in helpless laughter while her leading man became more and more frustrated.

"But Carlos, he taught me—I mean, he showed me..."

There was something about the way she fell silent.

"You slept with him? But he's..." I thought about the wrinkled cheeks, the walnut flesh.

But then I remembered how he was, how he changed somehow, the way his visage had adapted to each role he played. The way his eyes seemed to sink right into his skull when he was angry. The way his lips screwed up and wheedled, making him a born miser. The way his cheeks smoothed over, the way his forehead lengthened somehow, as he romanced the invisible leading lady. Then he was a lover. And I understood.

"It's part of the method," she whispered. Her voice became reedy, defensive. "And it was—you know—good. I mean, I never knew anyone like him. His hands. His lips. It was... warm. Special. And you know, when I'm in front of the cameras, between the sheets, I don't know, it's like all the cameramen and the lights vanish and it's just him and me. And it feels good, and right, and natural."

She paused again.

"And when I went up for *Catch All*—the director said he never saw anyone like me. He said I set the screen on fire—"

Her voice broke. She took a deep breath. Was that tears I could hear? Her voice was smaller.

"But it's never the same."

"What?"

"You know. When I'm with someone. Not on set, I mean... with a man. Even Steve. I just can't—oh, I don't know, it's like Carlos is there. Watching. Sneering, maybe. And I can't—"

"You can't..."

The line clicked, and Stella was gone.

At first it was all right. I started to read, and something about Carlos, about what he did, reached up from that center of pain inside and I felt the character waiting. And when I opened my mouth, it was her words that came out.

I heard the casting agents fall silent. I was aware of it but I didn't care. It didn't matter, because I was just a woman speaking. There was no division between me and her, between character and actress.

But then something happened. My inner voice awoke and told me, No, you can't be doing this. You're not her. How can you be? How can you be a star, you, who only waits tables? And it fell apart. Suddenly I was stumbling over the lines, and she was gone. There was only me and a script that surely didn't belong in my hands.

Afterward, the pain was gone. But the price of failure was in my mouth, and it tasted like ashes. It reminded me of his face, of the texture of Carlos' skin, his clothes. The way he was. It was like he was standing over me, judging me.

He didn't smile when I returned from the audition. It was like he knew. Maybe he knew I had called Stella, too.

Sometimes Carlos looked at me and I felt he knew everything.

I half expected him to close the door in my face. But he didn't. He appeared almost kind as he beckoned me in.

"Next time," he said, "you will win."

And then he said I had to stop comparing myself to her, the golden goddess, the perfect starlet. "When she came here," he said, "her teeth were crooked. Her hair, unlike yours, was a problem, a big one. She was too fat. I had to train her, make her diet. Did you know that? I had to literally shape her body."

He looked me up and down. I knew I looked good. Since these lessons, since I'd started to hope, I'd been working out. My muscles were hard from training and my skin glowed.

"I knew that wasn't your problem. And something else. Although I taught her, coached her, showed her a new way to act, there was a limit to what I could do. Because she hasn't got what it takes."

Stella? Perfect Stella, frequenter of Hollywood parties, of every audition going, hanger-on-the-arm of her perfect boyfriend?

He nodded. "She'll only go so far," he said. "You, when you lose yourself in a part, people will watch and they will cry. They will laugh with you, ache with you, suffer with you. Because you have it."

I shook my head.

He nodded. "One day," he said, "you will know this."

Stella never had a chance to prove him wrong. I didn't even find out through her friends, her family; I found out through the headlines.

Stella had locked herself in her apartment and drawn herself a bath, a long, hot bath. I wondered what she thought about as the water rose. She poured herself a drink. She chose champagne. Goodbye to all that, perhaps. Then she sank into the warm water, the starlet's foam-filled water, and she'd opened a vein.

Steve, the perfect man to go with her perfect life, was seeing someone else. Apparently, he had needs. Needs that weren't being met. He was with a new actress now, a hot new actress on the scene, someone from his latest movie set. I wondered who she was, really. Behind the picture in the paper, behind the black and the white. I wondered what she thought, whether she felt anything for Stella.

I still had that picture in my hand when I wound up on Carlos' doorstep. He didn't seem surprised. Just beckoned, a sharp gesture.

"Stella." I said it as though accusing him of something. "She's dead."

"I know." He waved away the newspaper. "I told you. She didn't have your strength."

I pointed at Steve, the black and white dots. "But you know why," I said. "Because she couldn't feel anything with him. Because of you, what you did."

"Aah," he said. "She told you. I thought so."

He turned and walked inside, forcing me to follow. "A man has a right to choose, Miss Davenport," he said. "As does a woman. Stella knew what she was doing. She knew there would be a price, and that sometimes, the price would be pain."

He sneered. "But she couldn't handle it. And when a woman like that comes along..." he gestured at the picture of the new girlfriend. "Now, she's a talented woman. Strong. Together. You wouldn't catch her throwing everything away like that, all my time, my effort."

I looked at the girl in the picture, long dark hair flowing over her shoulder, over Steve's. I wondered again what she was like, where she had come from. What she had learned. And for the first time, I wondered where she had learned it.

"You?" I asked.

"Enough." He was all business again. "You have an audition. So concentrate, because this time, you are going to win."

I gawped.

He raised a finger, pointed at me. "I have invested much in you, Miss Davenport."

He picked up a script, threw it at me. I batted it away.

"And now it is time to pay."

He picked up the script and this time, struck me across the face with it. "Read!"

I stared, frozen. I tried to protest but then saw his expression, the resolve written there. His face had become steel.

I looked at the script. The black, the white. The words danced.

"*Massacre at Silver Creek*," he snapped. "Drivel, of course. Pure drivel. But you will get that part and you will lift it, you will make it something better."

"But, but this is..."

"Stella's role. Yes."

And I suddenly knew. I couldn't.

I threw it down and headed for the door, but he was quick, too quick. He caught me around the waist.

"You will give it life, Miss Davenport. And people will fear, because when they see you, when they hear you scream, they will hear the beast at their backs."

I couldn't. I knew I couldn't.

"You can."

And I knew that I would, that I would try, because when Carlos looked at me I was afraid.

Even so, I knew that I would fail. I couldn't do it, not a part like that. I could never scream like that, full bodied, in total abandon, nothing held back. Nothing wanting. It would be like before, ashes, ashes in my mouth.

I couldn't take her place. I pictured her in a short dress, ripped to the thigh, slashed to the waist. She was running, blonde hair flowing behind. She was running and looking over her shoulder, trying to see the thing that was chasing after her. It was Stella. But it was more than Stella, more than my old friend playing a part. This woman was more than that. This woman was in real trouble. Suddenly, she stumbled. But when she recovered, she realized the beast was never behind her at all. It was here. And she opened her mouth and screamed. And screamed. And screamed.

Slowly, her face began to change. And there was only Carlos, smiling softly. "That," he said, "is what you must become."

And then he placed a hand over my face.

I came to gradually, the room passing in and out of focus. It was a new room, gray and austere. I could not move. I saw Stella's face. Then Carlos. Him. Her. Him.

It was Carlos again and this time I knew it was real, because he was leaning over me and I felt his breath on my skin. I sensed that texture, the ashen texture of his flesh, the spidery sensation aroused by his touch. But he hadn't touched me. Not yet.

"I was hoping we wouldn't have to do this, Miss Davenport," he said. He leaned over a low table, set out with sharp things, silver things, cruel things.

"It was, of course, the last thing in my repertoire."

He pulled on my wrists, and for one wild moment I thought he was releasing me, but he was only testing my bonds.

He appraised my face. Perhaps to check that I was really here, that I was awake enough. To make sure that I would feel enough.

He turned, picked up something slim and gleaming and sharp.

He was going to teach me how to scream.

The Good Life

Michelle Mellon

Nancy opened the mailbox and shoved the package inside. She slammed the metal lid closed and sprinted back across the street to the safety of her front yard. Dylan Massey's black Lexus crawled into the driveway minutes later, as she knew it would. Dylan emerged from his tinted cocoon, removed the mail from the box, and continued up the drive to his house.

Nancy waited until the gate closed across the driveway, hoping against hope that Dylan had glanced at the package and noticed the address. But his car slid into the garage, closing her off from further spying. She finished trimming her sickly rose bushes and trudged across the patchy lawn to her own house, small and badly in need of new paint, new windows, new life.

She cast a glance over her shoulder at the Massey estate with its manicured lawn, landscaped perennial beds, and stately appeal. That was the life she was meant to have. She should be spending her days basking in the gaze of Dylan Massey, tending to their beautiful, intelligent children, walking their whippet and seeing her lean, fashionable self in the paper at gala after gala for the numerous charities with which she worked. Instead, she found herself reduced to this. She had become invisible.

The other neighbors no longer wrote letters to the city to complain about her yard or her old, noisy car, or the state of perpetual disrepair in which her house wallowed. She had hoped things would be different with the Masseys. From the moment the moving van pulled up on a Friday morning and gave birth to furniture in hues unimaginable to Nancy in her sterile wood veneer world, with boxes of items marked Fragile and Valuable, Nancy wanted to know what life was like for such people.

She called in sick to work and prepared a basket of homemade cookies and brownies. She changed into her best dress, an unfortunate paisley in shades of blue that only emphasized her pallor and the brown bramble of hair on her head. She marched across the street, basket in hand, to meet the new neighbors before the others could turn them against her.

Seth Massey was in the yard, tossing a Frisbee to his younger sister Amber. The wind was light, but Seth was wearing the varsity jacket he'd earned that spring. He paused when he saw Nancy approaching and arched an eyebrow. Both children were beset with a fit of coughing. Nancy continued to the door where Heidi Massey stood in the foyer, directing furniture placement in the living room.

"Excuse me," said Nancy.

Heidi Massey turned, her green eyes sweeping Nancy. She said, "I'm sorry, we're just moving in and rather busy. We're not interested today, but maybe some other time."

They stared at each other. Nancy was confused and unsure of how to respond. Heidi's eyes narrowed, contracting the rest of her perfectly tanned face into the wrinkled visage that lay about ten years ahead of her. With a huff, Heidi reached into her pocket and pulled out a small change purse.

"How much?" she asked, waving the purse until the coins jingled.

"What?"

"How much?" Heidi gestured at the basket with her purse.

"Oh. Oh no, I'm your neighbor. From across the street. Nancy Loewen. I just wanted to bring these over to welcome you to the neighborhood."

"Hmm. What's in here?" Heidi lifted the protective cloth and poked around in the basket. "We don't eat nuts, including peanut butter, and no chocolate or refined sugars."

She looked up at Nancy, spreading her full lips in a flash of a smile that also showed off her even, glow-in-the-dark-white teeth. "But thanks anyway."

"Honey, what's up? Who's this?" Dylan Massey came up behind his wife and put his hands protectively on her shoulders.

Nancy had never seen a man more beautiful. He was tall and tan like Heidi, and also had thick, blond hair, but his eyes were unnaturally blue, like in those colorized old films where everything looks brighter than real life.

"This is our neighbor from across the street. Nettie, is it?"

"Nancy. Nancy Loewen." She extended her hand but realized too late it still held the basket.

"I explained to N—uh, her, that we couldn't accept her quaint gift, but we must have her over sometime for dinner, don't you think?"

"Absolutely." Dylan smiled at Nancy but was looking down the driveway. "So, the house directly across the street?"

"Yes, that's the one. It, uh, needs some work, I know. But it's all paid for. I mean, I inherited it from my parents and they paid it off, which is good because there's not a lot of money in working as a librarian, but I do enjoy being around books. So if your children need any help after they get their library cards, you know, finding their way around and all, I'd be happy to help."

Nancy exhaled and Dylan looked down at her.

"Yes, well, thank you. It was nice to meet you..."

"Nancy. Nancy Loewen. And I'm usually around if you need anything. Just knock."

"Yes, of course," Heidi murmured.

She and Dylan melted back inside their house, leaving Nancy with a view of their perfectly matched living room ensemble in rust, green, and ivory. The French doors were open onto the slate patio that surrounded the pool and waterfall out back. Despite the failure of the basket, Nancy floated back across the street, wondering absently if she should return with some cough or allergy medication for the children, who were struck with another fit as she strode past.

An invitation to dinner. She couldn't wait!

But wait she did. Six months passed, and the Masseys remained hidden in their house, behind the security gate. Nancy had seen some of the other neighbors wander in and out of the Massey home. Once she thought she smelled barbecue and heard laughter and splashing from their backyard. Perhaps they were entertaining old friends or clients. The few neighbors she'd seen leaving had probably just dropped by, or attempted to crash the event. Nancy had too much pride to stoop so low. She would wait until asked.

Perhaps the Masseys needed a nudge. Perhaps they'd forgotten, in the frenzy of settling in, their promised neighborly gesture. That's how she came up with the plan. A tickler file, as it were. Nancy prepared a package, something too large to fit into her own mailbox, but still able to fit into the Masseys'. She would slip it in with their mail, as if it had been sorted incorrectly. The Masseys would have her name, and when they brought the package over to its rightful owner, they would surely remember their initial conversation.

A week passed. No package.

Nancy checked every day. The kids left for school, Heidi left for her various volunteer activities, and Dylan left for his job. No vacation, no illnesses, no excuses. Nancy was trapped. She couldn't ask the Masseys about the package without raising suspicion. And she didn't dare go around to her other neighbors and risk their cold, silent treatment.

She was annoyed. She was used to being lonely, but this felt like an extra snub, a secret joke at her expense.

One morning she stepped outside to get her paper and almost tripped on the package. Or what was left of it. Nancy was more upset by the fact that it had been left at her door in the middle of the night, than by her discovery that it had been opened and sloppily repackaged.

From her kitchen window, over her cooling mug of coffee, Nancy could see the Masseys loading luggage into the Lexus. Laughing and carefully placing the dog crate in the back seat while Seth and Amber squeezed in beside it. Dropping Precious off at the kennel. Skipping out of town on a trip. Leaving her package in the middle of the night. Wiping her off their radar, just like the rest of the neighbors. Just like everyone else throughout her life.

Not this time, Nancy decided.

She packed her own bag. She checked the street for any of the other neighbors and marched across to the Masseys'. Though their house looked imposing from the front, Nancy knew the brick wall lowered in height on the sides, behind the line of trees. From there she could either climb over the wall or walk around to the rear gate, which had a simple clasp lock that could be unhooked from the outside. Nancy walked around the pool, across the patio, and over to the back of the garage. She assumed the Masseys had turned on their alarm system, but knew from her father, who had installed the systems on most of the houses on the street, that the garage was not covered.

Nancy pulled a screwdriver from her bag and removed the vent cover. She shoved her bag through first, hoping it would sweep away any webs or crawly critters in her path. Then she hauled herself through and crossed the immaculate concrete to the door leading into the kitchen. Inside, Nancy dropped her bag in the living room and toured the house. Everything matched in wood tones and style. Nancy felt it was too soft and serene for people she had come to think of as hard and cool.

She returned to the living room, spread out a few things on the low, glass-topped coffee table, and moved her bag into the bedroom. She showered and tried to squeeze herself into Heidi's clothes, splitting a few blouse sleeves and popping a few pants buttons. She pulled on a silk robe, sniffed Dylan's shirts, cuddled with some of Amber's stuffed animals, and played one of the CDs from Seth's collection, wishing that she could be the one to yell at him to Turn That Noise Down! Eventually Nancy fell asleep, dreaming of Dumbo and the Ugly Duckling.

For the next few days Nancy lived the Massey life, minus the Masseys. She held conversations with herself at the table for breakfast and dinner, playing each person's role. She found the alarm code in Dylan's desk and disabled the system so she could enjoy afternoons sunbathing and swimming in the pool. She ate their food, and when it ran out, she had meals delivered.

By the fifth day, Nancy was bored. And still lonely.

She was snooping around in Seth's pockets—she found a joint in his jacket and a condom in a pair of jeans—when she came across some notes containing an ongoing dialogue between Seth and one of the girls from the neighborhood who was in his class. She was going to stop reading after the first few treacly exchanges, but then something caught her eye:

> Loser Loewen? Yeah, she's creepy alright. You don't know the half of it.
> —What do you mean?
> Don't you know about her hobby? Gives me the creeps just thinking about it!
> —Why, what is it?

Nancy ripped the notes again and again, watching as the pieces fell from her quivering fingers. She stalked down the hall to Dylan's office, where she typed up a note and forged his signature, copying it from one of the documents lying on his desk. Then she pushed the button to open the driveway gate, marched out the front door and across the street, got in her car and drove away.

"I, I don't know about this. I'll have to ask my supervisor." The girl behind the desk moved away, glancing back at Nancy and then down at the note in her hand. A couple of minutes later an older woman appeared at the desk, holding Nancy's note.

"Ms. Loewen?"

"Yes, that's me. I have my ID if that's the problem."

"Oh no, no. It's just that we've been taking care of Precious since she was a puppy and we've never given her over to a stranger before. I mean, the Masseys have never even mentioned something like this."

"It's just one of those emergency situations, you understand. They probably would have called you directly, but they had to change their travel plans and wanted to make sure Precious was with a friend, since they didn't know when they'd be able to return."

"Oh? Something serious, then? Well surely, Precious would best be left here if it's going to be a long time. Where she has instant care if she needs it."

"If you think so," Nancy said, pretending to walk away. "I'll just have Dylan talk with you when they get home after their ordeal and have to drive all the way over here to pick up Precious."

She drove back to the Massey house with Precious in the backseat of her car.

After unloading the dog in the backyard, Nancy parked at her own house and walked back across the street. She ignored the surprised looks from her neighbors, who were returning from their jobs and sure to rush inside to call each other to find out if anyone knew why on earth the Masseys would have chosen Nancy to house sit.

Nancy sat in the living room, alternately watching the large flat-panel TV mounted above the fireplace, and Precious, who was running around the yard and drinking water out of the pool. It was going to be a long afternoon.

Night fell, and Nancy woke at the sound of a slammed car door. She could hear the Masseys as they gathered luggage from the car and headed toward the front door. They were quiet as the key clicked in the lock, but Nancy knew there was no way they could guess someone was home.

That is, until they met Precious in the foyer. Or, more accurately, what was left of Precious.

Dylan said, "What the—"

Heidi screamed.

Precious sat, unblinking, unaware, preserved, and easily portable.

The Masseys moved into the foyer in disbelief, surrounding the stuffed dog and looking at each other in confusion.

Nancy stepped from her position in the entry closet. She closed and locked the front door behind the shocked family.

Slowly they turned to face her. She stood before them in her best dress. With one hand she adjusted her glasses, patted at her hair, and wiped small drops of perspiration from her upper lip. In her other hand she held a large, long knife.

"I only wanted to be a part of it for a while," she said, waving the knife to indicate the Masseys and the house. "All you had to do was invite me over."

Heidi looked at Dylan, who was trying to slip his cell phone out of his pocket.

"Don't bother," Nancy droned. "I canceled your account. All of your accounts." She pointed at each of them in case they had a similar idea. "I've canceled your commitments for the week, Heidi. And I let your secretary know, Dylan, that there was an emergency with your extended family and you'd be out of touch for a while."

She turned and smiled at the kids. "And I wrote to the school to let them know you'd have to extend your spring break for the same reason."

Seth wasn't too scared to scowl and give her the finger. Nancy decided she'd save him for last.

"This is crazy," Heidi said. "You can't do this. What do you want from us?" She paced in a tight circle away from the rest of the family. "Is this about that package?"

She turned her head toward Dylan. "I told you to take that stupid thing over right away, didn't I?" she shrieked. "Didn't I?"

Dylan shrugged, his eyes focused on the knife. Nancy smiled as he slowly slipped behind Heidi and the kids. She could hear him counting steps to the back door. She was tempted to play with him a bit, but the fun had gone out of living like a Massey, and the work getting Precious ready had been tiring.

Instead of tracking Dylan, Nancy simply watched the reactions of the rest of the family as he bolted for the back door. Heidi was confused by the motion, glancing uncertainly between her husband and Nancy. Crying, Amber remained rooted, eyes unfocused. Seth decided to make his own break and bolted for the garage door. Nancy sighed and forced mother and daughter onto chairs in the living room, where she secured them with clothesline.

Dylan stood at the back door, rattling the frame as if it might undo the lock Nancy had installed on the French doors. Seth, undaunted by the new lock on the garage door, ran to the laundry room to try the door to the sideyard. A poke in the back with Nancy's knife sent Dylan to a similar fate as the females, and Nancy watched as Seth tried the laundry room window, then returned to the kitchen and leaped onto the counter to force his way through the window over the sink.

"Something you learn pretty quickly as the daughter of a security expert..." Nancy addressed them all, but kept her attention on Seth, who was panting and slumped on the kitchen floor against the sink cabinet. "How to lock your doors and windows. All these years I thought it'd only come in handy because I lived alone."

Nancy entered the kitchen, where Seth remained on the floor, head hanging low.

"Why are you doing this?" He didn't look up.

"You have everything, and you don't care. You take it for granted. You take things and people and your perfect life for granted."

Seth mumbled a response.

"What was that?"

"It's not our fault you're a loser," Seth said, looking up, his eyes mocking Nancy like so many had done before.

Without a thought she struck him. The knife sliced across his neck, and his eyes grew wide before his head fell back against the cabinet with a clunk.

"Seth," Heidi screamed. "Are you all right? Seth? Seth!"

Nancy was annoyed again. She had hoped to save Seth for last, and now she'd have to work quickly. After all, the invitations had already gone out to the neighbors for the Massey family barbecue on Sunday.

She had outdone herself this time, Nancy decided as she opened the gate to the driveway. On her way back to the house she sprinkled petals here and there until the driveway looked like a soft spring rainbow. Inside, the Massey house shone. The furniture was glossy, the rugs clean and crisp-looking, the hardwood and marble floors polished and smooth. Everything smelled fresh, like the air after a cleansing thunderstorm.

Outside, she had swept and hosed down the patio, cleared the pool of debris, and fired up the professional-size grill. There was fresh-squeezed lemonade and a large basket of homemade cookies on one end of the entertaining island into which the grill had been built. A long picnic table sat on the strip of lawn next to the pool. Nancy draped the table with a traditional red and white checkered cloth, and set out sturdy white plates, plastic cutlery, and festive red drinking cups. Large bowls dotting the length of the table held potato chips, pretzels, and snack mix.

The bug-killing lantern she'd hung from the patio roof zapped, reminding her to check on what she had come to think of as the picnic area "adornments." Everything looked tip-top, although she wasn't sure how they'd hold up under the direct sun and heat of the afternoon.

The doorbell rang, and Nancy jumped with nervousness and glee. She floated through the house and ushered in the first of the neighbors, who seemed shocked to find her greeting them, but recovered when she offered them wine and cheese and crackers in the living room. The bell continued to ring and neighbors came in, equally surprised but unable to ask the question on everyone's mind as Nancy flitted about, playing hostess.

Soon the living room was full and Nancy feared the short attention spans of the children might lead to indoor disasters. She opened the doors onto the backyard and offered up the pool and picnic table while she went to the refrigerator to get the grillables. The neighbors exited the house in a rush of conversation, the kids shrieking and chasing each other around the pool.

Then everything went silent.

Nancy appeared in the doorway, wearing an apron and carrying a platter of sausages and burgers in one hand. All eyes turned to her. Some of the children hid behind the legs of their parents, whimpering, but they kept their gaze on Nancy just the same. As she moved forward, the neighbors backed away in an arch, away from the picnic table, nicely framing what Nancy considered to be her masterpiece.

Overall, the Masseys had never looked more gentle. She had taken special pains to dress them and make them up with exceptional care, but the shortened timeframe meant she'd had to cut corners.

The dog, in particular, was the source of a decidedly unpleasant smell. If she'd been at home, with her normal set-up and chemicals, she could have taken care of that and even found some glass eyes to fill in the now empty holes that stared at nothing. Nancy had placed Precious farther back on the lawn, so as not to offend the sensibilities of the guests at the picnic table.

On either side of Precious sat Seth and Amber, posed in the act of petting their beloved dog. Nancy was particularly proud of how she'd hid Seth's neck wound with a collared shirt and carefully placed leather choker. It made him look tough, she thought, and she noticed how some of the older girls couldn't look away. Amber looked sweet in her flowered dress and Mary Janes, and of course Dylan and Heidi were the height of casual fashion.

Nancy had placed them at the table, holding hands and gazing at each other. Well, not really gazing, since she had sewn all of the Masseys' eyes and mouths shut to keep out the flies. The ear and nose plugs were tougher, but some clear wax she had remembered to pack in her bag made all the difference. They'd start to smell like Precious soon, but that was nothing to worry about now. Besides, she wasn't without compassion on their big unveiling day—she had pulled all four faces into smiles with a needle and thread.

Nancy was so taken in by her own work that she didn't hear the screams and cries when they started. Several people were vomiting in the flower beds against the fence. Cell phones were out and numbers punched through tears of disgust, outrage, and fear.

After a while the platter grew heavy in Nancy's hand and she sauntered over to the grill and began laying the meat on the grate. Sirens wailed in the distance, but Nancy remained focused on her barbecuing. She'd have to gather the buns and condiments next, but had already loaded them onto trays in the kitchen.

As the food on the grill sizzled and sent smoke into the still, spring air, she smiled. This was the good life after all.

About the Writers...

Mary Aldrin, author of the mystery novel *A Double Dose of Murder,* is from Cleveland, Ohio. She has a graduate degree in Psychology and also received a master's degree in Writing Popular Fiction from Seton Hill University. You can email her at mary@maryaldrin.com, or visit her website at www.maryaldrin.com.

Kevin Anderson has worked as a marketing professional for fifteen years writing award winning copy for TV and radio. His fiction has appeared in speculative anthologies and publications such as *Surreal Magazine*, *Deathgrip: Exit Laughing*, and *Darkness Rising*. He lives and writes in Menifee, California, with his wife Hope, daughter Avalon, and new son Ronin.

Michael A. Arnzen (gorelets.com) has won the International Horror Guild Award and several Bram Stoker Awards for his fiction and poetry. He teaches courses in Writing Popular Fiction at Seton Hill University. *Play Dead* is his latest novel. *Licker,* a humorous novelette, is forthcoming from Novello Publishers in fall 2006.

K. Tempest Bradford is an Ohio native who travels the country looking for the best place to sit quietly and write. She has many talents and plays many roles—including editor, teacher, and enthusiastic debater. You can find her website at FluidArtist.com.

Sarah Brandel is a graduate of the 1999 Clarion West Writers Workshop and the MFA program at Hamline University. Writing "Hungry Ghosts" was an opportunity to continue exploring China after traveling there twice. She would like to thank Hilary Bienstock, Alberto Yanez, and Mike Frigon for lending her their expertise.

Leslie Brown works as a research technician in the Alzheimer's field in Ottawa. She has published four stories in *On Spec* and in several anthologies. Her website, which has been updated in this century, is at: http://www.geocities.com/labrowns2004/home.html. She's pretty sure she's violated commandments three, four, and ten.

Jennifer Busick stole the story of the fiancée in the deer stand from a male friend, and the ashtray made of horseshoes from her husband's grandmother. She hopes to atone for those thefts here. Jennifer's fiction has appeared in *Weird Tales*, *Black Gate*, and other scrupulously honest places.

Lawrence C. Connolly's stories have appeared in *Fantasy & Science Fiction*, *Cemetery Dance*, *Twilight Zone*, *Borderlands* (3 & 4), *Year's Best Horror* (11 & 12), and numerous other magazines and anthologies. A short film of his story "Echoes" recently won Best Cinematography at the Fusion Film Festival in New York.

Megan Crewe is a Toronto-based writer of young adult and speculative fiction. Her stories have appeared in *Brutarian Quarterly*, *Son and Foe*, and *On Spec*. You can reach her through her website at www.megancrewe.com.

Marguerite Croft is a recovering anthropologist who lives high on a hill in Idaho with her husband, two sons, dog, and cat. You can find more of her fiction in Two Cranes Press's *Scattered, Covered, Smothered* and *Say... what's the combination?*

Cristopher Fisher has published in *The Wittenburg Door, Infuze Magazine*, and *The Sam Houston State Review*. He is currently earning an MFA in Fiction from the Stonecoast writer's program, a low-residency graduate program hosted by the University of Southern Maine. He lives in Texas with his wife and four children.

John M. Floyd's short stories have appeared in a wide range of publications, including *Grit, The Strand Magazine, Woman's World*, and *Alfred Hitchcock's Mystery Magazine*. Several of his new stories are currently featured on Amazon Shorts.

Lee Forsythe is a travel writer who also enjoys an occasional fictional side trip. Among other places, his work has appeared in *Diversion, Travelers' Tales*, and *The Foreign Service Journal*. He currently lives in Moscow with his wife Rosemarie, who has never shared his apprehension about exotic destinations.

Eugie Foster calls home a mildly haunted, fey-infested house in Atlanta that she shares with her husband, Matthew, and her pet skunk, Hobkin. Her fiction has been translated into Greek, Hungarian, Polish, and French, and her publication credits include stories in *Realms of Fantasy, The Third Alternative, Cricket*, and *Cicada*. Visit her online at www.eugiefoster.com.

B. M. Freman stopped imagining and started scribbling and studying when her children were old enough to care for themselves and each other. Now, facing a PhD, she has two projects: modern language Shakespearean plays for junior school kids and turning all Parables into modern phrases set in Tanka-style verse.

Barry Hollander writes horror as an escape from teaching journalism and conducting academic research, though he's convinced horror is not so distant a step from being a university professor. He has sold over fifty short stories. He lives in Athens, Georgia.

Lee Allen Howard has published short fiction in *Cemetery Sonata* anthology, *Dreams and Visions* magazine, and other venues. Beautiful Feet Publishing published his first novel, *When the Music Stops*. He's a graduate of Seton Hill University's Writing Popular Fiction program. He lives near Pittsburgh where you can find him in the neighborhood gym.

William Jones has published fiction in a variety of genres. You can find his writings in *Darkness Rising 2005*, *The Strange Cases of Rudolph Pearson*, and *Horrors Beyond*. He also edits *Dark Wisdom* magazine, and when not writing he teaches English at a university in Michigan. www.williamjoneswriter.com.

Simcha Laib Kuritzky lives in the Maryland/DC suburbs. An active member of his synagogue, he has taught Kabbalah and Jewish history. He also collects and exhibits coins, medals, and amulets, and is widely published in numismatics. He works as a federal accountant for an international software and consulting firm.

Alison J. Littlewood has contributed to *Whispers of Wickedness*, *The Harrow*, *Dark Fire Fiction*, and *Prometheus Unhinged*. She lives with partner Fergus in West Yorkshire, England, where she spends far too much time dreaming and writing strange notes to herself on scraps of paper. See her website at alisonlittlewood.co.uk.

M. Stephen Lukac is a married father of three, a professional bookseller, and a still-aspiring writer. His first novel, *Oogie Boogie Central*, was released in 2003, followed by the collection *But Then Again, You'll Have This...* later that year. You can visit him at www.oogieboogiecentral.com.

Derwin Mak lives in Toronto, Canada. His stories are about ballerinas, Hooters Girls, cheerleaders, tiny aliens, vile U-boat captains, and unlucky Titanic survivors. His story "The Siren Stone" was a finalist for a 2004 Aurora Award, Canada's science fiction award. He has university degrees in accounting and defense management.

Barbara Malenky is a Texas resident. Her nonfiction work has appeared in national crime magazines and paperback anthologies, and her fiction in numerous publications, including the award winning *Borderlands 5* anthology, and the chapbook *Human Oddities*. She received honorable mention several times in *The Year's Best Fantasy and Horror*. She's a member of HWA.

Michelle Mellon is a freelance and fiction writer living in the Los Angeles area with her husband and two cats. She is currently working on a collection of short stories and a screenplay.

Jennifer D. Munro's work has appeared in *Zyzzyva*, *Best of Literary Mama*, *Best American Erotica*, *Secrets and Confidences*, and in many other journals and anthologies. She received an Artist Trust GAP Award and a StorySouth Notable Online Stories award. She has lived in New Orleans, Hawaii, and Seattle. Website: www.munrojd.com.

Derryl Murphy's short fiction has appeared in a wide variety of publications, on paper, and online. Most recently "Mayfly," a story written with Peter Watts, appeared in Gardner Dozois' *Year's Best Science Fiction*. As well, his collection *Wasps at the Speed of Sound* was released to excellent reviews in 2005. A novel, *Napier's Bones*, is coming soon.

Marc Paoletti—After fifteen years as an award-winning advertising copywriter, Marc decided to focus some of his energy and passion on fiction of a different sort. His well-reviewed short work has appeared in numerous anthologies, and he is currently at work on a crime novel. He lives in Chicago.

Dave Raines loves his family (wife Kathy, children Kevin and Becky), and his job as pastor. But ah, to be a writer, too! He once had an article published in the *Strat-O-Matic Review*, an obscure baseball-game fanzine. "Michael's Grave" is a decided step forward, and, he hopes, not the last.

Stephen D. Rogers—Over 300 of Stephen's stories and poems have been selected to appear in more than 100 publications. His website, www.stephendrogers.com, includes a list of new and upcoming titles as well as other timely information.

Lisa Silverthorne has published nearly fifty short stories. She dreams of becoming a novelist and writes to discover the magic in ordinary things. You can visit Lisa's website at: www.drewes.org.

Barbara Stanley lives in Southern California with her husband and one disturbed cat. She has written film reviews and commentary, and now devotes her time to writing creepy stuff. Her fiction has appeared in *SHOTS*, *The Lightning Journal*, and the annual *SubNatural*.

Chris Stout holds an MA in Writing Popular Fiction. He enjoys exploring the dark recesses of humanity that can be found in the twisted labyrinth of a writer's mind. "Bitter Taste of Memory" is his first professional sale.

Mark Tullius is a former no-holds-barred fighter who lives in Los Angeles. He opted for the much safer occupation of writing and now only inflicts pain on paper where his antagonists can't strike back. He is the author of numerous suspense and horror short stories.

Bev Vincent is the Bram Stoker-nominated author of *The Road to the Dark Tower*, the authorized companion to Stephen King's fantasy series, and nearly forty short stories. He writes for *Cemetery Dance* magazine and *Accent Literary Review*. He is working on a novel at his home in Texas. Visit www.bevvincent.com.

Heather Wardell is a full-time writer, currently working on her second novel and looking for a publisher for her first. She lives with her husband and many pets in Ontario, Canada.

Jacqueline West—Her stint as a performer behind her, Jacqueline currently lives, writes, and teaches in Madison, Wisconsin. Her work has recently appeared in journals including *Aoife's Kiss*, *Kenoma*, *Mytholog*, and *Not One of Us*.